MISTRESS
OF THE
THRONE

MISTRESS
OF THE
THRONE

RUCHIR GUPTA

Srishti
PUBLISHERS & DISTRIBUTORS

SRISHTI PUBLISHERS & DISTRIBUTORS
N-16, C. R. Park
New Delhi 110 019
editorial@srishtipublishers.com

First published by
Srishti Publishers & Distributors in 2014

Typeset by Eshu Graphic

Printed and bound in India.

*To the three most important
women in my life:
my mother, my wife,
and my daughter.*

CONTENTS

ACKNOWLEDGEMENT

This book could not have been possible without the unwavering support of several individuals whose advice was integral to its production.

First, I'd like to acknowledge my editor, Mark Orrin, who offered me the sour truth about my earlier versions of the book. His advice wasn't always easy to digest, and yet he delivered it in the most tasteful way anyone ever could.

I'd also like to thank the members of my writer's group, the Long Island Writer's Guild. On numerous weekday evenings over coffee, I learned how to write and develop my thoughts by listening to the works of these fine men and women. In turn, they listened to passages of my book, and gave me helpful hints that allowed me to strengthen my work. Most importantly, they made me believe I wasn't as far from my dream of writing a novel as I once thought.

Finally, I would like to thank my family members who read various portions of the book and offered their thoughts. I hope I never disappoint them. Most importantly, I want to thank my wife, Supurna. She must have read and reread more pages of my book than anyone else, and each time she told me that I can do this. Three years of such steadfast devotion and confidence in someone is a lot to ask, even a spouse. She once told me when this manuscript was rejected by someone to "not worry," and that I can continue to write "just for her". I decided then that if no one ever

Acknowledgement

publishes anything I write, I will still keep writing, knowing that my only reader is my devoted and loving wife. Luckily, this book has found a home and will hopefully entertain many people in years to come. However, even if it hadn't, I would've kept writing - just for her.

List of Characters

Afzal Khan	Friend of Shah Jahan
Arzani	Ladli's daughter
Asaf Khan	Mumtaz Mahal's father, Jahanara's grandfather
Aurangzeb	Shah Jahan's son
Bahadur	Jahanara's eunuch (fictional character)
Chamani Begum	Shah Jahan's concubine
Dara	Shah Jahan's oldest son
Dawar Baksh	Khusrau's son
Dilras	Aurangzeb's wife
Gabriel Boughton	British physician
Gauhara	Shah Jahan's youngest daughter
Hamida	Jahanara's distant cousin (fictional character)
Henna	Shah Jahan's concubine (fictional character)
Jahanara	Shah Jahan's oldest child
Jahangir	Jahanara's grandfather
Kandari	Jahanara's stepmother
Khusrau	Shah Jahan's brother
Ladli	Nur Jahan's daughter
Manbhavati (Manu)	Jahanara's Hindu stepmother

Mullah Badakshi	Member of Qadiraya order
Mumtaz Mahal	Shah Jahan's wife, Jahanara's mother
Murad	Shah Jahan's youngest son
Nadira	Dara's wife
Nur Jahan	Jahangir's wife, Shah Jahan's stepmother
Raushanara	Shah Jahan's daughter
Sadullah Khan	Aurangzeb's father in law
Sati-un-nissa (Sati)	Jahanara's lady-in-waiting
Shah Jahan	Jahanara's father
Shahriar	Shah Jahan's brother, Ladli's husband
Shuja	Shah Jahan's son

MUGHAL FAMILY TREE

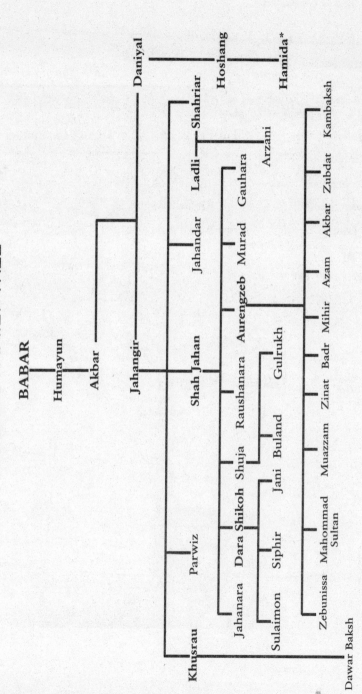

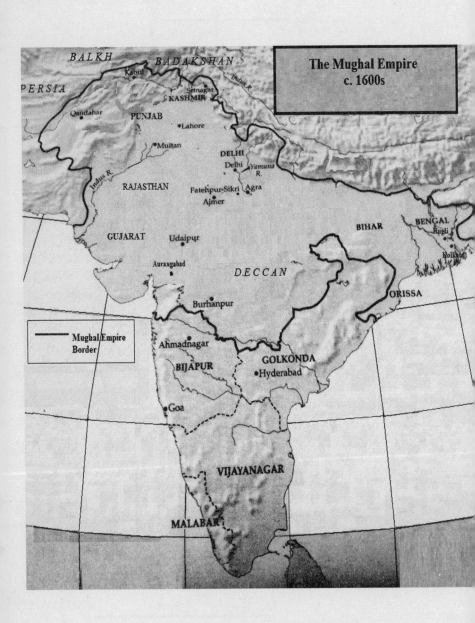

The Mughal Empire
c. 1600s

Mughal Empire
Border

1
THE REUNION

7th March, 1628

I'd spent the better part of last night tossing around on my silk sheets, moving my blue, velvety pillow from side to side, unable to find comfort in my new, expensive bed. It seemed this long sleepless night would never end. Eventually, the rays of the sun began tunnelling through the darkness, and with them the sound of kettledrums began, summoning the faithful to a balcony in the Red Fort – the Jharoka-i-darshan. From here the King would offer his presence – his *darshan* – to his subjects as proof that he still lived, and the kingdom was still secure.

I noticed more ladies awakening as soon as I got out of bed. A slave quickly brought warm *chai* to each maiden who desired it.

I could hear the hustle and bustle of slaves in the harem – the *zenana* – starting kitchen fires, sweeping brooms, and the gentle stirring of the men from the floor below. Then my stepmothers' and the royal concubines' whispering began:

"I need hot water *now*!"

"Where's my *kajal*?"

The women spoke simultaneously to the hapless slaves who rushed in and out of the zenana trying to fulfill several wishes at once, in a fluster of activity that arose almost instantly as the slaves ran hither and tither.

Splash!

"Look what you did, you fool! There's water all over my *choli*!" A poor slave had lost her footing and dropped a potful of hot water meant for Kandari onto Manu's blouse. (Manu was my father's only Hindu wife, all others being Muslim, like the rest of my family.)

Suddenly I felt a slap on the back of my head and a rage-filled voice – Kandari's: "What will you do with your allowance, Jahanara?" I knew I wasn't supposed to answer this question; more was to come. "Will you buy expensive oils for your hair while the rest of us die hungry?"

I just sighed, knowing not what to say to my stepmother. My father had granted me an allowance of six *lakh* rupees upon becoming the fifth Mughal Emperor of India, with a one-time gift of four lakh rupees. My mother received even a higher allowance because she was now the official queen: ten lakh rupees per year, with a one-time gift of two lakh gold pieces and six lakh rupees.

Kandari walked away but continued to crane her neck in my direction so I could see the fury in her eyes. Kandari had been a Persian princess bequeathed to my father before he married my mother. She was the first choice of my grandfather, Emperor Jahangir, for my father, and my father had married her only on condition that he could also marry my mother shortly thereafter. My grandfather acquiesced, but the marriage to my mother didn't come about for another four years. When it did finally occur, my mother was catapulted to the top of my father's zenana, placing Kandari downward in the hierarchy.

Kandari had supposedly been a beautiful bride: slim, with sharp features and bright blue eyes. But she looked nothing like that now. The 'official' word was that Kandari was also barren and sterile, and indeed no offspring had come from her. But rumours around the zenana hinted differently. As one of the concubines would say, "Why blame the pot for not cooking lentils when the chef never poured any lentils into the pot in the first place?"

With the passage of years, Kandari's bitterness had taken root, and her temper had grown ever darker. Wrongfully labelled barren and rightfully feeling unloved, she knew her life was ruined and desolate because of Aba's love for my mother; yet she wasn't permitted to show it.

Indeed, the zenana rumour was that no other wife but Ami shared the pleasure of his company. Still, my mother was treated well by these other wives despite her status, for not doing so would incur the wrath of my father.

At last I saw Kandari move her head away. I looked down, almost in shock that my daily taunts had begun so early in the morning.

I got out of bed and walked over to the mirror. For some reason, I felt filthy this morning. As I stared into the mirror I realised my eyes had been tearing this whole time. Everyone in my father's zenana hated me. If ever I awoke even a little late, they would say loudly, "The Begum Sahiba has been sleeping more these days, now that she has a title…" It was impossible for me to not feel their envy. Their jealousy showed not just in their tone, but in their eyes, and even when they appeared to make endearing remarks, their eyes divulged their hearts' true meaning.

Though there was no formal crown for a Begum Sahiba (Supreme Princess), I felt as if something overburdening and heavy had been placed on my head, and even now, in the comfort of my own room, I felt its crushing weight sink deeper and deeper into my skull.

Every time Aba asked me if I liked my new home I lied to him and told him what I knew he wanted to hear, though the truth was just the opposite. I'd been much happier before, living as a simple princess in exile in tents. Instantly I'd seen wisdom in the old saying about how it could be lonely on the heights. What I learned better, however, was how much lonelier it is *near* the summit. At least those at the very summit have their cronies who grant them their company and whatever pleasure is requested in return for favours. Those only near it, like me, receive all the agony the title brings, with no real power to do anything about it.

Now I heard Kandari say: "Let's get going, Begum Sahiba. You can't spend half the day staring into the mirror. We must be in the Diwan-i-am within the hour!"

And the commotion of the hundreds of spoiled women suddenly died as quickly as it had begun; we hurriedly adjusted our hair and garments to look presentable. Meanwhile, at a distance Kabuli, the chief eunuch, moved his big hands together as if motioning us to file in a single line and make our way to the Diwan-i-am. (Kabuli was my mother's eunuch, which meant he was also the chief one.)

Slowly we walked single-file, like a parade of ants. History was to be made in the Diwan-i-am today and no one should miss it. A hundred years from today, books would be written about today's events; future poets would compose sonnets commemorating them; false witnesses would paint images showing these events unfolding. My powerless title commanded my attendance, though I felt like a helpless insect stumbling through life, utterly oblivious to the world around it.

We all pushed one another, each hoping to secure the front spot for ourselves. The place for women in my society has always been behind grilled screens. Elaborate designs made of marble are carved in the shape of flowers and lotuses to form small holes, through which we see the world, but the world can't see us. My face, I was told, was only for my family, and perhaps one day, for my husband. Still, I was trying to push against the screen, sticking my thin, ivory-coloured fingers through the holes and pressing my sharp featured face against the cold marble gratings, until the imprint of the marble formed on my face.

The pomp and excitement of the moment reminded me of Aba's coronation, which I'd watched a month ago, from the same decorated screen. I remember that day vividly. The invocation prayer for my father and his subjects was read under his new official name –Shah Jahan the Magnificent. I was told runners had been sent out in every corner of the realm to spread the word proclaiming my father's ascension to the throne.

The empire he would rule stretched from Persia in the west to Bengal in the east, and from the northern Himalayas to the plains of the Deccan plains in the south. It would take a camel 60 days to travel from one edge to the other – and now it belonged to us!

I ran my eyes around the hall to see who else was in attendance. The hall itself was approximately 12,000 square feet in size. I'd been told that, made of red sandstone, it was painted over with white stucco to protect the stone and allow for coloured decoration. This was the Hall of Public Audience, hence the name Diwan-i-am. In the back of the hall was an alcove of inlaid marble that connected to the royal apartments behind. Here the emperor sat and would grant promotions and examine papers related to land grants, offices and salaries (do the regular administrative business of the kingdom).

I could see the orthodox mullahs arranged along the front of the hall. Their long beards and dark robes always intimidated me. I often felt they hated women, which is why Ami and they were in a perpetual state of conflict. Ami would ask for alms for the poor and protection for women in our kingdoms (sometimes from their own husbands), and the mullahs would scoff at the idea that Aba should listen to a woman.

Standing at the other end of the hall were the brave Hindu Rajput warriors. I tapped Sati, my lady-in-waiting, on her shoulder. "Why are they here?"

She replied, "They are here because of Manu. Look, that's her older brother, the one with the long mustache." Manu's family was Hindu royalty, and every Mughal king for the past three generations had married a Hindu princess to form an alliance with the brave Hindu Rajput kingdom.

The crowd suddenly went silent as the proclamation of the king's arrival was to begin. All eyes now fixed on the empty throne that awaited its master; it sat on an elevated marble platform, with four white marble pillars supporting the decorative canopy. Red drapes hung from the ceiling to add more colours to the display.

A voice formally intoned: "Presenting His Imperial Majesty, Shah Jahan the Magnificent!" This was, of course, not his real name. Originally named Khurram by his grandfather, Aba had received this title after his military victory in the unruly town of Mewar. The story of his success in Mewar was legendary, and all who recited it spoke of how brave and valiant my father was as a young prince.

Aba entered the hall wearing a blue robe with a crown turban – the turban being a relic of our nomadic heritage – with jewels and rubies glistening at a distance. Around his neck hung a beautiful necklace of pearls the size of a baby's palm. He wore a diamond-encrusted gold dagger around his waist. As he walked, jewels on his robe took turns glistening, and it seemed as if he himself was exuding light. He at last reached his imperial throne and sat down.

Behind Aba stood eunuchs who then began fanning him with peacock feathers; to his left stood the standard bearers, facing forward with their backs to the wall. He was surrounded by burly Uzbek bodyguards, and the executioner stood by at a short distance, to dispose of anyone who might have committed a criminal act.

Sati turned to me in excitement: "See how handsome your father looks! He's so happy whenever he sits on the throne!"

I sighed. To the degree Aba's title had brought him unimaginable joy, mine seemed to have brought me nothing but grief. I couldn't understand why I needed to be dragged into this. I felt that from that fateful day when I was crowned Begum Sahiba, people had begun treating me differently. Now I tried to be unaffected by my melancholy, for today was no day for lamenting, but instead for boisterous anticipation. Today my brothers, who'd been forced to live apart from us for several years, would finally be reunited with us.

I couldn't resist the suspense, and so insisted on moving to the front of the zenana so I could see my brothers clearly. I put my slender fingers through one of the holes, wishing I could push my entire body through so I might be able to stand right next to my Aba as the young princes were presented. My fingers hung from the lattice windows like leaves after monsoon rains.

Then burst an announcement loud enough for all of us in the audience to hear: "Presenting to His Majesty the Most Magnificent of Amirs, Yaminuddawla Asaf Khan!"

I saw my heavy-set maternal grandfather with his graying beard walk from the side to the centre of the hall and bow before Aba. Asaf Khan had helped Aba secure the throne for himself after my grandfather, Jahangir, died. For this aid, Aba gave him a special place at the court.

Aba smiled gravely. "Tell me, Asaf Khan, have you brought my sons?"

A pause ensued, each moment of which seemed like an eternity. I had spent many years wondering why my parents allowed two of their children to move to Agra at such young ages, separated from them. Why had they never visited and why had my parents never sent for them? A part of me almost resented my parents for having separated us siblings from each other. (Four of us, Shuja, Murad, my sister Raushanara and I, had lived in the Deccan with my parents, while Dara and Aurangzeb had lived in Agra.)

One day, Sati had told me the truth behind my brothers' suspicious absence from our lives: They were hostages! When Emperor Jahangir was king, my father launched a rebellion against him. To Aba's dismay, Emperor Jahangir's forces were too strong for Aba's princely army, and Aba suffered a crushing defeat. As his punishment, Emperor Jahangir's queen and Aba's stepmother, Queen Nur Jahan, exiled Aba to the Deccan and held my two brothers as hostages – a ransom against any future rebellion.

Now said Asaf Khan: "Jahanpanah, your sons had a good journey from Lahore to your presence. I would like your permission to present them to you at this court."

Aba nodded his head in acquiescence and gave the signal to allow his sons to be presented. I continued to press my face against the screen, my heart racing; this was what I'd so long waited for.

"Presenting Prince Muhammad Dara Shikoh!"

Dead silence fell upon the hall, which was now filled with several hundred attendees, all arranged by rank. I heard footsteps, and instantly concluded that Dara had grown significantly since I'd last seen him. We women of the zenana readily picked up subtleties like the footsteps' sounds; we'd learned to use all our senses in lieu of our limited vision to form complete pictures of occurrences on the other side of our screened windows.

The mullahs remained at attention, motionless, like everyone else. No matter what the proclamation or whoever entered, these old men would always stand still as statues. Sati sometimes said: "Perhaps they would benefit from pouring their 'lentils' into zenana concubines from time to time." I would chuckle at such comments. A certain concubine had once confided to me: "Many of them *do* pour 'lentils' into us. They just let no one find out!"

A shadow began to appear that told me my brother must now be at least 5'5" or 5'6" tall. Then I caught sight of a fair-skinned boy with no discernible facial hair, dressed in an orange robe with a turban on his head. He walked to the throne, bowed to Aba and kissed the ground, as was customary behaviour before the King. Aba blessed him, rose and hugged his son tightly.

My brother said, "Aba, Jahanpanah, I hereby present to you a thousand *mohur*s as a submission of myself to your service, and another thousand as a gift to you, my beloved father."

Aba accepted this tribute, commanded his oldest son, perhaps the future King of India, to sit at his side and presented him with a daily allowance of a thousand rupees as the ceremony continued.

I almost cried out in excitement to my brother, but Manu put her hand over my mouth to prevent me from committing this egregious offence unintentionally; court etiquette had to be maintained at all costs. I noticed Ami had begun sniffing as though she were weeping.

The ceremony continued with another announcement: "Presenting Prince Muhammad Aurangzeb!"

A softer stomp with a much smaller shadow appeared, of a lad possibly not even 5' tall and very slim. Then a figure more boyish-looking than Dara manifested himself, wearing an emerald-green robe and an orange turban.

Though the Prince was only three years behind Dara, he looked even younger. *He must not have started his growth spurt yet,* I thought. I also noticed other things different about him: the way he walked and his facial expression. He lacked that levity and enthusiasm Dara had shown when approaching our father. Prince Muhammad Aurangzeb seemed withdrawn, almost as if he was being forced to do this and considered he had better, more important matters to attend to.

Aurangzeb, like Dara, kissed the ground before Aba and was immediately blessed and hugged by his father, though the Emperor's emotion seemed tempered by the fact that this was the second child presented. Had Aurangzeb been presented first, he perhaps would have benefited from the enthusiasm that accompanied the first encounter – a reaction I felt couldn't be artificially summoned for the benefit of the second.

Aba had Aurangzeb seated on his other side and awarded him a daily allowance of five hundred rupees while the daily prayers were being read in the Emperor's name. Daily business was then attended to, as the princes stared forward, their faces showing completely contrasting expressions: Dara seemed hopeful and energetic (this was his father's kingdom); Aurangzeb was resigned and emotionless, as if unsure whether or not his presence here was even needed.

After the court finished its business, all the immediate members of the royal family reunited in the Ghusl khana, a private room near the zenana apartments.

Raushanara and I walked towards Aba and our two brothers, slowly picking up pace as we approached them. Aurangzeb came towards us at a leisurely pace, but Dara sped to us and scooped us sisters into both his arms. We began to laugh and smile and talk to each other incessantly, while Aurangzeb stood at some distance watching us. After a little while I slowly walked over to my awkward young prince. "I've missed you, Aurangzeb," I said calmly.

Aurangzeb just stood there without reciprocal expression or comment. I waited no longer; I hugged my brother as tightly as I could, and Aurangzeb instinctively put one hand around me in slight acknowledgement.

Raushanara was only a year older than Aurangzeb, though, and much shyer. I knew she didn't have it in her to run up alone to anyone and greet them, physically or verbally; now she just stood at a distance smiling at Aurangzeb. Aurangzeb walked slowly over to her gazed at her quickly and snapped, "Have some shame and cover your head!" In the corner of my eye I watched Raushanara cover her head as her smile turned into a resigned frown.

Then we all sat down on Persian carpets for a sumptuous meal for the first time in many years. As had been the case all day, Dara continued talking nonstop, asking us sisters how we'd been, for zenana gossip and about our journey. Aurangzeb just ate quietly, saying little.

Dara wondered: "How was life at Nizamshahi?" (Nizamshahi was the town in the Deccan where we lived in exile before Aba became king.)

"Nothing like Agra," I shrugged. "We had servants and ate off of gold plates and wore expensive clothes, but we lived in tents."

"You all lived in tents all these years?" Dara seemed shocked, perhaps thinking we'd lived in the dingy military tents used by the Mughal army.

"Yes," I laughed, "but these tents were grand, two-story structures, beautifully decorated with wonderful colours and ornaments. We had cooks, nursemaids and servants for everything."

Raushanara interjected: "And we each had our own rooms."

Dara appeared to pay no attention to her. "Where did you all sleep?"

Raushanara repeated, this time with contempt: "I just told you, brother: We each had our own rooms."

I tried to placate her. "Raushanara's right; the rooms were beautiful, even nicer than the ones we have now."

I knew Raushanara had always harboured resentment towards me, though I'd never intended to provoke it in her. But I looked very much like my mother: we both had olive skin, straight hair and thin frames. The zenana women always said I was a Persian beauty like my mother. I contrasted starkly in appearance to Raushanara, who was tan-complexioned, with curly hair and a rounder physique, resembling the South Indians'. I never understood why one look was deemed more beautiful than the other, but to us Mughals, a Persian appearance was considered regal and therefore desirable. It seemed that to us, perfection was Persian, and anyone who looked like a Persian was considered automatically royal.

Persians were considered disseminators of an elegant and sophisticated Islamic culture and etiquette. Mughal poets composed versus not in a native Indian language, but instead in Persian; official language at the Mughal court also was Persian; chronicles of major Mughal conquests by court historians were also written in great detail in Persian. Persian artistry, painting, and carpets, adorned our palaces and forts. We chastised the native Hindus as infidels needing change, while Persian was the gold standard they were to be changed to. Persians, in turn, had descended on Mughal India in droves. We were the wealthiest Islamic kingdom in the world, with riches beyond compare. This drew Persians at every level – artisans, poets, architects, businessmen – to our dominion, allowing intense intermixing of the two cultures. Among those who came to India from Persia looking for a better life had been my great grandfather; this made me part Persian myself.

Shuja and other slave kids would tease Raushanara as the 'ugly sister,' or the 'excess waste that needed to be dispelled somehow from Ami's womb.' I worried that talk like this had further aggravated Raushanara's feelings towards me.

Dara's eyebrows rose. "So you each had your own rooms in the tents?"

"Yes," said Raushanara, "and the playgrounds were bigger."

"Where did you all play?" asked Dara, as if he hadn't heard Raushanara.

I answered, "We played on vast, open grounds with no attention to boundaries. We were told it was all ours!"

Dara grinned. "I bet it wasn't as beautiful as the peacock gardens!" I'd heard of these gardens but still hadn't visited them. He added, "Shall we retire to the peacock gardens now?"

We played for awhile in the peacock garden; several peacocks ran up to us. Dara kept chasing them away as Shuja and Murad tried to grab them. The birds ran into the colourful bushes, where their own colours camouflaged them.

More peacocks then ran out, and also rabbits and pigeons. Soon the entire garden was filled with animals and just us six children.

Dara picked up Murad and tried to sit him on one of the peacocks, but they were too fast for him. Suddenly I noticed that a giant peacock stood next to me. I jumped back in mild excitement. It then spread its feathers wide in front of me, and I began to giggle. "What's wrong with this peacock? It's constantly looking for attention!"

Aurangzeb sneered, "Perhaps it has caught your vanity, sister!"

Aghast, I burst out, "Vanity? What vanity?"

Aurangzeb walked over to me, stomping his feet. "You walk around freely with your face uncovered. Why? Because it's too hot? It's March, yet you show your face for what purpose – because you want others to admire it?"

I looked down my nose at him. "Even if I do, what offence have I committed, brother?"

"Allah has condemned vanity as the greatest sin, yet all you people display it everywhere I go."

I shot back, "*You* people? Who do you mean, *you* people?"

"You, Raushanara, even Aba! What's the need for all these jewels and rubies? I heard Aba had an artist present today in the hall – to paint our reunion scene. Does he not know it's forbidden for our faces to be painted? That it's an affront to Allah?"

I decided to try reasoning with him. "That's fine in the mosque, Aurangzeb; but this is our home. What we do here is different."

He wouldn't relent. "So our homes shouldn't be mosques? They shouldn't be cathedrals we build to serve Allah?"

Dara intervened to my rescue. "Don't mind him! Aurangzeb, if you're so pious and we're so vain, why do you wear pearl necklaces around your neck? Why do you wear brightly coloured robes in court -- and why don't you donate all your allowance funds to the mosque?"

Aurangzeb's face lowered; he seemed unsure of how to react.

Dara went on: "There's plenty of time for piety, brother." He set a conciliatory arm on Aurengzeb's shoulder. "For now, let's all just enjoy each other's company."

Aurangzeb stomped off; I remained baffled at the encounter. What had happened to my younger brother? Prior to his imprisonment, he'd been an innocent and loving child who'd slept next to me all the time. He listened to everyone and respected everyone. Now, he'd been transformed into an arrogant young mullah who had strong words of condemnation for anyone who didn't see the world the way he did.

Dara told me then not to be upset, that he would explain everything later. Aurangzeb's behaviour had its origin in his imprisonment, Dara said. "In due time, I'll tell you the rest."

Indeed, I was eager to learn what had happened during their imprisonment to transform my little brother into a religious zealot!

✳ ✳ ✳

Soon Dara and I were spending almost every moment together. As the crown Prince, Dara commanded respect with the zenana ladies, so they began treating me better as well.

One day he asked me about the lost years from the time he was kidnapped to the moment of our reunion. It was difficult remembering every detail, because like most Mughal stories, this one, too, was filled with terror: fratricide, deception, betrayal and greed. At times I was astonished that my father had even taken part in all this.

I began by telling Dara how we lived a tranquil life in Nizamshahi, and though we always tried not to discuss it, the shadow of his and Aurangzeb's exile always eclipsed our happiness. However, everything changed when we received word that grandfather Jahangir had suddenly died.

Along with five of his closest allies, Aba then decided to ride to Agra from Nizamshahi. Aba had received a runner-message from our other grandfather, Asaf Khan, who was in Agra at the time, to hurry to the city before Nur Jahan declared my uncle Shahriar King. Jahangir had died in the hills of Kashmir, with Nur Jahan by his side. If Aba reached Agra before her, he could secure the kingdom before Shahriar was declared king.

However, during their journey they received a message that Asaf had already crowned our cousin, Dawar Baksh, King of India!

Dara looked puzzled. "But Dawar Baksh was just a boy!"

I told him this had been part of a larger plot by Asaf Khan. Indeed, Nur Jahan's choice for king was Shahriar and the fact that he wasn't crowned king spoke volumes about what was happening in Agra: that Nur Jahan wasn't in control, at least not at that moment. Asaf Khan had installed a puppet to buy them some time.

"So Dawar Baksh was just a puppet?" Dara was shocked. I nodded. I continued to tell him how Aba's next big obstacle to Agra was the tiny kingdom of Bijapur, a town loyal to the newly anointed king, Dawar Baksh. As Aba and his men rode slowly on their horses to the hill overlooking the main fort of the city, they quickly realised they wouldn't be able to cross the city with force. Thus, my father used trickery to cross the kingdom.

Dara appeared intrigued as I recited the story, as though it were some imaginary tale. My view of things differed: It had hurt me to see family members fighting for the throne while their father hadn't even been buried.

Dara swung both hands in the air and chanted: "One day I will be a valiant warrior like Aba!" I stared at him in mild amusement. He continued. "I will defeat my brothers and descend upon Agra to seize the throne after Aba is no more!"

From then on shivers went down my body whenever I thought that my brothers would likely quarrel among each other while we, his sisters, mourned our father's death. Dara cried, as he raised a wooden stick sword-like in the air: "One day, *I* shall be King of India!"

2

RETRIBUTION

29th April, 1628

Parties were one of the more enjoyable aspects of zenana life. Royal chefs would prepare authentic Mughal dishes for us: lamb in yogurt sauce, grilled *kebab*, lamb *pulav* garnished with raisons, chicken *korma*, and grilled fish in lemon sauce. Our vegetarian Hindu members like Manu were served vegetable *pilaf*, *moong dal*, yogurt with vegetables with *tandoori* bread and the like.

The palaces of the zenana were like a giant jewellery box with an almost limitless number of compartments, each connected through lush gardens and verandahs. In effect, the zenana was its own separate little society, with its own hierarchy and rules, the wives and relatives of the royal family on top, concubines and scullery slaves next, followed by lesser slaves. Room size and furnishing luxury were according to the occupant's rank.

Children were born in the *zenana* and grew up there. The Emperor would occasionally come to the *zenana* and spend the night with someone, either a wife or a concubine, and while competition and jealousy ran at all levels, no one dared show these to the King, as that would be deemed disruptive. A concubine or slave, for example, who won the King's favour would be left alone with him on the night of his choosing – but perhaps would be made to pay dearly the following morning, when the King was gone.

The ladies would spend literally a full day decorating themselves. When they finished, they splayed themselves on the velvety *divans*, awaiting the other ladies.

If we were lucky, during a kingly visit all the ladies would smother him, each for different reasons: the wives for gifts, the concubines for sex and us daughters to receive genuine love and affection.

Henna Begum was an eccentric member of our zenana. She had the annoying habit of walking around the harem naked as she readied herself. I found this odd and unnerving; because she was rather attractive, her body made me admittedly self-conscious.

Women in the zenana knew they could display such promiscuous behaviour because no unaltered male but the king was allowed anywhere near us. Our zenana was guarded by three different levels of individuals. The highest were the Tatar women, Uzbeks, who were women of gargantuan proportions, larger than even the largest of Amazons and stronger than many of the soldiers in the imperial army. The next level was the eunuchs, who played a central role in advising the individual wives and serving as their representative to the outside world. The lowest level women were regular female guards.

"Where is Henna?" Kandari sipped her usual glass of *arak* wine as she began what I suspected would likely be a jealous diatribe about the overly flamboyant Henna Begum.

"Probably running naked somewhere," sniped one of the other concubines.

Kandari grinned. "As long as she doesn't show up naked in front of the King, I'll be happy." From a distance Raushanara and I watched Kandari, resting semi-intoxicated on the divan. We still weren't sure whether, or even how, to participate in these parties, but their entertainment value was unmistakable.

Manu yawned, "What's the occasion for this party?" Manu knew her place here and never protested Kandari, because she knew well Kandari's belligerent and condescending ways.

"So innocent, Manu," Kandari's voice slurred. "Don't you know tomorrow is Nur Jahan's sentencing? Perhaps Jahanpanah doesn't want to see us after tomorrow for a while because he'll be executing the former Queen of India. It's not every day former zenana queens are killed!"

"Hush, Kandari," Ami chided, "there's been no word from Jahanpanah to attest to that. For all we know he may pardon her or exile her."

Kandari snorted. "How can he simply pardon that whore after what she did to him and all of us? We lived like animals in tents for so long!"

Ami said brusquely, "That's for the king and no else to decide!" When Ami spoke, others in the zenana knew to control their tongues. Her word was usually final.

Just then, Aba entered, and the women instantly smothered him as usual, someone handing him a glass of wine, another stuffing a small sweetmeat in his mouth. As he sat in their midst, one of them lifted his turban and padded his hair. Ami sat beside him.

The women weren't allowed to question him regarding stately affairs such as how he would punish someone, at least not publicly. Thus, all the women vied for his attention, hoping their night would be spent with the King, and that in the intimate privacy of his company they could both learn and influence forthcoming events.

Before long Henna Begum arrived, in a tight choli and salwar. The clothes hugged her skin so one could make out every contour of her flesh. Today she looked particularly stunning.

Aba stood up and removed himself from the company of women surrounding him. Ami pouted. Aba walked up to Henna, who stood at a distance, seductively smiling at him. She then performed the customary salute – the *kornish* – as she greeted the King. Placing her head in her right palm, she offered Aba homage. She would remain with her head bowed until Aba gave her permission to rise.

Aba said, "The zenana looked incomplete without you, Henna Begum." Henna looked away as if embarrassed by the compliment. Aba came to stand in front of her and put his hands on her waist. "Where did you get this stunning outfit?"

Henna slowly looked back at the King, staring down out of respect for him, for she wasn't 'good' enough to stare at his face. "The court tailors, Your Majesty."

Aba squeezed his hands into her waist. For a moment, it seemed the night would be hers. Then Aba removed his hands and began to inquisitively look at his fingers, almost as if the colour of Henna's tight salwar pants had rubbed off on his fingers.

"What's wrong, Jahanpanah?" asked Henna, frowning.

Aba moved away and looked more carefully at his fingers. "My fingers have blue paint on them." Henna looked at Aba's fingers. Then both craned their necks to see where on Henna's waist the colour could have come from. To everyone's astonishment, beige finger marks showed on Henna's waist at the exact location where Aba had touched her.

Kandari ran up to Henna. "You foolish girl! Did you paint yourself?"

Henna looked flustered, as though she was searching desperately for answers. "Jahanpanah… I… well… what I mean…"

Kandari cried: "She *painted* herself!"

The women broke into mocking laughter. Aba, apparently unaware of just what was happening, stepped back a few feet and said, "Let me see – my God, woman, you're *naked*!"

The women laughed harder, and Aba began to join in. Now everyone, including the children of the zenana, was laughing at Henna Begum as she stood in the middle of the room, painted but naked. Henna began blushing and sweating with embarrassment, and soon the sweat rolled down her body, creating clear streaks of skin.

Aba guffawed: "Did the court tailors really not satisfy you, my dear? Yes, yes, Henna Begum… go – put some clothes on!"

Henna ran out of the zenana as quickly as she'd come in. Aba sat back in the midst of his wives; soon the laughter died out, and he resumed his eating and drinking. All wondered who he would choose for the night: a wife, a concubine or a slave. Most importantly, would the individual be a proponent for a harsh sentence or a mild one for Nur Jahan?

Aba began to yawn; the decision time was coming near. Kandari hissed, "It's your bedtime, Jahanpanah." If the night went to her, Nur Jahan would surely be executed; she'd made that clear even before Aba arrived.

Aba said, "Indeed, we should all get some rest. You ladies must be ready for tomorrow." That was the only public hint Aba would give about the forthcoming events. He looked at Ami and said, "My dear, let's go."

Heavily pregnant Ami helped Aba up and escorted him to her chambers. As nearly always, the night would be hers.

✖ ✖ ✖

Next day, we found ourselves in the Hall of Special Audience, the Diwan-i-khas. Nur Jahan was summoned to the Diwan-i-khas, with Aba and Ami seated together, the remaining zenana women watching from behind the screens.

The Diwan–i–khas was where the King handled more sensitive matters of State. Smaller than the Diwan-i-am, the purpose of this hall was merely to shelter the nobles and the royal family from the gaze of the common man. To the public, the royal family was still God's representative on earth, and the King was the personification of God himself. The debauchery of the harems, the drama of the household, the poisoning, political posturing and so forth were kept far away from the eyes of the public.

This was a rare display – Mughal women were never seated with their emperor husbands. A slightly plump, fair-skinned elderly woman with beautiful azure eyes was escorted into the hall. She looked like an older version of Ami – similar straight hair, dimpled cheeks and red lips. I now understood why men in her time had admired her beauty so much. I was tempted to think she must have aged more in the last few months, having lost not just her husband but also her kingdom.

Nur Jahan was not only my step-grandmother, but ironically also my mother's aunt. My grandfather had fallen madly in love with her, married her, and then given her as much power as she desired. Rumours even whirled that she was the true ruler of India, while my opium-addicted grandfather was merely a puppet.

Aba said: "Begum Nur Jahan, you have been accused of sedition and plotting to kill me and my family in your quest to place your son-in-law, Shahriar, and your daughter, Ladli, on the throne. Is there anything you would like to say in your defence before I announce my verdict?"

Nur Jahan had originally wanted her own daughter, Ladli, to be the next Queen of India; thus she had demanded many years ago that my father marry her and make her his primary wife. My father had flatly refused, saying he could view Ladli as a sister, but never as a wife. Nur Jahan had retaliated by having Ladli marry my father's younger brother, Prince Shahriar.

Prince Shahriar was never much of anything. He had neither military skill to boast of nor artistic talent to display. Much younger than my father, he was clearly a weak choice to be king, and though Nur Jahan was influential at the royal court, even her influence wasn't able to displace my father as the rightful heir to the throne of India.

Now Nur Jahan spoke: "Jahanpanah, you are the Emperor, and I a former love of your father." Staring straight ahead, her spine arched backwards as though she were still the queen. She avoided eye contact with anyone, adopting an almost mocking posture. "What bargaining can I do with *you*? I ask that you understand that I did what any loving mother would have done for her daughter, and that is, give her a happy, prosperous future."

Ami yelled, *"Even if it would trample on other people's happiness?"* This was a rare display of anger for a woman as sober as she. The entire harem gasped in shock; Nur Jahan remained motionless before the royal couple.

It was surprising that Ami, related to someone as calculating as Nur Jahan, should emerge so innocent and selflessly loyal to her husband. She had gone from campaign to campaign with Aba never questioning or rebelling, but always supporting and strengthening his resolve. She was a rare combination of modesty and candour, a woman highly intelligent but, happily, not shrewd.

While my father was subduing a rebellion in the Deccan, Nur Jahan had made plans to make Prince Shahriar the heir apparent. My father's rebellion against her and his puppet father had failed, and he'd been forced to live in exile in the Deccan, while my two brothers were held as virtual hostages by Nur Jahan as insurance against any future rebellion. Prince Shahriar had become the heir apparent, just as Nur Jahan had envisioned.

Nur Jahan added in a low voice while staring at the ground: "My daughter is now a widow, as am I. She has a small daughter who will never know her father. Do what you will to me, but please look after my children. They are your own flesh and blood."

I'd learned from Sati what became of Prince Shahriar. Upon reaching Agra and seizing the throne, Aba ordered the execution of all of his rivals. Prince Shahriar, Prince Dawar Baksh, along with two nephews of my father, were blindfolded and brought to an open field and shot to death by an executioner.

Living with the knowledge that my father was a murderer had proved difficult for me, so I'd tried to forget about this horrific aspect of him. But at moments like these the horror would resurface again, and I'd be reminded of how much blood my Aba had on his hands.

Now he said: "Begum Nur Jahan, it would be untrue for me to say that I am happy with the way you have treated me and my family. You took my children from me and forced us to live like refugees in our own home. You even turned my father against me so he spent his final years cursing me and offering none of his blessings to me or his grandchildren. Yet I do not wish to tarnish my father's memory by having you harmed. You are after all, the *former* Empress of India."

I knew Aba had emphasised the word *former* to make it clear that Nur Jahan should understand her place. I'd like to think I was at least partially successful in telepathically communicating with my father, for what he would do next shocked all in the hall.

"I would like you to remain in a private home, right here in Agra," he went on. "You will be given an annual allowance of two lakh rupees, but you must remain in the home. You are not to meet with any dignitaries, nor attend any court events. You will not be given command of any cavalry or ships, and you cannot leave your house without the expressed written consent of myself or the Empress, Mumtaz Mahal."

"May people visit me, Your Majesty?"

"Yes, you may have anyone common visit you as you like, but you will refrain from any involvement in state affairs. I suggest you devote your remaining days to prayer and good works."

"You are too kind, my King," said Nur Jahan, as she performed the royal salutation.

I suspected that Nur Jahan had received a much weaker sentence than she'd thought she would. Even Ami, who was a calming hand on the bellicose Mughal throne, looked surprised that a stricter sentence hadn't been levelled against the former Empress. Perhaps Aba didn't want to be seen as an executioner of an old lady, a mother, grandmother and stepmother. Perhaps he wanted to save face with his children now, since we knew our father was a murderer.

3

THE POISONING

5ᵗʰ June, 1628

Our elephant was right behind Ami's golden-canopied one. As she was the royal Empress, hers had to be the grandest. Behind us rode over 100 Uzbek bodyguards with silver-tipped spears, along with dozens of eunuchs on horses. Our elephant was among the countless beasts that rode as the official royal zenana.

When summer arrived, our entire royal family decided to retreat to the summer capital in the northern hills of Kashmir to escape the oppressive heat. The pleasure gardens there were supposedly paradise on earth; we kids had only heard of them, but were now anxious to actually experience their glory ourselves.

Gardens held a special meaning to my people. Paradise after death was considered to look like a pleasure garden. By creating beautiful pleasure gardens all over our kingdom, we Mughals tried to attain the closest thing to a paradise possible here on earth. Nowhere was this truer than in Kashmir. Nestled in the northern part of the Indian subcontinent, the Kashmir valley was south of the inhabitable Himalayan terrain, but north of the plains of Agra. It therefore had perfect summer weather, with cold damp winds and clear breezes. My grandfather, Jahangir, often went there when his asthma attacks would start to worsen. It was believed the climate of Kashmir was better for the breathing of an asthmatic.

India was now akin to a patient recovering from a deadly illness. The unchecked virulence of Nur Jahan and her politics had wreaked havoc on the kingdom, with six years of political posturing and intense infighting. The entire royal family had been torn apart, and it seemed at times no one – save Nur Jahan – had been happy with her actions.

New Empress Ami stood in complete contrast to her predecessor. Aba consulted her on all private and public matters of state. She was not just his favourite wife, but also his closest adviser, confidante, and on certain matters, even co-regent. I now shared my elephant, its canopy decorated in gold and azure, with Dara; Raushanara rode with Murad and Shuja. Aurangzeb insisted on having an elephant all to himself.

Aurangzeb still seemed like an enigma to me, an entangled coil I somehow needed to unravel within the confines of my own quiet private world. I wasn't sure how I would do that.

At times I felt all of Agra had left with us. The centre of the empire was the King, so wherever he went would be the centre. Thus, the centre was moving north and with him, all of the luxuries and responsibilities of the kingdom would go also. A total of at least 80 camels, 30 elephants and 20 carts were devoted just to carrying the royal records. An additional 100 camels carried over 200 cases of Aba's clothes alone; 50 elephants carried jewels to be distributed to those individuals who had pleased the King with their words and deeds; 100 camels carried cases loaded with silver and gold rupees; another 100 carried water for drinking and bathing; several large carts carried the *hammam* that Aba and his wives would use for bathing.

At a distance of one *kos* in front of us was a horseman with the finest white linens, whose job it was to cover the carcass of any animal lying on the ground, to prevent the Emperor from viewing such a dastardly sight.

Two 'metropolis' cities travelled as part of the entourage, one always set up in advance of the other so the emperor wouldn't have to wait if he wanted to relax. Anticipating the Emperor, the Grand Master of the royal household always picked a scenic location at which to set up his city. These temporary cities featured red imperial two-storied tents lined with gold, silk and velvet each complete with its own Diwan-i-am and Diwan-i-khas as well as zenana apartments in the rear. A guard of nobles surrounded the area; a separate tent was filled with sweetmeats, fruits, water for drinking and betel leaves. Added were separate tents for the kitchen, the officers, the eunuchs and the animals.

I found myself alone often with Dara during our journey in my new makeshift tent chambers. We enjoyed each other's company so much, no one objected to him entering the zenana, and many of the zenana ladies even flirted with him, which I think he enjoyed.

On this night, I decided to prod Dara to tell me what had happened during their exile to make Aurangzeb so different. Though reluctant at first, he did tell me the whole story:

"When Aurangzeb and I first arrived at Agra from Nizamshahi, we were incredibly homesick, and the separation from Ami and Aba was especially difficult for Aurangzeb, who was very young at the time."

"How so? Did he weep often?" I inquired.

"Yes, he wept all the time. He began acting infantile; he started wetting his bed and falling ill. Nur Jahan was ruthless to him, teasing him all the time and calling him a girl and a begum."

"Oh, my God!" I was appalled. How traumatic it must have been for a child, especially a boy, to be called a member of the opposite sex by an adult!

"Aurangzeb's depression and agony went on for several months, as all of Nur Jahan's servants, especially the female ones, continued taunting Aurangzeb. As you yourself noticed, he also wasn't growing at the same rate as me because he would hardly eat anything – the grief he was enduring stole his appetite. Having received full licence from Nur Jahan to taunt Aurangzeb, the female servants grew ever more cruel to him. One day they sneaked into his room, pinned him down, put makeup on his face and told him he was small because he was really a girl, and he should accept that he was only a princess, not a prince."

As I continued to listen I was filled with both rage and sadness. I couldn't help but suspect that this mistreatment had been suffused with Nur Jahan's virulence.

Many years ago, when my father returned from his campaign in the Deccan with Arjun Singh, the leader of a rebel group that had played an instrumental role in the agitation there Aba assumed Arjun Singh would be imprisoned or executed like most rebels. Instead, Nur Jahan had Arjun Singh imprisoned and given a large cup filled with an elixir of opium seeds. Arjun Singh was allowed no food until he finished the full elixir. Over the course of several weeks, Arjun Singh, who'd been known for his physical strength and masculine leadership skills, drifted more and more into opiate senselessness. Several months later he was completely emaciated and had the wits of an imbecile. Nur Jahan then had his legs severely broken and threw him into the streets of Agra to live the rest of his days as a disabled beggar, unable to even clean himself.

I asked, "Did they also torture you, Dara?"

"They tried to, mainly by cursing Aba in my presence; but soon they realised that they couldn't upset me, so they directed all their energies at Aurangzeb. I tried to protect him, but they usually kept us apart."

"But this still doesn't explain his religious zeal?"

"I'm about to arrive at that point. With no one there to ease his torment, and me being forcibly separated from him, he began reading the Koran for comfort and wisdom. The more Nur Jahan tortured him, the more he would read. He began to sew caps for prayer services and donate them to the mosque. Whenever the servants would come to taunt him, he would recite the Koran, and the Muslim servants would walk away out of fear that they were doing something unjust while the Koran was being read aloud in their ears."

"Did that stop the torturing?"

"Yes, it did. When Grandfather Jahangir fell sick, Nur Jahan even asked Aurangzeb to lead her in prayer for the Emperor's life."

"Was he happy then?"

"He was. He would wake up at any time of the night to recite the Koran if requested to do so. He would speak out against any injustice, such as a drunken man beating his wife or a mullah accepting a bribe. His religion, oddly enough, was rooted in a pure desire to further himself spiritually through the Koran."

"And you, how did you become spiritually enhanced?"

"I didn't," smiled Dara, "at least not according to Aurangzeb. I read the Koran once, but since he and the mullah always stuck to just their own interpretation of it, I began to learn some other religious literature."

"Such as..?"

"Such as the Gita, the Hindu scripture. One of the zenana girls was a Hindu whose daughter's name was Gita, and one day I asked what her name meant. She told me it's the name of a sermon delivered by God to a soldier just before the soldier was about to go to war against his family for the Kingdom of India."

"Like Aba!" I said.

"Yes, but not exactly..." Dara continued telling me the whole story of the Gita, mesmerising me with this tale of chivalry, duty and sacrifice. It wasn't as if I'd never heard these principles before, but I'd never before been exposed to any non-Islamic scripture. I never thought something non-Muslim could be so interesting, yet many people, including my younger brother Aurangzeb, considered it blasphemy to draw strength from any religious edict other than the Koran.

It seemed Dara took a special liking to not just the scripture but also the girl who was its namesake. I asked him where she was now, in hopes of making her part of our zenana. Dara looked away at the ground. "She's dead, Jahanara."

I didn't bring up Gita again to Dara, ever-mindful of the traumatic experience he must've endured knowing that his first love was dead. I was slowly learning that Mughal men rarely needed prodding to pour their most heartfelt thoughts out to me. Whether it was Aba, Dara, or sometimes even Aurangzeb, in due time, they would tell me everything. Thus, I decided to put aside all of my worries about my family and simply enjoy the summer in the foothills of the legendary Kashmir valley.

We were indeed amidst an absolute paradise all summer, swimming in Dal Lake and having our lessons on different picnic grounds that adorned the summer capital of India. Aba and Ami spent a great deal of time together, even though Ami was pregnant all summer. Since their wedding, there had been hardly any time that Ami was not either pregnant or recovering from pregnancy. In their 28-year marriage, she would have 14 different pregnancies, almost half ending in miscarriages.

Dara increasingly drew close to Manu, who would serve him as a teacher of Hinduism. Through Manu's stewardship, Dara slowly began to master all the different Hindu texts, including the *Ramayana*, the *Mahabharata*, the *Upanishads*, and so on. He, along with my other brothers, also began to learn Persian, and he grasped it surprisingly quickly.

Aurangzeb was unnerved by this unholy alliance between our brother and his Hindu stepmother. He felt Muslims weren't supposed to learn about other religions, and that a Hindu even being brought into a Muslim household constituted a sacrilegious act. In fact, he continued to feel that much of what was transpiring in Mughal Indian culture was sacrilegious. He spoke out against intermarriage between religions, social liberation for women and the abolition of the *jiyza* (a tax on non-believers that was detested by Hindus but welcomed by mullahs). Our parents, though troubled by his attitude on these matters, were comforted to know that their son was equally passionate about his opposition to bribery, domestic violence, theft and drug abuse. Aurangzeb had a pure heart, he just needed some appropriate guidance, thought Ami. Ami spent many days with Aurangzeb alone and slowly began to change him, even convincing him to play with all his brothers and sisters and enjoy his youth, not spend all his time praying.

Raushanara succeeded in winning the love of Aurangzeb. He would take her wherever she wanted to go, and though he continued to talk down to her, no one else was allowed to. Once a servant raised his voice at the young princess; Aurangzeb had the servant lashed ten times and dismissed from his service. Raushanara made sure her brother was always included in her activities, and in turn he never allowed her to leave his sight, either.

For me, this was indeed paradise on earth. I wanted to capture this moment, seal it in my heart and never let it escape. I had everything, I felt: My father was the emperor; my brothers were reunited; I'd developed a strong friendship with Dara; and I was beginning to make inroads into Aurangzeb's heart, which was slowly thawing from the trauma of imprisonment. If only nothing changed, life would be absolutely perfect.

However, winter would arrive in a few months, and this paradise would slowly have to disappear into the depths of the cold, I began to fear. But it would return again, I figured, next summer, and life would be perfect again.

By February, our entire family was back in Agra. Dara's mysticism was growing stronger and stronger, and he began to attend Hindu prayer services, *pujas*, held at Manu's palace.

Aba, meanwhile, had begun to construct a special throne for himself. He often complained that the current throne was grossly inadequate for him, and that he needed something that would better reflect his status as ruler of the world.

Aurangzeb saw this desire as yet another blasphemy. According to him, people weren't supposed to engage in the sort of self-indulgence our own father and previous monarchs had. He began acting as though in his mind matters were beginning to spiral out of control: the pseudo-conversion of his brother to Hinduism, the vanity of the court, the celebration of non-Muslim idols by Manu in the kingdom.

"Jahanara, come quick! Something's wrong!" cried Ami one morning from a small apartment in the zenana.

I ran to my pregnant mother, fearing her health had deteriorated.

But she cried, "Manu is vomiting blood! She's barely lucid and can't keep anything down."

I entered to see a feeble Manu lying on a blood stained bed, her head in my mother's lap, blood pouring from her mouth like lava from a volcano. It seemed as though I was staring at death itself. "How long has this been going on?" I asked.

"I don't know, Jahanara." Ami wrung her hands. "I just noticed it this morning when I came to see her. Go get the *hakim*!"

I instructed the slaves to fetch the court hakim (physician) at once, informing him it was urgent. The hakim came right away and began examining Manu. He couldn't determine the cause of her symptoms, but asked the servants to place her discharges in buckets and deliver them to him for closer analysis. He also gave her a tonic to drink, which, surprisingly, she didn't vomit back up.

Over the next several days, Manu's condition remained stable, but she continued to move in and out of consciousness. This saddened Aba noticeably, and he remained with Ami at Manu's bedside. I slept in the same room as Manu and Dara stayed at Manu's feet, tears drying on Dara's face and his eyes red from sleepless nights.

This whole episode just sucked the happiness from our lives as if some ill-wisher had cast an evil spell on our happy home. Ami was clearly in no condition to nurse Manu, but fearing what the rest of the zenana would say about her, Ami put her own health aside and gave Manu absolute attention.

I also began to wonder if Nur Jahan had cast a spell on our home as an evil 'gift' for departing from our lives. Based on the tales I'd heard about her, she wasn't one to slowly walk into oblivion, and I feared that by sparing her life, my Aba may have left his worst and most powerful enemy a chance to destroy our lives.

Finally, after a week of supportive treatment, Manu's fever subsided, and she began to eat full meals. She no longer vomited blood or anything else, and she started to regain her energy. In gratitude Aba ordered prisoners to be released and forgiven and bags of gold coins to be distributed among the poor. The hakim was rewarded handsomely, but what he was about to say was worth almost as much as what he'd done to save the imperial wife. He'd learned the cause of Manu's illness: She'd been poisoned.

Aba was furious. He thought he'd dismissed, imprisoned or killed every 'snake' and traitor in his kingdom and now could rule with peace in his heart that all those who surrounded him wished him well. However, now someone in his kingdom was plotting against him and had tried to assassinate his wife.

He ran from the zenana without speaking to anyone, while I looked helplessly at Ami in disbelief and heard him shout, as he ran: "I wish to meet my advisors in the Diwan-i-khas—*now!*" We all stared at each other in bewilderment.

All the nobles and advisors gathered in the hall, their heads held low, in part to show respect to the monarch, but also to show sadness at the news that foul play had been involved.

Aba roared, *"I wish to know who has dared to invite the wrath of the Emperor of India!"*

The nobles stood patiently, waiting for their monarch to finish his rant.

"I wish all those who dare question my authority to know that the punishment for attempted murder is just as severe as that for murder itself! I want all of you to scout out through your contacts and spies and find out who was behind this! To start with, I want a full list of everything the queen ate, and who prepared it."

The chef for the royal zenana, Hamid Shah, was summoned before the King and brought out in chains by the royal guards. He begged, "Jahanpanah! Forgive me, Lord, but I cannot tell you who made me do this!"

"You fiend! You tried to kill my family. I'll have your entire family fed to dogs and have you crushed by an elephant if you don't tell me who was behind this."

"But I cannot, my Lord. If I do, I'll be killed, but if I don't, *you'll* kill me. Either way I am doomed!"

The Kind ordered: "Imprison this man's family! I want this man crushed by an elephant next Tuesday!"

Animal fights were infamous in the Mughal courts. All sorts of animals – elephants, lions, leopards – were made to fight while huge crowds watched. The execution of criminals by placing them in rings with the fierce animals was a favourite and therefore somewhat rare form. A criminal had to work hard to incur such wrath of the Emperor as to be sentenced to such heinous punishment. By attacking a member of the royal family, Hamid Shah had secured this fate for himself, and 'Bloody Tuesday' would be his day of reckoning. Though the shows went on every day, with pauses on Sunday for prayer, Tuesday was a favourite because it was considered *the* Day of Blood. Fortunately for Hamid, he was sentenced on Wednesday, so he had almost a week left to prove his innocence should he desire to do so.

Aba retired for the night to his private apartments, not visiting his zenana at all. As a man, it seemed he felt ashamed to know someone had tried to and succeeded in harming his wife, so he refused to face his zenana until he found the perpetrator and brought him to justice in front of Manu.

I was in my apartment crying; Dara lay by my side. He said, "This whole episode brings back so many memories."

"Memories of what?" I asked.

"Gita." He paused. "Her symptoms were the same. She and I used to meet in the courtyard every day and spend the entire day together. She's the reason I became so infatuated with religion. Were it not for her, I would never have learned anything but Islam. She taught me Hinduism, and I began to see how we all share essentially the same religion."

"But what does this have to do with Manu?"

"Gita was fine until I came into her life. Then, suddenly something happened to her. She, like Manu, started vomiting blood one day. She got sicker and sicker."

"What did the royal hakims say?"

"Royal hakims? Jahanara, Gita wasn't a princess so no royal hakim was going to attend her. She had to settle for what the neighbourhood women gave her for her sickness."

"But she was your friend. You could've gotten a hakim for her."

"No, I was a *prisoner*," Dara said. "Nur Jahan would never listen to me, and Grandfather Jahangir was barely lucid in those days. First her and now Manu. Someone is killing people because of me, I just know it."

I prepared some *khichdi*, a bland gruel of rice and lentils, for Manu myself, because Ami feared no one else could be trusted with her meals until the perpetrator had been found. Manu was still too weak to feed herself, so I fed her the khichdi myself.

As I did I heard behind me the same caustic voice I'd grown to detest: *Kandari's*. "See how life can transport a person from one place to an entirely different one! How awful– you were riding atop a massive elephant just a few months ago, and now you're made to cook and feed the Queen like a servant girl."

I slowly turned livid. I tried ignoring her as always, but to no avail.

She sneered, "Manu, make sure the lentils in the khichdi aren't too hard, or else *you'll* have stomach pains." Yet another backhanded slap at my cooking. I prayed she'd leave. But she peeked over my shoulder into the bowl and added: "That doesn't look like khichdi…"

"*Begum Kandari*!" I yelled. "This is khichdi! I know because I cooked it, because the Padishah Begum commanded me to. She could've commanded you, too, and you would've had to do it, because she's the Padishah Begum and you're not!"

Kandari arched backwards in astonishment, but I wasn't finished. "Maybe she didn't trust a minor begum like you, so she had me, the Begum Sahiba, cook for Manu. Now, as the Begum Sahiba, I command you to leave Manu's chambers. Perhaps I will have you make us some ginger tea later! Understand?"

Kandari began to shake, and tears swelled in her eyes. By now an entire crowd of zenana women had gathered and were murmuring, hands over their mouths. "Hay Allah, listen to this girl! Hay Allah!" But none dared address me directly. One of them then grabbed Kandari's hand and began to lead her away.

As the women cleared off, I noticed my mother had been watching and listening to everything in the back, and she now slowly made her way forward. I was too nervous and upset to address her, for I knew she'd be upset with me. I turned my back to her and resumed feeding Manu, as though I hadn't noticed my mother was there.

I heard her walking towards me, but didn't acknowledge her. In my mind I began reciting what I'd say to her if she reprimanded me for speaking rudely to my stepmother: I'd tell her I'd had no choice because the taunts were becoming unbearable; how to some extent Ami herself was responsible for this outburst because she never came to my rescue; how I never coveted this title, but was being abused by everyone in the zenana; and the person responsible for this abuse was Kandari, who was inciting everyone to treat me this way.

Ami put her hand on my shoulder. I was ready for her. I would tell her this much and more. She slowly lowered her head while I continued to feed Manu, and looking the other way she said quietly, "Well done, my child!"

We all congregated in the Diwan-i-khas a few days later to witness the sentencing for Manu's heinous poisoning. Aba had learned from his spies the identity of the culprit who'd instructed Hamid Shah to poison Manu. We were all disillusioned to learn this, but we had to keep our emotions private.

The women of the zenana were looking from their grilled screens as Dara and Shuja stood next to the throne, with Aurangzeb a short distance away. The nobles all stood in front of the Emperor as Hamid Shah was again brought in.

Aba shouted sternly, "You have been accused of aiding in the plot to murder Begum Manbhavati! And we now know that the person who instructed you to mix poison in her food was none other than my own son, Prince Aurangzeb." There was a short pause. Everyone was shocked by this disturbing news.

No one knew for sure, but the rumour around the zenana was that Aurangzeb was opposed to all the Hindu rituals Manu was bringing into the Mughal household. Fearing that she was polluting the household, he'd tried to kill her

Aba said, "I cannot excuse what you did, but I also cannot punish you more harshly than I do my son, because his crime was graver than yours. I therefore nullify your earlier sentence of death and instead banish you from my kingdom. You are not to show yourself in the Mughal dominion ever again. Should you do so, be assured an elephant's foot will meet your chest!"

The prisoner began to weep but didn't beg for a softer sentence. Sensing he'd just narrowly escaped death, he probably took the banishment as a boon.

"Now, Prince Aurangzeb. Because you are my son I cannot treat you like a criminal; and after so many years of separation from you, I cannot bear the prospect of distancing myself from you anymore. Your fate shouldn't be decided by this disciple of Allah. For you, another disciple must make this decision."

Here is what I gathered from later reports about what happened next:

Aba escorted Aurangzeb from the Diwan-i-khas to the Pearl Mosque, built in solid white marble, with so very ordinary and unpretentious an entrance that an individual would be hardly prepared for the majestic beauty and unaffected expression of religious fervour that characterised its interior. Rarely could one find any Mughal building whose beauty reached such heights with so little ostentation of jewels, silver or gold, but solely with perfection of proportion and elegant harmony of constructive design. Inside the mosque a mullah was waiting for him.

Aba thus asked the mullah to evaluate Aurangzeb's actions based on Islamic doctrines from the Koran: "I will present to you the facts of this episode, and if my son wishes to interrupt me and correct anything I say, he has my permission to do so."

Aurangzeb, visibly frightened at everything that was transpiring, patiently listened, unsure of what Aba was up to.

Aba said, "Speak now, mullah – how do you find my son's actions?"

Aurangzeb is said to have looked at the mullah and given him a smile, as if the winning hand was now in his palm, and his father was about to be embarrassed in his own kingdom.

But the mullah replied, "Your Majesty, Prince Aurangzeb's actions are un-Islamic!"

Aurangzeb's eyes widened, I was told. How could anyone call *him* un-Islamic when he'd devoted so much of his life thus far to serving Allah? This was the greatest insult anyone could give him.

The mullah continued: "In the Koran, the attacking of women and helpless children is strictly forbidden by the Prophet. Yet the Prince harmed a helpless woman. And what makes his offence even more sinful is that the person he harmed was his own stepmother!"

The mullah then looked at Aurangzeb and shouted loudly: "Does the Koran not say paradise is at the mother's feet, you fool?!?"

The words were said to have echoed in the mosque several times after the mullah finished speaking, amplifying his already loud voice as they reiterated his statement to the young Prince.

"You have offended Allah and Islam for several generations! Your whole family will have to answer for your sins on Judgment Day."

Then the mullah levelled against Aurangzeb a punishment befitting his crime: He was not to be allowed to enter the mosque for a period of 60 days; he was to continue to pray and ask Allah for his forgiveness; he must offer his apology to Manu, and also have ten lashes laid on his back.

The next day, we siblings stayed in the zenana apartment while Aurangzeb was escorted to a private room to receive his physical punishment. The air seemed thick that day. Everyone knew what was to occur, but no one dared speak of it openly. Very little laughter and levity was heard in Agra on this fateful day. Quietly we all waited for the nightmare to end.

Aurangzeb, pursuant to the sentence proclaimed by the mullah, received ten lashes on his back. With each lash, he cried out and begged for his Aba to have mercy. Aba, standing outside the door of the torture chamber, told me later he closed his eyes with each cry and shed tears after the fifth stroke. Aba begged forgiveness of Allah on his son's behalf and asked that he be pardoned on Judgment Day for what he'd done.

After the tenth lash Aba left, not wishing to be seen by anyone with tears in his eyes, as such a sight would indicate weakness, which a king isn't supposed to possess. My young brother put his long shirt on and began to walk back to the royal zenana where he lived. With the same urgency a traveller has approaching his destination, I fixed my eyes in the distance as I waited for my wounded, troubled brother.

Finally in the distance I saw a small, skinny figure nearing. I noticed he couldn't walk straight – his back must have stung as he walked – and he had a limp as he returned to the apartments.

We were waiting in Angoori Bagh (literally meaning 'grape courtyard'), which was located within the harem apartments. We knew Aurangzeb would pass from there, and we hoped to see him up close as he entered.

The small, olive-skinned, five-foot-tall figure came into sharper focus as he neared, and I noticed dried tears on his face. As he walked, he sounded as if his every step was painful. His head hung low, as if he wished to avoid any embarrassing eye contact with us siblings, all of whom by now knew what had transpired in the mosque behind closed doors.

With a pang of concern I asked him, "Aurangzeb, my brother, how are you feeling?"

"I'm fine," he whispered hoarsely.

"You don't look fine."

I noticed a trail of blood drops along the path he'd walked. "You're bleeding?"

"I said I'm *fine*; I just want to go to my room."

Still a head taller, I ran up to him and quickly embraced him, weeping myself. "What did they do to you?" I cried, pressing his wounded body against mine. "You're just a child; it's monstrous that they made you bleed. Please let me take care of you; your clothes are bloody; let me help you my brother."

Dara then broke in: "He doesn't need your help, Jahanara. He doesn't need anyone's help. Do you, brother?"

"I just want to be left alone," he muttered.

Dara snarled, "Did you leave *Manu* alone?"

"That's all settled now, Dara," I shot back.

"What about Gita?" Dara said bitterly. "Is that all settled too?"

My eyes widened in shock and I slowly shifted my gaze from Dara back to Aurangzeb: I hadn't made the connection in my mind that perhaps Aurangzeb had orchestrated that murder as well.

Dara grabbed Aurangzeb by the collar, pushed me aside and cried, "Listen, Aurangzeb, just tell me the truth once: *Did you poison Gita?*"

"I just want to go to my room," he sighed wearily.

"Not until you answer my question. Did you murder Gita?"

"I said, leave me alone."

Dara pushed Aurangzeb to the ground; his back landed on the hot pavement; it hit his bloody wounds like a hot iron on soft flesh, and he screamed in agony.

"Did you kill her?"

"Yes, I poisoned her, okay? I did it! I poisoned Manu, I poisoned Gita! I killed the non-believers. I did what I *had* to do!"

Dara, visibly, furiously hurt by the admission he must have known for several days now was forthcoming, lunged on top of my younger brother and began punching him in the face repeatedly. I stood at a distance and struggled to keep myself from jumping in to save Aurangzeb. Then I glanced at Dara's fists; they were now covered in blood.

I struggled between the two and covered Aurangzeb's body with my own. "Stop hurting him! Hit *me*, stop hurting my brother! He's just a child! What's wrong with you people?"

Dara kept trying to punch Aurangzeb through the spaces my body couldn't cover, and I felt a sharp blow on my back that caused me to cry aloud.

Aurangzeb heard me scream and looked up at me. I don't think anyone had ever before tried to protect him. His earliest memories had been of being abandoned by our parents in a political game and tortured by his captors. Nobody came to his rescue – not even the mullah. Now, for the first time ever, someone was defending him and had actually taken a blow meant for him.

Dara jumped back in horror from having hit me unintentionally. I got up still weeping and held my brother in my arms and cried, "No one needs to hurt him anymore! *No one!* He and I will leave this kingdom right away. We *need* no one! *I'll* take care of him! You don't have to do anything if you think he's a monster. He'll be my responsibility!"

Having heard the commotion, Ami came running from her apartment. Shocked to see not only Aurangzeb dripping blood, but also me crying while holding him, she yelled: "Are you kids already continuing your ancestors' tradition of killing each other?"

All us children looked away in shame at our otherwise pacifist mother's scream: "At least they waited till the King was dead to commit such a sin. If you can't wait that long, can you at least wait till after I die?"

We reeled in shock at our mother's words. Still heavily pregnant, Ami's health was deteriorating with every successive pregnancy, yet this was the first time she'd ever brought the inauspicious word 'dead' to her mouth. "Jahanara," she ordered, "take Aurangzeb to my room and tell the servant to prepare a warm bath for him with some sponges for his wounds!"

She turned then to Dara and commanded, "Go to your room! Now!"

As we stood there in stunned silence for a moment before moving, I felt as if she'd foretold a prophecy, predicting a calamity that awaited the Mughal Empire in the years to come.

I took Aurangzeb to Ami's palace and asked him to take his shirt off so I could see his bare skin's wounds. As per Ami's wishes, I sent the servant to fetch some warm water. Raushanara hurried in after me and we soon began using warm, wet cloths to wipe our brother's dried blood off his back.

Ami came in after we, his sisters, finished washing his back clean. She was aware of and understood everything that had happened the past few days – the censure by the mullah and the rift now widening between Dara and Aurangzeb. Did she feel herself guilty of failing Aurangzeb as a parent? Could she now play a greater role in his upbringing, and would this be the moment from which she began that new journey? Time would tell.

"You are a prince, Aurangzeb; don't let these wounds destroy you," she said as she applied more warm water to his blistered and scarred back. Aurangzeb moaned at each touch. "You have a gift. You understand morality probably better than anyone your age."

Aurangzeb seemed stunned to hear Ami compliment him.

She went on: "But as you pray, you must remember what it is you're praying for. Your actions from now on must be such that if someone writes about them, he'll think he's reading a verse of the Koran!" Aurangzeb's eyebrows lifted inquisitively and he moved his head closer to Ami's.

"Imagine if someone wrote about your actions: What would they say? 'Aurangzeb, messenger of Allah, sneakily poisoned his idol-loving stepmother to prevent the infidel culture from prospering in the land of Allah?'"

Aurangzeb listened silently.

Ami continued: "We Mughals were a small tribe of nomads who came to this country. 'Hindustan' means 'Land of the Hindus.' We are in *their* country. We face not east toward the rest of the country, but west towards Mecca when we pray. We are outsiders. Nothing about this country is to our liking... not the food, nor the religion, nor even the customs. Yet we are here, and we're slowly bringing more Indians to the grace of Allah. How? *By convincing these people, Aurangzeb.* Bring Allah into your heart, and the voice that emanates from your mouth will convince all the non-believers to convert!"

Aurangzeb seemed stunned by what Ami had just uttered to him. Till now, no one had ever truly explained the complexity of India's culture to him. The heterogeneous, multicultural heritage of India was never discussed in the Mughal household, and teachers often glanced over it as if it was insignificant. Ami, I think, understood this relationship and knew that we children must appreciate it also if we were to maintain the empire after her.

"We Mughals," she said, "are to Hindustan what a veil is to a face. We can cover it with our mosques, but we can't change what lies beneath it." She then turned him around, cupped his cheeks in her hands and kissed his forehead. "I want to give you something now, which only you deserve to have."

She got up, went over to her jewel-studded cabinet and moved her jewels from one of the shelves. She found behind them a small black box, returned to Aurangzeb's side and handed it to him. She said, "Open it and see what's inside – but don't touch it."

Aurangzeb slowly opened the lid from the box and found a few brown stands of hair inside; but obeying Ami's instructions, he didn't touch them. He said, "What are these, Ami?"

"This is the most valuable treasure in the world, one passed down to me by my mother and to her from hers. I want no one else to have it because I don't think anyone but you would treasure it with the respect it deserves. These are actual strands from the beard of the Prophet."

"Mohammed?"

"Yes, the Prophet Mohammed. Before he died, he gave a few strands of his beard to each of his disciples. Few people today still have the originals; you are now one of them."

Aurangzeb looked awestruck at what he was being given. Never before, I presume, had he been given any gift of true personal value to him – he thought his father's riches worthless.

"But son," Ami added, "you must promise me this: Now that you have these, you will never do anything that violates the Prophet's teachings ever again. You will never hurt any Hindu or Christian or non-believer, ever. Promise me!"

"I promise, Ami," cried Aurangzeb, and he hugged Ami for the priceless present he'd been given. "I'll never do anything to harm anyone, I promise."

4

THE EVIL HAND

3rd September, 1629

Ami closed her eyes, placed her palms before her, and began to utter words softly aloud so I could faintly hear them as I sat beside her. "Allah, hear my prayers: Please help me make Aurangzeb a better person."

I opened my eyes and looked at her. Her demeanour had been sad for the past several weeks, and I knew why: She'd suffered another miscarriage, and with each of these, Ami had told me she felt as though she herself was dying. Were all these miscarriages a prelude to something much more serious and tragic? Keenly aware of her own mortality, she began immersing herself in service to the unfortunate, perhaps hoping that helping those in need would absolve her of any sin she might have committed, and that she'd be granted a long and prosperous life, alongside her first love – Aba.

Now she prayed: "You've taken seven of my children, I've never questioned your will, and I don't dare do so now. But, Creator of this World, understand a mother's anguish at watching her child take the path of evil. To watch as your child, whom you've held and hugged and kissed, walks the path of injustice is unthinkable. Give this peasant servant of yours this one wish: Take my life, but spare Aurangzeb's soul!"

I looked at my mother in surprise, but then quickly closed my eyes and resumed my own prayer. I couldn't bear the thought of losing my Ami, the anchor that held everything together. If there was one person against whom no one in the family had any complaint – not even Nur Jahan – it was Ami. Her leaving this world would be a disaster not only for me, but the entire imperial household. I began to pray more fervently, hoping that my prayer and not my mother's would be answered.

"Please take *me*, Allah," I pleaded in my mind. "Take all my riches, and let me live my life in the mud huts on the far side of Agra, and give me a painful death. Deny me any children and any love, and I will still say my life has been blessed. But please spare my mother. Don't let her die!"

On the far side of Agra were districts where the peasants lived in simple huts made only of mud and straw. These would often disappear during extreme weather, as the wind and rains washed the inhabitants into the river along with their homes and belongings. While the nobles were often rewarded with hundreds of acres of lands and cavalry, the peasants, the backbone of our revenue system, toiled all day in the fields and gave more than a third of their income in taxes and bribes to corrupt officials. A poor harvest wouldn't preclude the peasant from paying such taxes, and often he'd have to mortgage his farm during such seasons. Continued poor harvests would cause the peasant to default on his mortgage payments and lose his land and livelihood. Such was the sad, ugly truth behind the opulence of the Mughal Empire. For all the wealth that existed in the royal household, the average citizen's lot was far from comfortable. Ami understood this and upon Aba's coronation, she began spending vast sums of money to feed the poor, and she even gave regular audiences to women whose husbands had died and who now needed to feed their families.

I was tormented by my mother's anguish and felt compelled to help her somehow. Was Aurangzeb's intolerance his own creation, or was an evil hand misguiding him? I began pondering the possibilities. I asked my eunuch, Bahadur, to find out who had been in contact with Aurangzeb after we returned from Kashmir. I was certain someone was pulling the strings, and my little brother hadn't concocted the plan on his own. Bahadur was a gentle soul who never engaged in zenana gossip for her own amusement. After being assigned to me, she became almost an older sibling, protecting me from the dangers that lurked in unthinkable places in the palace. The other women of the harem feared her, and their treatment of me changed once I was placed in her charge. I now commanded respect; my suggestions were no longer met with taunts and sarcasm, and the women would go out of their way to include me on trips and hunts.

She now told me, "Begum Sahiba, both your brother and your sister, Raushanara, have been paying regular visits to the former Empress, Nur Jahan."

I froze in horror. I'd heard of Nur Jahan's vindictiveness, but I couldn't believe her tentacles could run so deep into the fabric of my family. "Bahadur, are you sure? I can't act on a rumour…"

"I assure you, Begum Sahiba, this is no rumour. Several of my sources, including Nur Jahan's own eunuch, Hoshiyar Khan, have attested to this."

I resolved not to make either parent of mine privy to this information; I opted instead to take matters into my own hands. With Bahadur by my side, I took a detour on my way to visit the mud huts of Agra and personally confront the former empress.

A small haveli began to come into focus as our palanquin made its way towards Nur Jahan's home. There was an uncomfortable feeling in my stomach as we approached, as if Nur Jahan had placed a curse on the air around her haveli.

Yet, I was determined to not be intimidated by this woman. She had caused so much grief in my life that I opted to do what was right for my family and confront her. By this age, I'd developed my mother's sense of confidence and sophistication in dealing with difficult matters.

Bahadur approached the haveli first and made contact with Hoshiyar Khan. After the two eunuchs discussed the purpose of the visit, Bahadur escorted me to the main room where Nur Jahan would receive me.

Though we exchanged the customary salutations, I didn't waste any time on casual conversation, instead forthrightly saying: "Aunt Nur Jahan, I'm here to tell you plainly: leave Aurangzeb alone!"

Nur Jahan smiled slimly. "What makes you think I've said anything to Aurangzeb?"

"He told me!" I lied. "I know everything. I know how you manipulated him to poison Manu and told him it was God's will for her to die. Why won't you leave him alone? Why do you wish to turn him into a fanatic?"

If Nur Jahan was surprised at my boldness, she didn't let on. Instead, while I was speaking, she began walking around her room, rearranging figurines on her table as if she were preoccupied. She replied calmly, "I'm not saying anything his own heart's not telling him."

"He's a child!" I nearly screamed. "You're poisoning his mind!"

Nur Jahan continued to fiddle with her tea, avoiding eye contact with me.

"How did you become like this?" I probed.

She froze and moved only her eyes towards me. Realising I'd just struck a nerve, I prodded her more. "You couldn't always have been like this..."

Before marrying my grandfather, Nur Jahan had been in an abusive marriage with a Persian soldier, Sher Afghan, and those many years had made my grand aunt a tough individual who always plotted and schemed for her own interests, and whose cold ambition knew no limits.

She waved dismissively at the air. "As I said, fair Princess, you cannot understand any of this!" She walked away from my chair.

"I can't understand any of this?" I replied bitingly. "You're poisoning my happy home and trying to destroy your own niece's family. What more is there to understand?"

"Is *my* home not destroyed?" she shrieked. Is my daughter not a widow who refuses to remarry because she's so traumatised by what your father did to her husband? My grandchild is raised in this house like a prisoner, afforded none of the luxuries you and your siblings enjoy!"

I fought to remain calm. "Will punishing Aurangzeb for my father's mistake fix everything?" I pressed.

Nur Jahan took a deep breath to regain her composure, and then went on: "You can't understand. You've never been poor."

"What does wealth have to do with this?" I retorted. "My father gave you a handsome pension to live on; you have plenty of money."

"Women in this society have to fend for themselves, she replied, "… always…"

"How can you say that?" I shot back. "My mother has more riches than any woman in the history of India. Women are getting more rights every day under my father."

"Not the same as men."

"Almost!" I countered.

Nur Jahan just stared at me as if laying me bare to the bone with her eyes. She must have felt my unease. "You are very beautiful, Jahanara," she said, "a true Persian."

Embarrassed, I looked away and replied in a low voice, "I'm only half Persian."

"Oh, no, my dear! You're fully Persian! Those long slender fingers, that olive skin, those sensual eyes, and that silky black hair could never belong to a Hindustani. You're a Persian. Maybe your naiveté and peaceful demeanour is Hindustani – we Persians love war – but physically you're a Persian beauty."

I sensed she was trying to toy with me now. I composed myself and hurled back, "What does my appearance have to do with the plight of women in India?"

Nur Jahan just smiled, as if amused by my outburst. "Tell me, Jahanara. You're how old now? 16, 17?"

"Fifteen."

She chuckled. "We Persian women develop fast, don't we? My body was also fully developed by this age. My breasts were more developed than my Hindustani maid's, and she was 20!"

She began to run her finger along the edges of my face, and I looked away, feeling myself blush at her compliments. She purred, "Have you ever been in love, Jahanara?"

Stunned, I stared at her. "I love my parents. I love my family."

"That's not the love I'm talking about."

My shyness and her comment's directness made me even more uncomfortable. I looked away, and she said, "Have you ever loved a man who wasn't related to you?"

"I don't think that's any of your concern, Empress Nur Jahan."

"Oh, but you see it *is*. My dear, no matter how beautiful you are, how sensual your face and how well developed your body, it will never be touched by any man. That's the sad truth of the Mughal Empire."

My eyebrows wrenched in confusion and anger as I felt Nur Jahan take control of the conversation and steer it into uncharted territory. "What are you talking about? My Aba will find a prince for me!"

"Is that what he told you?" she laughed condescendingly. "He lied. No Mughal daughter of the Emperor is allowed to marry. None of your aunts married, and none of their aunts married. You and your sisters have been damned to a celibate existence, while your brothers will enjoy harems of 300 women each."

I started to feel suffocated. I'd come here to talk about Aurangzeb, and somehow we were now talking about me? My head throbbed with a strange mixture of emotions: embarrassment, disgust and rage. I spat back: "More of your lies!"

She chuckled again and moved her hands sensuously over my lips and neck. "I wish they were. No matter how good you are, my dear, no man will touch you. Sensual intimacy will never be yours. Get wise before it's too late, and find an heir to the throne to groom in your image. If you wish to survive, that's the only way."

I wrenched Nur Jahan's hand from my face and shouted, "Is that what you're trying to do with Aurangzeb? Groom him for your own ends?"

"Why should I groom him? My days in this world are numbered. By the time he or any of your brothers becomes king, I'll be but a memory. I have other reasons to groom him..."

"Like what?"

"Oh, you'll see. No one has ever wronged me and lived happily. Even if it's from beyond the grave, I'll get even with your father," Nur Jahan replied ominously.

"How? By turning Aurangzeb into a zealot?"

"Precisely."

"That's a strange way to get revenge."

"Your own life will tell you why it's not strange."

Consumed with rage, I turned to storm out of Nur Jahan's residence, but before I'd gone some distance I whirled around and spat, "If your life is dedicated to destroying Aurangzeb, then *my* life will be dedicated to *preserving* him!"

Nur Jahan's chest heaved and her eyes reddened with rage at my challenge.

I continued: "You and I are made of the same Persian blood, eh? I swear to you, I'll see my father's image in whoever becomes king, and I'll help him rule Mughal India to the best of my abilities. I'll never cross my king!"

Nur Jahan pursed her lips as if about to reply, but I never gave her the chance: "You tried it your way, Nur Jahan; I'll do it mine!"

5

PIT OF DEATH

4ᵗʰ January, 1631

Are you getting more comfortable with these elephant rides?"
Ami smiled.

I didn't think anyone would ever be comfortable riding on top of these massive beasts, but I was getting more used to it. "Yes, Ami!" I would lie just to make her happy.

Nearly two years had passed since Manu's poisoning, and Ami was pregnant yet again. Having miscarried many times before, it seemed this time she was determined to give birth to a living child. This was now her fourteenth pregnancy, her previous 13 having resulted in the birth of four sons, two daughters and seven miscarriages.

As fate would have it, there was yet another war to be fought, this time in the Deccan, and as always, Ami insisted on being by Aba's side during the war, even in pregnancy.

We set out for the Deccan with the entire kingdom at our disposal. Not everyone came though; Dara, Shuja, Aurangzeb, and Raushanara remained in Agra while I, along with young Murad, accompanied our parents. I was riding with Ami in her palanquin due to her health.

She moaned, "Try being pregnant on these rides! Every bump feels like a contraction." Ami was beyond modesty at this point. She would continue lamenting her condition to me. Not knowing how to respond, I would simply smile.

I could tell we'd left Agra because the scent of sweetmeats and kebabs was fading, gradually being replaced by that of woods and forests. The bumpiness of our ride made me realise the heavily vegetated mud paths of the wilderness had replaced the paved streets of Agra. Day and night we travelled, stopping more frequently than usual so Ami would have sufficient rest. At times, Ami protested to Aba that he was making her feel like a burden by slowing down his troops en route to war, but Aba would not relent. He continued to pamper Ami, as if she were still in Agra.

The journey was long. Travelling with the Emperor was very different than travelling with anyone else. Even during the march to war, Aba paused to hold court every day at noon, dusk and dawn to anyone who wished to pay homage and present gifts. The local nobles – the *ranas, amirs, divans, maharajahs* – gladly paid us homage as the Emperor passed through lands they claimed to rule, knowing full well they were ultimately subservient to us.

Several days into our journey, I began to sense yet another change in smell. *Was it the Deccan?* The Deccan had a vague but familiar scent that is very difficult for me to even describe. The Deccan was really nothing more than an endless mass of jungle with interspersed pockets of isolated villages run by petty princes. Oddly, it was comforting to me. This is where I'd grown up, and though life was much more fulfilling now, I often thought of the Deccan with nostalgic joy, for this land was where I had spent many happy moments with my parents.

"Not there yet," Ami would correct me. "But we're getting close." We'd actually taken a detour through the state of Gujarat and were several days from the Deccan.

Suddenly, the air was filled with the most putrid stench of waste I'd ever known. "What is that smell?" I choked. I began coughing and moved my shawl over my nose to attempt a partial escape from the stench. "It smells like death."

Ami looked equally disgusted and worried. We moved the curtain of the canopy with our hand and looked out for answers. "Allah have mercy!" cried Ami.

The shock in her voice was nothing compared to my own feelings. I utterly lost my voice. Perhaps Ami had seen such a disturbing scene in the past, allowing her to be in simple dismay, but for me this was a sight unlike any other that had ever met my eyes. My breath quickened.

"Where are we, my child?" Ami asked rhetorically, probably aware I had no answer.

To our dismay, dead bodies of all ages and types were lining the streets. The road was littered with them: men, women, children, goats, cattle, dogs, horses. Those not yet cremated or buried had been partially consumed by jackals and vultures. This desolate village looked completely devoid of any inhabitants. The air was dry and suffocating, making it impossible to even breathe. "Allah have mercy!" repeated Ami. I stared at my mother as she again invoked God. Yet one devastating scene gave rise to another even more horrific one. I held my breath at the stench of the beggars now filling the air. I didn't want to risk inhaling their affliction.

"Two *dam*!!!" yelled a man. so skinny I could see every bone is his body. He held a baby in his hands out to us.

"What's a dam?" I asked Ami, trying to sound unmoved. She told me a dam was made of copper, and was the lowest form of currency; I had never seen nor heard of it before. As royalty, the lowest denomination I dealt with was the rupee, made of silver; but more commonly, I just used the *mohur*s, made of solid gold.

"Allah have mercy!" Ami continued as she gazed at the man. "They're selling their children for money!" With no food for entire villages, the inhabitants had resorted to deserting their own children. As Ami and I stared at the devastation, we saw a group of men fighting each other for rights to a pile of dung to see if there was a piece of undigested grain they could eat. "This is the real India, Jahanara," said Ami. "This is what you must fight for. The true sin and offence against Allah is poverty."

"Wait! Wait! Please, we need your help!" A pale-skinned man at a distance pleaded with our caravan to come to a halt. Our soldiers immediately surrounded the poor man for the offence of stopping the King. Ami and I, seated in the palanquin behind Aba's, heard bits and pieces of the conversation. Ami asked one of our eunuchs if the man was old or young, to which the eunuch replied, "He is young, handsome, and slender."

As the caravan resumed its journey, I snuck my head from behind the gold-embroidered curtain on my elephant to look upon the village again. As I did so, my gaze settled on a man wearing a white shirt tucked into dark pants with sweat pouring down his face. Tall, with blond hair and green eyes, he was truly the most handsome man I had ever seen, though I couldn't understand why I felt the need to stare at him. As the elephant rode by, I continued staring at him though he wasn't looking at me. Finally, he moved his head up and towards me and our eyes met. He smiled at me, sending me into a quiet fit of embarrassed joy, and I ducked back into the palanquin. When I gathered the courage to peek my blushing olive face out of the palanquin again, the man was gone, and I was filled with a sudden sadness because I knew I would never see his handsome face again.

That night we camped in the outskirts of the famine-stricken town. The stench had left the air, and the royal cooks had begun to prepare roast chickens, curried lamb and mixed vegetables for our dinner.

As always, Aba insisted on having dinner with us. Ami asked, "What was the commotion with that *firangi?*" as she sipped her soup sporadically, as if with a depressed appetite.

"His name is Gabriel Boughton," Aba replied. "He's a physician with the East India Company." The East India Company was a corporation of British merchants who lobbied the Mughal emperor for trading rights in India.

"What's he doing here in this desolate land?" inquired Ami, taking the words out of my mouth.

Aba said, "Well, though he's a doctor by trade, it seems his official profession now is a commercial traveller for the East India

Company." Aba took another bite of his chicken, seeming little interested in saying anything more about this man who, I was embarrassed to admit, had piqued my growing interest. "He seems to have travelled from Surat to Gujarat on his way to Agra, but seeing the devastation from the famine caused him to remain here."

Gabriel pleaded with our generals for food and supplies and a small garrison of soldiers to protect him and those with him from robbers. In response to his request, Aba ordered half of all rations travelling with the caravan to be given to Gabriel, to be distributed as he saw fit; imperial tents to be used as safe houses, living quarters, and hospitals; and 200 troops were set to guard his supplies and men. Aba also ordered 5,000 rupees to be distributed every Monday among the deserving poor. As for the governors of the Deccan, who had sat silently and increased their treasuries during this time of destitution, Aba ordered them to be relieved of their duties and sent back to Agra immediately.

That night, Aba bid Ami and me goodnight with his kingly kiss on our foreheads, oblivious to how his story of Gabriel's courage and heroism had affected me. As all girls do, I dreamed of romance. Was it just lust or something much deeper I felt for this man? I had read poetry devoted to this thing called 'love' and of how numerous people along the ages had withered and died from this strange illness. But to me, love was nothing more than an illusion, a concept meant to be heard, not felt. Still, I decided that with time I would approach Ami about how I was feeling and let her guide me. My inner feelings were too raw and fragile to be shared with anyone else.

✻✻✻

The Burhampur fort was a much smaller building than our fort in Agra. Made of brick, it reflected the undeveloped and simple character of the region it was located in.

As our caravan finally arrived in the fort of Burhampur, I continued to think about the pale-skinned man with whom I'd shared but one moment of eye contact. I wondered how people in his country lived and what traditions they followed. Unlike most Mughals, Gabriel had no facial hair; his head-hair was blond; he wore tight English trousers; his eyes were hazel green. Yet here he was, thousands of kos from his home, yet he'd stopped the royal caravan to plead for rations for my people, while we, the royalty, were ready to merely drive past the people's plight. Such gentleness was rare in the Mughal household. Perhaps Dara had it, I thought, but even he now spent more time on religion than in practical community service.

As we arrived at the imperial fortress in Burhampur, I helped my pregnant mother to the harem quarters, using the opportunity to talk to her about this encounter with the firangi. Though only three months pregnant, her face had turned pale white, and she was losing weight from her face and arms, as if this child was literally draining the life out of her. She was unable to walk without the assistance of another, and even then she moaned with every step.

The marble staircase in the fortress was poorly maintained, its edges cracked and uneven. One could see the wear and tear on the tiles of the steps, on which thousands of people had stomped through the ages. Ami moaned every time she raised a leg to take a step up.

I asked her, "How long was it before you knew you loved Aba?" as we limped up the stairs.

Ami looked at me as if annoyed that I would choose such an inopportune time to ask such a question. "How many times do I have to tell you the story?" she asked me wearily. I stared at her feet as we continued to climb, pointing her where to step and trying to bear her weight as she leaned on me.

"I know the story," I replied, "but you never told me how *long* before you *knew*."

Still moaning and limping, she huffed, smiled at me and said: "Instantly!"

Indeed, I'd heard the story of my parents' romance many times. In fact, nearly everyone in the Mughal kingdom knew it. It had become somewhat of a legendary fairytale. While every king and queen would have some stories recited about them praising their beauty and greatness, my parents didn't need any court chronicler to create a mythical tale about them; their story was popular long before they were crowned – and it was factual!

My parents had met 23 years earlier, in 1607 at the royal Meena Bazaar, a private marketplace where the women of the aristocracy purchased dyes, oils, waxes and perfumes that were essential for their elaborate daily beauty rituals. Men were strictly forbidden, however, and any man caught in the bazaar would have his hands and feet cut off at the minimum. Certain dates, however, were reserved as 'contrary dates' during which men and women were all welcomed in the bazaar regardless of rank. The bazaar on these dates looked less like a traditional marketplace and more like a lusty pleasure garden, with courtship and flirtation flowing in both directions between men and women.

Some otherwise passive and docile aristocratic women and concubines would even reverse their roles and become noisy shopkeepers, selling goods from behind the store pavilion and flirting with the young male customers, who, momentarily emancipated from the restrictive routine, would show off their courtly wit by asking prices in rhyming Persian verse.

One such stall was being managed by my mother, the daughter of the then Prime Minister, Asaf Khan, which prevented otherwise interested young courtiers from approaching the stall or striking a conversation with my immensely beautiful, fair-skinned mother. But if there was one courtier who was intoxicated by her beauty without being intimidated by her title, it was the young Mughal Prince, my father. Aba wasn't intimidated by anyone else's title or status, much to the chagrin of the other young men there. He moved from stall to stall, flirting and charming, but realising that as a prince, bargaining was beneath him, so his act of doing so was only to entertain the fair maiden and afford him the opportunity to flirt with her and give her the chance to flirt back. And though he knew he was off-limits to most of the young maidens, he enjoyed the game of flirtation.

But when my father reached Ami's stall, he's said to have stopped in his tracks. This was no maiden to be flirted with. She didn't even look typically Indian; she had Persian skin tone, and was tall and slender, and yet, for all these attributes, decidedly well-mannered and polite. Both their eyes are said to have gazed at one another for several minutes before Ami smiled and said, "Is there anything in my stall that pleases you, sir?"

"Much in this stall pleases me," he replied. "This stall stands unique; it is the pride of the entire bazaar. If all the other booths were removed and only this one remained, it would be enough for me to come here every day and stay until it closes."

Ami told me her face had turned red. After all, what wasn't there to love in my Aba? Ami was a 15-year-old maiden, in her sexual prime, and here she'd met the future Emperor of India, just one year older, who was already a veteran of one war and a famous poet; a poet and a soldier, with good looks, artistic abilities, her age and a Muslim aristocrat. What girl wouldn't fall in love with him? But she was not to be won over easily. She was to be a wife, she thought, not a concubine. Nor would she accept being second to any other wife. If she was to be Aba's wife, she'd only be his if she knew she'd be the primary one. For this, she needed to know that Aba really wanted her.

She asked him, "Are you here to purchase something?"

"Depends," he smiled back. "Is your heart for sale?"

"A heart is not a piece of property to be bought, but a reward to be won, Sir."

"How may I win yours?" Aba asked.

"Well, why don't you start by purchasing something expensive from my stall so I can tell everyone that I, too, am a good shopkeeper?"

"Then why don't you sell me this large piece of glass shaped like a diamond?"

"Sir," she blushed, "this piece isn't just shaped like a diamond, it *is* a diamond!"

Ami knew she was addressing the royal Prince, but she didn't want to give him the satisfaction of knowing that. If he knew she was aware of his identity, he'd expect to be spoken to as royalty, and any back-talking or snide remark would be interpreted as an insult to the King. This way she could plead ignorance and also show Aba she wasn't like those other girls who'd happily flirt with him and be taken by him anywhere, under any role.

She fingered the diamond sensuously. "Not even a prince could afford this gem, sir."

"Why? How much is it?"

"10,000 rupees."

Aba immediately took 10,000 rupees from his left pocket, grabbed the piece of 'glass' from her hand and disappeared into the crowd.

Ami told me she knew from that moment that if she got married, it would only be to Aba, but she didn't know whether her stand-offish attitude had turned him off. She'd acted so to show confidence, but had she gone too far and made it seem she was arrogant? She remembered what her equally beautiful aunt, Nur Jahan, had told her on her 15th birthday – that because Ami was beautiful and fair-skinned like her, it would be important to show as little conceit as possible. Nothing is more attractive, confided her aunt, than a person who can be arrogant, but chooses not to be.

Summarily, Aba went to his father and asked for permission to marry Ami. My grandfather was a reigning contradiction: though an alcoholic, he'd outlawed the drinking of alcohol in his kingdom. Though he'd received a modest punishment when he rebelled against his own father, the Emperor Akbar, Jahangir had punished his own son Khusrau's rebellion by torturing Khusrau's men in front of him and then blinding him. Such contradictions were a staple of my grandfather's kingship and would surface yet again at this request.

He told Aba: "Marriage for Mughal princes is a matter of political gain, not fulfilling passion. For passion, you have the harems with the concubines. So make this woman your concubine – you can do with her whatever you'd wish to do with a wife, even give her children and let those children be eligible for the throne."

But Aba wouldn't relent; he was convinced that my mother could be no concubine, but must truly be the future Empress of India.

His father went on: "I've already given the King of Persia my word that you will marry his niece, Kandari Begum. We have a tenuous relationship with the Persians, and I therefore command you to do this for not just my, but also the empire's sake."

Thus Aba agreed to marry Kandari first, and make her his primary wife; Ami would be second – but that was a promise Aba knew he wouldn't keep.

Jahangir was pleased to hear this, but he levied yet one more condition: my father must wait ten years before marrying Ami. This would give the public a chance to see Kandari as the future empress. Aba reluctantly accepted, but four years later, Nur Jahan herself wooed and married King Jahangir. Understanding the intoxicating effects of love and the happiness that ultimately comes when one surrenders to it, Jahangir must have felt ashamed of how he'd treated my father.

Nur Jahan began exerting her influence over the King instantly. She jockeyed to be the favourite wife, displacing Aba's mother, Jagat Gosini. Upon becoming the primary wife, Nur Jahan began filling the top posts with her own confidantes, including her brother Asaf Khan. She commanded, and Jahangir followed. The ten-year wait for Aba became a relic of the past, to be tossed into the rear of the palace with the other wives and advisers. New 'management' took charge, and within a year of Nur Jahan's marriage to Jahangir, Ami was married to Aba.

Ami moved her arm from around my shoulder, sat down heavily on her royal bed and added: "When it's real and true, it only takes an instant." Then Ami smiled, as if all this had reminded her of a better time with fewer responsibilities and worries and more time for romance and chivalry.

I blurted out, "And what do you do when love happens?"

She shook a finger. "You hide it! There's nothing more attractive for a man to be denied something. Don't make it obvious, make him work for it. Your grand-aunt, Nur Jahan, taught me that."

I began to feel sorry about how Nur Jahan's life had turned out. Back when my parents met for the first time, she was their staunchest ally. Not only did she tutor my mother on how to pique the interest of a man, but upon her marriage to my grandfather, she used her influence to hasten my parents' marriage from a ten-year engagement to a much more tolerable five years.

I said, "That's what you did with Aba!"

Still in pain from the walk, Ami smiled again at me and said, "Well, it's a little harder when the guy is the Prince."

I shared a laugh with my mother at her comment, but then I began to wonder if Gabriel was royalty back home in his native land. Then I would be a queen if I married him. "Do you know who that firangi was, Ami?"

"No, I've only met a few Europeans in my life, and he wasn't one of them."

"Do you think he is the head of the company?"

"I don't know Jahanara, maybe he just works for them." Her eyes narrowed. "Why so many questions about love – and this man?"

"Just curious. Who knows, one day I might marry a firangi?"

Ami's smile quicky disappeared, and she seemed to be searching for an excuse to change the subject. But I kept prodding her to say whether my father would approve of such a union. Finally, she succumbed to my insistence and said, "You know Mughal princesses can not marry."

My face dropped, and I just stared at my mother in disappointment as if this rule was her creation. Perhaps she didn't make it, but how could she tolerate it and allow her daughters to be raised in a household where such a rule existed? Why give birth to daughters if their sole purpose was to just sit like the possessions of a man in a closed fort?

Ami's voice broke. "It *is* one of the most grievous injustices in this kingdom. No Mughal princess may ever marry or have children. She will never be anyone's love."

She tried to reach out to hug me in consolation, but I pushed her away. "How can you say that? Is it our fault we're girls? Do we not have feelings? What's the reason for this?"

Ami just nodded her head with tears in her eyes, and I repeated the question. At last Ami broke her silence and cried, "There is no *reason*! It's a male-created rule, without justification! Those who seek to rationalise it say it's because they don't want descendants of Mughals to be raised outside the Kingdom, for fear their paternal relatives will poison them against us and encourage them to fight us for the throne of India."

I moved closer to my mother. "That happens anyway! All the brothers rip each other's heads off!"

"I know, my child," she sighed. "But what can I do? I'm trying to get your father to reverse these decisions. Give me just a few more years, and I'll convince your Aba to rescind this rule once and for all."

I breathed a sigh of relief. "Promise?" I asked cautiously.

"Promise!" was her welcome answer.

I wanted to upset my mother no more, given her health. I was confident my mother's assurances were good, and I knew she was the one person who would never lie to me. For now, I let her promise suffice.

6

BIRTH AND DEATH

1st June, 1631

Aba's forces ripped through the rebel army of Lodi, inflicting severe damage on his men's morale. We suffered heavy casualties, but our Hindu Rajput allies helped our army force the rebels into retreat. Several of Lodi's allies deserted him, and finally Lodi himself was killed in battle. Aba, ecstatic at the prospect of returning to Agra and putting this rebellion behind him, ordered Lodi's severed head be brought to the fort and mounted at the gates as a warning to anyone else who might consider revolting.

Though I knew we were coming to the Deccan for a battle, the brutality and bloodshed of war added to the aura of death and devastation that was surrounding us at all times. For the past several months, beginning with the famine on the route, to the deaths of thousands of soldiers on both sides, death had been accompanying our family as our uninvited guest. Now, for the remaining four months of her pregnancy, whenever Ami would look out from the front of the fort, she would see the severed head of a corpse staring back at her, as if it was still alive and about to grab her at any time. Yet, she didn't want to bother Aba with these thoughts, probably aware that doing so might jeopardise his motivation to finish routing out all the rebels.

Ami had lost a considerable amount of weight in the months since our arrival. Her arms were literally the width of bone; her eyes were sunken in her head; her hair had begun to show some strands of gray; and the only part of her body that didn't look like a skeleton was her belly. Nursemaids and hakims expressed concern about whether their Queen was receiving enough nutrition, but it didn't matter. No matter what she ate, she was constantly vomiting and looking weaker every day. No one dared say it, but at times she looked not much different from the people we saw in the famine-stricken Gujarat. I began worrying that she would experience yet another miscarriage.

In mid-June, I happened to see a letter she'd received from Sati:

To the gracious Mallikaye Hindustan:

I hope this letter finds you in good health. As per your command to me, I have been looking after the well being of the royal princes and princess. I am pleased to inform you that Dara has mastered Persian and writes poetry in his spare time. He is getting taller, and handsome, just like his father, the esteemed Jahanpanah. Raushanara is also getting prettier, though she has inherited her father's Hindu features and looks less like you. She is learning courtly manners and is developing nicely. Finally, Aurangzeb is a delight to have. I don't know what you did to him, but he is everyone's sweetheart. Still praying three times a day, he has decided to become more charitable also. He knits Muslim skull caps to sell at a nominal price to pilgrims before Friday prayers. The proceeds he then donates to the poor. He has abandoned all talk of religious intolerance and is slowly beginning to reject the views of some of the backward minded mullahs. He is also getting taller, almost at Dara's height, and has a small moustache. He also is a very skilled archer and swordsmen, more so than Dara. He has inherited his father's military acumen and will extend the domains of Mughal India to the frontiers of the world.

How are you, Your Majesty? Has the pregnancy been tolerable? Pursuant to your instructions, I am taking care of your children well, but please come back soon. The city is not the same without you. Women gather at your balcony every morning in hopes that perhaps your caravan arrived in the dead of night and you will offer them your sight. For the poor, helpless, and unfortunate, you are the mother of this land. Please return soon.

Your Servant and Friend,
Sati

I wondered why Sati's letter seemed so morbid. Did she know something about Ami's health that others didn't? Were my mother's weakness, weight loss, and constant stomach pain really indicative of something wrong with her health? For the first time, I dared to ask myself the forbidden question: Was she dying?

Ami's sleep now was the first restful one she'd had in a long time. In the afternoon of the following day, she went into labour.

Already weak from a pregnancy that had drained the life out of her, she started to scream in agony when the child would not expel itself from her. She began making superstitious comments: "Will the child arrive only after all the life has been drained from me?" Persian and Indian astrologers hovered over her with astrolabes and charts. The entire household waited impatiently for the news of the birth of a prince, so drums could be beaten.

Ami fell in and out of consciousness, with sharp belly pains pushing her to the verge of death. Aba, oblivious to how his wife's condition had deteriorated, and purposely left unaware of what she had been feeling since the child's conception, merely thought this was like any other birth. I stayed by Ami's side begging the hakims to give her something for the pain.

"Have her suck on this!" The chief hakim handed me a powder of opium and told me this would make her sleepier, but also would take away her pain.

I told her, "Ami, the hakim wants you to suck on this powder. Don't ingest it right away." Ami popped the powder in her mouth and did just as she was told. Her pain was relieved, but I could tell she was still in distress. This was not like her other pregnancies. I myself began drifting to sleep as I lay next to her. The labour was exhausting us both. A few hours later, I felt a tap on my shoulder.

"Jahanara, get the hakim! The baby is coming!" I ran outside to fetch him.

He shouted: "Empress, please spread your legs so I may be able to see the baby's head!" Ami did as she was told, while I applied cool bandages to her forehead to wipe off her sweat.

"What do you see, hakim?" my mother uttered through her exhaustion. The Hakim wouldn't answer, making Ami more nervous. Finally he looked up and said, "Your Majesty, you have not yet dilated. I can see nothing."

"How could that be?" she yelled in exasperation. "I feel the baby descending! It *has* to come out! I can't take it anymore!"

I began panicking as well. I'd never seen my mother so beaten and distraught. She spoke as if she knew how all this would end and was fearing the inevitable.

I said, "Can you do something to help her along?"

The hakim ignored me. He rose, pushing Ami's knees toward one another, and said, "Malikaye, please take some more opium and rest. There is nothing more we can do right now."

Another 30 hours – a full day and a half – passed; then Ami's contractions began anew.

"Get the hakim!" she screamed. "Get him! I feel like I'm exploding!"

I ran out again, this time more panicked and nervous than ever, and found the hakim. He ran in and again bent down to look for the baby's head. She cried, "Tell me you can see the head, Hakim. Tell me I'm dilated... please!!" The hakim didn't answer, but from the side I caught a glimpse of his face. He seemed worried.

"What's wrong, hakim?" I asked.

He wouldn't look at me, but he said to Ami: "The baby is breech, Your Highness. We can't pull it out this way. If we try, we risk tearing your uterus."

Ami began weeping. During the past 30 hours, she'd come to look as though she'd aged considerably. It seemed wrinkles had formed along the lines of her cheeks as she cried and shrieked incessantly.

"Do something, hakim! I can't take this anymore! I'll die if you don't do something!"

The hakim continued to apply pressure to Ami's belly, hoping to rotate the baby in the uterus so the head would turn down. Frustrated by his inability to do so, he began to push more vigorously, causing Ami to yell out in agony.

I shouted: "She's not a goat, she's a human being, hakim!"

"I know, Princess," he said wearily, "but both the mother's and the child's lives are at stake." Soon more hakims ran into the room, massaging Ami's belly as though it were some ball of dough. One of them bent down to look between Ami's legs as another pushed from above.

"I see the feet!" one of them yelled.

"We don't need the feet, we need the head!" interjected another.

"Well, the feet are better than the buttocks we've been seeing all along!" The hakims continued to ramble. Head, feet, buttocks, what were they talking about?

"I'm pulling the baby from the feet; we have no other option!"

"You'll shear the uterus and cause bleeding."

"If I don't, she and the baby will die!"

I froze. Die? It was one thing when my mother was saying it (I'd assumed it was her pain talking). But now the hakim was saying it? Was it true? Was my mother really dying?

Finally I heard the shriek of the infant rend the air. Ami cried to me that this was a voice different from the voices she'd heard in her previous births. Perhaps it was due to her own dilapidated state, I reassured her, that the voice sounded different. She cried that she still felt she hadn't given birth to a healthy baby – her weakness had prevented the child from receiving the proper nourishment.

The hakim called out, "It's a girl!"

"Is it healthy?" she murmured.

"Yes, Malikaye, she's absolutely healthy!"

Ami smiled as she leaned into my shoulder; she'd given birth to a healthy child after three unsuccessful pregnancies. I began to cry with joy, even as I noticed my mother's head getting heavier. I looked over to Ami and realised that her eyes had rolled back into her head. I cried, "Ami, wake up! Hakim, look at Ami!"

The hakim sent one of his assistants over as he continued to manage the bleeding that was issuing from her birth canal. He said, "She's losing a lot of blood, Begum Sahiba. Lay your mother flat so that blood can rush to her head!"

I didn't know what to do. I ran to fetch Aba; I needed him now more than ever. But the hakim asked him not to enter, as he needed space to work.

After three hours' work, the hakim walked out of the apartment and told Aba about his wife's dire condition. "Here in Burhampur, Your Majesty, I simply don't have the instruments and tools to help the queen."

"Hakim, what are you saying? Make sure you think before speaking. I want the truth. Is my wife well?"'

"Your Majesty, your daughter is healthy, and your wife is alive. But I couldn't stop the bleeding. I've packed her bleeding in hopes that it will eventually stop on its own. The body has a way of healing itself. But…"

"But what?" Aba's voice was wary.

"The Queen's blood was thin to begin with," replied the Hakim. I don't know if she has the energy to hang on long enough for her body to heal itself. If this were Agra, I could stop it. Here I cannot."

Aba squinted and bit his lips. He looked up to the sky. "Why did I let her come here with me? Why did I allow her to get so weak?" He paused. "May I see my wife? Is she awake?"

"Please, Your Majesty, go in quickly and stay as long as you like; she may not have much time left."

Aba and I entered the room. We each grasped one of Ami's hands with tears in our eyes.

"I need you to get through this, Arjumand," whispered Aba.

Ami opened her eyes and smiled at her torn husband, his eyes red and his face dripping with tears. She breathed feebly, "I'm very comfortable, Khurram." They were now addressing each other by their original names, as if the time for ceremony and tradition needed to be halted. Right now they weren't the King and Queen of India, but just Khurram and Arjumand, two people who'd loved each other as soon as they met and had never stopped loving each other since.

"We really didn't need another child, Arju," Aba said, smiling.

"Yes, we did, Khurram. You told everyone you wanted children only from me. So I needed to make up for all your other wives."

"No, you didn't," claimed Aba. "We had six already. Who needed more?"

"We would be here, Khurram, just as we are, you there and me here, regardless of the pregnancy. This is how it was meant to end for us."

"Please don't say that," Aba pleaded. "I can't live without you, Arju. I'm like the moon, and you are my sun. The moon has no light of its own, it's all reflected light from the sun. Were it not for the sun, no one would ever see the moon." Ami kept smiling at Aba's analogy. "I draw my strength from you. I draw my light from you. Were it not for you, no one would ever see me. I am the moon, and you are my sun."

Ami briefly lifted a hand toward him. "Our love was the light that allowed the world to see you. Our love doesn't have to die with me."

"Not like this," insisted Aba. "Who is going to help me take care of all of these kids?"

"Jahanara will." Ami turned her face toward me and said, "Jahanara, from this day forward, you are both their sister and their mother."

I began to weep relentlessly, and I begged my mother not to leave us and to fight harder. I wanted her to stand still and transform this moment into an eternity, for her doing so would prevent the passage of time to a world where my mother was no longer alive.

Aba wept openly now. "How am I supposed to keep our love alive without you, Arju?"

Still smiling, yet getting weaker by the moment, Ami said, "Keep our love alive by doing whatever it is that you like that's inspired by our love. If you wish to sing, then sing about it, if you wish to paint, paint a scene from it, and if you wish to build, build something that allows the whole world to see how we felt about each other. As long as you remember it, it will give you the light you need to shine, my love. It will be your light."

In her dying moments now, she uttered the religious words every Muslim must say before dying. Aba and I stared at her and watched her release her final breath.

Instantly as she died, Aba led out a loud cry, screaming *"No!"* multiple times in horror, his voice only silenced by desperate, noiseless cries that followed before he could gain his breath and repeat the sequence. As though forgetting he was a king, he began tearing hairs out from his own beard.

I beat the bed and cried out, "Ami!" I couldn't control myself, and I eventually started to pound my own chest; I felt I didn't want to live in a world without my mother in it. She's not been just my mother, but my best friend and confidant. My agony turned to incoherent screams of horror and disbelief. The hakims and the harem women ran into the room, and joined us in our mourning.

Ami exhaled her final breath shortly before dawn on Tuesday, 17th June, 1631. She was 38 years old. During her short life, Ami had become unquestionably the most popular Empress of India. She had initiated multiple reforms in the kingdom to help the poor and needy and continued to serve her husband with the utmost loyalty.

Though born into a family where political posturing was practised more than anything else, she treated Aba's plight as her own, and lived however he kept her. On endless journeys with swollen bellies, she'd accompanied him from one military campaign to another. No one, not even Nur Jahan, who hated everyone in the royal household, had anything negative to say about her. Her brief four years as empress gave the country a much needed figure of imperial decency and charity. The days of mourning to follow would be uncharacteristic of any royalty in that time, save for possibly the King.

It was as if India had lost its first ever 'Mother India'. A true embodiment of beauty, grace, tolerance, and modesty, she represented all India aspired to be. It was she who taught me to wear my title of Begum Sahiba like a medal and use it to further those causes I believed in. By the time she died, she'd already raised me to be independent and free thinking. Her son was multicultural in the spirit of the legendary Akbar, the most popular Mughal king. Her other children were too young to have learned this, but her counsel had started Aurangzeb on a course of reconciliation and service. She treated all of her husband's wives with respect and candour, not cruelty as had been the practice of other empresses. Never before, and perhaps never again, would India fall in love with such a figure as my mother, the legendary Mumtaz Mahal, and no Mughal king would feel for his empress what Aba had felt for his. A remarkable human being in every sense, Ami thoroughly deserved the timeless monument Aba would one day build in her honour.

7

HEALING BROKEN HEARTS

18ᵗʰ June, 1631

One of the Muslim nobles began reading the Koran's 'O Man' chapter as Ami's body lay beside him. Another mullah turned her head towards Mecca. As the mullah spoke the Koranic verses, her body was cleaned and washed by a female washer and wrapped in a white shroud consisting of five pieces of white cotton.

The mullahs continued to chant in unison: "I bear witness that there is no God but God, who is One and has no co-equal. I bear witness that Mohammad is His servant and is sent from Him." All around me women cried while the mullah chattered: "Say God is One! Say I seek protection of the Lord of Daybreak! Say, I seek the protection of the Lord of Men!"

Kandari walked up to me and said, "Jahanara, we need to gather at the entrance of the fort to begin the procession." I willingly left the room, not wishing to see my mother's lifeless body anymore.

As we congregated, all the zenana women continued to weep, some out of obligation, I thought others with genuine grief. I joined them in their mourning, still both stunned and devastated. The tatars then motioned us to stand at the side as the mullahs escorted Ami's remains to the entrance.

Ami's body was then removed from the fort, head first so as to prevent her ghost from finding a way back to the fort. All this was customary.

The chief hakim then approached me. "Begum Sahiba, we must now go to the banks of the Tapti river. The mullah has chosen that location for the burial."

The entire day continued to feel like a surreal experience, and I often felt like I was in an alternate reality. I felt dizzy, and my vision was foggy all day.

Aba looked less like the king of a vast empire and more like a fakir, a street wanderer, crying and chanting religious verses. The zenana ladies continued crying the loudest, as if their own child or mother had been taken from them.

I don't think I ever stopped crying. From the minute Ami died to now, I think I'd been crying all along, so much that it didn't even seem abnormal anymore. My tears flowed down my cheeks like water flows down a snowy cliff on a warm day. I began to feel my throat closing, and I began gasping for air as the procession marched on.

"Begum Sahiba, take long deep breaths!" The zenana women tried to help me catch my breath. My cheekbones began to ache from weeping. Yet I felt the need to cry more. "My head is going to explode," I said, gasping for air, my mouth wide open.

The slave girls, themselves weeping, tried to restrain me. "You must remain calm, Begum Sahiba. We can't afford to lose you, too!"

Was I having a nightmare? This couldn't be real. I started pounding my chest with my hands. *Wake up Jahanara! This isn't real! This can't be real! Your mother is fine. You're having a nightmare. We're still in Agra; we never left!* The Deccan, this jinxed Deccan, which many years ago took away my brothers from me and was the site of our exile, now had taken my mother. The maids grabbed hold of my hand.

"This is all my fault," I cried. "I must have committed some offence; that's why Allah took my Ami away. Forgive me, Ami!" The zenana women literally dragged me for the duration of the procession, begging me to control myself, though I continued to fall apart.

I somehow found myself finally at the burial site, a journey of several kos that seemed like it had taken no time at all. This was where I would say a final goodbye. The slaves began lowering Ami's body into a shallow grave, and the mullah poured a fist of dirt on it.

"No, stop that!" I cried out, breaking free from the maids holding me back. "You can't lower her in that grave. She can't breathe in there. Take off that cloak! She's fine!" I began hallucinating and then lost all sense of self.

The hakim stared back at me with pity in his eyes. "Hakim!" I cried, "I am the Begum Sahiba! I order you to open the cloak and stop this! I'll have you crushed for insubordination!"

The hakim stared fixedly at me. "She must rest, Begum Sahiba," he said calmly.

I continued to resist. "You all are committing sedition against the King!" I shouted. "You're killing the queen, and you'll burn in hell!"

I couldn't see straight, the tears had blurred my vision so badly, I scarcely knew where I was. Blinded by my tears, weakened by my weeping and hurting from my sorrow, I suddenly realised I was making a spectacle of myself. Kandari put my head on her shoulders and led me to the side of the grave. I continued to weep as Ami's body lay in the grave with its head pointing north and turned towards Kaaba, the shrine in Mecca that contained the legendary black stone given by the Angel Gabriel to Abraham.

Chanted the mullahs: "Say God is One! Say I seek protection of the Lord of Daybreak! Say, I seek the protection of the Lord of Men! Say God is One! Say I seek protection of the Lord of Daybreak! Say, I seek the protection of the Lord of Men..."

My vision went dark after that, and I can't recall much of what happened the rest of that day. Different women counselled and nurtured me. I don't recall eating or sleeping. It was as if the candles in a room had been extinguished and all that remained was sheer darkness. In such darkness, one often loses track of time. Such was the case with me.

The next several days continued in a haze of confusion and bewilderment. Though officially only 40 days of mourning were to follow, the actual melancholy of the empire would last much longer.

No court events were held, no special food was made, and the immediate family members wandered around the fort like zombies themselves. It was as if everyone had lost a sense of purpose. A wet nurse took care of Ami's newborn, named Gauhara, making sure at least someone in the royal family was getting the proper nutrition.

I started having daily nightmares of my mother dangling off of a cliff as I stood helpless, unable to pull her back up. Slowly my mother's arm was slipping from me, inch by inch, until the arm was released and my mother fell to the ground, screaming for help along the way. I would wake up from these dreams devastated and crying; but unlike before, my Ami was no longer with me to comfort me when I awoke. The servants tried to play her part, but theirs was not the comfort I yearned for.

In my grief, I turned to the one person my mother had told me during our stay at Burhampur to look to if I needed anything: Sati. I awoke from my nightmare one day, distraught as always with servants rushing in to comfort me. I realised this couldn't go on indefinitely, so I wrote a letter to Sati asking her advice:

My dearest Sati:

As you may have heard in Agra, Ami is no more. The light of our lives has been taken from us, and there is darkness everywhere. No one laughs or smiles anymore. The songs, festivals, poems, and shows have all ended. Ami took all of our smiles with her when she left this world. There is no hope for anyone now, it seems. We all stay in bed and wish to sleep in hope we may be visited by her in our dreams, but all that I see are nightmares. Nightmares where she is dying over and over again and I can't help.

I can't help but feel this is somehow all my fault. Maybe if I had done something different, Ami would be with us right now. Aba has lost all will to live. He took off his crown jewels and decorated robes and now wears only white shrouds. He has pulled all the hair out of his beard in grief, and what he has left of a beard has turned white, to match the shroud he wears always. I went to seek his comfort a few days ago and saw him crying out in pain over the loss of his best friend. How could I seek comfort from him? We both lost our best friend, but his grief is at a whole other level than mine.

I sometimes open Ami's cabinet just to smell her scent, which is still in her clothes and possessions neatly tucked in drawers. But, Sati, I opened it yesterday and the smell is fading. Even her scent is fading from her belongings. I'm so sad, no words can describe how I feel. I've stopped eating and have lost so much weight. Yet I still vomit, though I've eaten nothing. I feel like I'm falling and no one is here to catch me. Please help me, Sati. I need you more than ever. Please catch me, please help me find a way to live again.

> *Yours always,*
> *Jahanara*

As I would later learn, Sati received this letter amid the grief that had overcome Agra as news trickled in of Ami's demise. She reported to me that all the royal children were overcome with dismay and insisted on visiting the Deccan to attend our mother's funeral, but their demands were put to rest by the news that her body had already been interred before news of her death even reached Agra. Aurangzeb took the news especially hard, and he now regressed to the state he'd assumed as Nur Jahan's prisoner. He fell into a depression, during which his only companion was the Koran; it was his only comforting potion. I believe that like me, Aurangzeb felt like he was falling; but unlike me he was being caught by the mullahs who were counselling him about the Koran. For me, no such place of safety existed, nor would I have wanted one. As Sati wrote back to me:

> *My Dear Jahanara:*
>
> *Your pain is pure, and were it not for the greatness of your mother, perhaps it would not be so deep. We all grieve with you at your loss. Losing a parent is never easy, especially one as special as*

the Empress. She was a lone star in the midst of a vast darkness. Yet, your mourning must eventually pass, for you must fulfill your role now as both a daughter and a sister. You are the oldest female of the royal family. Your father, the King, needs you as do your siblings. You must not let your grief prevent you from taking care of them.

Dara and Raushanara cry all day. Shuja and Murad have stopped eating. And Aurangzeb? Aurangzeb has again sought refuge in religious doctrines and sequestered himself inside the Pearl Mosque, claiming that's the only place he finds any peace. Jahanara, your family needs you. It is up to you to lift this family out of despair. They will listen to you in ways they will listen to no one else. You have your mother's gentleness and grace. The future of this great family and this country is now in your hands, my dear. I am here to catch you, but YOU must catch THEM. Don't let your mother's legacy be simply that all she cared for died in grief over her death. There are still battles to be fought, causes to be championed and hearts to be healed. Come back to Agra and give us again a reason to live again, my child.

Love,
Sati

I was deeply disturbed to hear how my siblings were reacting to my mother's demise. I tried to be brave in my loneliness. I began to cope with the harsh reality that my mother's voice and scent had permanently floated into the vast depths of eternity and now would be known only by God.

I went to Aba's chambers and found him as always sitting in front of his copy of the Koran, sobbing as he chanted the prayers. Dressed in white robes from head to toe, he looked as if he'd aged ten years in the last ten days. He'd lost considerable weight, and his beard was now so completely gray, I thought for a moment he must have dyed it this colour to match his robes.

I sat right next to him, but was unable to distract him from his prayers even for a moment. He seemed mentally in another world. I put my head on his lap as he stared forward, his palms facing upward, praying. Then he suddenly looked down at what was in his lap, and for an instant he must have thought Ami had returned to him: the same silky black hair, olive skin, the same scent, even the same features as Ami were lying in his lap. "Arju?" he muttered.

I corrected: "No, Aba, it's me, your princess."

As if suddenly waking from sleep, Aba sprang back to reality. "Of course, Jahanara. I don't know why I got confused."

I got up and looked at my father directly, worry etched in my face. "Aba, you were confused because I look just like her. Everyone thinks so. Sometimes I look in the mirror and even I think I'm staring at her. I even show some of the same facial expressions she did... you know... like when she knew you were lying to her, the way she'd put her hand on her waist and begin nodding with her finger? I did that the other day, just so I could trick myself into thinking she was alive again."

Aba listened with a helpless look on his face, as if he understood exactly how I felt.

"But Aba," I went on, "she's gone! You can't just keep mourning like this. You are the *king*! Your family, including your new daughter, needs you. The kingdom needs you. *I* need you!" My voice cracked as I told Aba of Sati's letter and how Aurangzeb had locked himself in the mosque and the other royal children were punishing themselves in equally horrific ways.

"But I am so lost without her," he confessed, gazing helplessly at me. "I can't even get up from a chair, I feel I would fall..."

"You are a *Timurid*!" I insisted. "Timurid men have fought greater battles and endured greater hardships than these. What would your father, Emperor Jahangir say? That his kingdom was shattered because the King's wife died? The House of Timur cannot be shattered by just the death of a queen!" As untrue as I knew this statement to be, I also knew that I needed to appeal to his manhood and familial legacy to jolt him out of this despair. Aba nodded and silently, if reluctantly, began to pull himself together. First he allowed the barber to trim his beard and even dye it black. This was my idea. I didn't want the public to feel that their emperor was an old man. I had his royal robes cleaned and ironed, but he refused to wear them, insisting instead on wearing his white robe, which looked more like a loincloth than a royal garment. So I had him sequestered in the rear palanquin when we set for Agra, so no one might view their emperor in such a dilapidated state.

The royal caravan left Burhampur with the same number of people as had arrived with it from Agra almost a year before, except for Ami, whose presence was replaced with infant Gauhara Begum. I stayed in the same palanquin as the King, convinced that he was unable to travel alone.

I made sure the royal caravan took the same route it had taken on its journey to the Deccan. This was intentional – I had to see if the royal relief efforts had borne fruit in the famine-stricken regions. Of course, this might also afford me an opportunity to steal another glance at Gabriel, though this I never admitted even to myself at the time.

As the procession approached the former famine-stricken regions, I saw in complete surprise that the villages I'd seen less than a year ago were now drastically transformed. As if I were travelling in some other region that had been unaffected by famine, these villages now had homes, people were working and children playing; it seemed the economy had completely revived here, in this former pit of death.

Peeking from behind the royal curtain of the palanquin, I remarked to one of my attendants, "This can't be the same place!"

"Your Majesty, this is indeed that same village."

"Is the young firangi doctor still here, or has he left?"

"Your Majesty, I've been informed that he's still working here."

"Tell him we would like to see him and set up the royal camp on the outskirts of the village. We will camp here tonight."

The imperial camp was soon set in the grandiose manner typical of the Mughal times. As if palaces themselves, its golden embroidered tents were raised in lavish contrast to the mud and brick shacks that existed a few yards away in the village.

I arranged an audience with Gabriel from behind a thin screen that allowed us to see only halos of each other, without ever revealing who was truly on the other side. I thanked him for his service and offered him 100 mohurs as a reward for his good work. But he shared some displeasure at not having an audience with the King.

I explained: "As you know, the Queen, my mother, is no more."

Gabriel bowed his head to acknowledge his sadness at this news, which, I would later learn, he'd known for some time, though he hadn't yet had the chance to express his condolences.

"The Emperor would be barely alive without me." I confided. "His body exists, but his mind and heart are gone. He can't even dress himself or shave. He has lost weight and is barely recognisable. If my mother were alive, we would surely have come here and given you the full court audience you deserve. But I cannot grant such a favour, nor would my father be capable at this time of meeting with you."

For reasons I couldn't fathom, in those moments together Gabriel made me feel more like a desirable woman than just a member of the royalty. He addressed me repeatedly as 'fair maiden,' a term I liked. At the end of the audience he asked to shake my hand in thanks for the gift of the 100 mohurs.

I replied, "But that would be impossible! Mughal women are not allowed to be seen even by our people."

"Well," he said cordially, "I'm not one of your people, and surely you've shown your hand to people, just not your face."

Hesistantly, I extended my hand from the side of the curtain; the firangi doctor took it and gently kissed it, then hurried from the tent

My hand remained outside the curtain, posed just as if he was still holding it, and I felt a sudden veil of shyness descend upon me.

The royal caravan eventually made its way into Agra, and the entire city gathered to see it without the Empress. The drumbeats seemed more sombre than usual, a sign that our arrival was steeped in sorrow. I leaned my head out of the canopy to see the people who were now to be my responsibility.

The citizenry moved closer to the edges of the procession as our caravan grew nearer, like relatives holding an all-night vigil at the bedside of a dying patient. I watched their faces, horrified. Some of the women, overwhelmed, began sobbing uncontrollably. Many of the men, peasants who probably never directly saw Ami, stood with their farming tools, tears dribbling down their faces. No matter where I looked, I saw people crying, looks of profound helplessness having possessed them. Eyes blood-shot, layers of tears caked on both cheeks, there wasn't a dry eye in that sea of people that flooded the streets...

During the months that followed, Agra was like a ghost town. No celebrations took place, no exchange of presents for Hindu or Muslim festivals, no music or dancing of any sort. Everyone merely went about their business and in their spare time stared outside their windows waiting – waiting to live, waiting to die, waiting for answers that would never come.

I had convinced Aurangzeb to leave the Pearl Mosque, into which he and Raushanara had locked themselves for several months after hearing of our mother's death. Now in his chambers he'd become more orthodox than ever, believing that he was responsible for his mother's death by having committed sins such as observing Hindu festivals and tacitly condoning idol worship. The mullahs used this time of vulnerability to mould him in their image. Raushanara was his partner, following him wherever he went and inciting him to proclaim himself the heir apparent.

Dara moved oppositely. Devastated by Ami's untimely death, he began learning more about other religions, all in hopes of understanding a higher meaning of life and death. He also began publicly labelling the mullahs 'enemies of a diversely cultural India,' chanting that the only way he could keep the empire strong after Aba's reign would be to appeal to both Hindus and Muslims.

Aba became more lucid as time went on, but he also began blaming unorthodox religious practices for Ami's death. Like Aurangzeb, the mullahs succeeded in filling an answer vacuum for both father and son. God was punishing them for their un-Islamic ways, they claimed.

I found myself nestled between my orthodox relatives and the overly ascetic Dara. Though I thought about Gabriel all day and hoped that somehow I could tell him how I felt, I realised the future of the family was in my hands. As much as I could, I tried reasoning with everyone, but grieving was different for everyone. Some were angry, others resigned; everyone coped with grief over Ami's death in their own – albeit self-destructive – ways...

Then, like a cool summer breeze in the middle of a hot arid day, a letter came to me from the Deccan... from Gabriel:

Dear Princess,

As per your request, I am updating you regarding the progress here in the once famine-stricken regions of the south. The summer rains were good to us, the harvest is sufficient. New homes have been built, and the economy of the village is solid. My good friend, Mirza Diwan Baksh, who is the governor of the region, is an honest man well able to take care of matters from here on. I ask your permission to continue my journey now. I will be travelling to Hugli, in the eastern border of His Majesty's Empire. The Portuguese have a flourishing business there, and I hope to learn more about it from them.

As your friend, I assure you this is not farewell, and I will write to you once I arrive in Hugli. Till then, please accept this rose as a token of my friendship with you. When we met, you gave me 100 mohurs, but at the time I had nothing to give you in return. I hope I am not being too forthright, but we Englishmen have a tough time being passive, as you may have already noticed. Give the Emperor my respects.

Warm wishes,
Gabe

I wasn't sure what to make of this letter. I smelled the rose repeatedly, though it had withered considerably in the journey from the Deccan to Agra; but I wasn't sure if this was an admission of some attraction he also shared with me or simply a chivalrous gift given by an awkward-feeling firangi unsure of proper etiquette towards eastern royalty. I read and re-read the letter, looking for signs or hints of how he felt.

I thought: *did he abbreviate his name Gabe, instead of Gabriel, to indicate that he feels comfortable enough with me to talk to me like an ordinary person?*

After spending hours holding and caressing the letter as if *it* were my lover, I began to wonder where Hugli was and if it might be possible to visit there. I learned that Hugli was a trading port of the Portuguese in Bengal, Eastern India. Vessels of India, China, and Manila were repaired in great numbers in this port city. Persians, Armenians, and Mughals all came here to fetch their goods. In addition, the Portuguese carried on a very profitable salt trade here. If the British East India Company was to be successful, it would have to begin operations in Bengal.

Unfortunately, relations between our empire and Hugli were never very stable. Originally, the arrangement was that the supreme power would lie with the Mughals, but they were content with leaving the governing up to the Portuguese, as long as the empire received revenues. The spiritual government of Hugli was vested in the Brethren of St Augustine, an enemy of the Islamic mullahs of Agra.

So Hugli was an unlikely place for me to ever visit. Though my title of Begum Sahiba placed me above the confines of protocol my siblings had to adhere to, thereby allowing me to travel just about anywhere, why would I tell Aba I wished to go there? Why would a Muslim Princess visit a Jesuit colony that had been at odds with the Mughals ever since my father ascended the throne?

As always, I would visit my forbidden destinations only in my thoughts and dreams. I would imagine walking around this Europe-like city, free from the bondage that my heritage and title trapped me in. I would imagine an alternate reality, and in that imagination, I would find the strength to deal with my current state. Dreams, I learned a long time ago, are always good – they help you deal with reality.

8
DEFEAT

5th March, 1632

It's gone! I thought. *Everything is gone! There is nothing more left to mourn or fear the loss of, for nothing remains. Everything is gone. Hugli has been burned to the ground, and all its people have perished under the wrath of Mughal intolerance.*

Today, as the court assembled in the Diwan-i-am, the Mughal General paid his respects to Aba and informed him that he had been successful in rooting out the infidels from our kingdom. Apparently the mullahs had incited Aba a few weeks ago to obliterate the colony, as punishment for its tacit support of my uncles during the war of succession. Now, in Aba's quest to win the favour of Allah, he listened to the ill advice of these fanatical mullahs who were abusing their role to raze Hindu temples and destroy Christian churches.

I tried requesting an audience with Aba, but in the weeks leading up to taking this fanatical course, he'd become very dismissive of everyone else, including me. Getting an audience with him was impossible, and even if I did, what would I say? I didn't know the art of manipulation and evasiveness others in the empire practised. I'd never learned to ask questions without divulging my own emotions and intentions. What would happen if somehow I revealed that I had feelings for Gabriel? Aba would be horrified, and I'd be a disgrace in the household.

I grew dejected and withdrawn and stopped attending court sessions. The massacre in Hugli had left me in a drowning despair. I retreated into my palace and remained there for the next several days.

I lay on my bed as the sun set in the distance. The hot summer air blew my curtains inward, as if the wind itself was angry this night and wanted to make its presence known. I walked up to the balcony and viewed the town beneath, watching the still grief-stricken townspeople go about their business. At a distance where once a beautiful stone temple stood, Hindus had constructed a makeshift shrine on the rubbles of their lord's home. The shrine would be short-lived, however, for the mullahs were trying to convince the King to use the rubble to make stones for the steps of a mosque, to be constructed on that very site.

Further along the Jumna, I could see a Jesuit priest rummaging through his belongings, for our soldiers had thrown all his possessions onto the street from the Mughal guesthouse where my Ami had given him permission to stay as long as he wished.

The Muslim citizenry, unhappy to see their fellow townspeople mistreated, were helping their non-Muslim neighbours with rations and places to stay, but they had to do so discreetly or face the Emperor's wrath.

I have never understood why men force others to follow their religion. Is it because they themselves are insecure in their beliefs, and thus feel that if others follow their faith, perhaps they alone won't be thought of as fools if their beliefs turn out to be false?

The Jumna river, usually calm this time of year, was rushing along with powerful waves, as if it wanted to leave our jinxed city and irrigate someone else's fields. Its waves struck the shores and collapsed against the stones, seeming as though it, too, was cursing us as it ran by.

Before I knew it, my eyes became so filled with tears, all these ill-fated images turned a brownish blurry, in which the houses of worship were destroyed, a whitish blur where the moon reflected on the angry river, and reddish blur where the burgundy-coloured Mughal military men continued executing their king's sinful orders. I had lost everything, I felt; my mother, my chance at love, the well being of my people, everything. Even Aba existed for me in name only; the nurturing father I'd always known no longer existed. He might as well have been buried alongside my mother on the Tapti river.

Utterly demoralised, I went to Aba to inform him of the decision I'd made: to leave Agra and spend my days in prayer at Mecca.

"That's great news!" my father exclaimed. "I'll come with you! Lately, I, too, have been feeling that I haven't visited the birthplace of the prophet for some time now. Your mother always wanted to take me, but alas, it was written that we wouldn't go together. Anyway, having you with me will be just as pleasant."

Staring at the ground, ashamed to clarify the situation to my father, I said in a low tone, "No, Aba. Not with you. I wish to go by myself."

"Yourself?" He thought for a moment and then turned his head and sighed, "If you want to, fine. I'll arrange for you to go, and after you come back, I'll go with your sister."

I paused. "I won't be coming back, Aba. I wish to go to Mecca and stay there. I want to devote my life to service of the pilgrims."

Aba's face purpled, and he shouted: "What is this nonsense, Jahanara? You are a royal princess. You can't just go to Mecca and live like a fakir."

"I don't want to be a princess!" I fumed directly at my father. "I have no pleasure in being a Mughal princess anymore! I want none of this! I hate my life!"

Aba's face softened. He leaned close to me and held my hand. "I know the death of your mother has saddened you, but you can't give up, my child."

I couldn't believe how oblivious my father was to the sin he was committing and the toll this was taking on me. I replied: "It's not her death that saddens me. It's you!"

Aba jerked backwards, clearly startled.

I railed on: "You've turned into a monster! You kill people for petty crimes, you tear down temples, and now you've burned an entire city just because it was Christian!"

Aba stared wide-eyed at me as I went on: "Remember what Ami told you as she died? She said to keep your love alive, and you'll shine. Do what makes you happy. Sing, write poetry, build. But what have you done? You've destroyed and torn down other people's homes! You've not even stopped to think what Ami must be thinking as she watches all this in heaven!"

I broke into tears; Aba looked shocked and speechless. Indeed, Ami's soul would be turning in its makeshift grave if she knew what went on here.

Aba said calmly, "But they were infidels, Jahanara..."

"So are you, Aba," I retorted. "*You're* three quarters Hindu. How can you treat your own kind this way?"

"Allah took your mother from me because I was too tolerant."

"Where in the Koran does it say that being tolerant is a sin?" I shot back. "Was Akbar a sinner? Was Ami a sinner?"

Aba stared hard at the ground; I shook my head in dismay. "I'll leave by the end of the week for Mecca, Aba. I've decided. You and the mullahs can continue to rule India however you please. If you wish to tear down temples and churches, then do so. But I won't be here to witness it."

This said, I stormed from Aba's chambers and began making preparations in earnest to depart for Mecca.

News of my decision slowly began permeating the household. Dara and Aurangzeb seemed devastated to learn of my leaving, but Raushanara was openly ecstatic at this dramatic turn of events. Doubtless she figured that with me out of the picture she could posit herself as the next Begum Sahiba and eventually perhaps even become the empress.

Dara and Aurangzeb both tried to talk me out of leaving, each in his own way – Aurangzeb by lecturing me about the duties of a woman towards her father as called for in the Koran, Dara by describing to me what he'd learned from the mystic Sufi saints about the essential oneness of religions

I was flattered that my brothers wished for me to stay but not enough for me to reverse my decision.

My day of departure soon arrived, and the royal caravan was assembled to take me on my one way *hajj* to Mecca. My brothers gathered in front of my apartment to say a final farewell. Dara, holding infant Gauhara in his arms, seemed on the verge of tears. The ladies of the harem gathered opposite the princes.

Each in turn hugged me and gave me something of use for my journey. I fought back tears lest my determination to continue on my hajj be brought into question. Soon I found myself before Afzal Khan, whom I regarded as an uncle and addressed as *chacha*.

But I looked past him and asked, "Afzal Chacha, where is Aba? I wish to pay my respects."

He looked at me with glistening eyes and a soldier's smile. "My dear Jahanara, he is waiting for you in Samman Burj. Please go and see him, just once."

The Samman Burj was an apartment in the Red Fort overlooking the river. Previously the home of Nur Jahan, and then of Ami, this was the most beautiful apartment in the entire fort. Since my mother's death it had remained empty, but it was still cleaned and repaired every day, as if royalty were still residing in it.

I walked into the Samman Burj, not having done so since my mother's death, and to my astonishment I saw a glittering figure in the distance, facing away from me towards the river.

"Aba, is that you?" I said in wonderment.

Aba turned around and reached his arms out to me, smiling for the first time I'd witnessed in almost a year. He was wearing his jewel-studded turban and his dagger; pearl necklaces, rings and other ornaments adorned his entire body.

I smiled and walked towards him, mightily baffled. I held my father's hands, and he leaned towards my forehead and kissed me. We walked over to the balcony overlooking the river. He said, "I want to show you something…" He paused. "…I intend to build."

The light reflected red from the rubies on his dagger, and I squinted to avoid the glare. He said, "You see that site over there, past the river? It belongs to my friend Raja Jay Singh. I'm going to buy that from him and build there."

I shaded my eyes, trying to discern which mansion he was referring to. "Build what?"

"I will build a mausoleum for your mother. Look, I already have several ideas."

He led me to a drawing he'd made on a wide sheet of paper. We bent our heads over the massive parchment that covered the entire surface of the table it was resting on. Aba continued: "You know how the Koran says that paradise contains gardens? Well, we're going to have four walkways and fountains that lead to a central pool. The flowers and shrubs in the garden are emblems of life, and along the walkway we'll have cypress trees. Do you know what they represent?"

"What?"

"Death and eternity, Jahanara. Death and eternity."

My eyes began to glisten. I hadn't seen my father show such enthusiasm or utter such coherent, lucid thoughts since before my mother's death. True to my Ami's advice, it seemed that only a hobby such as building, which my father had enjoyed since his childhood, would be able to bring him out of his despair. My mother knew my father better than anyone, and even in those final moments when life was draining from her, she must've been cryptically offering the cure to my father's inevitable melancholy and depression she knew would follow her death.

"And here…" Aba went on, waving his pointer up and down, "… here will be the mausoleum itself, pure white, just like your mother. It will be located where the Koran says paradise itself is, within the gardens. As your mother reclines on the thrones of paradise in heaven, her body will be forever housed in this paradise on earth."

"Aba?" I said as I stared smiling at the drawings. "When did you have time to do this?"

"Ever since you told me you're leaving, I've done nothing but think about building. I searched all of the other drawings on Mughal architecture to devise this. I want the domes of the building to be modelled around Akbar's tomb, because like your great grandfather, your mother, too, was a tolerant and beloved ruler. Everything will have a symbolic meaning, Jahanara."

We stared at each other, as if two lovers had found each other after a long period of exile.

Aba grinned, "I'm back, Jahanara. Somewhere between Burhampur and Agra I lost myself. It took a while, I know. But I've come home."

I fell into my father's arms, wept and hugged him as tightly as I could. As he embraced me, I sensed his familiar scent, and a memory rose from my childhood in the Deccan when we played games together in our exiled world. Hoping he never would leave me again, I tightened my grip so he would be a part of me for a lifetime.

"Does this mean you'll stay?" asked Aba with both tears and a smile.

"What about all the broken temples and churches?" I asked.

"All the temples destroyed shall be rebuilt and an allowance for their maintenance will be given every year from the royal treasury. The Christians will be free to practice and convert as they choose. And I am having the mullahs removed from the Diwan-i-khas. Raushanara has been visiting Nur Jahan regularly, and she was the one who incited the mullahs to advise me to attack Hugli."

"But why Hugli? Why not some other Christian city?"

"I don't know, but she has been reprimanded, and Nur Jahan is now being banished to Lahore. She will not be allowed any visitors, certainly not any of my children. From now on, Dara will advise me on religious matters. I am anointing him the heir apparent!"

Aba took my hand, and we walked across the marble floor towards the Jharoka-i-darshan. Afzal was waiting for us there along with my brothers, who by then, I presumed, had been told by Afzal about Aba's plan to convince me to stay.

The *dhundhubi* beat began as we walked closer to the *jharoka*. I stopped a pace before reaching the balcony so Aba could offer his darshan to his people alone, as was customary -- but he seized my arm and gestured for me to walk with him.

I walked out onto the balcony with my face covered, standing right next to my father, just as Ami always had since his coronation.

Staring at us across the pale horizon was a sea of people with faces upturned like black dots with white clothes. Thousands upon thousands stood below, forming their own fluid river, filling the narrow gullies in a massive flood of humanity. At such an elevation, one's vision begins to change; the world shrinks and the way others view you changes as well. Aba raised his hands to acknowledge his faithful subjects, as if to give them his blessing to officially end their mourning and resume their lives.

9

THE PROCLAMATION

10ᵗʰ August, 1632

I was livid about Raushanara's involvement in Hugli. Until now, I'd sympathised with her and wished to have a close relationship with her. But now, I felt as if something inside me was changing. It was almost as if my heart and mind were undergoing a metamorphosis, and I began feeling rage and – dare I say —hatred towards her. Oh, my God! Was I becoming a Mughal in the spirit of all those before me who killed their siblings for the throne? But though I couldn't prevent the change occurring in me, I was determined not to act on it. I simply would watch Raushanara and be more wary of her from now on.

As news of my remaining in Agra permeated the royal household, my brothers and the other members of the harem rejoiced. Later that week, Aba ordered the first official celebration. A royal banquet was convened in the palace. Rich carpets of silk with golden and silver embroidery were laid on the ground to form tables. The most fragrant perfumes were burned to give the air a sweet aroma. The Emperor entered, preceded by several beautiful women wearing golden silk garments. My maternal grandmother and I walked on either side of him.

Then entered Dara, followed by my other brothers. It seemed to me they, too, were satisfied with their royal titles. Perhaps because of my decision to stay or simply because of the majesty of the moment, their faces featured wide grins, as though this were now their kingdom. The drums began to beat, and those present bowed their heads as we entered.

Boom! Boom! Boom!
"Padshah zindabad!"
"Padshah zindabad!"
"Padshah zindabad!"

I had never walked alongside Aba into such a room since he'd become emperor. Surprisingly, I found the feeling empowering. For once I felt I had the power to make a difference and that others cared what I thought. I held my face high, acknowledging my father's subjects, and walked into this elegantly decorated hall.

The drum ceased beating and music now began: Light sitar plucking and whines filled the air. An ambience was thus set, majestic yet mellow. As the royal household sat at our respective locations, four women came into the hall. Because these were slave girls, their incredibly thin veils revealed each girl's different ethnic origin. The first, who had Turkish features, laid a white cloth in front of the King; the second, who was of undoubtedly Kashmiri descent, placed a jewel-studded golden vessel with a hollow centre covered with a fine grating in before him; the third girl, who looked Persian, came with water to wash the King's hands over the vessel; and the fourth, with Uzbek features, handed him the towel to dry his hands.

After the King had been served by the four maidens, 12 more entered to do the same for the Princes. The eunuchs, wearing different-coloured trousers and white coats of the finest transparent muslin, brought out the royal dinner in sealed golden dishes. Four placed themselves next to the King and handed dishes to the two women, the Turk and the Uzbek, kneeling on either side of the King. I saw Aba motion to the Uzbek girl to serve him his favourite dish: roast lamb steeped in spiced yogurt. As was customary, the seal was broken, the food was sampled by the girl, and then handed to the King. While the Uzbek served him, the Turkish girl, as if she'd been trained by one of my father's servants, served him naan along with two, not three, pieces of tandoori chicken. The women continued to place the dishes before the Emperor, hand him drinking water and remove the dishes he no longer desired.

The plates we ate from were of gold, and the feast was the grandest Agra had seen since Ami's death. In addition to the Emperor's favourite dishes, there were also bowls of chicken *chaat*, *mugli masala*, mutton *saag*, and tray after tray of *seek* kebabs, *shammi* kebabs, *do peesah, roghali josh, shahi* korma, with every imaginable fruit our kingdom had to offer: grapes, pomegranates, mangoes, papayas, watermelons, oranges, guavas, pears, custard apples and watermelons. All told, there were over 100 different dishes, served with lemon juice, mango juice and different types of wines.

I noticed that some Europeans had also been invited and situated a certain distance away. I asked Sati, who was seated next to me where the firangi might be.

She shrugged, "I have no idea, I can't tell white people apart."

Then the desserts came out: European style pastries and cakes served by slaves. Aba remarked that the pastries were Portuguese and added that the Europeans would be a great people if only they didn't eat pork and washed themselves more often. To this comment, one European replied to Aba, "Why generalise, Your Majesty? Not all Portuguese are like that."

"But they still eat pork," sniped Aurangzeb.

I looked at the European directly and asked him, "Are you Portuguese?"

"Yes, Your Highness. His Majesty is right," he remarked with a grin on his face, "some of us can be filthy."

"Have you spent time with other Portuguese in India?" I asked.

"Yes, Your Majesty, in Hugli. My name is Sebastian Manrique."

I was pleasantly surprised, but didn't have the courage to show my emotions in full public display. I said off-handedly, "Did you know a doctor there named Gabriel?"

Sebastian began laughing, but couldn't speak with a mouthful of food. Aba and Dara looked at each other in disgust at the poor etiquette and table manners the traveller from Europe was displaying.

Manrique gulped, "Yes, Madame. Very well. He was with me in Hugli."

"Where is he now?" I asked.

Sebastian's smile turned to a frown. Perhaps knowing he couldn't criticise the King directly at a royal banquet, he seemed at a loss for words to describe the horror in Hugli. I later learned he had narrowly escaped death himself by playing dead and sneaking out after the Mughal soldiers left. "I believe he was wounded in battle, but I don't know what became of him. I'm sorry."

I nodded unemotionally. "I wish to employ your services for our Jesuit mission in Agra, sir."

"As you wish, Your Highness."

"You will be escorted by my eunuch, Bahadur, to the zenana quarters tomorrow," I said with a bit of royal cockiness I was now becoming accustomed to.

Aba then began making an announcement. The crowd's chattering halted as the heart of the empire, the King himself, demanded their attention: "My fellow countrymen and esteemed guests, I wish to inform you of something truly historic. Not too long from now, you will see the construction of a mausoleum for the Empress Mumtaz Mahal, across the river from the fort. I am assembling artisans from all over the world, even Europe," he said nodding to Sebastian. "I intend this to be the finest structure the world has ever seen, and it will require my undivided attention. I am commanding my daughter Jahanara to manage this project."

The crowd began chanting and cheering. *"Padishah Zindabad!"* *"Padishah Zindabad!"*

But Aba wasn't finished. "I am also letting you all know that a kingdom without an empress is like a body without a heart. India shall once again have an empress, and she will be someone in whom we see our beloved *former* empress."

Dead silence fell upon in the Hall as Aba turned towards me and began walking in my direction. I wasn't sure what to expect, and my heart began beating faster. Finally he stood in front of me and handed me an object that was too large for my hand, as though it had been made not for a woman's but a man's. I clumsily held it with both my trembling hands and began examining it. Made of solid gold, it had Persian writings on the side and a large diamond on top. Even with both hands I had trouble holding it, and I struggled against its weight pushing my palms down.

Then beside me Sati gasped, "The *muhr uzak*!" I was shocked: Could this truly be the legendary muhr uzak, the royal seal so important, no command, not even the emperor's, could reverse its authority once stamped? It all made sense now. No object this grand could be for a small task. In its grandiosity lay its true purpose.

Aba then cried: "Ladies and gentlemen, Jahanara Begum is no longer Begum Sahiba; she is now the *Padishah Begum*!"

I was overcome with emotion; something inside me stirred as if another soul was trying to possess my body. Padishah Begum? Was I really worthy of such a title? What had I done to deserve this extraordinary honour?

The crowd now roared, "Long Live Padishah Begum!" and continued to roar, and my stomach began to churn and my heart raced. Was this how all the empresses had felt when first given this title? The *muhr uzak! This seal has changed so many hands. So many powerful, intelligent women have held it, and now it's mine to hold?*

I noticed my brothers rejoicing. It seemed my betterment was the one thing that had brought Aurangzeb and Dara together. But Raushanara, seated on the far corner, ran out of the room in rage; hardly anyone but me, even noticed.

Sati embraced me tightly and whispered excitedly in my ear: "You are the first ever Empress of India not to be married to a king. In bypassing all of his wives and bestowing this title on you, the King has redefined a daughter's role in the royal household. You now control the throne. You are its mistress." Mistress of the throne? What did that even mean? Was this a new title carved out just for me? Would some new, unknown responsibility accompany this title?

Sati continued: "You can now exercise more control over state affairs than any prince or even the Emperor." I immediately began feeling to feel a sense of this new-found power; such was the effect of the *muhr uzak*. And I already knew what I would do with it: I would learn from Sebastian Manrique what had happened to Gabriel in Hugli, and then determine why my sister chose Hugli of all places against which to instigate an attack.

The words immediately began resonating in my mind: *More power than even princes!* I didn't covet this power, but since it was bestowed upon me, I could now redefine a woman's role in my society. I could finish the work Ami had begun, to stop the male domination of my kingdom. I hadn't seized power; power had seized me; and I would now seize this opportunity to set right what in the past had gone wrong.

"*Padishah Zindabad!*

"*Padishah Zindabad!*

"*Padishah Zindabad!*

The crowd continued to chant louder each moment. I nodded to my constituents and bowed to my father in reserved appreciation. Did he have any idea what he'd just done?

10
HIDDEN SECRETS
29th September, 1632

I soon found my life as empress more exhausting than I'd imagined it could be. Sure there were perks: slaves would bathe, dress and perfume me over the course of hours, for this was customary for empresses. I was waited upon by countless eunuchs, slaves and Tatars and at times I felt as though I was drowning in all the attention. However, there were also strict requirements of me, and this made being an empress very arduous. Every word, gesture and movement I made was noted, interpreted and discussed. I was now required to move with the demeanour of an empress around the zenana. My mother had made all this look so easy; perhaps it came more naturally to her.

As I struggled to adjust to my new title, I took the first step in fighting back against my wicked sister. I assembled a team of spies consisting of slave girls, eunuchs, maids and Tatar women to inform me of Raushanara's whereabouts in a given day, to see whom she interacted with and what mischief she was planning on wreaking on the royal household. Now that I knew she'd spent time with Nur Jahan, I was convinced she'd learned some of Nur Jahan's manipulative tactics and was not to be trusted. It was still unclear to me where her loyalties were, but I was convinced they weren't with me or Aba.

The head of this team was a burly Tatar woman named Isa.

At a gargantuan size of seven feet two inches, her biceps were the diameter of the strongest of Mughal men. She was at once both loyal and fierce. With her in charge, the other members of the team would remain in line.

The announcement came: "Padishah Begum, the firangi, *Sahib* Manrique has arrived."

Sebastian Manrique was escorted by Bahadur to the special screened window at which he would have an audience with me. By promising him employment for Agra's Jesuit mission, I'd lured him close enough to me to ask him what had happened at Hugli and what had become of Gabriel.

He began: "Your Highness, I am at your service as you requested."

"Very well, Mr Manrique. The Jesuits have begun to hold services here again in Agra, and the emperor wishes for you to meet with the head priest and determine the best way to tell those in neighbouring suburbs about his mission. As a traveller, you have the ability to reach thousands of Christians within the Mughal domain."

"Her Majesty is too kind. It would be my pleasure to offer assistance to the head priest of the church."

"I have another matter to discuss with you. You mentioned you knew of Gabriel Boughton in Hugli. What else can you tell me about him?"

Sebastian hung his head low, for he was not permitted to stare at the marble window behind which I stood. He abashedly said, "I told you, Your Highness, I knew him. What else can I tell you?"

"I wish to know under what circumstances he arrived and what became of him."

Sebastian said: "Much of what I'm about to tell you I heard from his own mouth..."

Gabriel arrived in Hugli a few weeks before the arrival of the Mughal regiment and found the port busier than any he'd seen since arriving in India. Ship after ship of cargo was being exchanged at this port, and for a moment, Gabriel began to feel as if he was back in Europe, with all the churches and light-skinned people. It was as if someone had plucked a town out of Portugal and planted it in India.

Not sure of where to go, he made his way to the Church of St Augustine, where the Brethren of St Augustine's head, Pastor Reverend Frahlo, was Gabriel's contact.

Gabriel spent the next several days learning from the Portuguese the secrets of the profitable trade, especially the salt trade that had made the Portuguese very powerful and wealthy in this area.

One night, as Gabriel was sleeping in his guest quarters, a servant came running to his room and informed him that an army was gathering at their doorstep.

The two men peeped out of the small window of the guest quarters, and Gabriel saw an entire division of men carrying torches with the Mughal banner off to one side. This military cordon was dressed on war footing, and Gabriel wasn't sure what to do or where to go.

Gabriel ran to the church of father Frahlo, where he met Sebastian Manrique. The men decided to pursue diplomacy and try to negotiate with the Mughal generals.

Sebastian Manrique slowly walked over to the general, who was mounted on a horse and asked what his grievances were. The general informed him that this colony had been accused of committing heresy and teaching infidel religion contrary to the teachings of the Koran. Sebastian pleaded with the general to understand that it was the King's own father, Jahangir, who'd given the colony the power to build churches and practice their religion as they pleased. But the General was clearly looking for a pretext for attack, not interested in debating or discussing any issues. He made his demands clear to Sebastian: "Surrender your leaders, tear down all religious buildings, burn all Christian books and accept Allah as your saviour. Anything short of this will mean swift annihilation."

Sebastian went back to the church, which by now had swollen into a town hall gathering of all the Europeans in the colony. As he told everyone what the Mughal general demanded, the entire crowd cried out in an uproar.

The firangis decided to organise and mount resistance. One by one, men volunteered, until the number of people ready to do battle swelled to over 100. Aware that they were drastically outnumbered, the men began to devise a strategy whereby they could sneak behind the army and attack them from either side with bullets. The soldiers would be so surprised, they would run in whichever direction they could find cover.

Gabriel volunteered to use the underground tunnel linking the church to the port, to lead a group of men to the far side of the field. There, they would grab weapons from the ships docked at the port and sneak up behind the rebel army.

As the hours passed by and the time allotted for the Europeans' surrender drew near, the Mughal army began making preparations to storm the church. Pursuant to Aba's orders, the European missionaries were to be burned within the church, while the women and children would be brought back to Agra as prisoners.

Gabriel and his men made way through the tunnel and snuck into one of the cargo ships carrying munitions. Gabriel reached the storeroom and grabbed rifles, which he began handing out to each of his men as they entered in single file.

As the men loaded their rifles, one of the men accidently fired a shot into his own shoulder. The loud sound, along with his own scream as he was writhing in pain, alerted the Mughal army that something was occurring at their rear.

The men began running towards the church, launching cannonballs at the different wings. Haphazard firing from the church also began, but was too disorganised to mount any serious challenge to the Mughal army. The merchants-turned-soldiers were no match for the Mughal army, and one by one they began to fall. The women and children all gathered in the rear of the building under the guidance of Father Frahlo and began to pray for help. "Lord, have mercy on us. Christ, have mercy on us," the crowd chanted as the bombs continued, while the women watched their men drop like flies.

"Lord, have mercy on us. Christ, hear us, Christ, graciously hear us."

"God, the Father of heaven, have mercy on us."

More men continued to die and cry out in pain; women watched their husbands, children watched their fathers fall.

"God the Son, Redeemer of the world, have mercy on us. God, the Holy Spirit, have mercy on us."

The Mughal army mercilessly pursued the Christians. For every one Mughal soldier that fell, ten Portuguese merchants died.

"Holy Trinity, One God, have mercy on us."

The women and children knelt on the ground and closed their eyes, flowing tears as father Frahlo continued to lead them in what would be their final prayer. "Holy Mary, pray for us. Holy Mother of God, pray for us. Holy Virgin of virgins, pray for us."

Finally the shelling and bullets stopped. There was utter silence. The congregation opened their eyes slowly and awoke to a scene of horror no person would wish upon their kin. All their men were dead. There was smoke and rubble everywhere. The front of the church had been completely blown away. Sebastian Manrique lay at a distance playing dead, so he might survive to tell me this horrific story one day.

Then the front door was blown open, and the general arrived with blood in his eyes.

Meanwhile, at the other end of battlefield, near the port, the Europeans apparently had better luck. They were able to position themselves at different locations in various ships and engage in sporadic fighting against the Mughal army. Here, for every one European that fell, ten Mughals fell. However, the ratio was apparently not enough to help the Europeans – there were too many soldiers overall.

Gabriel fought off several soldiers, but then noticed one of his men was hit. As he tried to run towards the man to help him, a shot hit him across his neck and he fell into the Bay of Bengal. The remaining men each fell, either to their deaths, or into the Bay, or both.

Back at the church, the families of the fallen were all chained around the stage where they'd been praying, the crucifix and the statues of Christ overlooking their imprisonment. Their heads were covered with black cloths as they continued to pray and recite their religious chants.

"Lamb of God, who takest away the sins of the world, spare us, O Lord. Lamb of God, who takest away the sins of the world, graciously hear us, O Lord. Lamb of God, who takest away the sins of the world, have mercy on us..."

Then the Mughal general ordered the entire church and all its occupants, burned. Though Aba had merely ordered the death of the missionaries and was silent on what should be done to the families, the battle-enraged Mughal general, not content with killing the men in armed combat and merely imprisoning the families, decided to avenge the deaths of his soldiers in a much more ferocious way.

As the women, children and Father Frahlo began to smell smoke, everyone screamed and writhed trying to free themselves from their bondage, but to no avail. Children could be heard screaming for their mothers; women screamed at the fumes that smothered their dresses; some continued to pray: "Christ, hear us. Christ, graciously hear us. Lord, have mercy on us. Christ, have mercy on us. Lord, have mercy on us. Lead us not into temptation, but deliver us from evil!"

The Mughal army watched this spectacle at a distance and began celebrating, as if they were watching a fireworks display. Some even began drinking wine in celebration. Soon the sounds of people began to die out, and the smell of burnt flesh permeated the air. By morning, the entire church had burned to the ground, and no European in Hugli seemed left alive.

✳ ✳ ✳

A full month later Isa paid me a visit at my apartment, with an update on her assignment.

"Your Majesty," she said, "when you're not in your apartment, Raushanara Begum welcomes herself here and looks through your belongings!"

I gravely looked at Isa, nodding gently, trying to hide my disgust and horror at learning of this invasion of privacy. "Anything else?" I asked, staring straight at her.

I believe Isa understood I had to purposely refrain from showing any emotion. Doubtless sensing the gravity of the news she'd just given me, she added, "Mallikaye, I have worked in this zenana since before you were born. I know what goes on here. If you have kept personal items such as letters or presents in your apartment, I suggest you check them."

I was appalled to learn that my quarters were being routinely ravaged by Raushanara in my absence, and then restored as if nothing happened. After Isa left, I opened my drawer to search for the one token I had from the man I felt something akin to love for: Gabriel's letter.

Opening my copy of the *Ibn Majah hadith*, a holy book for us Muslims, I turned to number 2771. Number 2771 of the hadith stated 'Paradise is at the mother's feet.' I'd purposely hid Gabriel's letter there because of all the hadith messages, this one held a special meaning for me, as my Ami existed now only in my thoughts and prayers.

I turned the pages, anxiously trying to reach number 2771, hoping Raushanara hadn't touched, and if touched, not stolen, this memento. I finally reached the number 2771, and the only thing staring at me was the message, *Paradise is at the mother's feet*. There was no letter.

I picked up the book by its cover, opening it like a bird's wings and shook vigorously from side to side, hoping the letter would shake out.

Finally a small piece of torn, flat paper folded into fourths popped out, that must've gotten caught in the seams of one of the pages. Though Raushanara must be sharp enough to know that I'd again look for the letter one day and, not finding it, would suspect something amiss, she hadn't realised I'd kept the letter in a special place, with my Ami, and that if I didn't find it there, I'd know someone had moved it. So Raushanara knew about Gabriel and me, and this is why she must have incited Aba to burn Hugli.

11
THE WHITE SERPENT

28th May, 1633

Aurangzeb had seemed like an awkward boy for several reasons. First, his odd personality and cold intellectuality repelled anyone who might have found his skinny, peach-fuzz physique even mildly attractive. Secondly, he wasn't interested in athletics or music, the two things women of the zenana saw as prerequisites in a suitor. So Aurangzeb went through childhood with no real friends or admirers, burying himself in the one companion that couldn't abandon him: religion. And he began acting as if he owned it; only his interpretation was valid, and any deviation from his standards was heresy against Islam. He found admirers in the marginalised mullahs, who were still reeling from Aba's rebuke following the massacre at Hugli.

The mullahs had seen for several generations the laws and tenets of Islam being stretched widely and skewed creatively to form an inclusive, pluralistic society in India. Beginning with Akbar in the 1500s, intermarriage between Muslims and Hindus was accepted, and Hindu traditions were observed in the Mughal kingdom. Jahangir and Aba continued this tradition, each taking Hindu wives and expanding the scope of our kingdom to now include Christian missionaries from the west. All this had led to a counter-revolution by the Islamic purists, who were, in their opinion, observing the incremental destruction of Islam by non-Islamic forces.

Thus far, though, no prince of any merit had taken up the mullahs' cause as his own. For Shuja and Murad, life was about wine, women and wealth. Dara was a continuation of the infidel tradition of Aba, according to the mullahs. But Aurangzeb was the antithesis of Dara. Where Dara was inclusive, Aurangzeb was stringent; the more Dara spoke about the oneness of religions, the more Aurangzeb spoke about the strict letter of the law. The mullahs rightfully saw in Aurangzeb their opportunity to win back the kingdom and mold it according to religious doctrine as set forth in the Koran.

Aurangzeb, now 14, was becoming a handsome young man. He was now tall, well built, he had facial hair and a firm understanding of warfare. He had Aba's physical frame and military acumen, and Ami's skin tone and charisma. Aba had effectively shunned him numerous times, no doubt at the instigation of Dara, who still held resentment towards Aurangzeb for poisoning Gita. In fact, Aba called Aurangzeb the 'white serpent,' a stinging reference to his pale skin.

One day, in the northwest city of Lahore, Aba was seated at the royal balcony while 40 fighting Bengali elephants were presented to him. As the Padishah Begum, I was observing from behind the marble window, while the four royal princes watched the event from horseback. Suddenly, I noticed that one elephant, instead of fighting its opponent, began charging towards my four brothers. Dara, Shuja, and Murad all fled for their lives, but Aurangzeb stayed mounted, unwaveringly staying his ground. As the elephant continued to charge towards him, Aurangzeb, a spear in his hand, stared directly, without blinking, into the elephant's eyes.

"Allah ho akbar, Allah ho akbar," he murmured – and then to the amazement of all, the elephant moved around Aurangzeb and passed without harming him.

"All hail Prince Aurangzeb!" yelled the riders on the elephants and the guards at the gate. Aba smiled and nodded approvingly to his son (recognition Aurangzeb rarely received).

Then the crowds suddenly stopped cheering. Aurangzeb, looking towards Aba, and noticed the people in the balcony fall to worried looks. He suddenly turned his head straight and saw that the first elephant's opponent was now charging Aurangzeb in pursuit of his earlier rival.

Still with spear in hand, Aurangzeb again began to mutter his religious verse. "Allah ho akbar, Allah ho akbar."

As the elephant came charging, Aurangzeb rode his horse into the beast's path: an immense shape against a 14-year-old prince. Every moment seemed a day long; we hovered on the edges of our seats, our voices unable to leave our throats and make a sound. I was terrified though protected behind the screen. Suddenly Aurangzeb let out a loud cry and hurled his spear at the elephant, piercing its forehead. Though hurt, the elephant swung its trunk and knocked Aurangzeb off his horse, and the crowd gasped in horror.

The elephant didn't advance further. Aurangzeb lay on the ground, his legs bent, his knees up. Dara, Shuja, and Murad all stood at a distance watching, no one intervening. Dara placed his hand on Shuja's shirt as if trying to shield himself from any danger. Aurangzeb scrambled for his spear, took hold of it and threw it at the elephant's head again, this time turning the elephant away in agony. The crowd together breathed a sigh of relief; I finally released my breath and began breathing normally again. Aurangzeb waved to the crowd to acknowledge their applause, while my other brothers remained standing at a distance.

Aba then descended from his balcony, as servants and nobles rushed to Aurangzeb to examine and tend to his injuries. Aurangzeb walked slowly over to the King, and our grandfather, Asaf Khan, said, "You're walking slowly towards us, and it's the Emperor who's in an awful state of panic!"

Aurangzeb smiled grimly and quipped, "If the elephant was still here I might be walking faster, but now I see no reason to be worried!"

Aba hugged his son, immediately presented him with 100,000 rupees and said, "Thank God it all ended well, my son. Can you imagine what tragedy it would have been if things had turned out differently?"

Aurangzeb accepted the gift, but retorted, "Regardless of how things ended, the real tragedy is, my brothers, even the older ones, didn't stay to protect me or defend their honour."

Asaf Khan interjected, "But Aurangzeb, what were they to do? You chose to stay and take that risk."

The Prince replied, "Are they not soldiers, Grandfather? If soldiers should stay and face danger, was it right for them to run away and hide in shame?"

"There, there, Grandson. You must not take this personally. Besides, we all know that in the art of military tactics you have no equal."

Aurangzeb was now visibly angered that the adults took sides with my other brothers, particularly Dara, who hadn't stayed in the arena to defend him. He stormed towards the exit of the arena past his brothers, all of whom hung their heads low. On his way he shouted to Shuja, "I don't blame you, because you fell off your horse while running, but at least the heir apparent should have had some courage!"

He stopped momentarily, and Dara shot back: "Courage for what? For you?"

"For the kingdom! For our honour."

"Honour?" Dara exclaimed. "You stayed in the arena to look like a hero, and trying to save you, I might have been killed. That's what you would've liked, but I'm no fool. If you're going to act foolish, do so at your own peril. Besides, beasts should fight beasts, not men!"

Aurangzeb looked appalled at Dara's words. He dismounted, walked up to Dara, who was now equal in height to him and said softly, "I can't wait for the day when you and I face each other on the battlefield. I will bury you!"

Dara smiled back, "That'll be the best day of both our lives, *brother*!"

✳ ✳ ✳

The year before I'd sent Shuja and Sati to the Deccan to bring Ami's remains back to Agra. I instructed that along the way bestowal of enormous sums of money and food be made on the people along the countryside, the vast majority of whom were Hindus; and with each charitable act, the penniless peasants blessed the dead Empress' remains with all their heart.

Aba and I received word from a runner when the remains were a few kos away, so the two of us and Dara went to the Samman Burj to view the caravan bringing the remains to the intended site, which was owned by Rajah Jay Singh and bought from him in return for four mansions in Agra.

We watched as the caravan reached the banks of the Jumna. A provisional tomb was constructed to hide the site of interment from public view. The spot was instantly converted into a sacred site for Hindus and Muslims. Hindus during their morning prayers would fold their hands in that direction, as if seeking blessing from a deity. Muslims would treat the shrine as a mosque in itself, though no one could enter it.

After the remains of my mother were interred in this new site, Dara and I walked down the stairs from the Samman Burj to the Macchi Bawan, a large hall located on the main floor. My father was already there with two other men, discussing the overall plan of the site.

A wooden model of the mausoleum had been constructed by the lead architects, Ahmed, a Persian astrologer and engineer who frequently directed Aba's most ambitious architectural projects, and Ali Mardan Khan, one of the court's great statesmen and architects.

Aba was telling the two men: "I want to make use of the number four. It is the holiest of all numbers in Islam, so I'm envisioning a garden laid out in a quadrate plan, with two canals running at perpendicular angles to one another."

Ahmed asked, "Do you have any idea what you want at the intersection of the two canals?"

Piped in the architecturally obtuse Dara: "You could have the actual building in the centre."

"No!" said all three men at once.

Aba said, "My son, you aren't taking advantage of the reflective power of the canal."

"How about a reflective pool in the middle?" said Ali Mardan. "That way, the visitor will see a mirror image of the structure in it."

"Precisely!" said Aba. "Not just that, but all along the canal, the structure will reflect into the water."

Dara and I gaped at the men discussing these ideas, hardly able to understand how such theoretical ideas could be developed and executed.

"But I'm concerned," said Ahmed, "about the seepage into the Jumna, Your Highness."

Aba put his hand on his chin and raised his eyebrows, pondering this challenging dilemma. The sheer size and weight of the structure would indeed place a tremendous burden on the already soft ground by the river. Then he said: "We're going to have to excavate an area the size of fifteen kos by fifteen kos and fill it with sediment."

The two men continued to discuss plans, as Dara and I watched from a distance and rejoiced to see our father coming alive once again. He wasn't excited about *building*; he was excited about building for *Ami*. He was communing with her through art and celebrating his love through his work and keeping it alive, honouring his lover's last wishes.

***

Aurangzeb told his partner Raushanara about the elephant incident, and I learned that the two apparently discussed how biased our father was towards me and Dara, and how they were always playing second fiddle to lesser-quality siblings. Raushanara, as I would learn from Bahadur, had pursued a dangerous course ever since I was proclaimed empress. Not only did she encourage Aurangzeb to openly challenge Dara for the throne of India, but while chastising Dara's unislamic ways, she engaged in sexual promiscuity in her own chambers.

Every night servant men were brought to her, and she bedded
them, often committing lewd sexual acts some of the zenana
concubines had taught her. Sometimes she bedded several men at
once and even had the men commit sexual acts with each other. On
occasion, she would ask to have the servant men bed servant women
while she watched. If ever she was displeased with any of their
service, she would have them secretly killed by the prison guards on
trumped-up charges of theft and burglary.

Princess by day, whore by night, Raushanara's promiscuity
was effectively hidden from all of the household members, even
Aurangzeb. As intolerant as Aurangzeb was, he was equally critical
of Muslims committing immoral acts such as premarital intercourse
and adulterous affairs. She must've concluded that should he learn
of this, she would lose her last ally. By inciting one side to fight
another, the household members were kept warring with each other,
with no one having time to learn of her affairs.

I was torn about what I should do with this information. There
was no doubt in my mind that once Aba or anyone else learned of it,
Raushanara would face the harshest of punishments, possibly even
execution. Not wanting to be responsible for a family member's
death – not even a malicious family member's – I decided to keep
my mouth shut so long as her sexual deviance was affecting only
her.

Seeking more allies to censure Dara for his passivity, Aurangzeb
came to me one day. "I know what happened, Aurangzeb," I nodded.
"I was there. I'm sorry. You're right, Dara should've intervened."

"So will you censure him?" Aurangzeb seemed both hopeful and
demanding.

"You know I can't censure anyone, but Aba and I will speak with
him."

Aurangzeb's face dropped. "Aba is on his side!"

"You know Aba doesn't take sides," I reminded him.

Aurangzeb looked sharply at me. "Are you blind? Do you know
Dara refers to me behind my back as 'the white serpent?' What did
I ever do to him?"

I just looked at the ground. I knew Aurangzeb was right, and that as the only surviving parent it was Aba's duty to give all his children the love of both a father and a mother, but I was powerless to do anything. I had talked to Aba already about equalising his treatment of all his sons, but to no avail. I also was aware of this derogatory nickname he'd given my light-skinned brother.

"Go, Aurangzeb," I told him. "You've made your point. I'll do what I can, brother. But in the meantime, please don't carry ill in your heart against Dara. You know he'll be wed soon, and I want to put a unified 'family' face for the people to see. This will be our family's first wedding."

"First wedding… huh! First wedding, for the first son, who's first always. Do you realise that my only fault is that I wasn't born first? Were I older than Dara, *I'd* be Aba's favourite, I'd be the heir apparent, and I'd be wed first. For my wedding, everything will be second-rate."

"No, Aurangzeb, I swear that on your wedding I'll spend just as much as on Dara's. I'll work just as hard…"

"I know you will Jahanara, but somehow Aba will remind me then also that I'm second-rate in his eyes. No matter what I do, it never stops!"

Having said these words, Aurangzeb left my apartment – and me to plan Dara's wedding. I was disappointed by my inability to pacify my brother, but what could I do? I left him to rot in his self-pity and rage, unable to fathom how it might one day grow into a fury even he wouldn't be able to control.

❅ ❅ ❅

With Sati's help I went to great lengths to plan for Dara the most extravagant wedding the country had ever seen. Nuptial costs alone exceeded 30 lakh rupees, of which I contributed half from my own savings. Dara was dressed in his mansion overlooking the Jumna. All three of his brothers, including Aurangzeb, gathered at his mansion and accompanied him to the Diwan-i-am, where the nobles and public were gathered. Aba then put a pearl necklace on Dara and a groom's crown on his head.

Dara rode behind Aba on his own horse, wearing a burgundy *sarapa* covered with emeralds, pearls, amethysts and gold embroidery. The younger brothers rode on lesser decorated horses behind him, as velvet and rose petals were showered on the ground in front of them and nautch girls whirled in ecstasy in front of the procession. The music was loud but peaceful, preventing anyone from hearing the sounds of silver and gold coins being showered as father and son passed by.

Over 1,000 nobles attended the wedding, and the gifts from each noble were paraded and then marched off to the royal treasury to be catalogued and recorded. (This show of wealth was out of respect for the king more than for the marrying couple.)

As they reached the house of Dara's new bride, Nadira, all the royal men dismounted and stood at the gate, sunset's rays shining off the diamonds on their turbans. They were greeted by Nadira's family and escorted into her house. The men sat across from the women; the mullahs sat in the centre. I noticed Nadira's hue from behind the screen, for she wasn't permitted to see or be seen by anyone during this ceremony. I was told her *churidar* was made of the finest silk, and her *ghaghara* had streaks of gold running down its length. She wore a necklace with pearls the size of grapes and earrings made of emeralds.

The mullahs read a passage from the Koran, and then shortly after midnight proclaimed Dara and Nadira married. A great celebration ensued, with Chinese rockets providing a fireworks display and music thundering through the red sandstone halls of the fort.

Equal in beauty to Ami, Nadira shared Dara's thirst for higher learning of other religions and had won his trust and love even more deeply than Gita had. Indeed, Dara first consented to the marriage when he noticed how closely Nadira bore a resemblance to Gita. It was as if Gita had come alive again, aged, and then had been presented to him as a Muslim royalty. Dara, in turn, proclaimed that he would never marry another woman, adamant that the role that Manu and other wives of Aba had in the household shouldn't be inherited by any others in future.

The zenana rejoiced in the privacy of its own quarters. There were copious amounts of wine and opium for those who desired them. Henna Begum, as usual, began disrobing in front of the other women as one of the eunuchs sang in the background to light, distant sitar music. Henna was so heavily intoxicated, I wasn't sure she would even remember this event the next morning. At a distance, I saw Raushanara, also heavily intoxicated, carrying a giant jug of wine she poured into the mouths of the zenana women.

She growled thickly, "I command you to open your mouth!" Her eyes were glazed over. "You have to obey me, you are a mere concubine!" The women reluctantly opened their mouths, and as Raushanara poured the sour wine into their mouths and ordered them to swallow, the concubines squinted. I wasn't pleased to see this forced intoxication. Standing next to her, holding her hand, was Gauhara, my younger sister and only sibling never to have known Ami. She, too, was drunk.

Raushanara and Gauhara slowly made their way to one young concubine who begged, "Please, Begum Raushanara, I do not wish to consume wine. I never take any intoxicating substances."

"Oh?" Raushanara rasped. She walked up to the concubine, a young 16-year-old beauty with Turkish features. "Such intoxicating beauty, but no intoxicating substances?" This, I knew, was Aba's favourite concubine, who had won several favours from him, much to the chagrin of the other zenana women. "You intoxicated my father, but no one can intoxicate you?" She then motioned to Gauhara and commanded, "Gauhara, hold her hands down!" Then Raushanara held the concubine's mouth open with her hand and began to pour wine into her mouth.

I yelled: "Raushanara, stop it!" There was silence as both Raushanara and Gauhara loosened their grips. The concubine ran out crying. "Stop forcing people to drink if they don't wish to!"

Henna Begum purred, "Begum Raushanara, may I have some of your love juice!" She continued dancing and disrobing, and Raushanara and Gauhara walked over to her, waggling their hips to emulate Henna's moves. Henna opened her mouth and Raushanara began pouring the wine in Henna's mouth as they both bumped and ground, causing the wine to spill onto her face and down her bosom. Henna laughed, "Gauhara, the wine is expensive! Don't let it fall – lick it!" Gauhara licked the wine off of Henna's neck and slowly went down to her nipples and the women laughed loudly at their debauchery.

I shouted: "Gauhara, what do you think you're doing? Go to your chambers! Bahadur, take the wine from Raushanara; no more drinking tonight!"

"Sorry, Padishah Begum," Raushanara said. "Aba has issued a proclamation that there will be boisterous rejoicing tonight to celebrate the heir apparent's wedding. You sealed it with the muhr uzak!"

"Then I can unseal it also!"

"No, Jahanara, you don't have the authority to unseal it. The King makes the decision, and you approve or disapprove, but you cannot initiate a decision already taken. Sorry!" She then began fondling Henna's breasts and looked towards me, openly defying my orders and challenging me. Gauhara, completely inebriated from the opium and wine Raushanara had fed her, continued licking. I left the room as the women laugh and mocked on. I hoped my mother wasn't watching from her place 'beyond.'

❈ ❈ ❈

The wedding having occurred with much fanfare, I was lauded by the King for my efforts and given more time now to manage the building of the mausoleum. This structure was preordained to be one of the most eclectic structures of all time. Designers from all over the world descended upon Agra and were presented to me in the Macchi Bawan, located behind the Diwan-i-am.

Ahmed and Ali Mardan presented their choices for the different parts of the structure.

"Empress," said Ali, "may I present to you Ismail Afandi, from Turkey? He is a designer of hemispheres and a builder of domes."

I asked "Tell me, Ismail, have you constructed many mosques for your former masters?"

"Yes, Your Majesty. I have built several domed structures for both mosques and palaces, and I wish to make the domes of your structure perfect to the final inch."

"What makes you think your construction of domes will be the finest?"

Ismail looked at me confidently. "Your Highness, I have spent a lifetime building domes. Though you may not see the subtle differences in domes, I assure you there is a significant difference from one structure to another."

I probed his eyes deeply: "And I assume you know the difference?"

Ismail explained to me further how the domes differed and the techniques he would employ. This dome, he went on to tell me, would have a special fullness he felt would bring out its beauty. Satisfied with this self-described expert of domes, I moved to the next mason.

"Your Highness," Ahmed said, "I now present to you Qazim Khan, a native of Lahore, a renowned expert in precious metals."

A tall, slender man with a trimmed beard and moustache rose; I noticed his hands were covered with thick calluses, doubtless reflecting a lifetime spent welding metal. "Are we to have metals for the structure?" I asked.

"Yes, Your Majesty," bowed Qazim. "I will be the artist to design a golden structure atop the majestic domes you create."

"Does the drawing call for metal elsewhere?"

"Not to my knowledge, Your Highness, but perhaps the doors to the mausoleum will be of a fine material such as silver."

How opulent this structure would look with giant doors made of pure silver! Almost embarrassed that I didn't already know about the metals planned for the structure, I moved on to the next artisan.

Ali spoke: "Your Majesty, I now present Amanat Khan Shirazi, master calligrapher from Shiraz."

A heavy-set middle-aged gentleman very gracefully rose and greeted me. Unlike the other artisans, this man seemed non-athletic; his art wouldn't require him to build muscles or a chiselled physique. Rather, he was a poet, artist and master calligrapher with a visual acumen that would see the subtle flaws of everyday writing and thus create the most flawless depiction of prose wherever he put his ink.

I said, "Tell me, Amanat, where will your calligraphy find a home on our structure?"

"Your Highness," he said with quiet assurance, "I will write Koranic verses on the entrance to the structure, so that Allah's words will remain always a part of your mother's home."

I smiled and nodded to this exquisitely polite gentleman, whose name would ultimately be the only signature on the structure.

One by one, Ahmed and Ali Mardan presented more men to me. To the best of my abilities, I tried to question each in his area of expertise, only to find they'd been well pre-screened by my two chief architects; these were simply the best in their trades to be had anywhere. After several days of interviews and questioning, 37 men were chosen to form the nucleus of the project, with over 20,000 actually commissioned to work on the structure. Marble was to be dug from the quarries of eastern India in the state of Rajasthan and transported to Agra with ox carts for hundreds of kos. Red sandstone was to be brought from the abandoned city of Fatehpur Sikri as well as from local quarries. The precious stone inlays came from much more far and remote regions: turquoise from Tibet, lapis from Ceylon, chrysolite from the Nile, carnelian from Baghdad, rare shells from the Indian Ocean and jasper from Cambay. Forty-three different types of gems and precious metals were to be used in the structure, including diamonds, rubies, silver and gold.

Aba and I spent the next several years steeping ourselves in the work for the new structure. Not even having a name yet, we referred to it simply as *The Structure*. Labourers and masons from all over India poured into Agra to help with the construction, and a ten kos ramp of bricks was constructed to haul the large marble slabs up to its highest portion.

As we viewed the area from the Samman Burj I remarked to Aba: "There's more life out there than there is here in the fort."

"Yes, indeed," he smiled. "In fact, they're calling that area Mumtazabad, after your mother I presume." It was beyond amazing to me, how on a clear barren field along the banks of the river, an entire metropolis had erupted, chaotic-looking but dynamic.

I said, "Mumtazabad? Hmm... I guess it has its own streets and avenues and lanes. They even have a bazaar and playing grounds for the childrens' servants."

"Everything you'd expect to find in a city," replied Aba. "In fact, a caravan from Baghdad went through our city yesterday and stopped only in Mumtazabad, not Agra, because they felt there was more business for their goods there than here."

"Really?"

"Not only so, but some people are openly saying they're residents of Mumtazabad, not Agra."

"Did they receive your approval to say this, Aba?"

"No..." he said hesitantly, as if reflecting for the first time on the illegal nature of such a claim. "Yet," he nodded, "I guess as long as they're honouring your mother's name, I'm content. In truth, were it up to me every town would be Mumtazabad."

I looked again at the makeshift town of Mumtazabad, marvelling at how the former empty riverside location was now bustling with life: children were playing in the streets; vendors were selling goods. I then turned to my father and said excitedly, "Next time we go to survey the structure, can we also visit Mumtazabad, Aba? I want to see just how much it has developed!"

Years had passed since I first interviewed the master artisans for the mausoleum. I continued to coordinate changes to the design as well as negotiate with other kingdoms for precious stones, but I left supervision of the actual construction to Ali Mardan and Ahmed. Now, as Aba and I set out to survey the progress, I wasn't sure what to expect.

As we dismounted from the elephant, I felt in utter awe of how, amid the debris of broken lumber and bustle of half-naked labourers, their ribs visible and faces darkened with dust, there was rising a luminous, snow-white structure that looked as though it had fallen from Allah's very paradise for our earthly pleasure.

Along the side of the construction area, I saw rows of burly, muscular men gathering in long lines to give their names and areas of expertise, and if they were lucky, to receive their new assignments. Indians from all over the country came to us to seek employment, and each according to his skill would find employment to help build my mother's shrine.

I could tell many of the labourers were drinking, quite possibly to find comfort from the long, hard days their new job required. At a distance, labouring women balanced basins of earth on their heads, while their male counterparts dug with iron piks and dumped the earth into the never-ending line of empty basins. Slowly, the actual direction of the river was being changed so it might be brought closer to the site.

As Aba discussed the progress of the structure with his architects, it seemed to me that the architects were torn over a dilemma: How would the structure simultaneously exemplify both the opulence and grandeur of the Mughal King and the utter simplicity of the Queen it meant to immortalise? This quandary seemed born from Aba himself, for he would vacillate between what the monument was supposed to signify -- the greatest architectural glory of Shah Jahan the Magnificent – or the enduring love and devotion of his modest wife, Mumtaz. He would make one comment supporting the former and then regress and make a completely different comment supporting the latter. Ali Mardan motioned to me not to be concerned, though. The end – he would tell me – would perfectly combine both.

❈ ❈ ❈

We decided to venture on foot through the tented city of Mumtazabad. Much to our amazement, we learned that the makeshift town had indeed blossomed into a major metropolis. Tents were arranged in a specific section, with narrow streets leading to a main avenue where larger carts could be found. There were bazaars for several kos, where all goods one can imagine could be bought and sold. Of course, the residents of this town were all labourers on the structure being built, so many of the goods were cheap items they could afford – no noble would be caught shopping here.

As we made our way back to our elephants near the structure, the sun began to set. On our way back to the fort, I decided to talk to my father about his treatment of Aurangzeb. Still concerned about the nickname he had been given, I was equally troubled by the biased treatment I saw with respect to both the elephant incident and overall inequalities between the treatment of the royal siblings.

"I never called him that to his face!" my father protested.

"It doesn't matter, Aba. You must understand that your nobles can't be trusted. Anything you say can poison your relationship with your son. And as bad as he is, is it your belief that calling him a 'serpent' befits a king as great as yourself?"

Aba pouted. "Are you aware of the offence he's committing since I made him Governor of the Deccan?"

Aba had sent his sons to govern different regions of his kingdom. To the west was sent Murad, to become governor of troubled Sindh and Afghan regions; to the east was Shuja to govern the more passive Bengal region; and to the south was Aurangzeb to govern the Deccan. Dara remained in Agra to oversee the capital and reap the pleasures of the city.

Aba said, "Ever since your brother was sent to the Deccan, I've received regular complaints from the people there of different temples he has destroyed. In Fatehnagar, he levelled a 6th century Hindu temple and used the statues to make a staircase for a mosque. His reasoning was that every time a believer in the Koran walks to the mosque, his feet should crush the infidel's idol to show the supremacy of Islam!"

I shook my head in shame. I hadn't been aware of what he'd done, but I knew he had it in him to do such things, and he was no more willing to change his ways than was my father.

"He purposely usurps my authority whenever he can. No other son does this but him!"

"But should you call your own son a serpent?"

"I only said that a couple of times in a moment of rage," Aba replied, his voice even more tense at being confronted about this matter.

I continued: "I know Aurangzeb could never be king, and I know he's intolerant of non-Muslims, but for you, he always tries to do well. He has always yearned to please you; always wants to be just like you. He's mastered military matters better than anyone, and he does it because he wants to be just like you."

"Well, if he wishes to be like me, I suggest he start with more subtle approaches, such as respecting religious minorities. You know…" he continued, leaning near me, "he doesn't even approve of all this," he said twirling his finger in the air.

"All what?"

"This… the structure, the mausoleum for your mother. He says it is un-Islamic because it shows vanity."

"Then what does he want?"

"He said the mud and wood covering we have on her grave is sufficient. We should be building mosques or conquering territories with the money we're spending on this."

I just sighed. No matter how much I tried to help my brother, his actions and words always made it very difficult for me to convey my message and win him any allies.

Just staring straight at the road, not even looking me in the eye, Aba continued: "No mausoleum, no music, no poetry, nothing that makes life worth living is acceptable with that son of mine. That's why I sent him to the Deccan. Live there however you please. Just stop bothering me."

We, father and daughter, stayed quiet for the rest of the journey. I noticed my father was just staring out into the sky sadly, as if he felt devastated to see how Aurangzeb had turned out and felt helpless and frustrated at his own inability to mold his son into a better man. As if just giving up on him altogether, he'd merely banished him from the kingdom, but done so in a politically appropriate manner by calling him the Governor of the Deccan and giving him some limited power in a region that wasn't very important to us. Aba concentrated almost entirely now on Dara and Dara's newborn son, Sulaiman Shikoh. It was as if they alone were important to him. I didn't even bother re-approaching the topic of the elephant incident. For every one incident in which Aurangzeb was wronged, there appeared to be ten in which he was committing offences. Any discussion seemed futile.

12
THE ACCIDENT
5ᵗʰ April, 1644

I could barely breathe, my nostrils were so clogged with soot and ointments filled to treat my burns. My mouth was so dry, I was perpetually thirsty but never received any water because of my inability to communicate. My head ached as if someone was poking it with sharp needles all day and night. Every part of my body ached, except those parts I could no longer feel. Every time I tried to move, I felt as though my body was covered with layers of bandages, but perhaps it was just scars from the accident that had swollen and developed into atrocious blisters of fat and skin.

I slept most of the time from the opium they seem to have been giving me for the pain. Though I'm told I was never alone, I have barely any recollection of those months of my life.

Ami would visit me in my dreams on some nights, but whenever she did she looked like she did when we were in Nizamshahi, not in Agra. It was as if my memory chose to recall her not as the grand Queen of India, but as a simple princess back when power and status meant very little to our family.

In her sweet yet stern voice she would say to me, "Jahanara, stay close by; don't run into the forest after any rabbit or deer!" I felt as though I was looking through a window transported in time, for in my dreams, I saw myself as a ten-year-old girl, running carefree, wanting nothing more than a beautiful deer to admire and a beautiful baby sister or brother to give way to my perpetually pregnant mother who through her days with a swollen belly, would run after me and pick me up in her arms.

She was with me during those days when I lay in bed on the verge of death, my body badly disfigured from the flames that had consumed it.

I don't know how my family members were coping with this, especially Aba, whose voice would occasionally echo in my ears when I went in and out of consciousness, barely aware of my surroundings. But honestly, as much as I cared about them, I was in too much agony to think of their needs at this time.

After we arrived in our palace from Mumtazabad that fateful day, I was walking back to my apartments, newly remodelled in the past several years, after I'd finished checking up on my father. Four female servants accompanied me as I walked through the marble and red sandstone corridors. On this night, I wore muslin I'd purchased from Mumtazabad. It was a beautiful turquoise colour, but was a little bit big on me. As I walked, the bottom portion of the rear of the muslin swung in the wind behind me like the train of a bride.

I was enjoying the wind gusts created by the corridor of the palace and I began to walk faster, hoping the wind would hit my face harder as I enjoyed it on this hot summer day. I closed my eyes so they wouldn't dry out from the cool, brisk air that was embracing my face. Suddenly, the bottom portion of the muslin already gliding in the air must have hit the flame of a candle and caught fire. At first, I didn't even notice what had happened, but then the fire crept up my back and the flame touched my soft, olive skin. I turned around and saw that my muslin had caught fire and began to scream. *"Help! Fire! Ahh! Someone help!"*

A number of female servants threw themselves on me, hoping to extinguish the flame, but it reached up my neck and then set my hair on fire.

"Someone help us!" cried one of the female attendants. I then saw one of my attendants, Sharda, who'd rushed to me first, herself now on fire. Her hair, longer than mine, had caught fire as soon as she ran towards me.

The other female attendants were now trying to extinguish flames burning us both. Then one of the other girls, much younger than Sharda, moved away as her scarf caught fire. She threw it off, but it was too late; she was already on fire. The last of the attendants smothered me, trying to choke off the flames, but to no avail. Each one by one was catching fire while trying to extinguish it. The flame engulfing all four of us was destined to permanently scar our bodies for life, or whatever would be left of our lives after this.

"Get some water, help!" I yelled.

My arms were now on fire, too; only my front side, from where my tears had wet my entire face, was left unharmed. "Wake up!! Someone help!"

All I could see were four flame-embroiled shadows surrounding me.

"Help us!" somebody yelled.

I cried: "Where is everybody?"

Every moment seemed like an eternity, and my body seared with pain I'd never known was possible.

Finally two guards came running. I began to lose consciousness and everything turned into a blur. The guards were shouting that there was no water tank nearby to fill buckets with. I knew this area of the palace. The only deposit of water was in the fountains – beautiful, glistening fountains that looked like floating crystals in the sunlight. Though aesthetically pleasing, they would take time to fill water buckets. By then, we would all be dead.

"Aba! Help me!!" I cried, my back completely covered in flames.

I heard one of the guards shout, "We must do something besides just pour water, or they'll die!"

My attendants' cries began to die out, and I feared they might have succumbed to the flames. Were they dead or was I? I wondered. Then suddenly two women covered me with a heavy shawl.

I murmured half awake: "Save Sharda. Save my girls..."

"Yes, Your Majesty," replied one woman anxiously.

After several more minutes, they completely extinguished the flames. I then lost consciousness.

❊ ❊ ❊

During my recovery, some of my dreams involved visions of heaven. As pictured in the Koran, there were lush gardens with fountains and many rose bushes, and on the paved walkways people didn't stand, they glided by. No one had feet, souls simply floated in air, with faces implanted with smiles that never eroded and happiness that never faded. I tried to run across this garden, searching for my mother, but realised soon that I myself wasn't running, but gliding. Was I dead too? Was this dream in actuality my new reality? I continued to float, my skin tone no longer olive, but now a glistening golden, like a ray of the sun; my fingertips were pointed like the edges of a sword; my eyes were pointy and thin, like simple slits. Would I even be able to recognise my Ami if everyone looked as different?

The weather was very warm, but we didn't sweat, instead just absorbed the light as if we were a part of it. Wherever I went in this never-ending paradise, everyone greeted me like a long-lost friend. Was I drunk or simply enlightened? Was this paradise or simply an opium hallucination? I kept searching for my mother, crossing wondrous landscapes in my quest, floating and gliding past waterfalls and fountains – and then I saw a tall woman at a distance, wearing the same clothes my mother wore. She didn't glide, nor was her colour gold. Instead, she simply stood as though she were still human.

· I glided towards her, crying, "Ami! It's me, Jahanara! I'm here. Turn around!"

Slowly the figure turned, and it indeed was my beautiful mother, her belly no longer swollen, smiling, and she stretched her arms out to hug me.

I ran into her arms like a child bruised on the playground would run to her mother. She wrapped her arms around me, and I was able to smell her aroma – an aroma that had long since faded from her belongings. "Oh, how I've missed you, Ami" I cried, with no tears to run down my golden-hued face. I was now convinced I had died and was in paradise, for here you couldn't cry. The only emotion you were capable of was happiness.

I asked my mother why she didn't look like everyone else. Why was her colour not golden, why were her eyes not thin as lines, why were her legs still present?

"I will be like this until my family is safe, Jahanara."

"Safe? We're all fine, Ami. The King is building a mausoleum, Dara is married, and the brothers are all governors. Raushanara and Gauhara are doing well too!"

"Until my family is safe," she said, a fixed smile still across her face. "Not until they are safe."

What is my mother saying? I wondered. Was she telling me something I didn't know? Was there some impending danger I needed to save my family from? Was she telling me that she would never find salvation in heaven until we were all safe, and that I was the one who needed to protect us from some impending danger?

Then my dream ended, and I could again hear voices as I came in and out of consciousness. I was unable to question my mother further.

❋ ❋ ❋

I heard:

"You cannot look at the Empress!" The voice sounded like that of the court physician, Wazir Khan. "It is absolutely forbidden for an outsider to look at her."

"How can I treat someone I can't even see?" said the firangi in irritated, broken Persian.

"You will stick your hands out through a curtain, and someone will guide your hands to where they need to go. If you wish to see something, tell the eunuchs and they will tell you what they see and describe it in detail."

"Are you serious!?" yelled the firangi. "What rubbish is this? The Empress is dying, and you speak of vanity?"

I was 'dying'? But I wasn't dead yet? So that whole experience had been just a hallucination? *It couldn't have been,* I said to myself. *That odour, that energy, they had to be my mother's...*

"These are our rules!"

"Well, they're bloody stupid rules!"

"Doctor, watch your language!"

"If His Majesty wishes to play these games, he must find someone else to take care of the Empress; I can't." There was a pause.

The first voice finally said, "All right, fine, do as you wish. But don't tell anyone I allowed this!"

"This is the Empress?" asked the firangi.

"Yes, why? What's wrong?"

"Nothing. Did the former Empress look like her?"

"Yes, sir. You'd think they were identical twins."

"Now I understand why so much time is going into the 'structure,'" replied the firangi.

✻ ✻ ✻

Over the next several weeks, as the firangi was treating me, I slowly began regaining consciousness, though I was still unaware as to who was taking care of me and exactly what had happened during the last few months. My wounds were beginning to heal, and in a matter of a month, my skin had grown in the areas where it had been burned. I still wasn't back to normal – that would take another month – but I began to follow commands and react to instructions.

Finally, I opened my eyes and after blinking a few times, experienced my first clear vision since the accident. I thought I was having another dream, possibly a hallucination, for now I was staring at someone else who was no longer in this world: Gabriel. A white, chiselled, clean-shaven man with shoulder-length blond hair and sharp features was staring straight at me.

Too weak to talk, I simply smiled. I knew I was staring at a figment of my imagination, so I had no desire to make a fool of myself again and embrace him as I did with my mom. Yet, I wanted to finally wake up and face whatever reality God had now chosen for me. With all my energy, I concentrated on my throat and tried to utter a sound from my vocal cords. I finally formed a sentence: "Am I dreaming?"

The firangi called, "Arif, she's awake!"

Another man came running in. *Who is Arif?* I wondered. I'd never known any *Arif* before. Aloud, I said, "Where am I?"

"You're in your chambers," said Arif anxiously. "You were in an accident, but you'll be fine now. The doctor has cured you."

For the first time in months, I felt actually awake. I could smell the Agra air, and soon I realised that the firangi sitting next to me was indeed the man I thought had died in Hugli: Gabriel. I was both surprised and grateful to have Gabriel in front of me; only my pain and weakness dampened my enthusiasm.

Gabriel and I continued to smile at each other, neither uttering any words, but both speaking volumes through our expressions. I don't think Gabriel had any expectations of me. He probably didn't even know I cared for him. Yet we continued to stare at one another, unable to move our eyes away and grace other objects with our vision.

I said weakly, "I don't have words to thank you, sir."

Gabriel raised his eyes, smiled more broadly and said, "You needn't say anything, Empress. You probably don't remember, but we met many years ago in Gujarat, and you honoured me with 100 mohurs."

I closed my eyes for a moment and still smiling said, "Yes, of course I remember. How could I forget? You were the only man who would dare return a gift from royalty."

"I won't this time, Your Majesty."

"Well, you won't get just 100 mohurs either," I continued. "My Aba will grant you whatever you wish.

"Just your full recovery for now will do."

"You cut yourself short, doctor. You can secure for yourself a very handsome estate with official title for helping the Empress."

"How about just a promise to accept my companionship and not banish me after you regain your strength?"

I replied, "I'm sure something can be worked out."

"Rest then, my dear." Gabriel, perhaps forgetting for a moment that he wasn't talking to just a fair maiden from the English countryside, but instead the Mughal Empress, leaned into me and kissed me on the forehead. For me, the experience was very passionate, as no man had ever touched me except my father, and even then only with a kiss on the forehead or a cheek. I felt overcome with both emotion and confusion. After nearly dying, I couldn't have experienced an awakening more special than this. For one moment – if just that – I chose to forget I was a Mughal empress, bound to a life of celibacy. For now, I offered no protest, emotional or physical, to the otherwise modest advancement of the charismatic firangi.

Arif, who'd watched the whole episode like a viewer in the front seat of a *tamasha*, seemed shocked at the firangi's provocative moves on me, and unsure whether or how to intervene. But sitting still and smiling, I offered my approval to Gabriel's advances and within myself wholeheartedly welcomed more future rendezvous with him.

❧ ❧ ❧

"Jahanara? My child, are you awake?" I heard my father's voice and his footsteps running towards my apartment.

I slowly opened my eyes, turned my head towards the door, squinted and said, "Aba!"

Aba ran to me and hugged me as tightly as I'd hugged him many years ago when he announced plans for the mausoleum.

Choked with emotion, he said, "I prayed every day for your health, my child. I spared no expense. Healers from around the globe have visited this city in the last six months."

I kept hugging my father and just let him speak on of his tribulations during this time: "We gave alms every day in your name, and then your brother, Dara, brought a mullah to me."

I frowned, fearing he'd reverted to the advice of mullahs.

He shook his head. "No, no, Jahanara. Not your typical mullah. This one was a Sufi saint. Indeed, a saint! He goes by the name of Mullah Shah Badakshi, and he's the one that told me to do charitable acts and embrace *every* healer, even the firangi ones."

Then Aba told me the whole story: how during my illness, Dara brought Mullah Shah Badakshi to visit. Aware that our father was deteriorating in health and purpose, Dara took the role I'd once taken at the death of our mother, to bring our grieving father out of his turmoil.

Mullah Shah Badakshi was a well-respected Muslim Sufi who'd introduced Dara to the head of the entire Qadiriya movement, Mian Mir. Shah Badakshi had built strong support for the Qadiriya movement from Lahore in the northwest to Bengal in the east, and Aba respected him well, though the two had never met. Originally sceptical of involving any mullah in his private affairs, Badakshi won Aba's heart with his words and message. It was he who suggested to Aba to become more charitable by giving gold and silver from the treasury to beggars, in hopes that they, too, would pray for my health.

Taking Badakshi's advice, every night Aba placed silver and gold valued at thousands of rupees under my pillow and dispensed them the following morning to beggars. Thousands of prisoners of petty crimes were released, death sentences commuted, and offerings of truce to neighbouring states were made. Oddly enough, it seemed my sickness brought a sense of tranquility in India not seen since before Ami died. People's eyes began shifting away from their own disputes and towards my bed, as every religion and sect began reciting verses in my name every morning. Dozens of new baby girls were given my name, including Dara's newborn daughter, whom he named 'Jani.'

Aba summoned healers from all corners of the kingdom to offer advice and help me. Several months passed since the incident, and my precarious state remained. In the interim, two of the four female servants of mine who'd tried to save me succumbed to their wounds, a morbid reminder of what awaited me if something didn't happen soon to reverse my own downward spiral.

Here in time present Aba said, "He recommended this man, Gabriel Boughton. Did we know him from somewhere?"

"Yes Aba," I continued. He was the man we met in the western state of Gujarat on our way to the Deccan – the one who brought relief to the famine-stricken villages."

"Yes! You're absolutely right," exclaimed Aba. "Now I remember... You know, it seems whenever we need him the most, he always comes to our aid."

I just smiled at my father, not wanting to divulge too much to him on the subject of Gabriel, lest I risk exposure of my true feelings for him and create a political calamity for the firangi.

Aba said, "I think he should stay with us for a while, perhaps be our royal physician. At least until you're fully better."

I smiled and just nodded my head, not letting a word escape my lips on the subject.

"You rest now, my child. There will be celebrations louder than the world has ever seen once you're feeling strong again!"

He leaned to kiss me on my forehead, his favourite place since I was a little girl. But I moved my face and pointed his lips to my cheek, hinting it was there I wished to be kissed. My forehead had already been graced by Gabriel, and I wanted to keep that location his, at least for a few more moments.

✳ ✳ ✳

In time I slowly began catching up on everything that had occurred while I was in my semi-comatose state. Work on 'the structure' had all but ceased, as the men and women working on it lost all their enthusiasm while the royal family mourned my accident. I felt at once both guilty and humbled by all of this attention. Yet now that I began to regain my strength, I insisted the work on 'the structure' continue, for not going on meant that my mother's remains would stay interred in a makeshift grave.

Meanwhile, conflict had arisen again between Aba and

Aurangzeb. I was disheartened to hear of this because my own relationship with Aurangzeb had turned tense before my accident. It all started shortly after his marriage to Dilras Banu Begum, the daughter of the military noble Shahnawaz Khan. As per my promise, I spent more money on Aurangzeb's wedding than Dara's, and Aba himself honoured him with jewels and gifts. For one day, Aurangzeb was the centre of attention and felt like the king. Though I did all the work and arranged everything, it was of course Raushanara who fronted the affair and acted like the favourite sister before the zenana. Whether her feelings were genuine or politically expedient, she wished to show the world that as far as she was concerned, this, not Dara's, was the first marriage of this household.

So in the same breath he thanked me for the wedding preparation, Aurangzeb made me a shocking request: "I plan to challenge Dara for the throne of India. Do I have your support?" I was dumbfounded! Aba had made it clear that Dara was his heir apparent, and as the king, this was his sole decision. Besides, Aurangzeb's intolerant attitude and closeness to the mullahs might well turn India into a war zone and splinter the fragile coalition of Hindus and Muslims.

I said, "You can't challenge Dara, Aurangzeb. There's to be no competition; Aba has already made his choice."

"I don't propose war, sister; I merely want to make it clear to Aba that *I* should be the next king of Mughal India. I want to challenge Dara to a series of competitions of strength, mind and body."

"It's not for you to challenge anyone, Aurangzeb. Again, Aba has made his decision."

"Do I have your support if I go to Aba with this?"

"No, you do not!"

"Then consider this farewell!"

Aurangzeb left for the Deccan soon after, and we never had a chance to resolve any of these matters. After my accident, Aurangzeb had taken three full weeks to arrive at Agra to offer his help and assistance. Though I'm told he showed genuine concern once he did arrive, it had been too late – Aba was already angry and hurt at the lukewarm interest such a delay reflected to him, and once again father and son fought.

According to Bahadur, Aurangzeb was again repeatedly referred to as the 'white serpent' by Aba, and far worse, relieved of his post as Governor of the Deccan. Aurangzeb felt devastated at this public humiliation and left Agra to find his peace and home elsewhere.

Before setting on his journey, he met with Bahadur and asked again about my condition. By that time, Gabriel had arrived and I was slowly recovering. Unable to endure Aba's taunts or the pain of seeing me in such a state, he simply gave Bahadur a copy of a letter he wrote to Aba, asking Bahadur to show it to me when I awoke. It would explain everything, he told her.

Dear Aba,

If His Majesty would like that of all his servants I alone should pass my remaining days in dishonour and eventually perish in an unbecoming manner, I have no choice but to obey. I know I am not the son you want as a successor, and perhaps no matter how hard I try I can never make you proud of me. I also know that some of those you are closest to wish me the most harm and incessantly poison you against me. I therefore request your permission to leave His Majesty's service and devote my remaining days to charity, prayer, and service as a hermit. I do not wish to cause any more uneasiness to anyone's heart, and I wish to be saved from the harassment of my foes. I will leave your kingdom by noon tomorrow unless I hear objection from you.

Yours Eternally,
Aurangzeb

Aurangzeb left for Fatehnagar, a city north of Goa, where some years before he'd destroyed a 6th century Hindu temple to use its rubble for the staircase of a mosque, and then lived there as a hermit. Fatehnagar became his abode, where no one would bother him or accuse him of any misdoings. I was torn as to how to resolve this conflict. Thus, I simply decided to wait till I fully regained my strength to address the matter.

13

LOVE OR LUST

1st May, 1644

To my pleasant surprise, all of my burns, which had consumed my entire back and rear, completely healed. It was almost as if I'd never been burned.

Celebrations occurred all over Mughal India as news of my recovery slowly permeated into the most remote of villages. Their empress was back, and no one would take her from them again. It didn't matter what religion or creed the person belonged to, it seemed the emotions from my tragedy had rippled across all races, creeds and castes. I was now referred to by the court chroniclers as 'the people's empress,' and now that I was better, the residents of Mumtazabad returned to work on the structure, buoyed by celebrations. If before they were building to mourn Ami's defeat at the hands of death, it now seemed they were building to celebrate my triumph over illness. This was now my monument too. I was its manager, and in its successful completion lay the dignity of not just Ami, but mine as well.

But as my wounds healed, the time Gabriel was permitted to visit me in the zenana also shrank. When he did visit, we talked for hours about our lives. It was during this time that I learned about what had actually happened to him in Hugli.

Severely wounded by the Mughal army during the massacre at Hugli, Gabriel fell into the Bay of Bengal and was saved by fisherman near a village named Kalikata. Finding himself saved by the very servants he'd often called 'stupid,' and 'illiterate,' he was humbled to be in their nurturing company. Though not a surgeon like Gabriel, one of the village doctors sewed the wound on the side of Gabriel's neck well.

Though he'd originally hated the entire country of India, especially our intolerant, racist monarchy that had massacred innocent women and children of Hugli, he slowly began to see the goodness of India in its villages. Just as he'd nurtured the masses in Gujarat, the masses were now taking care of him, giving him attention day and night, and bringing to him the cleanest water they could find as well as the healthiest food.

When his strength returned, the village gave him a hero's farewell, and he vowed to return to Kalikata one day to help their village become better and stronger and one of the greatest cities in Bengal. He then left for the port city of Surat to help with the trading operations of the company. It was here that a pipe-smoking, swollen-gut Englishman name William Bruton conveyed to Gabriel that a request had been received from Agra asking for his services to help heal the ravages of my accident. Gabriel wished to leave at once, but before leaving, he needed to secure the permission of his captain.

Captain Bruton was a businessman in the purest sense. He only gave leave to Gabriel on condition that if Gabriel was successful in curing me, he would ask Aba for exclusive trading rights in Bengal on Bruton's behalf. Unconcerned with achieving such gifts for himself, Gabriel reluctantly agreed to the trade-off so he might be able to leave quickly for Agra.

I was humbled and grateful to Gabriel for travelling to Agra to help me, especially after all the trouble he'd endured at the hands of our army. And my feelings for him began to deepen as I started seeing the goodness in his heart.

I didn't know how – or even if – I should tell him how I felt. The zenana women began teasing me about Gabriel, how beautiful he was and how obvious it was that he liked me. It seemed these women were most interested in the gossip that would be created if I confirmed their suspicions by revealing to them the true nature of my feelings. Still, I found it hard to not be influenced by their talk.

My mother had told me about this thing called love. I'd read poetry about how it can give life to even the stone-hearted and weaken even the strongest of men. But with Ami's death I never thought I was ever going to experience it, for I wasn't permitted to do so. I just assumed my life would be spent in a loveless existence, and only through others would I celebrate this cherished sentiment that Allah had given man.

I began wondering if Allah had caused this accident just to reunite me with Gabriel and allow me to experience this strange thing called love. I felt like crying, not from sadness, but from the excitement that perhaps my life might not be loveless after all.

✳ ✳ ✳

Every night I'd lie in bed and woo sleep, secretly desiring to be courted by the firangi, but every night sleep evaded me. He was no longer welcome in the zenana now that I was well, and I hadn't seen him in weeks. Unable to see him in the real world or visit him in my dreams, I still yearned for his company. I felt he'd flown into an area of my being no one else had ever entered, and I felt almost haunted by his spirit. The pain in my heart was suffocating me. I instructed Bahadur to travel to the city and inform me about how Gabriel had been. To my excitement, Bahadur told me Gabriel had requested to see me several times but was turned away by the Tatar guards on instructions of the Emperor. She further told me that Gabriel wanted to request an audience with me in private.

I was torn as what to do, for allowing him in the zenana against Aba's wishes wasn't possible, and venturing out to meet him would raise suspicion.

But Bahadur said confidently, "*I* will arrange a private meeting. "It's the only way." I felt as though she didn't want to say she knew what was happening, but realised we two needed to meet, if just once. Love or lust, sincere or false, this uneasy feeling in my being cried out for some kind of satisfaction. If I was never to see Gabriel again, I needed to say farewell properly.

I had never ridden on a horse by myself; the closest I'd ever come was riding in a carriage drawn by four horses. I soon realised that riding on a horse by itself is much more turbulent than riding in a carriage. Maybe, I thought, if I could ride faster it would be smoother, but Bahadur didn't allow that because her horse needed to be right next to mine so she could pull on its straps if I lost control.

I rode at night, dressed as an imperial soldier to the people of Agra, escorting the chief eunuch; but in reality, of course, *she* was *my* escort. We turned our horses into the warehouse district of Agra because this area was completely empty at this hour, all the dealers having closed for the day.

Bahadur dismounted and then helped me to my feet. "Malikaye, he is inside. I'm here in case you need me. Take however long you desire."

Bahadur's words made me feel strangely liberated. For once, I felt free to do as *I* wished, though saying a simple goodbye was all I had in mind.

I walked into the warehouse and found him standing at a distance with a rose in his hand. I went to him with a smile on my face; he welcomed me with a courteous kiss on the cheek, but closer to my lips than I'd expected. His skin was so white, I felt dirty in his presence. His body was muscled and slim. I felt the warmth of his skin, and through my partially closed eyes, I admired his blond hair that curved down around his neck. I sensed desire in his eyes. I felt as if a sudden veil of shyness had descended upon me. I reluctantly stepped back from him at first, but then he moved towards me.

I never had thought a day like this would come. My dreams were my sustenance, and in their company I'd hoped to spend the rest of my life, with only memories to hold of what was once my beautiful body before this disfiguring accident. The thin, soft hairs on my arms began to stand out, and a strange sensation of nervousness and anxiety overtook me. This is what I wanted, so what was stopping me? I had told my eunuch I would just say farewell, and she was waiting for me... but didn't she say she'd wait as long as I desired? She would wait for my desire, and Gabriel would do what I secretly desired... was this the day Jahanara's desires would be fulfilled? Was I allowed to have desires, and if so, was I allowed to fulfill them? My heart started racing, and I began to sweat, still holding back but not pushing him away because my mind still hadn't resolved this conflict.

After a lifetime spent in such a provocative institution – the zenana – I'd heard of everything sexual but been allowed to experience nothing. Now, fate had brought me here, with this man I'd loved since I first saw him, and who'd saved my life. *He feels the same way about me, and I'm not supposed to allow that?*

I wanted to turn, run out, order Bahadur to take me away, but instead I waited as he touched me and kissed me. I kept expecting my mind to overtake my heart to resolve this dilemma, but my heart raced ahead, and I began feeling warmer, though I knew not where the heat was coming from. I was frightened, and at last I made a bargain with myself: I would allow myself to reciprocate just once, only to see how it felt; then I would pull back before I went too far. So I kissed him back, welcomed his advance, and then tried to pull back. But I was unable to. A voice inside me said, "Time to pull away..." but my body didn't listen. I drowned in my emotion; there was no pulling back.

I walked out of the warehouse shortly before dawn. My hair was dishevelled, and I felt dirty. Strangely, I also felt liberated. A goodbye had turned into an embrace, and that in turn into a kiss, and then into something I should have been ashamed of but wasn't. I felt I'd done something wrong, yet I wasn't angry. It had all made sense as it was happening, as if a divine power was guiding two beings together that I had no control over and no right to oppose. Was this what made the zenana women yearn for their secret lovers? Was it for this that they lied, cheated, deceived and broke all the rules just for one night with their forbidden loves? Would I, from this day forward, be considered one of them? Had I lowered myself to their level... or risen up to their level? My own confusion on the matter suffocated me.

The ride back to the fort was quiet. Bahadur's stony face spoke nothing, as if she wasn't interested in the details.

✱ ✱ ✱

Gabriel was presented to Aba in the Diwan-i-khas the next day. My knees were shaking as I watched the proceedings from behind the screen. What if someone knew about me and Gabriel and told Aba in front of the whole court? Surely Aba would have Gabriel executed instantly.

I tried avoiding Sati, who kept tugging me as she stood beside me, trying to remind me that I was supposed to be looking more at the Emperor and not the firangi. Then I saw Gabriel present his knife to the imperial soldiers guarding the entrance to the Diwan-i-khas, and I heard the announcing voice: "Presenting hakim Gabriel Sahib!"

Gabriel was now apparently the hakim, a literal translation of the word physician, but a title which nonetheless seemed oddly bestowed on a firangi.

To my astonishment, Gabriel appeared to be dressed in traditional Mughal attire. I suppose he wanted to make a good impression on the King yet take nothing for granted. I pushed my face against the screen hoping to catch a better glimpse of my Mughal firangi, whose long burgundy robe made him look like a true prince.

"I'm here Gabe," I wished to say but knew I couldn't. The other zenana ladies, noticing my interest in the handsome doctor, began to chatter.

I turned to them, a finger to my lips. *"Shshshs!"* I wanted to miss nothing that was happening.

Gabriel then made what seemed like a sloppy attempt at the *kornish*. I giggled under my breath as Aba shrugged at his nobles in mild disappointment.

Aba said: "You've impressed us with your skills as a doctor." Gabriel nodded, smiling modestly. "First in Gujarat and now with the Empress, there's no denying that you've helped our kingdom in our greatest hours of need. Tell me, firangi hakim, what do you wish of my kingdom: a mansion, a title, women, wealth – you may choose one or all of these!"

Gabriel took a sharp inward breath. Then he began speaking in the best Persian I'd ever heard a firangi utter, as if aware of my invisible presence and therefore wanting to impress me. "Your Majesty is too kind – but all I wish to ask for are exclusive trading privileges in Bengal for my company."

Aba laughed merrily. "You wish for trading privileges in Bengal? Here I'm offering you estates and titles, with hundreds of concubines if you so wish, and you merely want the writs to trade in the eastern port of Bengal?"

"I do not wish for titles, Your Majesty. I merely ask that you allow me to remain in Agra to finish my treatment of the Empress, and afford my company, East India Trading Corp, the rights to set up a trading post on the ruins of Hugli. I also ask that you allow my company to set up factories along the outskirts of neighbouring villages, including Suntanati, Govindpur and lastly, Kalikata."

"Hugli?" asked Aba incredlously, looking at the ground. "Hmm... Well, consider it done, then. I have no use for those neighbouring villages anyway."

I knew Aba was still reeling from the massacre at Hugli he'd ordered many years ago, perhaps he saw this as an oddly appropriate opportunity to make amends on this matter.

Aba added: "Still, I feel you deserve more for your service than just trading rights. What will people say? That the Empress' life was worth mere trading rights?" Aba's vanity was a function of both his titles and his heritage. Most Mughals cared more about royal appearances than anything else. I was glad to know Aba's love for me was a close second to his love for his own glory. Nevertheless, I was ecstatic at the turn of events.

Then he sighed, "Then if there are no more matters to be discussed, I will retire to the Moonlight Gardens along the Jumna."

"Jahanpanah," I interrupted from behind the grilled screens. "There is one more matter which I believe deserves your attention."

Aba turned his head toward the screens, keenly aware that the voice from behind was mine.

I said, "Jahanpanah, I ask that you grant me one favour after all of the hardship I have endured for the past several months."

"Anything, my child."

"I ask that you allow my loving brother, Aurangzeb, to return to Agra and be enlisted in your royal service once again."

Aba shot a glare of clear disapproval; he no doubt still angry at his younger son for having taken so long to come to Agra in the difficult time of my illness. He could have forgiven his son had he come late for Aba's own sickness, but not for coming came late for mine.

I said, "I know His Majesty must be upset by Aurangzeb's late arrival during my illness. But my informants tell me that news of my accident didn't reach his ears until very late, and I have only the deepest trust in his love and affection for me."

I had already learned that Raushanara was the culprit in this delay in news transmission, and while I wasn't privy to exactly how and why she went to such great lengths to deny him this information in a timely manner, I knew I had to use this opportunity to push back against her actions.

I added: "If he's not the Governor of the Deccan, so be it. But please, allow him to return to your graces, Your Highness."

Aba made no utterance; but did nod his head in the affirmative to Afzal Khan, who would now carry out his wishes on the King's behalf. Aurangzeb would be asked to return to court.

14
CHAMANI BEGUM

2nd September, 1644

I received this letter from Gabriel the following week:

Dear Jahanara,

I know not how love is practiced in the Mughal dominion, but in my country when you care for someone, you show it. I know you are the mperial Queen of India and I am only a common merchant, but my heart doesn't recognise these artificial titles. You consider me your saviour, but it is you who've saved me. Had you not convinced the King to show mercy to the Christians after Hugli, I would surely have been found by your soldiers during my recovery and executed. I began to respect you then, and my respect changed to love when I cared for you those many months when you were ill.

I wish to remain here in the midst of your company for as long as you and your King allow me and pretend there is nothing between us. We may continue to meet in secret, but know that it pains me to keep our love a secret. Yet we will keep this secret only as long as you wish to do so, for I have no fear of anyone's wrath.

Love,
Gabriel

By now, I had assumed Bahadur knew what occurred that night in the warehouse. Though a raw structure smelling of spices, the warehouse was so special to me because of my time with Gabriel there, that it seemed as glorious a structure as the Diwan-i-khas in my heart.

Bahadur received and transmitted messages from Gabriel on my behalf, and through our time together, I learned that Gabriel's feelings for me were as intense as my own for him. Yet I was always frightened of what might happen were our secret ever discovered. Surely I would be removed as Queen and possibly even exiled, but what about Gabriel? I had no doubt he would be executed, and the Christians would face the wrath of our forces yet again for something they never were a part of. I needed to find a way to keep my secret safe.

I sat before my mirror and looked at myself in intricate detail. I've always felt that in such moments of solitude, when no one else is nearby and we stare at ourselves in the mirror, the image reflected is different somehow than the one we always show to others. We strip veils of deception from our faces, thereby revealing our innermost secretive thoughts and our demons, so far hidden behind our angelic exteriors. What I saw there often frightened me.

I began decorating my face. My scars ironically helped the situation. My eyebrows had been burned off, and I'd used makeup to create beautifully arched eyebrows for myself ever since. Now I'd use the same makeup to give myself more boyish features. I opened one container of makeup after another to see what effect each could produce on my face. Finally, I perfected my look: I was a brown-skinned boy with a slight fuzz on the upper lip (made from a cream of crushed coal). I wrapped a blue turban on my head, having learned how to do so from one of the zenana boys whose mother washed our clothes.

I looked again in the mirror and realised I was no longer Jahanara. Staring back now was a young boy, a liar, a deceiver, someone who had to do this because in Mughal society, deceit was an absolutely necessary evil.

I began to visit Gabriel every day, seeking his company, his love and his counsel. With Gabriel I could dispense with the cloying formalities of the court. I felt as though I hadn't lived until now. I dress in a boy's apparel with a blue *kurta* and pajamas. The loose attire allowed me to hide my well-developed female physique. We'd decided earlier that dressing like an imperial soldier was too risky, because as a soldier people might expect me to intervene in domestic disputes of the bazaars if they saw me walking through the streets, and then my disguise would be discovered. Being a young boy was less risky and more discreet, so I would go as a young boy to Gabriel. I hoped my mother wasn't watching this from 'beyond.'

✱ ✱ ✱

Chamani Begum was her name. She had the levity of a young girl and the body of a goddess. Every day, every night, she was the whore who decorated my father's dreams. The name 'Chamani' literally meant 'garden,' and she would prove a sharp thorn in the pride of my family and to my reputation.

I never knew her, nor did I ever meet her, but my father was infatuated with her. He would have her come to his chambers on many occasions and share night after night with her, never seeming to even notice she was my age!

Afzal disapproved of this liaison, but this never stopped Aba. Always self-righteous and often self-destructive, Aba's indiscretions were destined to plunge our family forever into darkness. This woman, an unsuspecting silent player in our lives, did more to harm me than Raushanara or anyone else. Whether she may have meant well, I'll never know, for I never made her acquaintance and she never made mine. Our lives, thus, would exist parallel, but still influencing one another monumentally, like two giant magnets whose force fields kept colliding.

She wasn't even a royal concubine, but a street prostitute Aba brought into his harem. Here he was, the undisputed 'King of the World,' yet he chased a street whore with the excitement of a pubescent teenager.

To placate Afzal, Aba agreed to have Chamani meet him more discreetly, dressed as a young boy. Afzal, now unable to openly oppose his royal friend, acquiesced and tacitly gave his approval, confident that one day it would cause him and his family great harm if the truth ever came out.

And come out it would. Like an eruption of a volcano long contained, it was to wreak havoc on our lives, and we would all be consumed by Aba's vices.

❈ ❈ ❈

One rainy autumn day, I put on my blue kurta with my white pajamas and wrapped a blue turban on my head. As always, I applied sufficient makeup to hide my female attributes and look like the young boy the world had to know me as.

The weather wasn't my friend this day, and my biggest fear was that the rain would wash away the makeup I'd applied to give my face the masculine looks. Putting my faith in Allah, I walked out of the main gate of the zenana, squinting so as to avoid my eyes' invasion by the flying dust that roared through the sky. I kept my arms folded to hide the mounds of my chest which were still visible below the baggy kurta and my head down as I continued walking, hoping to escape the gaze of any onlooker who might be suspicious of my appearance. Though most people had never seen my face and so wouldn't tell who I was even if my make-up failed me, I couldn't risk that someone might be suspicious about why a woman was dressed as a boy.

"Salaam Walekum!" One by one, men gestured to me as I walked by, receiving but a nod and smile in return. Feeling somewhat confident, I dared to disguise my voice, using as deep a tone as my throat would allow, and reply, "Walekum Salaam!"

I was actually enjoying this, walking more briskly, with more confidence and conviction in my voice, to the shop owner, the butcher with his goat carcass hanging; I repeated the same salutation to the seller of grains and lentils, thoroughly convinced that my disguise was working.

Leaving the market, I was walking out of the main fort when the wind suddenly grew stronger, blowing more of my turban aloft, until suddenly I felt its weight lifted entirely from the top of my head.

I grabbed the edge of the headpiece as it began to roll down the street, and vaguely heard someone yell, "Guards!" Had I been spotted? I wasn't sure, but my hair, which was tied up to hide its length, had also begun to unravel, and as I chased my turban, I paid little attention to whether or not my face was visible and its expression still disguised.

Grabbing hold of the turban, I pulled it toward me like the rope of a struggling mountain climber who'd just lost his footing and planted it on my head, not caring whether or not any of my long strands fell down beside it. Gaining full control then, I tucked my strands inside, all the while hoping that no one was watching me, for I'd totally lost control of the situation.

I then ran as fast as I could; the time for vanity and self-confidence had passed. My only hope was that no one had seen me and if they had, that they wouldn't say anything.

✻ ✻ ✻

Aurangzeb returned to Agra the following month as per our father's orders, but he spent little time with me, only an obligatory visit to ask about my health. I remember vividly our candid conversation that day. He arrived in my palace wearing a humble yellow robe with a white turban. I often implored him to dress more like a prince, with golden or burgundy robes, but he wouldn't relent, insisting always that such attire was a sign of sinful vanity. Aurangzeb sat on the divan with his arms at his side. He seemed very confused and tense during this time. I was hesitant to prod him as to the cause of this. I feared he felt disillusioned about everything that had happened and almost embarrassed to now be the only son of Aba with no real title of governorship. He knew he'd only been allowed to return because of my help, and I think knowing this emasculated him further.

I sat next to him, my head still bandaged from my scars as Gabriel had instructed. I took a sip of my ginger tea and looked for a way to begin the conversation. At last I asked: "Do you like the structure?"

Aurangzeb continued to avoid eye contact. Was he angry at me for what Aba had done? He shrugged, "It's perfect for this kingdom."

This kingdom? This seemed like a typical Aurangzeb remark meant to ridicule the kingdom for its glamour and riches.

I put my cup down and mustered the strength to move the conversation along. "Aurangzeb, I know you received news of my illness later than everyone else."

Aurangzeb finally looked at me resignedly. He'd told Aba this, but his father wouldn't believe him.

I added: "I also know that someone in this kingdom intentionally blocked the news from reaching you."

Aurangzeb continued to stare at me, as if disinterested with this information. Then I offered, "Raushanara! My spies have told me everything!"

He looked startled. "How can you be so sure? Everyone here is engaged in political intrigue. How can you be so sure your spies are telling you the truth?"

"It's the truth," I insisted. "She's not your ally!"

Aurangzeb looked away, and then moved just his eyes in my direction. "How do you know Dara wasn't behind this?"

"Dara? Why would he do such a thing?"

"Why not?" he shot back bitterly. "Didn't he abandon me during the elephant fight? Isn't he the one who constantly poisons Aba's heart against me? With me out of the picture, he's free to be the hero... you know, the brother who attended to grieving Aba."

"Dara isn't like that..."

"Yes, he is! He's not the ascetic devotee you all treat him as. Behind his façade of Sufism is a calculating politician who's been trying to get rid of me since day one."

"I tell you, Aurangzeb, Raushanara is *not* your friend. No matter what you think, she's trying to poison you against the rest of us, specifically me."

"Why would she do that?"

"Because she doesn't like that I'm empress. She wishes to drive a wedge between me and as many people as possible. With you on her side, she can build her own team of confidantes."

Aurangzeb's eyes narrowed and he nodded slightly, as if in dawning acknowledgment of the truth of what I was saying. I knew that despite the fact that I'd supported his arch enemy for the throne, Aurangzeb respected me immensely and knew that Raushanara was exceedingly jealous of me. But could he let himself believe she would act on that jealousy? Like himself, she always seemed to be consigned to second place because of Aba's partiality.

Aurangzeb took a deep breath and sighed. "Jahanara, thank you for pleading my cause to the King, but I don't feel Agra is for me. I wish to continue spending my time in prayer and solitude. I'll be leaving for Fatehpur in the morning."

15
SHAHJAHANABAD

9th November, 1644

I hadn't seen Gabriel in almost a week, though I'd written to him a few times, never receiving a response. I'd grown concerned that perhaps something was amiss, but tried to convince myself I was being overly anxious. Bahadur finally arrived one day with a letter from Gabrel. The brief letter read:

Dear Jahanara,

I have received orders from my Captain Bruton to travel to Bengal and establish a trading post there.

What? Gabriel was going to leave Agra and travel elsewhere? The news sank my heart as soon as I read it.

I am prepared to leave the East India Company if you ask me to, but this is your decision. We have spent many months and countless moments together. If you ask me to leave the East India Company I will do so, but the request must come from you.

Love,
Gabriel

149

How should I answer? How could I interfere with the trajectory of his life, when I wasn't even willing to make him openly a part of mine? To keep him here in secret was wicked, for we weren't married and never could be. I agonised over how to reply to him.

"What reply do you have for me, " Bahadur questioned as he looked intently at me. I looked away. I was scared. I knew what I had to do, but could not summon the courage to do it. In my cowardice I began immersing myself in my official duties: issuing edicts, conferring honours on nobles, and advising the King. "There is no reply now," I finally replied after being questioned multiple times by Bahadur. "I must attend to court business! The King has requested my presence in the Macchi Bawan for some important news.

"Shall I accompany you, Your Majesty?"

"If you wish, Bahadur, but this matter will not be brought up!" Bahadur nodded in the affirmative but gave me the disappointed look I was slowly becoming accustomed to. We quietly walked to the Macchi Bawan, uttering not a word to one another.

As soon as we entered, Aba was hovering over large parchments with illustrations. I could not help but wonder whether a new building was being commissioned and if so, then in whose honour.

Aba remarked, "The city will be an imperfect semicircle, on the banks of the Jumna, not far from the ancient city of Delhi. It will draw on both Hindu and Muslim influences. The streets will be in the shape of a bow from north to south, with a central avenue piercing them at perpendicular angles in the middle, like an archer's arm or an arrow. The location of the new Red Fort will be the junction of the axis, an auspicious centre according to Hindu beliefs of Vastu Shastra."

Vastu Shastra, a Hindu concept, broadly defined which locations were auspicious for a home, and within the dwelling, which rooms should be placed in which direction.

"But the entire city, my child," continued my excited Aba, "will be like an actual man, because a man lives best in a physical environment that's similar to him. Look at the paper: Here is the palace, so imagine this being the head of a man, and this central avenue goes from the centre of the palace all the way down, like the spine. These streets are like its ribs, and this... look at this – what do you think this is?"

Aba pointed to a large structure off to one side of the main avenue.

I said, "It looks like a mausoleum."

"No," smiled Aba, "this is a mosque, the largest one outside of Mecca, and it will represent the heart, because the heart can only be where there is God. It will be the Jama Masjid."

I smiled to see my father so excited and was amazed at how much thought and work he'd put into this new city. Aba had chosen the banks along the Jumna near the ancient capital of Delhi as the city for his new capital for a reason:

Delhi had been one of the oldest sites in the history of India; some scholars believed as many as 12 different civilisations had existed within its borders in the previous 3,000 years. The Pandavs, the heroes of the Hindu scripture Gita, which Dara always quoted, were said to have built the first ever city on that land, calling it Indra Prastha, God Indra's City. Then came the Hindu Mauryan Kings, one of whom was named Dillu, giving the city the name Dilli, or Delhi. Then came a host of further successor states: The Tomars, the Chauhans, and then the first Muslim rulers, Ghori, Khilji, Tughluq, Sayyid and Lodhi dynasties, stretching the time clock almost to 1526, when my great-great-great-grandfather Babur invaded Delhi and established his kingdom. Delhi remained the capital of Mughal India for another 20 years, but in 1558, my great-grandfather Akbar decided to move the capital to Agra due to its closer proximity to the unruly Deccan. Since then Delhi had remained in relative ruin, a constant reminder of India's multicultural background as well as her violent heritage.

Aba wanted to link us Mughals back to Delhi, hoping that by doing so he would not only have the chance to be creative in building and planning a brand new city, but the linkage with Delhi would also offer the new city historical legitimacy. He had plans drawn up as early as 1629, but the actual work didn't begin until much later.

"But why, Aba?" I asked. "Why now? We're not even done with the structure."

"Who cares?" he laughed. "The structure is just about finished, just needs a few more touches. Besides, I can't live in Agra anymore; it's much too congested, and I cannot properly honour dignitaries here with all the congestion. A capital city should be open. *Shahjahanabad* will have gates leading into every corner of the empire!

"And I've thought of a name for your mother's mausoleum. We're not going to call it 'the structure' anymore, nor will we use something long and difficult to remember. It should be something simple, so even these firangis can remember when they return to their home. We shall name it after your mother – Mumtaz Mahal."

"Mumtaz Mahal?" I mused. "That does sound pleasant, but do you really want all the commoners saying mother's full name aloud. Would that not be disrespectful to her memory?"

Aba's brows furrowed; he gazed into the air and started blabbing: "Mumtaz, Taz, Mum, Mahal, Mahal Taz, Dastaan-i-mahal... no... mahal Taz mum, no..."

I just stared at him, keenly aware that when Aba started to think out loud, no one was supposed to disturb him when he was engrossed in deep thought. In fact, all his big ideas came from such moments.

"Mahal taz... Taz Mahal – that's it! *Taz Mahal*, so as not to be confused with Mumtaz Mahal. Simply Taz Mahal!"

"Taz Mahal," I echoed. "It's perfect, Aba!"

✖ ✖ ✖

We set out for Delhi the next morning. My elephant was the grandest, second only to Aba's; I rode under an azure canopy with a Mughal lion painted in gold. I chose to ride alone so I could be at peace with my thoughts and memories of my several rendezvous with Gabriel.

Gabriel and I had spent the previous several months meeting at the mansion Aba granted him alongside the Jumna. The location provided me with a clear view of the structure. I would enter Gabriel's mansion as a servant boy and he would receive me as such. I tried learning some basic words of English while also helping him perfect his Persian. He would tell me stories of distant lands he'd travelled to: Persia, China, Ceylon, Baghdad, and of course his homeland.

I felt strangely free whenever I dressed as a boy, as though a tremendous burden had been lifted off my head. I even visited the structure dressed as a boy, and enjoyed seeing how the everyday labourers lived and worked. Streams of sweat poured down the sun-darkened labourers as they toiled every day for my mother's future home. Women, some pregnant, balanced basins of earth on their heads. Sometimes low-level administrators would tap me to leave, telling me I was getting in their way. A lifetime as a royal made it difficult for me to bear ever being spoken to this way. But I would smile regardless, and move on.

I didn't question the morality of what I was doing with Gabriel; I just lacked the strength to deal with that question. I lived for the moment and chose to relish it.

As our procession approached Delhi, I could tell this land had seen great civilisations before. Ruined fortresses with walls as high and thick as our Red Fort in Agra were peppered around the city. Mud huts covered the landscape, presumably housing the descendants of the people who once owned these civilisations. Overgrown shrubs and untamed forests had reclaimed land that at one time must have been beautiful gardens and walkways. Makeshift homes were made from remnants of what once must have been civil buildings or mansions. Beyond the ruins lay endless jungles with smoke emitting haphazardly from their midst; signs of life existing even there.

I couldn't help but wonder if this was what would become of our descendants one day. The thought left me worried and in despair for a few moments. What led to this great civilisation's collapse? What could I as queen do to prevent this from happening us? My mind again drifted to my brothers and who would be king. I never had any doubts that Dara would be a great king, but would he be able to be a valiant warrior who could fend off invading forces? What about Aurangzeb? Would he really be as intolerant a king as he was a prince?

The people in the mud huts coalesced around our procession, begging for alms. Aba loved this part of his journeys. He distributed silver coins to all who desired tokens of what was to come to their destitute land. This would now be the capital of our empire, and they would be its proud citizens.

We dismounted from our elephants and walked around the city, eventually climbing a tower that stood by itself. I'd been told it had once been part of a grand palace, of which it was all that now remained.

"Why are we here, Aba? I'm afraid this tower may collapse at any moment, too."

Aba snorted, "Nonsense! This tower had withstood the elements all these years. Nothing our earthly bodies do to it will have an effect."

We climbed its spiral staircase with its steps partly broken in some areas. Finally, we reached the top and looked out on the landscape. I now understood why climbing this tower was so important to Aba: From here one could view the entire city of Delhi – the ruins, slums and jungles.

Aba pointed. "That's where our new Red Fort shall be, alongside the Jumna."

I squinted but could barely see the edge of the river.

Aba went on to show me where the city would be and its different buildings would lie. "Yet again, the queen shall be its manager," he declared.

"Me? But Aba, I know nothing about all this."

"Nonsense," he huffed. "You've learned much about architecture in the last several years. Come now, and embrace your father."

I looked out again. *My future? In this jungle?* I took a deep breath and then grew pensive. For a moment, I felt transported back to the time when Aba stood on the Samman Burj and proclaimed the riverside location as the new home for his mausoleum for Ami. Now, I stood here overlooking another jungle, being given the chance to build my own 'structure.' I burst out, "I'll do it, Aba!"

He smiled, and I continued: "I shall make this the most beautiful city the world has ever seen! You won't be disappointed."

Aba put his arms on my shoulders and kissed me on the forehead. "I never am with you, my child. Never."

As the sun's rays waned, our caravan began its journey back to Agra. I smiled as we left this now desolate land that was to be our new home in a few short years. Peasant children ran behind our caravan, as though they wished for us to take them back to Agra also. Eventually tired, one by one they peeled off till no one was left chasing us. We slowly rode near the Jumna river, and in the distance I could see the Hindu sadhus bathing in the water. These men looked extremely old, probably even over 100, but their bodies looked strong, and I'd often been afraid of them. The caravan slowed, possibly, I thought, due to a ditch or obstacle that it would have to overtake to continue forward. Such delays were common when we set out in the jungle.

I peeked out at the sadhus as our caravan continued to slow down. They all began shaking their heads from side to side, as if telling me not to do something. Old thin men, with chiselled, muscled arms belying their age, white hair and long white beards, all in unison continued to shake their heads as they made eye contact with me. Then, one of the sadhus raised his finger and began waving it from side to side as if insisting that I heed their message. Finally, one of the sadhus ascended from the river and walked towards our caravan. The imperial soldiers blocked him from coming close to my elephant, so he resisted and cried out: "Heed my advice! He who builds his city in Delhi is bound to one day lose it!"

I felt shaken by this naked man's challenge of our plans, for I sensed he knew the truth of what he was saying. "Nonsense, Your Majesty," scoffed Bahadur. "These sadhus always scare people. They probably want you to pay them to lift the curse on Delhi. It's just a ploy to extort imperial alms from you."

"No alms, oh Queen!" The sadhu didn't relent. "This naked fakir needs nothing but what mother earth has already provided! Do not come back here. He who builds here will be destroyed himself!"

Just then, the caravan began moving more quickly, and the imperial soldiers pushed the sadhus away and marched on with us. But the sadhu's voice followed us, more distantly: "Do not build here, oh Queen! He who builds a city in Delhi is bound to lose it!" And his words continued to echo in my mind all the way to Agra.

✖ ✖ ✖

Sitting in the Macchi Bawan where many years ago I'd interviewed the architects for the Taz, I now sat with Aba's drawings of the new city and tried to give his ideas the breadth and depth he'd given the Taz. The main avenue that was to run down the centre of the city needed to have some unique attribute that defined it. In its grandiosity would lay the magnificence of the entire city. I was rummaging through paintings of the other shrines and buildings that had been built both by Mughals and non-Mughals to draw inspiration.

One such painting was of the Hindu city of Varanasi; I noticed in it that at night the Hindus would light candles and float them on the banks of the river. The glow radiated into the buildings bordering the river, giving them and the people standing beside them a special sheen. This avenue, I felt, needed to draw on this imagery. There needed to be water and light on that avenue. Delhi (or Shahajahanabad as Aba renamed it) had a very arid climate, so water was necessary throughout the city, but the main avenue commanded its presence more than any other area.

I found myself almost possessed by this idea, and began to feel the way Aba often commented he felt when he was inspired to build. The imagery had entered my mind, but my eyes had yet to form a complete vision.

I was looking intently through images and rummaging through my thoughts when Bahadur entered. "Your Highness, you summoned me?" I motioned for him to have a seat as I gave him a heartfelt letter I had written for Gabriel.

I now realised that love involves pain. Though I had immersed myself in courtly matters: granting petitions, conferring honours on nobles, supervising construction of the mausoleum and impressing the *muhr uzak* on official edicts, I couldn't escape the reality that I had created for myself. My note read:

My Dear Gabriel,

Please forgive me for taking so long to respond to your letter. I have been torn as to what is the most appropriate course. I cannot ask that you leave your company unless I am willing to give you full acceptance here. I know the King will never accept a liaison for me, especially with a firangi. I ask that you follow your captain's orders and leave at once. If destiny desires, we will meet again.

Love,
Jahanara

My hands had hurt as I wrote these words to this man I had given every part of my being. He'd found the most special place in my heart, yet in a twist of ruthless irony, I now had to send him away myself. I now understood the sort of pain the other women in the zenana felt, and how difficult it is to leave him who owns your heart, regardless of the consequences. Your world begins to shrink, and all you see is *him*. And while your heart and mind remain with him, think incessantly of him and nothing else, your body is forced to live apart, in agony.

I tried to forget Gabriel, but sometimes one's mind isn't as obedient as we hope it to be. With Gabriel, I got away from the cloying formalities of the court and could be just myself and live in those moments for no one but myself. I often asked myself: Did I love Gabriel or what he represented to me – freedom, intimacy and companionship? As for most things, I didn't know the answer, and so I continued to live without prodding myself further; I just wept in my apartment in the Khas Mahal, feeling as alone as I had the day after my mother died. Indeed something did die for me that night – my dream. Besides being an Empress who wielded more power than any before me, I longed to have an ordinary family with someone I could love as much as my parents had loved each other. Yet, through no fault of my own, I would have to watch that love forever slip me by; and if I chose to protect it, I would have to tell lie after lie. I began to feel I had no one to turn to anymore.

I lay on my bed, my face staring out at the elegantly decorated ceiling of my apartment, my elbow bent and my forearm sitting across my forehead. I began to wonder who, besides Gabe, had taken care of me the most when I was on the verge of dying. My father cared, but he still was too unstable emotionally to be leaned on for comfort. Sati cared, but her message was always to just bear the burden, though it was unclear how one could carry such a heavy load a whole life. Who had come to me in my hour of need and offered me something new and different that perhaps could help me understand the world and my place in it better?

Then I turned my head to the side and saw a green curtain blowing in the wind. Though it may seem odd, this green silk cloth made me think of the green turban I once saw Dara wearing, an emblem of the Sufi movement Dara belonged to and had prodded me many times to join or at least learn about. I remembered the promise I made to Dara, to learn about his Sufi movement and understand the Qadiriya movement from my benefactor, Mullah Badakshi. In this hour of darkness, when all seemed to be failing, I would go to him.

❊ ❊ ❊

We all gathered in the Diwan-i-khas a few days later. Aurangzeb presented his dagger to the guard and asked to be presented to the court. He then presented a petition to Aba: He wanted to be the Governor of Gujarat. Gujarat bordered the Deccan on the north, so

Aurangzeb was familiar with the political landscape in that area. He said, "Staying in Agra, I am of no use to Your Majesty. Let me bring *this* chaotic region under your control."

Aba looked quickly at Dara, whose facial expression reflected, I thought, subtle opposition to the idea. I watched what transpired closely.

"No one in our family has been able to bring peace and order to Gujarat," continued Aurangzeb, glancing vengefully at Dara.

Aba returned Aurangzeb's gaze with his usual look of disapproval. He seemed about to speak when one of the mullahs broke in: "Begging Your Majesty's forgiveness, I'd like to suggest that Your Majesty carefully consider Prince Aurangzeb's request. As Prince Dara is being trained by you in the virtues of kinghood, Prince Aurangzeb's presence in Agra would be..." The mullah moved his head searching for the right word...

"A distraction!" Aba finished the mullah's sentence, and Aurangzeb rose in disappointed astonishment. Behind the windows, I sighed in dismay at the pain I saw on Aurangzeb's face.

Aurangzeb had begun delving even deeper into religion, but without political power, his rage and anger at non-Muslims had remained strictly confined to his heart. Yet it seemed he and the mullahs were becoming close allies, together watching the court with scorn and contempt. Rumours even persisted that the mullahs were encouraging him to rise up against Aba, by making Aurangzeb false promises about what they could do to secure support for his candidacy.

Then Aba said, "Very well; you *shall* be made the Governor of Gujarat."

Dara looked a mite upset, yet surprisingly content considering. Aurangzeb was receiving what he'd petitioned for, but clearly not in the way he had hoped – merely because he would otherwise be a 'distraction'? How could Aba have spoken that way to him, I wondered? It was worse than calling him a serpent. The mullahs put a hand on Aurangzeb's shoulder, and he walked out. I should have said something, but I couldn't cross my king. I couldn't chastise him for calling someone a 'distraction.' Instead, I only wished Aurangzeb a farewell.

16
REVERSE INVASION
1st June, 1646

Aba said: "Let it be written that it was during our time we reconnected the home of our ancestor, Timur, to the land of his descendants." Aba felt that with the Taz Mahal almost complete, construction on the new city begun and his three sons now in different corners of the empire with the heir apparent, Dara, at his side, the time was ripe for the kingdom to expand its borders, but not south as it had done for the last couple of centuries. Now, the conquest would be north, to the original homeland of the Mughals in Central Asia. "I will instruct Prince Murad to initiate the conquest of Central Asia, including the areas of Samarkand and Uzbekistan."

Murad was my youngest brother. Like my other useless brother, Shuja, Murad was interested only in extravagances such as opium, wines and engaging in debauchery with the women of his harem. Though he had political aspirations of his own, he was neither clever nor resolute as Aurangzeb had been while opposing Dara outright. Thus, Murad drifted in his existence like a passenger on a caravan whose direction had already been determined.

Now 21, he would be sent with 50,000 men to conquer the precinct of Balkh and Badakhshan. This was his big chance, his moment to prove worthy of the throne should he ever be chosen. Though the youngest, Murad must have been aware that age had nothing to do with inheritance. Aba wasn't his father's oldest son, and a major victory here could do for Murad what it had done for Aba many years before in the Mewar.

In 1615, just three years after his marriage to Ami, Aba went to Mewar to subdue its king, Rana Amar Singh, who'd evaded Mughal conquest for almost half a century. Using brilliant military tactics and arts of warfare, Aba was soon able to win over Mewar for the Mughals.

Maybe Murad, too, had dreams of returning to Agra victorious with the heads of the kings of Balkh and Badkshan, while the entire public cheered and chanted. When Aba was victorious, his father renamed him Shah Jahan, a name superior to his earlier name, Khurram. What would Murad's name be when *he* returned victorious?

Maruwwajuddin. This was the name he'd chosen for himself: 'The brother with Aurangzeb's military skill and Dara's charisma!' His comrades chanted this slogan on the streets of Agra when Murad was given the charge of the royal army the following week. He would be next in line after the death of Shah Jahan, they began chanting. This was his moment, and with the Mughal army behind him, he hoped to prove himself worthy of both the title and the throne.

I couldn't help but feel that the whole expedition was tactically insane. There was a reason why invasions outside India were uncommon and succeeded only rarely. In the course of Indian history, no more than two groups per millennium had ever crossed the rugged Hindu Kush mountains and succeeded in setting up an empire in mainland India. Yet here was my Aba, King of India, sending his troops led by his clumsy son to engage in a *reverse* invasion, from inside the fertile Indian subcontinent onto the inhabitable mountainous regions of Central Asia? Though I had the muhr uzak, in matters of conquest, which were the essence of male bravado, Aba listened only to himself. And the whole endeavour exuded an aura of madness, and only Murad's myopic, megalomaniac ego allowed him to agree to lead such an expedition, not realising what kind of a death trap it might be.

Balkh and Badakshan, which lay beyond the Hindu Kush mountains along the Oxus river, were believed to be the stepping stones to the ultimate invasion of Samarkand, original homeland of Timur. Timur the Lame, or Timurlane, made Samarkand the capital for a vast empire he controlled in 1370 that stretched from Central Asia to Turkey. Every time he conquered a region, he would bring the artisans and gardeners back with him as prisoners. Samarkand thus grew to become one of the most beautiful cities in the entire empire and Timur's people, we Mughals, became architectural geniuses of our time. A century-and-a-half later, when Babur, Timur's great great grandson, succeeded in conquering the capital of India, Delhi, he brought the culture of beautiful gardens and majestic palaces with him to India – a reverse importation. Most likely some of the original artisans of Samarkand were conquered people from northern India. Now, their descendants were being brought back into India to import their culture from Samarkand. We Mughals took great pride in our roots, referring to ourselves as *Timurids* and our family as the *House of Timur*, and this conquest was an ill-conceived brainchild of that pride.

The regions themselves offered no wealth. Badakshan was a sparsely populated, mildly fertile region with poor harvest that was ravaged by primitive, savage tribes. Balkh, somewhat more fertile, hadn't produced enough wealth even to sustain the army should it be victorious there.

Murad, dressed in traditional metal armour with a grated iron cloth hanging in front of his helmet, rode off with his 50,000-strong-army of Mughal soldiers. I felt a shiver crawl down my spine as I bid him farewell. I was convinced he would lose both the battle and his life, but I was helpless to stop the expedition.

I began spending more time with Dara, trying to learn more about the mystical world of Sufism, hoping to find some message, some omen, some magical inscription within their beliefs that would sanction my relationship with Gabriel and give me licence to run to Bengal to marry him. But cryptically searching for one purpose, I would soon find myself realising something else altogether.

Sufism was the occult arm of Islam. By preaching the oneness of Man and the totality of Faith, it had alienated the very orthodox wings of Islam; but by repeatedly chanting Mohammad's teachings it appeased the more moderate wings of Islam, thereby allowing it to remain within Islam's fold. And many Hindus visited Sufi saints, regarding them as having special powers and teachings.

Within the broader umbrella of Sufism, the Qadiriya order piqued Dara's interest the most. Pursuant to Qadiriya rites, Dara wore a green turban whenever he went to visit his Sufi mentors and insisted I wear one too (a request I initially refused to grant). Dara and I reconnected with Mullah Shah Badakshi, a man I hadn't seen in almost two years but already regarded as my benefactor.

Said the pleased Badakshi, "It's good to see you again, my child. Your scars are virtually gone."

"It's all because of your blessing," I replied gratefully. "Were it not for you, I'd be dead right now."

"Only Allah decides who will go to him, my child. We merely serve him. But it's good to see you here."

"Mullah Shah," interjected Dara, "Jahanara wishes to learn more of the Qadiriya order. Like me, she, too, believes that in a city where an orthodox mullah resides, no wise man is ever found."

Badakshi laughed and said sarcastically, "Why do you think we live so far away from the fort? We are not orthodox, my child," he added, turning to me. "But instead of learning our teachings from me, I shall introduce you to the head of our movement, Mian Mir."

Badakshi escorted Dara and me to a room in his haveli and showed us a painting of a man sitting with Badakshi and Dara. The picture contained several people, but it was easy to discern who was who. The young, dark-bearded man was Dara; the two men sitting behind him were Shah Badakshi and Mian Mir. Mian Mir was dressed in all-white robes and looked older, while Shah Badakshi wore a white turban with black robes and a gray beard.

"Mian Mir is no more." Dara stared morosely at the picture. "But somehow I feel every time I look at this painting, he's speaking to me. Remember when I become ill, a few years after my wedding to Nadira? Well, for the four months I suffered, no one was able to help me, not Wazir Khan or any other hakim. One day Mian Mir came to my bedside and gave me a cup to drink, and within a week I was better."

Badakshi broke into a smile. "Mian Mir had a very deep relationship with your brother."

I was partly cynical and partly amused by everything I was seeing and hearing. Trying not to sound rude, I continued to force myself to have an open mind.

Dara continued: "One day Mian Mir had me take off my shirt, and he took off his. Then he hugged me. I wasn't sure what he was doing, but he hugged me so tight I could barely breathe. After a few seconds, so many lights came emanating from his heart into mine that eventually I implored him to release me, fearing that any more transference of this illumination would cause my heart to burst."

I was pleased to know that there were established sects within Islam that preached tolerance, and I began believing that my brother had indeed become more enlightened than most men in our family. I now admired him not just as a man but also as a statesman and a friend.

He would often say, "Hands begin to stink once they're soiled with gold. Drive egoism away from you, for like conceit and arrogance, it's also a burden."

Here was the heir to the Mughal throne, ready to inherit entire palaces made of gold and gems. Yet he was denying gold and shunning the ego? Under his tutelage, the empire would either disintegrate or achieve such a high level of spiritual enlightenment that wars and conflicts within its realm would end.

Shah Badakshi didn't treat me as the Padishah Begum in his company, but merely a follower and he spoke to me as an equal. I prayed with members of the order, then sat to eat with them, men and women together, something unheard of in traditional Islam. As I bid them farewell, I knew in my heart this order would be an integral part of my life from this day forward.

✳ ✳ ✳

Afzal Khan paid a surprise visit to Agra later that year. Originally stationed in Lahore to keep an eye on Murad and provide him with reinforcements from this northeast city, he rushed to Agra on this fateful day and asked to be announced in the Diwan-i-khas.

Aba greeted him. "What news have you brought, friend, that you journeyed overnight in terrible weather to tell me in person?"

Afzal looked at Aba with sad eyes, keeping his hands folded in front of him, yet maintaining his composure. "Jahanpanah, Prince Murad has arrived in Lahore."

I widened my eyes, not sure what would come next.

Aba motioned, "Go on, Afzal, your face tells me there's more." But Aba didn't sound encouraging.

"Prince Murad has won both Bukhara and Badalkshan for us, Jahanpanah, but he returned before a formal surrender was made. His men are still in the mountains of the rugged terrain – with no leader!"

"Prince Murad left his men? But why?"

"I don't know."

"I command him to return to Agra!" Aba was rightfully upset. By abandoning his men on the battlefield, Murad had committed the gravest offence a military commander could commit. That day Afzal showed our family the respect of not reciting the whole story in the presence of nobles in the Diwan-i-khas. Later he would tell Aba and myself of the whole sordid affair:

After several months of dangerous trekking through the uninhabitable mountains of the Khyber Pass, the Mughal army finally arrived at the doorstep of the provinces they wished to conquer. First was Balkh. Balkh and Badakshan were both protected by the Bukhara people. Their army was aware of the terrain they lived in, and they used it to their every advantage. The army of the enemy mounted guerilla warfare daily against the Mughal army. The Mughals unknowingly settled in the valley and were caught by surprise by the enemy. Murad apparently tried to lead his men to fight against the enemy, but our losses continued to be very heavy. The Bukhara soldiers occupied the higher ground and fired down at the Mughal soldiers. Fearing near complete annihilation, Murad ordered his men to retreat, prompting jubilant roars by the enemy, who erroneously believed they'd defeated the invaders.

Murad's army eventually set up the imperial camp along the mountainside. His helmet off, his dark hair spreading to his shoulders, he sat hanging his head.

Murad is said to have begun feeling for the first time that this victory wouldn't be easy and might come at a costly price. The men in the tent brainstormed strategy for the next day. Outside the tent, the picture was even more bleak; men were running out of rations. Murad hadn't accounted for the long journey and the less-than-simple victory that would await him in this ill-fated military excursion. With no space to cook, the soldiers began cooking on the backs of elephants, and every soldier was given smaller rations to allow the supplies to last longer.

Murad listened to his generals, but also got both nervous and angry with them. This wasn't supposed to happen, he began to think. He'd thought this would be a simple victory; all he had to do was wear armour and lead the army; the generals would do all the planning; the soldiers would fight; and victory would be his. Now, at age 21, how was he supposed to know how to win a victory in a difficult terrain he'd never even visited ever before?

"I want answers!" he yelled, lunging up from his chair. "Answers! You're my generals; you're supposed to know about this!" Murad ranted on, pulling his long dark hair out of his head, his voice squeaking out his emotional temper tantrum.

The generals weren't intimidated by this skinny, foolish brother of mine. Rather, they feared for their own lives and their soldiers' if the foolish prince continued to lead them to battle without a winning strategy in the following days.

That night they calmly discussed their options again, this time without adolescent interference from Murad. Their battlefield, they remarked, was also inhabited by lawless tribes – Turks, Uzbeks, Mongols.

Mongols were our cousins, descendants of a common ancestor who hadn't been fortunate enough to cross the mountain pass with Babur in 1526 and live like royalty in India. As if running to the other extreme, they now lived in modest dwellings on snow-covered mountain peaks, trying to preserve what little they had. For our part, we Mughals didn't consider them allies, partly because we were arrogant and partly because we had no use for our 'cavemen cousins.'

But at this time the generals believed that if we could get them on our side, we'd get a better idea of the terrain and also some more fighters.

They also felt these tribes must have an arrangement with the Bukhara army that allowed them to live in peace in the Bukhara dominion in return for loyalty in times of war. If we could get them on our side, we'd be able to take the Bukhara army by surprise.

The Mughal generals now formed a strategy they believed would give their conventional army the advantage – bribery – and persuaded Murad that it might be effective. So in the dark of night, Murad sent emissaries to the neighbouring tribes, promising them estates in the Mughal mainland of India in return for their loyalty during the fight. The Bukhara army, which governed both provinces, relied heavily on local tribes for defence. By bribing the local tribes, Murad could cut one limb from the body. Yet in another stroke of military genius, he opted to keep the alliance a secret. No one but the army commanders would know that the tribes were on our side.

The savage tribes agreed and gave the Mughal army much-needed inside information about the layout of Badakshan. Murad devised a strategy to incite the Bukhara army to fight on open ground. When they enter the field, the tribes would fire arrows and guns at them from the hilltops. After the tribes had cleared the army, the Mughal army would go in for the final kill and raise the flag.

Executing the plan, thousands of Mughal soldiers gathered on the edge of the open field and raised the lion flag of the empire. The Bukhara army coalesced on the opposite side. The Mughal commander led the army onto the open ground.

As 20,000 Mughal soldiers poured into the field, 30,000 Bukhara soldiers countered on their side. Fierce battling ensued with muskets, clubs and cannon. The Bukhara army poured onto the open ground, confident that the tribes would offer aerial attacks against the Mughals. But the opposite happened; the tribes attacked Bukhara soldiers.

Once the Bukhara army was too far on the field to effect an easy retreat, a barrage of arrows and guns showered them from the sky. Those who survived the rain of bullets and arrows now faced the Mughal army, who stared gleefully from half kos away, ready to march in as soon as the shower of arrows ceased. Finally, the remaining 20,000 Mughal soldiers poured onto the field to overwhelm the already weakened Bukhara army and sliced and chopped the Bukhara soldiers like a flock of helpless lambs. No soldier survived the battle, as the Mughal soldiers dismembered even already dead soldiers. The battle lasted only a few hours. At last the soldiers stopped mutilating corpses and cheered victoriously. Both provinces were won.

The following day, the tribal leaders came to Murad for a final meeting to discuss how the tribes would be led back into India and given the titles they were assured. Murad asked that all the deserving men – commanders, soldiers, elders – meet him in a tent for a private meeting with him and his generals.

The tribesman all went, eager to learn about the reversal of fortune they'd now experience. From roaming the mountains aimlessly hunting for food, they would now live like royalty, basking in the glory of the legendary Mughal Empire.

But moment after moment passed in silence, making the tribesmen feel uneasy about their unholy alliance. Unaware of what awaited them, they continued to be patient. Finally, a voice shouted from outside: "All tribesmen in the tent are hereby ordered to come out with their hands raised!"

The tribesman grabbed hold of their weapons and walked out, ready for any eventuality. The 45,000-strong Mughal army completely encircled them, on a war footing. Even the tribesmen's weapons were worthless; they faced far too many Mughal soldiers.

One tribesman shouted, "We don't understand. We were promised estates and titles!"

A Mughal general snarled, "Ask Allah for estates and titles in heaven, you savages!" Then he ordered, "Fire!" and every tribesman was summarily slaughtered.

A sudden shiver ran down my back as I heard this account. Acts of deception like this were common in our kingdom, and I felt sad and disgusted every time I heard of another. Aba, on hearing this part, seemed elated, not surprisingly. In fact this seemed to be the part of the story he enjoyed most. I couldn't help but feel at that moment that we were almost of different bloods.

Murad, ecstatic at these dramatic events, wished to celebrate instantly. The generals wished to teach him what ought to occur next in the process of winning over a territory. But Murad wasn't at all interested; instead he insisted that the generals handle the formality of receiving the kings' surrender and accepting royal gifts from them. The generals were astonished to see that Murad had been sent to oversee the army without even being versed in the basic etiquette of how a victory – and one in which many lives had been lost – should be properly handled.

Furthermore, Murad left that night, complaining that the weather and lack of women were distressing him. The generals pleaded with the young Prince not to leave, promising him the wrap-up wouldn't take much longer and that leaving by himself would be both dangerous and irresponsible. But Murad had made up his mind; he would leave by nightfall and go back to mainland

India, and when he reached Lahore send a runner with news of his victory to Agra.

Afzal now said, "I decided to come in place of any runner, Jahanpanah. I can only imagine how much worse you would have felt had a lowly runner brought you this news."

We all stared down dumbfounded, soaking in this whole episode. "'Maruwwajuddin' the idiot calls himself!" said Afzal bitterly. No one spoke further.

✽ ✽ ✽

I said, "Her Majesty needs to be made aware of this at once!" Bahadur had learned from her spies that Gabriel's order to move to Bengal had actually been influenced by someone from Agra, and she'd come to my chambers to tell me.

I was puzzled by the news. I said, "But who would want Gabriel to leave? He was the official court physician, and the King was indebted to him for saving my life. Do you think anyone knew about us?"

Bahadur said softly, "I can't answer Your Majesty's question, except to tell you that the origin of this account was within the zenana."

The zenana! How could I doubt that something so malicious and deceitful would have its origins in the zenana, the single most political and belligerent society in our dominion? "Do you have any guesses about who was responsible?"

"Your Majesty, I truly don't know. But it was reputedly one of the King's wives."

Wives! I thought intently. Of my father's wives, Manu would never do a thing so malicious, so it had to have been Kandari. I spoke sharply: "Do we know where Begum Kandari has been for the past several months."

"I thought the same thing, Your Majesty, but Begum Kandari has been severely ill for the last year."

"Ill? Bahadur, that woman never lacks energy to engage in vengeful attacks!"

Bahadur and I went to Kandari's apartment to see what her health was truly like. Ever since I'd been anointed Empress, her health had progressively declined, and at her own request she'd received an apartment far from everyone else. I'd always assumed that was so she'd very seldom have to address me as Empress.

We asked to be announced in her chambers. Upon entering, I beheld an image I hadn't seen since the days of the Gujarat famine: a dark, emaciated individual with bulging eyes stared at us. "Mother Kandari?" I managed.

She smiled, looking almost content, but her voice was weak and rough. "You finally decided to visit your mother?"

"Mother Kandari, I thought you never wanted to see me." Tears welled in my eyes, and I felt almost ashamed for having thought someone so feeble and ill could've plotted against me.

"I couldn't compete with you, Jahanara." She coughed several times. "First your mother and then you; there was never any place for me in the palace, so I just moved myself out of the way."

I began to weep. I knew everything she was saying was true, but how could I tell her that? This woman came to us as a beautiful 16-year-old bride, and in another time or place she could have wielded extraordinary power and riches; but because of my father's intense love for Ami, Kandari had never experienced a husband's love. She was forced to wrongfully embrace the lie that she was barren and thus never had the pleasure to be anyone's mother or love. For some reason, I felt as guilty as if I had been responsible.

I said, "Please forgive me, Mother Kandari. I should have told Aba *you* should be the next Empress, as was your right. Instead, I wrongfully accepted the muhr uzak. Please forgive me."

Kandari smiled on, as if unmoved by my words. "Silly child. Don't you know that, whoever holds the muhr uzak has the worst luck? First Nur Jahan, whose daughter was widowed and she exiled, then your mother, who died suddenly, and now you."

I was confused. Yes, I thought my life had been filled with misfortune, but how did Kandari know that.

Then she said, "I know about you and Gabriel."

"How?"

"When you were sick. I watched how he cared for you. Then I watched from the curtains when you first awoke and stared into one another's eyes. I knew then."

Profoundly embarrassed, I softly asked, "Is this why you moved to have him sent away?"

"Sent away? No, my child." Kandari reached out to touch my face. "As someone who was never touched, I felt your pain and couldn't bear the thought of you ending up like this. I was happy for you."

I paused and then said, "Mother Kandari, I need to know who else knew about me and Gabriel."

Kandari began coughing forcefully and for a moment I thought she was about to die. "The ladies that your Aba put in charge of nursing you during your illness, only they knew."

I had heard from Gabriel that Aba didn't want all of the zenana women hovering over me because the hakims had warned him about how susceptible I would be to infections, so Aba had appointed a select few of the zenana women to coordinate my care. I never really delved into who was in this small circle, but now I needed to know.

I looked away from Kandari and at Bahadur. "Who else besides Mother Kandari was nursing me?"

Bahadur looked up as if trying to jolt her memory to remember something so esoteric. "Queen Kandari, Queen Manu, Princess Nadira and..."

"And?"

"And that was all, Your Majesty. Just three women were required."

I began to think. I knew Manu would never harm me, and Kandari's words seemed sincere. That left Nadira, but as Dara's wife she was especially close to me, so what was her reason? Was she also jealous of me because of my closeness with Dara or did she fear me the way Ami feared Nur Jahan when she first married Aba? After all, Nadira would be Empress one day. But she and Dara always showed me intense love. They even named their daughter after me, Jani.

Why would she name her first child after me if she had ill feelings towards me? Could it be that she was two-faced? Could she have committed those good will gestures so no one would suspect her of trying to harm me? Was she afraid Dara would keep me as Empress after he became King while she would be discarded the way Kandari once was? I would go to Dara to learn the truth.

✳ ✳ ✳

Much to Murad's surprise, no jubilant signs of celebration awaited him in Agra's streets. No crowds gathered, no drums beat, no jubilant sign appeared anywhere. I could see from my balcony Murad slowly ride his lone horse into the main street of Agra, people barely noticing him, as if he was just another royal casually going about his business. At one point he had to stop so a cart drawn by two over-worked, sweaty bulls on their way to the Taz Mahal could carry stones across the street.

Murad's face looked discouraged. Here he was, dressed up in a jewel-studded turban, wearing royal silk garments with pearl necklaces and gold bracelets, coming victorious from battle – and being treated this way? While his horse stood still, he moved his head side to side, looking for any signs of celebration. In the deep distance I heard some loud music, but I soon realised it came from a wedding party, and the music slowly faded away as the party moved closer to its destination.

Now visibly upset, Murad stormed through the streets, even running over a limping beggar who was unfortunate enough to cross the street just as Murad reached it. He ordered that gates to the fort be opened, rode his horse to the outskirts of the Diwan-i-khas, dismounted and slowly walked to the hall to be presented to Aba. I went over to the marble window and prepared to see my brother's and father's encounter. Aba eventually entered, and the zenana women waited in the corner while Dara and Afzal Khan stood in their respective places.

"You idiot!" Aba raged. "I sent you on the most important conquest of my reign, and you deserted your army and ran back here!"

Murad hung his head, unable to offer an explanation for what he had done. He looked utterly pathetic there, wearing more jewels than even the emperor, seeming dressed as if for some reward banquet. Yet he was being scolded like a child in front of all of the nobles.

He stammered, "Aba, I-I..."

"Did you know that in your absence the king of the region refused to surrender?" Aba roared. "And in your absence no reigning general can command all of the imperial forces! Now the generals are quarreling with each other. Don't you see this is why we send *princes* with our armies – to prevent such quarrels and maintain a united front? Get out of my sight!"

Murad left the hall, remounted his horse and rode back towards Lahore to resume his governorship of the region. At least the King hadn't robbed him of his title, he must have thought. I saw him pause in the distance near the crowd that gathered around the lifeless body of the beggar he'd run over. But as if unaffected by the incident, he merely threw off his expensive pearl necklace and threw it in the body's direction. Then, with a haughty look after giving the poor man's life the value of that necklace, he rode away.

Aba was clearly devastated by this turn of events. What should have been the crowning military glory of his reign was now the biggest military debacle of all times. He moaned aloud about the Mughal men now dying of frostbite and pneumonia in the unforgiving snowy mountains of the Hindu Kush.

I'd always found the geography of this area fascinating. Sati once taught me the origins of the rugged northwest. These mountains were created ages untold ago when the continents were first split from the earthquake that gave the globe its current geography. The land mass that would one day become India broke off of present day Africa and floated in the Indian Ocean for several hundred years, gradually floating north to collide with Asia. As the land mass collided with the southern region of Asia, the sheer force of the collision created the Himalayan mountains. Thus, India developed borders along its northern frontier in the shape of the world's tallest mountain range, which included the highest peak in the world, Mt Everest.

Nowhere were the effects of this collision greater than in the northwest region of India, where several layers of mountain ranges continued to form, making the area almost uninhabitable. As a result, the people who lived there were a coarse group, used to a rugged lifestyle and unafraid to die. Their lives were a far cry from the opulent Agra, where parties and celebrations occurred every day while cool water chilled the arid climate in the summer months. Yet here were tens of thousands of Mughal soldiers from all over India, freezing to death, their remains not even receiving proper burials in the process.

We all realised something had to be done, and someone reliable had to be sent to do it. Though Aba thought about going personally to the area to supervise the reinvasion of the region, I was reluctant to let him leave the city without its King, especially given the construction projects still underway. Besides, if he were to be captured or killed in the process, India would be plunged into chaos, I felt, and all would be lost. Too much was at stake for him to put his life in danger; he had to send someone else, I implored.

He considered sending Dara, but he was too concerned about the danger to Dara's life. Besides, Dara never showed much of a military mind; he'd often been rebuked by his teachers for not concentrating enough during his training with muskets and arrows. And since no other of his sons showed much political promise, Aba was reluctant to send his future heir into harm's way. He next considered my other brother Shuja, who was the next oldest after Dara. But Shuja was at the time in Bengal on the eastern front of the Empire. To summon him from there and send him northwest would take too long; everyone now in Balkh would be dead by the the time he could get there.

So Aba knew who had to be sent; he just couldn't muster the will to say it. I told him, "You know who needs to go, right Aba?"

He looked away from me and said, "The generals could handle it on their own if I made one of them the supreme commander." But there was no confidence in his voice. He knew that was a ridiculous proposition; no military expedition of this magnitude could hope to succeed without a prince at the helm.

I said, "Tell me to send for him."

Aba made no comment, his face frozen as if defeated.

I repeated: "Tell me to send for him."

Again he ignored my plea, and now I implored: "He has military acumen like yours, and we need to bring our soldiers home. He alone can defeat the enemy and deliver the regions to us!"

Aba looked at me with resignation. "I must send for him, yes?" Now Aurangzeb would be ordered to Agra.

✼ ✼ ✼

"Presenting Prince Muhammad Aurangzeb!"

Dead silence reigned in the Diwan-i-am as we awaited the arrival of the Prince. The nobility always stood on edge whenever his name rose. Now a broad-shouldered, muscular young man with fair skin and a neatly trimmed beard, he walked slowly, with confident strides into the hall, the gold and pearl necklaces around his neck chiming in rhythm: *Clink, clink, clink.*

He came to a halt on the thick Persian carpets and saluted Aba.

"My son…" Aba extended his hands as if to hug Aurangzeb metaphorically. Aurangzeb stood politely at a distance, motionless. "How you've grown since last I saw you! I have heard of your successes in Gujarat and am pleased with your work." (Though Aurangzeb had disappointed in the Deccan, he'd impressed the Emperor in Gujarat; under his leadership robbers and rebels had been dealt with firmly, bringing peace and order to this previously lawless region. He'd even received a raise in his allowance and an increase in his estates in return for his good work there.)

He bowed deferentially. "Your Highness is too kind."

The mullahs at their distance all smiled broadly.

Aba went on: "As you have heard, your brother, Murad, has abandoned the royal troops and rushed home to quench his thirst for all sorts of vices."

I was amused to hear Aba refer to Murad's philandering nature as 'vices,' considering Aba's own indulgences in the same. It was rumoured that Aba was now engaging in intense sexual activity in the court. Several of his affairs were with wives of nobles; assignations were announced to him in cryptic ways, such as, 'Your morning breakfast has arrived,' 'your lunch is here,' 'dinner is ready.' These alliances were outside even his harem of over 300 concubines.

Much worse, Aba was now said to be engaging in yet additional promiscuous behaviour, even fornicating in the Shish Mahal, the Palace of Glass, so he could watch himself mirrored during sexual acts. All of these incidents added to my perception that when it came to earthly pleasures, Aba now observed no bounds whatsoever. At times I thought Raushanara must have gotten her voracious sexual appetites from him. Alas, the Mughal Kingdom was now a bastion of hypocrisy.

"I need you to bring the perishing Mughal men in the northwest home, son. Only you can do this task." Aurangzeb stood silently at attention, head bowed in mild deference to the royalty in whose presence he now stood. He glanced over to Dara, who himself gazed intently at the ground; he was doubtless annoyed at this lavish praise thrown at Aurangzeb. Meanwhile Aurangzeb might rightly have felt disappointed, still trying to decipher why Dara was the favourite if everyone, including the King, knew Dara couldn't be trusted with this expedition.

Aba now ordered: "Go now, to the rugged northwest and bring our troops home!"

"As Your Highness wishes," said Aurangzeb, "I will leave immediately."

Aurangzeb spent the night in Agra, but didn't visit me before he left. He and Raushanara were becoming dangerously close, and I didn't know what to do about that. Still, I felt if Aba continued treating Aurangzeb as his son and not a 'serpent,' Aurangzeb would slowly come to our side and stop being swayed by Raushanara.

The Aurangzeb who had just appeared before the Emperor was very different from the one who'd arrived a few years ago from the Deccan during my accident. He was now more charismatic, he held his head high, his accomplishments radiated from his smiles; he seemed very much aware of his destiny.

Fully understanding that he now possessed unmatched military prowess in the Empire, he gladly accepted charge of converting the worst debacle in Mughal military history into a triumphant victory over the enemy.

17
MISTAKEN IDENTITY
1st February, 1647

I think you need a smaller turban," chuckled Dara as he looked me over. I'd reluctantly decided to wear the signature green turban of the Qadiriya movement whenever I attended their meetings.

We knelt on the floor before the pictures of Mian Mir and began to pray for guidance. Shah Badkashi looked towards me as if he knew I wasn't concentrating on the prayer but other matters instead. I avoided his gaze. It seemed he had some special power that I'd yet to learn of.

We rose after our prayer, and I casually approached Dara and said, "My brother, I need to speak to you in private."

Dara seemed preoccupied, still murmuring some prayer verses as I spoke to him. He raised his hand as if gesturing me to wait. A few seconds later he looked at me and said, "Yes, what is it that can't wait, Jahanara?"

His attitude annoyed me. Maybe he thought he could speak to me this way because we weren't in the palace but in the headquarters of a movement he thought of as his own.

I shot back: "It could wait! But not for long. It's about Nadira!"

Dara's face softened. I wanted to be delicate in my approach to this topic.

He put his hand on my shoulder. "All right, Jahanara. I'll come to the zenana later today and we can talk then."

I looked away, annoyed and frustrated. I already felt tortured about soon revealing Nadira's duplicity to a man who was one of the most genuine people I'd ever known.

Dara met me in my apartment later that day. I had the royal chefs prepare his favourite dishes and bring them to my chambers: mutton korma, tandoori chicken and grilled fish in lemon sauce. After he ate, I offered him *shirazi* from my special collection. Shirazi and Canary were in high demand in our kingdom. Both were imported from Surat, Gabriel's port, and took at least 46 days to arrive in Agra. The high cost of such transport prohibited its sale in the open market, but that cost had no meaning for the royalty or nobility. *Araq*, the native wine made from local grapes and unrefined sugar, was what most noblemen drank when the foreign wines weren't available.

Dara sipped his shirazi and started the conversation. "So, what matters concerning Nadira do you wish to discuss with me?"

I could tell he'd prepared himself for bad news. I began: "I never told you this, but I was very fond of the firangi hakim, Gabriel."

"We all were," he responded, squinting. I'd watched him imbibe a large quantity of the mildly sour drink.

"Not the way I was fond," I said. This was getting harder. I'd never disclosed the full nature of our relationship to anyone, and verbalising it now made me feel dirty and soiled. It would be hard for me to find words to make my liaison with Gabriel look pure and sincere. Would Dara think of me the way we both always thought of the zenana women?

I said, "Gabriel held a very special place in my heart. I can't tell you how or when, but perhaps the way he cared for me during my illness sparked something inside me, and he felt the same way. We met several times after I became well and…" I didn't know how to say the rest.

Dara nodded slightly. His eyes looked into mine unblinking, but without a judgmental cast. Rather, I felt he was sympathetic towards me.

I continued: "I just want you to know that I know I can never marry anyone, but if I could, it would be Gabriel. He asked me to leave with him and even offered to stay here so we could go on loving each other in secret, but his captain forced him to relocate to Bengal."

Dara raised an eyebrow, as though he hadn't expected such a twist in the story. I went on: "I've recently learned that someone from here contacted his captain and implored him to send Gabriel away, telling the captain that not doing so might result in the rescinding of the privileges Aba had given him in Bengal."

Dara stared away for a few moments as he must have been thinking of what to say. At last he said: "Why would sending him away be a bad thing if you'd already been making your affair a secret? I mean, the longer he stayed, the greater the threat Aba would find out. Maybe whoever did this was trying to protect you."

I'd never heard of anyone refer to my relationship as an affair, though that's precisely what it was. I said, "Don't you understand? If they knew enough of this relationship to send Gabriel away, and they were calculating enough to go to the captain and threaten him enough to send order for Gabriel to leave, who knows how else they might utilise this information?"

"And I presume you think Nadira did this?" Dara put his glass down and folded his hands.

"Who else could it be? The only women, I'm told, who took care of me during my accident were Kandari, Manu and Nadira. Kandari is ill, Manu is too sweet, so that leaves Nadira."

Dara looked puzzled. He picked up his glass and took another sip of the shirazi. This was his third serving, a considerable amount for Dara. He then looked again at me. "Jahanara, Nadira wasn't taking care of you when Gabriel arrived. She was initially chosen by Aba, but then when she got further along in her pregnancy she found she was unable to handle the stress."

I felt a bit foolish then, for not having pieced together that Nadira's pregnancy'd been far from simple. She'd been on bed rest, and didn't even visit me after I was well. A full month passed after I regained consciousness before I saw her.

Dara said, "Aba then asked me who I thought should take Nadira's place in your care."

I felt I was getting close to my answer. I anxiously said: "And who did you recommend?"

"Your lady-in-waiting, Sati."

I felt betrayed and devastated. How could the one person I'd confided in the most after Ami's death do this to me?

The following day I confronted Sati about what she'd done.

She said, "I did it because you're *foolish*, Jahanara! Mughal daughters aren't supposed to have such feelings. It's very dangerous for you to be involved with any man, much less a firangi!"

I sensed so much fury in Sati's voice, it was as though she'd forgotten I was her queen; she spoke fearlessly and as though I were still a child.

I snapped: "And you think *you* have the right to pass over me and make such decisions?"

"Yes! I vowed to you mother I would protect you!"

"You could have simply come to me and discussed your concerns!"

Sati placed her tea on the table and said, "Matters have gone far beyond discussion, Padishah Begum!"

"What are you talking about?"

Sati shook her finger up as if disciplining me. "While you were running around in a boy's disguise to see the firangi, your Aba has had a concubine, not much different in looks or age than you, also wearing boy's disguise, visiting *him*!"

I huffed dismissively. "That's nonsense! Aba has no need to disguise anyone. He's the king; he can do whatever he wishes."

Sati stared at me wide-eyed. "Not when it's a street girl! To appease the mullahs, your Aba was trying to limit his liaisons to just his zenana, but then a street girl caught his attention, and deeming she's not good enough to be an official part of the zenana, he's chosen to meet her discreetly, dressed as a boy. Her name is Chamani, Begum!"

"What does this have to do with me and Gabriel!"

Sati pouted as if disappointed in me. "Your sister Raushanara has started a rumour that *you're* Chamani, Begum!"

This news shocked and disgusted me. Immersed in the Qadiriya order and on the construction projects, I'd had little time to keep my ears open to what was occurring in the zenana.

Sati cried, "She claims you and your father are having an incestuous relationship, and this is why he made you queen!"

I sat in utter disbelief. What could I say? How could I console myself? Sati went on: "She claims she spotted you one day from her window, and you lost your turban in the wind. She saw your face and tried to have the guards seize you, but you vanished quickly. Later that day, knowing he would be livid, she went to your father to tell him you were escaping from the zenana wearing a boy's uniform. But when she arrived at his palace, she saw him in a compromising position with a woman who from the back looked just like you, and whose clothes on the floor resembled the same boy's clothes you'd been wearing. The coincidence seemed too unlikely to dare question, but I know you and know you could and would never do such a thing!"

Sati began weeping. How she must have secretly suffered, hearing these rumours and fearing for me! She said through her tears: "I reckoned it was time for the firangi to go so the visits would end; then the rumours would die out. But they've only gotten worse!"

I said, calmly as I could, "Does Aba know of the rumours?"

"No. The nobles have protected your father, fearing his wrath."

"And Raushanara's continuously fuelling these rumours?"

"I'm afraid so. She wants you discredited so you have no merit in the kingdom. She wants to take your place!"

My eyes also began to tear. This had to be the worst day of my life. My love for my father had been perverted, and my own sister was the culprit. I said, "What should I do?"

Sati leaned toward me. "Discredit her! Everyone has secrets, Jahanara. Find out hers and exploit it the way she's trying to exploit yours! Discredit her before she can discredit you! Then no one will believe her."

I thought this over for a moment, and decided indeed, revenge was in order. Now I asked Sati, "But what about the rumour that's already out there about me? Should I address it in the zenana, perhaps issue an edict banning anyone from speaking such ill thoughts of the King and their Queen?"

"No!" shouted Sati. "You mustn't say anything. Right now it's just a rumour, but if you as the queen address it, it will become a *story*, and you'll only give it validity."

"So I should let the rumour stand?"

"Rumours have a way of dying, my child. Right now it's new, so people are talking. Eventually, something else will come up, and this story will be forgotten. But in the meantime..."

"...I have a score to settle with my sister!"

18

REVERSAL OF FORTUNE

3rd March, 1647

When Aurangzeb arrived at the Central Asian frontier with just 10,000 soldiers, he hadn't been fully briefed about the devastation that occurred there in the wake of a leaderless army. The 45,000-strong force Aba had sent with Murad was now but half that size, disease and famine having killed as many soldiers as had enemy attacks.

Aurangzeb quickly organised what now constituted the imperial army, sectioning the wounded and infected in one area so as not to let their diseases infect anyone else. He used the rations he'd brought to set up low-cost, high-energy meals for all the men. He then assembled the remaining generals and strictly forbade infighting, citing death as the penalty for such offences.

He then mustered his regiments according to size, the largest regiments in back, the smaller in front, then paraded them across the valley. The Hindu Rajputs wore orange, signifying their Hindu origin, though it was understood they were under the Mughal banner. The regimen from Agra wore green headbands – the colour of Islam.

The parade made for a massive show of force by the new prince-general, putting the Bukhara army on notice of an impending attack that wouldn't be a small, mere guerilla one based on bribes and treachery. This would be a serious, frontal assault by the new general.

Unlike Murad, Aurangzeb exercised disciplined control of the army and the whole situation. He had to make a repeat attack, but Aurangzeb was a savvy enough statesman to conclude that this region wasn't worth much fight – neither Balkhh nor Badakshan could even provide the salary of a second-rate Mughal noble. Indeed, the entire region would be a drain on the treasury and the empire's resources. Rather than expanding north into this snow-covered, dead region, the empire would be better served expanding south, into the diamond mines of the Golconda region of the Deccan. Thus, Aurangzeb resolved to end this conflict as quickly and at lowest cost as possible.

His plan was to let our army invade head on with a smaller number than the enemy's, but letting them believe we'd underestimated their forces. Once they thought they were winning, they'd release their remaining soldiers to finish our men off. Then our Hindu Rajput contingent would rise from the trenches and overpower them; they'd have no time to retreat, and we'd slaughter them summarily.

The day of the first battle came and Aurangzeb ordered his Rajput officers to bury themselves in trenches along the rear edges of the valley. The Mughal men, swords in hands, met the Bukhara army in close combat, slashing and being slashed in return. The Bukhara army seemed to be overpowering the Mughal men, moving deeper into the Mughal-controlled area of the battlefield, while Aurangzeb watched from the hilltop. Thinking victory would be theirs, the Bukhara army released their reserves, overpowering the doomed Mughal souls who would be the first regiment sent to their deaths on this battlefield. When the last of the Bukhara regiments charged in, Rajputs attacked from the trenches using muskets – routing the unsuspecting Bukhara army.

The Central Asian men ran from the battlefield in all separate directions. But to Aurangzeb's surprise, these men had made holes in caves alongside the valley, and using tunnels they'd linked the caves to allow themselves safe passage home. So Aurangzeb's hopes to destroy the enemy in one day were dashed – but he'd won an important battle. Half of the enemy troops had been annihilated, including numerous commanders who'd rushed the battlefield hoping to achieve glory by capturing Aurangzeb himself.

The trumpets of victory sounded as the Mughal soldiers, Hindus and Muslims, cheered at their general who'd given them this much-needed victory after months of death and disease.

In repeated engagements that continued for the next several weeks, Mughal muskets and arrows triumphed over the Bukhara army's primitive weapons. Aurangzeb gradually plugged up the caves, and the Bukhara army's clever cave-tunnel structure collapsed.

Though far from home and away from any mosque, Aurangzeb prayed regularly during this time and insisted on holding daily prayer services. A tent was designated as the provisional mosque where all Muslim men could pray. Aurangzeb believed this was important both for morale and for the continued blessings of God on his endeavours.

Slowly the Bukhara resistance thawed. Many began to desert and either go home, or in some cases join the Mughal army in return for clemency. And unlike Murad, Aurangzeb stayed true to his word and delivered to these poor souls what he'd promised.

Finally a turning point came in this months-long battle for an unworthy prize. During one late day's battle, Aurangzeb, heavily bloodied from the fighting, began to notice it was time for him to say his daily prayer. The young Prince rode his horse to a clearing at the far side of the battle field, dismounted and spread a rug across the floor. The commanders of both armies slowly turned his way, each unsure of what the Mughal was doing during this raging battle. Aurangzeb kneeled and performed his prayers, completely oblivious to the vicious fighting around him. His men were in awe, as were the Bukhara generals. The Bukhara king, seeing this unrealistic vision from a hill top couldn't believe his eyes, and is to have felt a wave of emotions overcome him.

"Islam is about brotherhood," muttered the King to the soldier standing beside him. "If this man believes so much in the Koran that he's willing to risk his life to pay homage to Allah on the battlefield, then I can fight him no longer. To fight such a man is to invite one's own ruin."

The King ordered his men to retreat and then he himself walked out onto the battlefield. As the Mughal soldiers were about to charge him, the generals stopped their men, convinced that this wasn't an attack but possibly a surrender. Aurangzeb, still kneeling on his rug with his eyes closed and chanting his verses, realised the fighting had stopped and something unusual was happening, but he refused to be disturbed during this moment.

The Bukhara King walked over to the Prince and laid his sword in front of the kneeling, shut-eyed Prince Aurangzeb. "Open your eyes, brother," said the King calmly. "I cannot fight the truest believer in the Koran I've ever met. Take what you will from our humble kingdom. It's yours."

Aurangzeb rose, and the King continued: "This will be our understanding, brother. You go home now with our treasures and tell your King you've won. I will stay here and rule my people as I see fit. You don't control me, and I won't cross you. Officially, we are now a part of your empire, but for all intents and purposes, you will have no control over us. We won't send men into your army, nor allow you to tax our people. On paper, though, we're now a part of you."

Aurangzeb embraced the Bukhara King, effectively accepting his truce; but he exacted one condition: the King had to submit a formal submission, plus a request for a pardon. To everyone's astonishment (and delight), the King acquiesced.

The war was now over, essentially as a stalemate. The day of the surrender arrived but much to Aurangzeb's chagrin, the King himself didn't show up, instead sending his two grandsons to bow in his place. Though livid at first, Aurangzeb did reluctantly accept these substitutes.

✱ ✱ ✱

While the war in the northwest raged on, a war needed to be won here at home as well – between Raushanara and myself. I'd never asked to be at war with my own sister, but now that she'd spread such a vicious rumour about me, I was ready to fight back.

My other sister, Gauhara, was slowly coming of age, and like other women of the harem, she was taking delight in the pleasures of the zenana. Like Raushanara, it was rumoured that she, too, was enjoying the company of a man (though Raushanara had many more than one). Gauhara's lover was a soldier named Imtiaz Khan; he'd visit her every night, promptly at one am (at least, that's what my eunuch told me).

I began to befriend my sister, the love child of my parents born on the day my Ami died.

"Shirazi?" Gauhara's olive skinned face lit up. Gauhara, with her fair-skinned complexion and slender, sharp features, looked more like me and Ami. This had only served to alienate Raushanara, who deeply resented her own tanned complexion and round features. What's worse, every summer Raushanara would break out with the worst case of acne, and the hakims would give her every herb and potion they knew to clear her skin, but to no avail. Both Gauhara and I had clear skin, and this enflamed her even more.

I asked, "Do you know Shirazi wine, Gauhara?"

She chuckled, blushed and then nodded in the affirmative.

Then I asked, "Tell me, have you had any other wines?"

She laughed profusely and reached to take the Shirazi from my hand. I moved it behind me to evade her grasp. "Jahanara!" she lamented, whining like the child I felt she still was inside.

"Have you also had Canary wine, because I have that too?"

"So this is what you do with you title?" she tittered. "You import foreign wines and horde them in your chambers? Well, I'm tired of drinking araq," she pouted. "It has a tangy flavour and makes me sick the next day."

"No araq for you tonight, sister! *Shirazi* awaits!" I poured her a glass of Shirazi, expecting her to just sip it slowly as I normally would. As if she were a thirsty traveller receiving water, Gauhara drank it all down in one gulp.

"That was fast," I said playfully.

Gauhara squinted as the final gulp drained down her throat. "Mmmm! That was good!"

I poured another glass. This was going to be easier than I thought! After several more glasses, Gauhara splayed herself across her divan and looked at the carefully carved ceiling. "Oh, Jahanara! Allah made wine for women like me... so we can drink our sorrows away!"

Clearly drunk now, she began confiding in me. This is where I needed her to be, but I knew I had to tread slowly. I said, "Why such sorrows, sister?" Not that I really cared; I knew why she was sad because she wasn't with her Imtiaz. But I wanted to let her do her talking, and I gently steered the conversation towards Raushanara.

"She's a bitch!" she blurted out. I was surprised. I'd thought she and Raushanara were friends. Why would she say such a thing about her? She rolled onto her stomach and purred, "I have just one love, and all I asked her was to pull some strings to make sure he wouldn't leave for the northwest to fight there."

I sipped my Shirazi but swallowed little. I needed to be sober for this, so I could learn more, and clearly. "And did she?" I sighed. Of course I knew the answer, but I wanted to prod her more.

"That bitch *ignored* me! She hushed me out of her apartment and told me I was being a nuisance."

"But why?"

Gauhara took another sip of the wine, as if she needed more fuel to spill the secrets. "She had her own lovers hide in the baths next to her apartment!"

"What?" This sounded strange, even for Raushanara. "But why?"

Gauhara moaned. "She is *soooo* wicked, Jahanara!" Then she whispered: "Even after I told her about Imtiaz, she wouldn't let me know who *she* was having sex with." She took another sip.

"So she hides them in the baths?"

"Yes! And most nights she has more than one! Raushanara rarely has sex with one guy at a time!"

I just nodded my head. I couldn't make Gauhara privy to my plan. She mustn't know why I was prodding her. "Is there any specific time of the month she has these 'lovers' over?"

Gauhara swayed drunkenly and the side of her mouth dripped wine. She slurred, "She does it when the hakims tell her she's least likely to be fertile!"

Pregnancy was the most feared outcome of sex for the zenana women. It was clear to us that we belonged only to the King; thus, if one of the King's women he hadn't visited turned out pregnant, that was proof she'd been unfaithful. And in the case of us daughters, we weren't to be touched by anyone, so how could we be pregnant? "So when is that time?" I ventured.

Gauhara thought for a moment. Then she said stuperously, "Around the 10th of every month. Just visit her then, and you'll always find men hiding in her baths!"

Visit her? I wouldn't need to visit that witch who took from me the love of my life. No, the person who'd visit her on the 10th of next month would be the King himself!

✳ ✳ ✳

For the Mughal army the march back from the northwest was cruel and unforgiving. Most of the pack animals died or got injured, making it virtually impossible to bring back any treasures from the region to Aba. Those men already sick or injured at the start of the journey almost all perished somewhere along the way. The price of this war was high – most of the original 50,000 soldiers deployed under Murad were now dead, including generals. Aurangzeb started out insisting on a proper burial for any Muslim soldier, including a recitation of the hymns; but he eventually gave up and chose not to be informed of further deaths, forced to embrace the 'bliss' ignorance can at times bring under such conditions.

When Aurangzeb returned to Lahore, he did carry a gold dagger from the King of Bukhara that he managed to keep through the journey, hoping to present it to Aba in Agra. Aba couldn't help but be disappointed, not with Aurangzeb, but at the disastrous cost in resources and human lives of this campaign. He chose to remain in Agra, consoled by his art and architecture and not greet his son in Lahore, as Aurangzeb had hoped. He further told Aurangzeb not to bother coming to Agra but to instead go to Gujarat.

It seemed there was but one victor in this entire war – Aurangzeb. After having spent a lifetime treated as a black stain, he only could claim credit for bringing home the deserted army from the Central Asian debacle. He secured the submission of the enemies' royalty, and he cut hard spurs in the icy grounds of the torrential northwest. More importantly, he won the admiration of Mughal generals, who'd seen in him both the discipline and the strength of a true military commander.

To me, his success and strength were both exciting and scary. I was proud to see my brother be victorious, but I feared his strong military acumen along with the allies he must have made in this expedition would embolden him to challenge Dara for the throne some day. With time, Aurangzeb would need friends in the military should anything happen to the King. Aurangzeb's fortunes were beginning to turn, and I became increasingly worried.

19
JAHANARA'S TAJ

7th **March, 1647**

M y relationship with Gabriel now began to stabilise into
extremely close friendship, not the lustful dependency it had
been while he was in Agra. One day I received a letter from him:

My Love,

*My work here in Hugli is complete. The factories have been set
up, and Kalikata, the once-impoverished village along the Hugli
river, is fast turning into a major commercial centre, and along with
the neighbouring villages of Suntanati and Govindpur, it's now being
reorganised into a central city, renamed Calcutta. I'm returning to
Surat at the end of the month and from there will go back to England
forever.*

*I want you to come with me. Leave your family and make it
seem like an accident. You can have a new identity, a new name and
a new beginning. Leave all this – the gossip, the fighting, the kingdom
– and let's begin our new life together. You'll fit in perfectly with
English society, your olive skin a refreshing tinge of colour among
the pale crowds that await me in England. We can start a family,
and you can give them all Muslim names if you wish. All I want is to
begin our life together, in the open.*

I'll meet you in your new capital of Shahjahanabad (Delhi) at

the end of the month, and then we'll escape in the darkness in my
bullock cart to Surat. From then on you'll be known as my 'bibi,'
someone I met and married in Bengal. No longer Jahanara, you'll
have a new name, a new identity, but the same love. I'm tired of
hiding and hurting. This isn't how it has to be. Do what's right and
shake off the chains that have bound us for so long. I'm willing to
leave it all for you. Will you for me?

> *Love,*
> *Gabe*

I'd meet Gabriel in Delhi, but I had other plans than he suggested. I
worked tirelessly for the next several weeks to complete construction
of the new city, to make sure it was perfect when he arrived.

I divided my time between planning out the details of the city
– locating gardens, canals, parks, havelis – and learning about the
Qadiriya order. Just as Aba had after Ami's death, I was coping with
the loss of Gabriel by immersing myself in architecture, using Delhi
as my pallet.

I remember discussing the planning with Aba many years ago.
He'd asked me, "What do you wish to do with the water on the
riverside?"

I replied, "I think we can use it to make canals all across the city,
just as you did for the Taj Mahal."

"*Taz* Mahal, Jahanara," corrected the King, "not *Taj*."

"You know, Aba, I think Taj sounds better, and everyone's using
that word now. Nobody seems to be able to remember it's Taz. Let's
just go with that: Taj."

Aba wasn't particular about names, and as long as the shrine was
devoted to his deceased lover, he had no problem with that minor
distortion.

"Aba, the climate of our new capital is even more arid and dry
than Agra's. But if we flow canals all through the city, into the
private chambers and all around the fort, it will cool the city on the
hot days."

"It shall be like paradise!" said a proud Aba, commending my budding architect's mind.

"The Paradise Canal, Aba. That shall be its name."

Now Delhi would be *my* Taj Mahal. Here, I'd fight the depression of losing Gabriel *and* celebrate through architecture the love that I shared with him. I took trips to the city regularly, no more than a few hours each way.

The entire city was a semicircle enclosing over 1,500 acres, was walled, with eight gates, each named after the city toward which it was pointing: The Lahori gate led to the city of Lahore; the Kashmiri gate led north to Kashmir; Ajmeri gate to the Rajput western city of Ajmer, and so on. The design of eight gates was also intentional: Four gates represented the four directions; the other four represented the gates of heaven. Within the walled city was another walled structure – the new Red Fort, situated in the west. The west was an important direction for us Mughals for this reason – it faced Mecca. All prayers were done facing west; mosques – including the Jami Mosque – opened their doors facing West.

Built of stones quarried from the abandoned city of Fatehpur Sikri, the walls of the fort formed an irregular octagon. Four large gateways, two small entrances and 21 towers lined the walls of the fort. A deep moat surrounded it, filled with water and fishes, beyond which were gardens of jasmines, roses, frangipani, violets and mango, apple and banyan trees.

The Paradise Canal pumped water several kos upstream from the Jumna and ran through the harem apartments into all areas of the Red Fort and the city at large, feeding pools and sending fountain jets high into the air, creating rainbows wherever they went. Flowers and trees surrounded the canal, but were often barely visible behind the drifting spray of the fountains. The largest apartment here was mine, and I created it with the utmost care and attention to detail, just as Aba had taught me.

The princes' mansions were situated outside the Red Fort's walls, each haveli looking itself like a miniature fort. The new Red

Fort was the first building completed, at a cost of 60 lakh rupees, almost half spent on the lavish design for the new Diwan-i-khas.

The Diwan-i-khas was made of solid marble, with inlays like those of the Taj Mahal. Built entirely of white marble, its outer wall was studded with agates, pearls and other precious stones. Sheets of gold in a threefold pattern decorated the ceiling; shards of glass sent sparks of light bouncing across the hall.

Gabriel had sent me a message informing me of the date of his arrival at this majestic new city. I'd already arranged for him to stay in a dwelling near the military encampment, the Urdu Bazaar. I myself had moved into my apartment, but I wouldn't stay there this night. As was customary with our meetings, I would put on a boy's outfit and a turban – green for the Qadiriya order and Mian Mir's blessing – to meet with him.

Now I watched from a casement as Gabriel's bullock cart made its way to the Urdu Bazaar and the servants of his quarters quickly unloaded the boxes from the carts and unpacked them for him in the haveli. Gabriel slowly walked into the central courtyard of this haveli, and must have noticed it looked a lot like his mansion in Agra. The bedrooms, bathrooms and kitchens, all opened into this main entrance. He entered one of the rooms where the servants were placing his belongings. I was waiting for him in the bedroom, dressed like a boy, wiping the furniture.

We embraced and then we talked for hours. I told him of the Qadiriya order and he told me about Bengal, which was slowly turning into the East India Company's stronghold on the Indian subcontinent, as the village of Kalikata became bigger and more westernised. The trade was extremely profitable, and Gabriel was being credited with its success, in no small part because it was he who'd secured the trading rights from the Mughal King.

Gazing in wonder, Gabriel smiled, "This place is truly amazing!" It's like walking through a Persian paradise."

"It is great, isn't it?" I giggled, my smile wider than any that had graced my face in the last couple of months. "Aba calls it 'Paradise on Earth.' When he visited it last month he said, 'If there is a paradise on earth, it's this, it's this, it's this!' I liked what he said so much, I'm having it engraved on the walls of the new Diwan-i-khas."

Gabriel and I spent the rest of the day walking through the majestic city of Delhi (conceived by Aba, but perfected by me). I showed him the different towns and told him what the names meant.

We walked around the town of Khari Baoli, meaning 'Salty Well,' so named because the salt water from the well in this area was used for animals and for bathing. Other towns – Churi Wallan, meaning the town where bracelets were sold, Chauri Bazaar meaning wide market, Darya Ganj meaning river trading post – reflected industry rather than honouring dignitaries or historical figures. I showed Gabriel how the city was to function like a well-oiled machine with everyone knowing where to go for what purpose, with no time wasted. This was the capital of India and it needed to function as such.

Gabriel wondered: "So did the people name the neighbourhoods, or did the neighbourhoods define the people?"

I said: "Well, we watched where the merchants and traders and artisans settled, and if we thought where they did made sense in the overall picture of the city, we allowed it. And then the town or neighbourhood got a name that reflected its purpose."

As we walked, Gabriel was extraordinarily impressed with how much thought and analysis had gone into every nook of this new city. We next stumbled on a mosque, not the grand Jama Masjid that Aba had built as the heart of the city, but another, much smaller one.

I said, "This is Fatehpuri Masjid, Gabe, built by one of my stepmothers, Fatehpuri Begum. She's very religious and always wanted to build a mosque, so I thought this would be a good opportunity to fashion one for her."

Gabriel looked in awe at how I'd built this city, every lane and avenue of it.

I led Gabriel to a beautiful garden, Persian in style. "This is Sahibabad, meaning Garden of the Sahiba." It recalled Persian gardens where men would kill one another over a dram of water, and where a small stretch of shaded land meted each day's journey against the hot sun and arid climate, and such gardens were always filled with water pools and fountains, their trees and shrubs aligned unnaturally. These unabashedly artificial-looking gardens had no signs of natural variation; all were geometrically shaped to reflect semi-religious concepts. The lines of trees, the carefully pruned flower beds, the marble canals, were all created to give the inhabitant a semi-divine pleasure as he enjoyed the surroundings. Such were the gardens of the Taj Mahal, and such were the gardens now of Delhi.

Eventually the sun began to set, bringing the moment I was waiting for. I wasn't going to let Gabriel see this part of the city until the time was right. It was now about 9:00 pm and the sun had just set, leaving the city in lamp and candlelight. We walked out of the garden and passed Fatehpuri Masjid, and I now led Gabriel to a wide avenue – the main one of Delhi.

This was the 'backbone' Aba referred to. It ran east-west, spanning the entire city and ending at the Red Fort. At a width of 40 yards and a length of 1,520 yards, it was the largest single avenue in all of India. Through its centre ran a water canal, on this moonlit night reflecting that orb in its water. The moon's glow and reflection in the canal lit the entire avenue, with some help from lamps along either end's far side. Just as in Varanasi, the glow of the lamps and moon in the water illumined the surrounding buildings and the people standing beside them.

"Gabe," I said, staring into the avenue as Gabriel held my hand, "when my mother lay on her deathbed, my father told her she was like the sun and he was the moon. The moon has no light; its light's all reflected from the sun. Without the sun, no one would ever see the moon. She was his sun – his light. Without her, no one would see him."

Gabriel waited silently, and I went on: "My mother said it was their love that was the sun, and as long as he kept that love alive, he would glow. I named this Chandni Chowk, meaning Moonlit Avenue, to represent the light, the energy and illumination *your* love has given *me*."

Gabriel looked at me silently, clearly speechless with emotion.

I said, "Before you, I lived for everyone else – the kingdom, my family and my people. You made me want to live for myself. I'm not ashamed of that anymore; it was my right to do something for myself. But here it must end. Gabriel, India is my life; its people are my children; and its king is the only man I can love." I paused, and then said, "You not only saved my life, you gave me another, and this avenue is my love's expression of that. This is *my* Taj Mahal, Gabe."

Then Gabriel and I walked in silence the mile-long Chandni Chowk, watching other people holding each other's hands, enjoying the romantic, sensual experience this corridor gave us all.

I told the heartbroken Gabriel I couldn't leave with him for England, and that by refusing his invitation I realised I was in all likelihood saying goodbye to him forever. As enjoyable as the past few years had been for me, and as much as I valued his love, I wasn't born to marry him – I was mistressed to the throne of India. Like any mother, I treated my children not equally, but uniquely, hoping to bridge the divide I knew was building and possibly avert the bloodbath every previous succession crisis in Mughal India had precipitated. I'd promised my mother I would take care of my siblings as if they were my own children. So I couldn't leave. I was meant to be the Queen of India. The Daughter-Queen.

Gabriel understood my dilemma and though ravaged emotionally, had to accept my decision. And I knew that by denying myself this last opportunity to escape, I'd forever tied my fate to that of the Mughal Empire. That empire and I were now one entity, and there could be no further room for Gabriel in my world.

Though we knew this could last no longer, that night we pretended tomorrow would never come, wishing to stay as long as we could in that present, walking up and down our own Taj Mahal.

20

REVENGE

10th April, 1647

Aba went to visit Raushanara on the 10th of the following month, as I'd advised. I didn't want to bear him bad news, but I hinted to him that something amiss was occurring in the zenana, and that if he visited her on that day, he'd surely find out what it was. He later told me what transpired:

Aba began: "You must miss Aurangzeb since he's been on the front lines for so long?"

Raushanara lamented Aurangzeb's plight as usual. "You have no idea, Aba. I can neither sleep nor sit. I worry for my brother and my countrymen all the time."

"You are a good princess! Tell me, how do you feel the Taj is coming along?"

Raushanara answered quickly, "Wonderful, Aba! It's your finest work yet!"

Aba felt Raushanara had answered too swiftly, almost as if she wanted him to leave, just as I'd cautioned him she would.

Her head moved from side to side slightly. "Aba, we have something special happening tomorrow, just the zenana ladies. May I ask your permission to rest?"

Aba smiled thinly and asked, "My child, when was the last time you took a bath?"

Raushanara replied, "Why, today, Aba!"

Aba nodded. "My child, this summer heat is destroying everyone. Do me a favour, bathe again before you sleep. Your face shouldn't rest tonight with the chemicals and substances of the flesh sitting on your otherwise beautiful skin. Let's light the cauldron and heat the water at once!"

"N-no Aba!!!" she stammered. "I prefer *cool* baths in the summer!"

"Nonsense! I can't risk you getting sick!" Aba motioned to one of the eunuchs to light a fire under the cauldron to warm it for Raushanara. Raushanara must have felt near-panic, wondering if and how her lovers might somehow escape.

The cauldron was lit, and Aba sat in front of Raushanara with a fixed smile, knowing full well that this wasn't what Raushanara wanted.

"Keep the fire hot, eunuch!" he ordered. He glared now at Raushanara, a slick smile crossing his face. Raushanara looked downright fearful.

Just then, loud men's screams echoed from the baths. Aba stared fixedly and ordered firmly, "Keep the fire burning, eunuch! And let no one escape the cauldron!"

Men's screaming grew louder, and now sounds of struggle rose. Burly Uzbeks eunuchs must have been pushing the men trying to get free back into the cauldron.

"Aba, please don't!" cried Raushanara.

"The bath must be sufficiently warm now," said Aba wryly. "Keep warming that cauldron, eunuch!" he called cheerily.

Some time later the excruiating sounds died out, and Raushanara wept openly under Aba's relentless stare. The eunuch appeared, slowly walked towards Aba and said, "All who were in the cauldron have been boiled, Your Highness."

Aba smiled at Raushanara and shouted, "Good! Now, go feed them to the dogs!'

Aba then forced Raushanara to go to the courtyard and made her watch as her former lovers were indeed devoured by the dogs.

I was sad to hear of this cruel outcome of events. I'd thought perhaps Aba would simply imprison the men. Angry as I'd been at Raushanara, I couldn't help pity my sister.

I heard she just lay on the ground wailing as the soldiers laughed at the sight of her lovers being devoured. Eventually the animals finished their meal and dragged off whatever bones were left, and Raushanara was left alone.

❊ ❊ ❊

Dara, Gauhara, Aba and I went to the site of the Taj Mahal on a bright day in 1648, to witness the removal of the choking ramp constructed around it. We all dressed in expensive robes, with Nadira Begum taking care of Dara's children in the Agra heat.

Dara now had three: Sulaiman and Siphor Shikoh (sons) and Jani Begum (daughter). Aba loved his grandchildren from Dara immensely, but was only lukewarm to his grandchildren from Aurangzeb: Mohammad Sultan, Muazzam (sons) and Zeb-un-nissa, Zinat-un-nissa and Badr-un nissa (daughters).

Already within this generation, political alliances were forming: I was close to my namesake Jani Begum and Aurangzeb's eldest daughter Zeb-un-nissa, while Raushanara always clung to Badr-un-nissa. Raushanara even went so far as to convince my brother to change Badr-un-nissa's name to Mehrunnisa, Nur Jahan's original name. Upon my objections, Aurangzeb declined to do so, reserving Raushanara's suggestion for some future progeny, perhaps.

On this day Aba's other children were absent. Only Gauhara, Dara and I went with our father. Shuja and Murad sent gifts for the occasion with their apologies, while Aurangzeb wasn't even invited by Aba, though he'd won Aba's debacle in Central Asia less than a year before. Raushanara stayed back at the palace, still in mourning.

Drummers and elephants were present at the event while the crowds danced in jubilant drunkenness. Dara looked to Aba and asked him when the scaffolding would be completely off.

I said, "They're saying three weeks, but they'll remove the bricks from around the central dome today."

Aba looked at me, as if he knew a secret I had yet to know. "Tell the men I want the scaffold off *today*, and whatever bricks they remove, they can keep for their own homes."

This order was read aloud, and the 20,000 workers removed the bricks in a flurry of panic, each hoarding anything they could find in large bags and sacks. Peasants loaded containers with what they collected, with every small cart claiming an owner within minutes. The Mughals watched standing atop the raised platform of the central pool, while at a distance the Taj Mahal revealed itself, looking like a beautiful Persian maiden slipping a thin gown from off her perfectly shaped, olive-skinned body.

None of us Mughals moved; the heat didn't bother us. We were witnessing an event none before us and possibly none after would ever be able to experience. How often does paradise unveil itself before you, while you enjoy a perfect view? This was the unveiling of a sculpture, disrobing of a goddess, exposure of a masterpiece. Hours and hours passed, and every eye stayed fixed on the Taj, no one moving even once to see what others may have been doing. A firecracker could have exploded behind us and we wouldn't have moved.

Finally, the last of the bricks were removed, to reveal the solid white structure on a raised marble platform. It was perfect, its symmetry accurate to the final inch. All the stones were placed according to design and shone in the distance.

Aba calmly said, "Your mother is at home in paradise, my children." I saw copious tears flow from his eyes as he contemplated what he'd created for her.

During the past 22 years, 20,000 labourers had constructed the world's finest monument, at a cost of 3.2 crore rupees. Of course, this price didn't include the 1,036 sacks of gold used to cast the railing surrounding the sarcophagus and the equal amounts of silver used for the doors.

Mumtazabad, now having its own civil affairs department and police force, had been settled around the Taj to offer it non-stop logistical support. Yet it was the *act* of building the Taj that Ami had truly craved, more than the building itself. By immersing himself in this project for so long, he'd been able to celebrate his love rather than mourn his lover's passing. Nearly a quarter-century had passed since her death, and Aba had now found other reasons to awaken every morning: his children, grandchildren, and perhaps great grandchildren (should he live so long). And he had territories to conquer, buildings to commission and poetry to compose. Life was now too full to remain in melancholy. Ami had succeeded in her mission – to give Aba new life after her death.

✻ ✻ ✻

Aurangzeb was promoted from Governor of Gujarat to Governor of Multan and Sindh, further north. Aba, realising Murad was an ineffectual leader in the troubled border province, had chosen to assign Aurangzeb that post. Aurangzeb, with his wife and five children, moved to Lahore and began ruling the province. Raushanara returned to Agra, content that Aba and I had now moved permanently to Delhi.

Kandahar now became the focus of Aba's attention. Always a contentious city, its location was strategically important to both the Persians and the Mughals. Merchants from China, Persia, Central Asia and India all crossed through this Silk Road city. Control of it assured control of trade. My ancestor, Babur, first took the city, but it soon fell into Persian hands. Babur's grandson, Akbar, then regained control, only for his son, Jahangir, to lose it. Aba then won it back in 1638. Under the weak and politically inept Murad, the Persians felt confidant Kandahar would be theirs for the taking. Thus, they launched a fresh assault against it in 1648, and by February 1649, Kandahar had fallen to the Persians yet again.

Aba asked me to stamp the royal seal on this letter he would send to Aurangzeb, delineating his instructions.

My Dear Aurangzeb,

As you know, we have lost Kandahar, in no small part due to the ineptitude of your brother Murad. It is now up to us to win it back and drive off the Persians once and for all. Certainly we can win Kandahar back; it has been done before – by me. I need you to march on to Kandahar, right now merely to reinforce the troops already stationed in the area. I myself will be leaving Delhi by the time this letter reaches you and staying in Kabul, to act as a rearguard commander. Make me proud, son, just as you did in Balkh. I know you will win Kandahar back for the Mughals and defeat the enemy again.

Yours eternally,
Aba

I said, "Aba, you're putting a lot of faith in Aurangzeb."

Without looking at me, choosing instead to rummage through his papers, he mumbled, "Yes, yes... he's the only one who can do this..." He moved to the other corner of the room, put his papers down and added, "Unfortunately..."

The word slipped from his lips, it seemed. I felt almost as if he hadn't wanted me to hear it, but for some extent didn't really care if I did. He looked up at me. "Just make sure this letter gets to the runner at once. I'm needed in the Khas Mahal."

✱ ✱ ✱

As per the royal instructions, Aurangzeb set out for Kandahar. He chose to leave his wife, Dilras, behind in Lahore with their children. My most beloved of her children was her oldest daughter, Zeb-un-nisa. Having failed to reach Aurangzeb, I had succeeded in befriending this child of his, who exhibited my characteristics more than her father's. Aurangzeb had a complicated relationship with her. My traits – my independence, candour, strong opinions

– Aurangzeb tolerated because I was his older sister. Women like Dilras or Zeb-un-Nissa who depended on him; he viewed as his inferiors, his property.

Dilras had learned through time not to cross Aurangzeb. He'd beaten her several times during their marriage, but hadn't struck her since she gave him a son. In his mind, he seemed to think beating a wife was the right of a husband, and if she disobeyed him, it was absolutely necessary that he beat her or he wasn't a real man. Most of Dilras's beatings, I heard through sources, were the result of unknowing offenses against Allah – failure to cover her face when looking from the balcony, skipping a prayer session, and worst of all, complimenting her husband's physical attractiveness. While the rest of us would have lauded Dilras Banu for one, if not all these things, for Aurangzeb such behaviour was worthy of a beating with a belt. Thus, Dilras during their marriage had aged considerably and now lived her days according to the wishes of her husband, never crossing him, and probably realising her fate was intricately tied to his interpretation of her role in Muslim society.

Aurangzeb set out in May for Kandahar, having not procured for himself any cannons or artillery of consequence, just a reinforcing contingent, as our father had instructed.

What he saw on reaching the city was yet another debacle. Letters from him later told us of how poorly equipped the Mughal troops already stationed in the area were for war, and how many had died in unsuccessful raids. Their ammunition had been stolen, their men slaughtered, and their morale was low. Aurangzeb said he tried to use his prowess as an orator and a military man to change the equation and mounted several attacks on the fort between May and September of 1649, all in vain. A particular letter explained his failure and his frustration.

Dearest Aba,

As per your instructions, I arrived here some months ago with a reinforcing contingent, but without any heavy artillery or cannons.

To my dismay, the condition of the Mughal troops here was worse than those of our troops in Central Asia. I've tried to turn the tables on the enemy many times, but to no avail. I'm therefore requesting permission to return to Lahore and prepare a proper expedition, when the time and resources are right to reengage the enemy at Kandahar with a proper force. You, Aba, may return to Delhi at your will. Your presence in Kabul will only alert the enemy that an impending attack is on the way.

Humbly Yours,
Aurangzeb

It seemed to me Aurangzeb was furious that Aba had misrepresented the battlefield conditions he would meet, and he must have contained these emotions as he wrote the letter. He would clearly prefer instead to launch a counter-offensive on his terms, with his men, on his time. I feared this would be a dangerous course for him, though, because with no one else advising his next move, Aurangzeb would become prime owner of the next battle. Should he succeed, glory would be his and his alone. However, failure would also find no other home but on his doorstep.

✕ ✕ ✕

Gauhara continued to lose weight over the next several months. Though my height, she was now but almost half my weight. Her eyes had sunk into the bones, a dark blemish appearing around each one. Her cheekbones were now more evident; the slight slither of fat that had always collected under them was now completely gone; and every time I saw her she looked like a woman in despair. I summoned Bahadur to my chambers to learn of the cause of Gauhara's deteriorating health. She said, "I'd be lying if I told you I know, Your Majesty."

I didn't want to use my spies to invade Gauhara's privacy, especially since it was Bahadur who'd given me the ammunition I needed to take my revenge on Raushanara. Besides, my relationship with Raushanara was so complicated, Gauhara was the only sister I had a chance to have a real relationship with.

I went the next day to Gauhara's chambers to question her directly. Her palace was the smallest among the princesses'. I had the largest as the queen, and Raushanara had whined her way to the second-largest. After that, Aba's other wives were given palaces, probably more as a consolation prize for never being visited by their husband, who now only kept sexual company with concubines.

Gauhara wasn't in her chambers when I arrived there, so I chose to sit on her divan and wait. I confess I was in the habit of rummaging through other people's things – such was the culture of the zenana and I was a victim of it. I initially resisted the urge to go through Gauhara's dresser drawers, but eventually I began finding and reading notes and diaries she'd kept. I learned more about my sister, including her interest in polo and her desire to study poetry. She'd even composed some verses, though they weren't very good. She had some roses pressed in her books, no doubt from her lover now engaged in our northwest wars. I read from her diaries, then her poems, and then eventually read from her letters:

Dear Gauhara,

I've abridged conscience a mite and told the commander of our unit that my mother has gone ill. He thus released me from active duty and gave me permission to return home. I will cross Delhi before going on to my village, and I wish to see you.

It has been very hard without you, my love. Please wait for me on the night of Eid. I will cross into the city and await you at your balcony.

Love,
Imtiaz

It seemed evident to me that this melancholy that had consumed my sister was none other than simple heartache. Perhaps Imtiaz had betrayed her or worse; perhaps he'd never made it here as he promised he would. This would be understandable, though not worrisome. Who hadn't been through heartbreak? In the zenana, women were used to being betrayed and forgotten by the men they thought loved them.

I waited a little longer for Gauhara to arrive, but she didn't come. I was about to leave when I saw her thin figure in the distance.

Both ecstatic and concerned, when she arrived I exclaimed, "So there you are! I've waited a long time for you!"

Gauhara sighed dully. "What do you want, Jahanara?"

I walked over to her, smiling. "I want to know what's wrong, Gauhara. You seem unwell to me. I wish to know what ails you."

Gauhara wouldn't confide in me, even after I offered her shirazi, as before.

I said firmly, "If you don't tell me, I'll go to the Mahaldar and tell her not to give you your allowance!" (The Mahaldar, chief lady officer of the zenana, kept an eye on all important matters of the zenana, including distribution of salaries.)

Gauhara looked shocked. I think she felt violated and clearly threatened, though I didn't intend to make her feel so.

She spat, "Keep the Mahaldar out of this! I need some time by myself, Jahanara. Please leave me alone." I wasn't used to being addressed like this, but I couldn't bring myself to protest my emaciated, clearly devastated younger sister's stand against me. Something had happened to her, someone had hurt her, and I would find out who it was.

21

KANDAHAR

3rd April, 1652

Iinformed my eunuch ahead of time, "Arzani and Hamida will ride with me on the main elephant during this trip." So Aba reluctantly let three women leave alone on this long journey, after I explained to him that several regiments of soldiers and cavalry men would be escorting us.

I was setting out from the imperial palace in Delhi to our fort in Lahore to visit Dilras. Ever since Aurangzeb had gone to Kandahar, Dilras had essentially lived alone in the fort with just her children. As both an older sister and the Queen, I wanted to see for myself whether they were safe and being well cared for.

Arzani and Hamida were both Salatins, descendants of previous Mughal kings whose lineage hadn't been fortunate enough to lead towards the throne. They were my cousins, some twice removed, others thrice, but to whom Aba and other members of my immediate family paid virtually no attention.

Once many years ago I accidentally found myself at the rear of the Agra palace, the home of the Salatins. The doors opened just for a few moments, and out poured a stench of disease, poverty and death. Here were the unfortunate descendants of legendary rulers like Babur and Akbar made to live in penury. They couldn't leave because the royals feared they might challenge the sitting monarch for the throne one day, yet they couldn't live in dignity either, and their allowances were scant in relation to the princes'.

I determined when I constructed the Red Fort at Delhi to create a small quarter for the widows and dependents of former emperors. Though not all the Salatins would live here, I could at least assure that widows and children of former emperors were well cared for there.

Hamida and I had the same great-grandfather, the legendary Akbar. My grandfather, Emperor Jehangir, and her grandfather, Prince Daniyal, were brothers. Though my grandfather had been anointed king, Prince Daniyal remained in the Red Fort with his son, Prince Hoshang. When Aba's men massacred Shahriar and his other relatives to gain the throne of India, one of the casualties was Prince Hoshang, who had also been a contender for it.

I still felt traumatised every time I thought of how these innocent uncles and cousins of mine, some not even teenagers, had been killed execution-style by Aba's orders.

When I began my quest to improve the lives of Salatins, I met Hamida, the only surviving kin of the deceased Prince Hoshang. I immediately took a liking to her. She had Aba's nose and eyes, and I could see similarities to my own in her mannerisms and expressions. Always a sweet girl, she simply looked to me as an older sister and always did whatever I asked of her.

"What's there in Lahore, Empress?" she asked, widening her inquisitive, innocent eyes.

I just stared at her smiling as we sat in the canopy atop the elephant. She reminded me of myself when I was just a young girl travelling to Agra for the first time with Sati and Raushanara. She had the same innocence, playfulness and candor; in her I was seeing my own youth.

I said, "We're visiting Princess Dilras. You'll love her; she's the sweetest person you'll ever meet."

"Not sweeter than you," blushed Arzani. Arzani was just a few years older than Hamida, 26 to Hamida's 21; but for me, now pushing 35, they both seemed like children. Oddly, as I regarded the two of them giggling and staring out of the canopy they'd never had had the pleasure to sit in before, I felt slightly jealous of them. In their limited world, a simple thing like a trip to another city was the event of a lifetime. Their existences had largely involved just tending to themselves. Mine had been for others ever since I entered Agra many years ago, and though people told me I looked young for my age, I already felt like an old woman.

"Will we visit Ami's tomb, Empress?" asked Arzani. She, also a Salatin, was related to me two ways. She was the lone child of Prince Shahriar and Princess Ladli, daughter of Nur Jahan. I was her second cousin through my mother and a first cousin through my Aba. She'd been brought to Agra by the wishes of her mother, Princess Ladli, shortly before she died.

My heart ached for Ladli, a beautiful human being who it seemed to me had been an innocent caught up in this bloodthirsty war for power and titles. She was nothing like Nur Jahan; she was simple, quiet and genuine, much like my Ami had been. I never saw the resemblance between Nur Jahan and Ami, but I could see how Ladli and Ami were related. Though both had wanted to marry Aba at one point, only Ami succeeded in winning his love, and the result was this: Ami is immortalised in the Taj Mahal while Ladli shares a tomb with Nur Jahan in Lahore. As Ami's daughter, I sit as the Queen of India, while Ladli's daughter lived in abject poverty as a Salatin until I rescued her.

The two girls played with each other, clapping hands together while reciting some rhyme. They commented on each other's new clothes, both given them by me so they would look like the princesses they still were. I rested my head back on my pillow and closed my eyes. As the girls' loud bursts of laughter now and then interrupted my tranquility I thought to myself: *Now I know what Sati must've felt all those years.*

I tried to fall asleep. My dreams were now my sustenance, and in their company I hoped to spend the remainder of my life. My mind slowly drifted to Gabriel. The pain of knowing I would never have him and always be alone humbled me. At once I felt like a beggar, yet I knew that unlike a beggar, I couldn't even ask for mercy or charity. I couldn't rise before dawn like other beggars and stand below the Jharoka-i-darshan and plead my case to the Emperor. When the wazir lowered the chain of justice from the jharoka, I couldn't send a petition. I couldn't ring the bell and scream, "Justice, justice, justice!" and expect to be taken seriously.

We arrived at the Lahore fort a few days later, having taken our tents to rest overnight at stops so the journey wasn't too taxing on anyone. Dilras had the fort glittering with decoration in anticipation of our arrival.

Arzani cried, "Wow!! This fort looks just like the one in Agra, but in white!"

I just stayed under the covered canopy, grinning. Many years ago, I, too, had been eager to see what lay outside my velvety prison, but I'd learned since. I was now the queen and I had to set an example for these two girls.

Poking her head outside the canopy, Hamida asked me again, "Why don't you live here, Empress?" Meanwhile, Arzani remained dazed by the image of the Lahore fort.

I said, "Because Lahore is too far west to govern from, my darlings. The King wanted a more central location."

The two girls shrugged at my explanation, almost as if my answer didn't matter to them. Their question, it seemed, was just meant to impress on me how much in awe they were of this site.

Dilras was waiting for us in the zenana quarters, her face veiled (just as Aurangzeb would've wanted), her daughters by her side. I introduced Arzani and Hamida to Dilras, and she held their heads with her hands and kissed each on her forehead.

Then she asked, "How was the journey for you, Your Highness?

I looked over at my two Salatin cousins, almost motioning them to answer in my place, still drowsy from my limited sleep in the presence of their incessant giggling. "Our trip went well, Dilras. So tell me: how have you and the children been since my brother left for Kandahar?"

214 * Mistress of the Throne

"Well! We go to pray in the Pearl Mosque five times a day, and we observe every tradition our lord has given us."

I knew this *lord*, my brother Aurangzeb, was very vindictive when it came to his family. He would leave strict instructions on how the women were to behave in his absence, and his spies watched over them, to inform him of any deviation on his return.

We spent the night in the zenana quarters, and for once Arzani and Hamida tasted what life inside the Mughal zenana was truly like. Dilras was gracious enough to give me the largest quarter. As I'd expected since arriving in Lahore, Zeb-un-nissa paid me an unexpected visit.

Looking anxious, she said, "Aba has banned any writing or music, Your Majesty," almost as if wanting me to overturn her father's orders in one swoop. "He told us we can't compose one verse even, and that to praise the beauty of any entity, even a flower, is anti-Islamic!"

I wanted to hear out this child, whose outlook on life had always been very similar to my own.

She confided: "I compose short verses of poetry and have formed my own little club in the zenana that no one knows about. We call ourselves *Makhfi*, the hidden ones."

I smiled and commended this child's cleverness at outwitting her father, but I also worried. "You mustn't cross your father, my child. Not only is it wrong, if he finds out, his temper has no limits, especially for women."

"I know, Your Majesty. I'm reminded of his temper every day when he's here. It's so suffocating. It's as if we're all truly in prison when he's here."

Zeb-un-nissa told me how Aurangzeb had spoken to Dilras before leaving for Kandahar. He'd ordered all the women to stay in the zenana at all times and observe the strictest of Islamic laws, including covering one's face and praying five times a day.

"If this zenana is any indication of what all of India will look like if my father becomes king, I fear for our country, Your Highness," cried Zeb-un-nissa, and tears began to roll down her cheeks. I remained composed on my divan, unmoved by what I'd just heard. By now, I was immune to hearing narrow-minded comments by my intolerant brother. Mostly when someone mentioned him, it was to complain of abuse he'd inflicted on someone else.

I said, "That won't happen, my child. Dara will be the next king, and he'll never let these practices stand."

I hugged my niece, bid her farewell and blew out the candles that had been lighting my room. After several days, I would finally sleep undisturbed.

I left Lahore a few days later, minus one companion: Arzani. She wished to live out her days near the tomb of her mother and grandmother, and it seemed appropriate to me that she do so. Agra and Delhi comprised the seat of Mughal power, and fraternal conflict would occur there. I wanted Arzani to remain far from all that. This poor child had already suffered enough.

***

Years had gone by since Murad's tragic loss of Kandahar, yet Aba drew now on the promise that his other son, his 'white serpent' who was now suddenly his hero, would win the prize back for us. But that hope had evaporated a few months ago when our counter-attack led by Aurangzeb had met a devastating defeat.

"I told you he was useless!" Aba stared at me, blood in his eyes. "He can't do anything right!"

As he walked away waving his hands in anger and frustration, I interjected, "He's the one who brought our troops home from the ill-advised Balkh misadventure!"

I was sure to use the word 'fiasco;' I didn't want Aba to forget his role in it.

"Who cares about Balkh! You can't feed even a small regiment with the riches from Balkh! It was Kandahar I wanted!"

Losing wasn't ever easy for Aurangzeb, especially when the battle involved physical strength. I could only imagine how personally defeated he must have felt. To learn what had happened in the past few fateful years, I summoned one of Aurangzeb's generals, Gulrukh Khan, to my chambers.

"Greetings, Your Highness," the General said.

I accepted his salutation and asked him how close he'd been to Aurangzeb during the conquest of Kandahar.

"I had the pleasure of serving directly under the Prince, Your Majesty."

"So I can trust your every fact, Gulrukh."

"Where you suspect inaccuracy, I ask you tell me and I'll clarify further."

"Will you embellish things to make my brother seem better than he is?"

"No, Your Majesty. I serve you and the King. Though I consider the Prince my commander, I owe my loyalty to you."

From this strong yet gentle man, I slowly learned first-hand what had happened in Kandahar.

❈ ❈ ❈

It took Aurangzeb three years to prepare a counterattack on Kandahar, searching for the right opportunity of vulnerability to do so. The Persian King had become ill, and during this time his forces were thought to have been working in a disjointed manner, each jockeying for greater power with the next monarch, should the present King's sickness lead to death. This was prime time for an attack, so with two crore rupees and 60,000 men, Aurangzeb again headed for Kandahar.

Aurangzeb commanded Gulrukh Khan to attack the Kandahar fort from the rear, making the Persians think the entire Mughal army was planning a rear attack on the fort. The plan was that while the Persians would engage our army in a rear assault, Aurangzeb would launch our cannons from the front!

Gulrukh Khan looked carefully at Aurangzeb's plans and found them elaborate and well thought out as if they'd been architectural blueprints for a building.

"Take 50,000 men in your assault," added Aurangzeb with urgency and conviction. "The Persians need to believe that the entire Mughal army is with you."

"Sire," interrupted Gulrukh, "are you sure 10,000 is all you'll need for the cannons? What if they open the gates and charge you?"

"I don't think they will," replied Aurangzeb. "You'll have to convince them with your strength that you're all we have here so they'll focus all their energies in your direction."

Aurangzeb's plan looked like it might just work. Gulrukh Khan marched towards the rear of the fort, causing the Persians to open the draw bridge and charge the Mughal army in arm-to-arm combat. When Aurangzeb felt the Persians were sufficiently bogged down with Gulrukh's regiment, he ordered cannon firing from the front.

The walls of the fort began to crumble. For a moment, it seemed victory was at hand, but then the drawbridge opened, and 40,000 armed Persians rushed Aurangzeb's contingent. It seemed he'd acted too soon; the Persians hadn't turned their eyes completely to their rear. Then men stationed to defend from the rear were rerouted to the front, and Aurangzeb's cannons weren't able to mount a lasting defence.

Aurangzeb fired cannons into the densest areas of the Persian army, but large smoke clouds impeded his vision after each impact. When the smoke cleared the Persians simply reorganised and released more men. Aurangzeb ordered more cannons fired, and men hastily loading them. More blasts went off and more Persians died, but to no avail. Eventually, Aurangzeb ordered his men to retreat. He'd lost yet again.

In the days to follow, Aurangzeb tried his best to salvage the report of the Kandahar blunder, but for all his boasts of being a military genius, he'd lost the most prized city in the region to his biggest foe, the Persians. To make matters worse, he'd waited three years and spent two crore rupees and 60,000 men, more than half now either dead or permanently injured.

When Aba heard of this devastating loss, he minced no words in a letter, commanding Aurangzeb to withdraw from Kandahar.

Dear Aurangzeb,

I hereby order you to leave not just Kandahar, but all of the northwest. It seems your glory lay in areas like the Deccan, so I am reappointing you Governor of the Deccan. Go there, destroy the temples and burn the churches. It seems your greatest strength shows itself when you attack the unarmed and helpless. On a battlefield with armed enemies, your talents are useless.

Every man can perform some work well, Aurangzeb, but had I considered you competent to take over Kandahar I'd not have recalled your entire army last week as I did. Men of experience need no instruction. You wasted two crore rupees on your misadventure, and in answer to your complaints that the Taj Mahal has leaky ceilings, had we spent that money on those leaks, we'd have been better served. Now do your father and your nation a favour and leave for the Deccan immediately.

Yours,
Aba

Aba's sarcasm in this sharply word attack was evident. I implored Aba to show some restraint, especially considering his success in Central Asia, but Aba took his anger at losing Kandahar out on his son. Aurangzeb begged Aba in subsequent letters not to send him to the Deccan, even offering to accept a subordinate position in the next assault, give him any opportunity to redeem himself, but it was too late; Aba wouldn't relent.

✷ ✷ ✷

Gauhara was now being attended to by the hakims. She'd attempted suicide a week before by drinking a potion she'd convinced one of the hakims to make for use on a prisoner. The hakim wondered why a princess like Gauhara would care to poison a prisoner, but didn't refuse her because she was royalty. Instead, he merely followed her and kept careful watch. After she mixed the potion in milk and began drinking it, he quickly ran to her and forced her to vomit it up.

The matter was brought to my attention before Aba's, and I chose to deal with it directly rather than let it escalate. Aba's justice often involved crushing someone's head under an elephant or something equally heinous. If Imtiaz had broken my sister's heart, though shameless, he was still a human being, undeserving of death for disloyalty to her.

Yet again I visited Gauhara in her palace. This time she was lying almost lifeless on her bed, looking skeletal, little different from the starving souls I saw many years ago when I went with Ami to the Deccan and witnessed the famine in Gujarat.

Gauhara was looking away, but I could tell she knew I'd entered. I sat on her divan and waited there for her to make some movement.

"Why are you here, Jahanara?" she said hoarsely. She didn't look at me, instead choosing to stare in the opposite direction.

I paused for a moment, then said softly, "I wanted to make sure you're well, sister?" Would she blow me off again? I really hoped she wouldn't. Gauhara continued to look away, but now fiddled with the curtain behind her bed.

At last she turned her head my way. I tried looking to her non-judgmentally. I smiled; I needed to comfort her. This was my Ami's only child who'd never had any direct interaction with her, never heard her voice, never felt her warmth. Was it just a coincidence that she'd been the only one who'd tried to hurt herself?

She said, "Why are you *really* here? Shouldn't you be in the Diwan-i-am, attending to the matters of state?"

We conversed in vagaries for awhile, but Gauhara eventually told me what was in her heart.

Raushanara intercepted Imtiaz's letter to Gauhara and sent three soldiers to capture him before he reached Delhi. The soldiers shot an arrow aimed at his left chest, but it pierced his left shoulder instead, forcing him off his horse to lie face down on the ground in agony.

The soldiers galloped towards their fallen prey and began to kick him incessantly, and he cried out for help. But no help would arrive.

One of the soldiers then grabbed a rope out of the bag fastened to his horse and tied Imtiaz's hands with it. He tried to break free, but was too wounded by the arrow still lodged in his shoulder as blood poured from the wound and his mouth.

Another soldier threw the other end of the rope over a tree branch and signalled to the third, who was standing on the opposite side, to hoist the ill-fated Imtiaz up several feet into midair, where he kicked his legs in mid-air desperately trying to free himself.

Meanwhile, Raushanara had invited Gauhara out on a hunting expedition. Feeling guilty for revealing to me Raushanara's escapades, Gauhara accepted the invitation, hoping perhaps to mend ties with her sister. Together they hunted deer, rabbits and boars. Raushanara then motioned for Gauhara to break with the hunting expedition and travel with her to 'a very special hunt.' The two galloped over fields and woods, eventually coming to a shallow cliff, which overlooked a lush, open meadow with a few beautiful trees.

Gauhara admired the view, which looked less like a work of nature and more like a Mughal garden. She said, "Why did you bring me here, Raushanara. I mean... it's beautiful, but why here... now?"

Raushanara smiled, her voice betraying a sense of victory. This was probably the moment she'd been waiting for. "There's still a hunt to be done, sister."

Gauhara looked puzzled.

"Look, over there," insisted Raushanara. "That looks like a good hunt!"

Gauhara squinted, and in the distance she saw Imtiaz dangling from a tree in agony, soldiers placing wood on the ground several feet under him.

"It's a party, sister!" Raushanara cried, raising her arms triumphantly. "There's a fire, some game, and plenty of targets for both of us!"

Gauhara gaped in disbelief. So this was why Imtiaz hadn't contacted her sooner! She'd assumed he'd been delayed on his journey; now she saw him screaming in agony. She begged, "Raushanara, please don't do this! I'll do anything you ask. I'll give you all my riches, I'll be your spy, I'll do your bidding. Just don't hurt Imtiaz, I beg of you, sister."

"Didn't you hurt *my* lovers, sister?" Raushanara snarled. "My own lovers were boiled and then fed to the dogs before my eyes! I couldn't even bury them according to Muslim rites!"

"But I never meant for that to happen! What I shared was misused..."

"What you shared!" Raushanara reminded Gauhara that her words had initiated the cascade of events that led to Raushanara's downfall. Gauhara began to weep and cry out her lover's name in anguish, though she knew he probably couldn't hear her.

Slowly she watched as the soldiers lit a fire on the pile of wood on the ground under Imtiaz's feet. The smoke rose, and gauged the fire's intensity by Imtiaz's cries. "Please, Raushanara, I beg you to stop this! I'll do anything! I'll leave the kingdom! I'll support your claim as empress!!"

Raushanara suddenly looked at Gauhara. Gauhara had hit a nerve, but would it work in her favour? "You'd support me as empress? What makes you think, you wretch, that I need your support to be the empress?"

Gauhara was speechless. Raushanara clearly wasn't interested in reconciliation with her sister. She ignored Gauhara's pleas and went on watching her victim being roasted.

Imtiaz's cries grew louder, it became apparent that he was now on fire, and both sisters inhaled the odour of burning flesh.

"You made me watch my lovers die. Now you'll watch yours die!"

Gauhara wept in unspeakable pain. Then she grabbed hold of her rifle and loaded it. Raushanara seized her own rifle, probably knowing she was a better shooter than Gauhara if it came to that. But rather than turn the gun on her sister, Gauhara aimed at the tree

Imtiaz was hanging from. She knew he was going to die; he'd been severely burned, his body was now blackened, and his cries issued faintly; still she couldn't bear the thought of him suffering anymore. She aimed her gun at his chest and shot, murmuring, "Forgive me, my love."

Shot in the heart, Imtiaz died instantly she said; Gauhara pierced the very heart she'd known belonged to her. As Gauhara watched her lover die, Raushanara broke into laughter. Eventually, the two returned to the hunting party, neither saying a word of where they'd been.

22

MYSTIC SOLDIER

4ᵗʰ December, 1652

Ireceived Aurangzeb's letter through a runner from Lahore, an uncommon location from which I might receive communications during the past several years:

Esteemed Empress,

I trust this letter finds you in good health and spirits. As you may have heard already, we have lost Kandahar to the Persians and everyone is blaming me. I am not in your presence to protect my name in your eyes, so I write this letter to uncover the veil of my ill wishers' lies and convey to you the truth of the matter. The King himself told me three years ago to travel to Kandahar with only a reinforcement regiment. Upon arriving there, I learned that our countrymen in Kandahar were grossly unprepared for war with the Persians; thus my reinforcement regiment was completely inadequate.

I then asked His Majesty to allow me to organise a counterattack on my own timing, on my own terms. He graciously agreed to this, but when we attacked three years later, the Persians exceeded my expectations and repelled our forces successfully. I have asked His Majesty to give me another chance, even if just as a subordinate, to win back this strategic location for us, but instead he has chosen to send me to the Deccan, telling me he has no confidence in my abilities and calling me incompetent.

My dear Empress, can the blame for Kandahar be solely laid on my door, when in fact the fort first fell not under my watch, but under that of His Majesty's former appointee, Murad? Can I be blamed for a failed counter-siege three years ago when in fact I was told to not go with more than a reinforcement regiment and upon my arrival, the reinforcement regiment proved to be inadequate?

We have lost Kandahar three times in as many years, and yet my folly is to blame for perhaps just one of these losses. Yet I am the sole bearer of the brunt of his Majesty's wrath, now sent to the Deccan against my wishes, told I am unfit for military endeavours and therefore undeserving of another chance. I ask you, sister: which of your brothers has more military acumen than I? Who among this generation of Mughals has consistently upheld our honour more than I? I ask for your help, to prevent this injustice from occurring and allow me to restore my honour and dignity in His Majesty's eyes.

> Your loving brother,
> Aurangzeb

I ran to Aba in the Rang Mahal, where he was enjoying light music and a dancing girl. I understood Aurangzeb's frustration and knew my father's unapologetic treatment of Aurangzeb over Kandahar was yet another manifestation of his bias against the young Prince. Yet, rather than discuss Aurangzeb, I chose to handle this situation by discussing the prince the Emperor was always fond of discussing: Dara.

I said, "Kandahar cannot be allowed to remain in Persian hands, Aba!"

Aba clapped his hands twice, gesturing for the dancing girl to leave the Rang Mahal and allow us privacy.

I continued: "It's a strategic location, and we've controlled it for generations. We need to recapture it."

"But we've already wasted so much money and manpower. Aurangzeb…"

"…Forget about Aurangzeb," I interrupted. "Let's talk about Dara. He's the heir apparent. He'll be king one day. Why not let *him* soil his hands on the battlefield."

So I was pushing for Dara to go to Kandahar. It was only fair – if Aurangzeb and Dara each considered themselves worthy of being king, then both should have a chance to fight the same enemy and be compared on equal terms.

Aba lowered his brow, appearing irritated. Finally he said, "Your brother Dara…"

"…Is ready for the task," I once again interrupted. I didn't want to let this opportunity pass. Aurangzeb would continue to feel unfairly judged by his own father if Dara remain the heir apparent while staying idle, though he and his other brothers were made to put their lives on the line defending the empire. "I think you should convene an assembly at the Diwan-i-khas and command Prince Dara to assume the task."

Aba stared straight ahead, unable to find reason to refuse my adamant request. He convened an assembly the following day.

Dressed in a royal blue robe and his jewelled turban, Aba looked down upon his assembly of royalty and nobles. As always, the nobles were arranged according to rank on the richly decorated Persian carpet of the hall. Standing on either side were Uzbek bodyguards, while Dara stood at the King's side next to the Peacock Throne as always, while I watched the proceedings from behind the marble screen.

"As many of you know," Aba began, "the Persians have illegally taken Kandahar from us. But as always, Allah is on our side."

The nobles anxiously awaited the Emperor's announcement of his next move.

"Prince Dara, I think *you* should now command our forces to free our Kandahar fort of Persian dominance once and for all."

Dara looked startled; the battlefield had never been his forte; war was for his childish, immature brothers, not for him. Yet, he couldn't disobey the Emperor in front of everyone, so he bowed his head to accept the command.

The nobles looked at one another, probably wondering if the King had lost his mind. Send a mystic to do a military man's work? Aba hadn't consulted any of his advisors prior to making the announcement; he'd (perhaps rightly) feared they'd try to talk him out of it.

Then a voice began chanting loudly, followed by more voices joining the chorus: "All hail Prince Dara Shikoh! All Hail!" The nobles then reluctantly joined in, not wishing, of course that their silence be considered disrespect to the King. Dara smiled to acknowledge the applause, and the Emperor forced his own smile onto his aging face. Then, while all eyes were still on the Prince, Aba gently moved his head towards the marble screen and where he knew I'd be standing, as though hoping his eyes would make contact with mine, and my eyes would give him confidence that this mystic Prince would be just as triumphant on the battlefield as he'd been in his other endeavours.

❋ ❋ ❋

Aurangzeb moved to the Deccan immediately after receiving instructions from Aba, devastated at being treated like a failure. So much time and energy planning and working for victory, first in Balkhh and then in Kandahar had all proved futile. Dara was still the heir apparent; Aurangzeb the forbidden leper. With Dilras and his children, he began the journey back to the Deccan.

The Deccan was essentially the southern peninsula of the India subcontinent. The Mughal Empire never really spread far into the Deccan, though it had been in our sights for nearly a century. Akbar's efficient revenue system from the peasantry thus never found a home in the Deccan because we lacked proper authority there. The peasants of the region continued to be overtaxed and burdened as different armies fought over and conquered the land. This, along with the wars from local tribes and the two other large kingdoms in the Deccan, Golconda and Bijapur, had caused many farmers to flee the region, and their cultivated land to degenerate into jungles. This was the legacy of the Deccan: a warring, unlivable, wasteland where our family never found peace, but instead a graveyard for some of its most cherished members.

I always wondered if anyone ever went to the Deccan willingly. It seemed the Deccan was always associated with tragedy. In this land my uncle Khusrau had been killed creating a deep divide between Aba and his father. When Aba was exiled by his father and Nur Jahan, it was the Deccan they sent him to, and this is where my generation spent the better part of our childhood until our father became king. Then the Deccan again came into the limelight three years later, when Khan Jahan Lodi rebelled against the Mughals, sending my parents to this jinxed land to wage war. There my mother died and was buried. Going to the Deccan was like telling one of us to pitch a tent by our mother's grave and be content with living in the cemetery.

I had a strangely vivid dream one night when Aurangzeb was travelling with his wife and children through this cursed land. Unlike my other dreams, which frequently had no meaning or were so strange and mystical I couldn't help but believe they were a product of my over-active imagination, this dream was more realistic. It was as if I'd been transported to the Deccan and was staring at this scene from many different angles, watching and observing everyone's expressions and movements.

The dream started with the royal caravan travelling through the Deccan's rugged terrain:

Aurangzeb asks the procession to travel to Burhampur before moving on to Daulatabad, the city Aba commanded Aurangzeb to live in. But rather than move towards the main fort of Burhampur, Aurangzeb directs the caravan to the Zainabadi garden, where Ami was initially buried many years ago.

Though her remains are no longer in that spot, the location is still treated like sacred ground, with a small, humble, makeshift memorial made by the locals in its place. To Aurangzeb, this may very well be the only memorial she needed and deserved – a humble, heartfelt, simple structure built with well wishes from the heart, not by gaudy riches from the world. This was Aurangzeb's Taj Mahal.

He has the caravan wait outside the garden while he and his family pay their respects to the site. Each in his own way comes forward, Dilras Banu tearing as she pays her respects to the mother-in-law she never knew. Of his daughters, the two oldest follow their mother's lead, each wishing that perhaps if only for a moment they might see and experience the grandmother that won the hearts of everyone they knew, even their seemingly cold-hearted father's.

Aurangzeb waits till after all his children and wives have finished, and then asks them to return to the caravan so he may have some time alone. As the royal family mounts atop their respective elephants, Aurangzeb looks again at Ami's grave, without a single tear in his eyes.

He bows his head before Ami and begins speaking to her, as if her remains are still there and her soul isn't in paradise as all claim, but rather here in this modest memorial.

"Ami, it's been so long since you left me, yet I feel as if it was just yesterday you were wiping my wounds and giving me the hairs of the prophet. I still have them, Ami. I've carried them with me in all my military campaigns, and I still have them with me now. I don't know why, really. I tell people because they're the hairs of the Holy Prophet; but to be honest, it's also because they're the only thing you ever gave me. You left me, Ami, but I never left you.

"I've tried so hard to win Aba's love, hoping he would give me the love you once did, that through him I would maybe feel your presence in our midst, but I've failed. He hates me; he blames me for all of his problems. I honestly think he wishes I were dead. When I'm completely helpless, I go to Jahanara seeking some support, but what can she do? She, with time, is becoming blinded with talks of rogue mixtures of cultures and is giving into her physical instincts and committing lewd acts that would devastate you if you were alive."

Rumours of me having an affair with Aba had indeed reached epic proportions, but what was I to do? Was I supposed to leave Delhi and Aba just to quell the dirty mouths of gossipy nobles? Almost everyone except Raushanara had no direct knowledge of a possible relationship, but as the rumours began to spread, the story began to change, and now even certain nobles were openly saying they'd watched Aba and me in compromising positions (though this was clearly at odds with the truth). But the vision proceeded, and Aurangzeb now said to the dream-Ami:

"I have no complaints from her, personally, Ami, but she's not you. She can't take your place, and her love can't substitute for Aba's. I'm here now, with you, in the Deccan, this destitute land of tragedy. I won't ever leave, because no one but you wants me. Perhaps this is why Allah brought me here, because this is where you'll forever be. Please guide me and give me the wisdom I need, Ami. Craving for your love and nurturing has long since passed; now just your guidance and wisdom will do."

Aurangzeb breathes deeply and releases a long sigh, as if a tremendous burden has been lifted from his shoulder. Though Raushanara is with him in this caravan, accompanying him to the Deccan, she never dismounts from her palanquin to pay her respects. Unlike Aurangzeb, she never felt she was loved by Ami, though Ami often tried to treat her well. She feels more alienated than even Aurangzeb, and if Aurangzeb vents his frustrations by destroying non-Islamic monuments, she releases it in her infamous orgies, which she continues to hide from our brother.

Aurangzeb rises and continues to the cramped fort of Daulatabad. There he speaks to his father-in-law, Shahnawaz Khan, who accompanies him to the Deccan. They discuss the conditions in which he is living.

"No marbles here, Mirza Khan," he claims. "No Paradise Canals, no gardens, just stones."

The two men continue to look around the stone hall as the workers unload the royal family's belongings.

"Your Majesty," says Shahnawaz Khan, his back arched against the wall as he sits in front of the Prince, "you must make the Deccan yours. Why are you staying here? Go to Fatehpur, where you were happy and safe, and at peace. Make that your home."

"Not a bad idea," says the Prince. "I mean, everyone's building cities today, why not me? If I have to live in this God-forsaken town, I need to make it feel like home."

"And name it after yourself!" says the aging Shahnawaz.

"Aurangzabad?" asks Aurangzeb.

"Remove the 'z', or else no one will pronounce it right," replies Shahnawaz. "Aurangabad."

"Aurangabad," says Aurangzeb, smiling as if content. "All right then, that shall be its new name, Inshallah.*"*

There my dream ended. The next day I received information from our sources in the Deccan that indeed Aurangzeb had travelled through Burhampur to Daulatabad and then eventually to the city of Fatehpur. As rumours claimed, many years ago, he saw a 6th century Hindu temple on a hill where temple prostitutes practiced sacred prostitution. Aurangzeb demolished it and used the stones from the temple as a staircase for a new mosque to be constructed on the plot. When a local Hindu priest protested the acts, he had him beheaded and then directed the prime minister of the region to keep quiet about the matter and not let it reach the ears of the King. Unfortunately, in our kingdom everything existed in abundance except loyalty and trust. News of the incident eventually made its way to Agra, and while it was unclear whether the Prime Minister had leaked it, he bore the brunt of Aurangzeb's rage, and was skinned alive.

I was at once shocked and frightened to learn of the similarities between my dream and the reality as it being told to me. I immediately went to Mullah Badakshi to ask him if he had any insight into what was happening to me.

"Ah, this is due to the grace of Mian Mir!" Badakshi stretched his arms out and looked upward as if waiting for a sign.

"What does Mian Mir have to do with this?"

Badakshi put his hand on my shoulder, making me somewhat nervous. "He protects us, my child. His followers always find miracles occurring in their lives once they begin to embrace the Qadiriya order."

I had heard of miracles of the order before, ranging from sudden cures of fatal diseases, to revelations that changed people's outlooks. I'd often treated such thoughts with scepticism, but I hesitated to do so this time.

"Perhaps Mian Mir is giving you the help you need to prevent conflicts in your kingdom. He's giving you sight and visions of events occurring thousands of kos away, perhaps in hope that you'll use this information wisely."

Badakshi took me to the river and asked me to hold his hands as we walked into the river. When the water reached to my breasts, we stopped. He said, "Close your eyes and meditate with me here."

I followed his command, slightly shivering in the cold water. He then put his hands on my forehead and then moved them to his own forehead, while instructing me to keep meditating.

The he said, "Open your eyes and look there." He pointed to the river. I followed his every command, somehow confident that he wouldn't mislead me. As I looked into the river, I saw not the reflection of the sun or the trees above, but instead Aurangzeb standing in the middle of a city I imagined must be his new Aurangabad. He was ordering people to harvest water and build tanks. He seemed like a man on a mission, fully in control of his destiny. Shahnawaz stood next to him, presumably assisting him in any matter he desired.

Badakshi said, "If you focus closely, you may be able to hear what they're saying."

I did exactly as I was told, confident that this man had special powers he was now giving me. I focused as hard as I could, hoping to hear any voices.

"Do you hear them?"

"No."

"Try harder."

I continued to focus, but to no avail. "I can't hear a thing!"

Badakshi smiled and put his hand on my back. "That's fine. You can't pick it up all at once. But at least now you know that Mian Mir is with you. Whenever you're curious about what's happening, come here and do as I showed you."

I nodded and retreated discreetly back to the fort. The people mustn't see their Queen wearing wet clothes.

23

AURANGZEB'S TAJ

26th December, 1653

"Chicken has been prepared in ten different ways as you requested, Your Majesty."

Zafar Khan had gentle but strong hands, making him a profoundly gifted head cook for the zenana.

"And lamb?" I reminded him. "The Emperor enjoys rogan josh with raisins."

Zafar Khan nodded, as though expecting the question. "It's been simmering since this morning, and I'll finish it myself."

I knew Aba wouldn't attend, but all zenana parties were arranged with the expectation that the Emperor would visit. He was the guest of honour even when he didn't show up.

Light sitar music played in the background as the evening festivities began.

Perfumed scents permeated the room as Persian carpets were laid around the floor. Giant flasks of wine were brought in to commemorate the first major party of the zenana in the new capital. Most of the women in this zenana were new additions brought in by Aba. The few exceptions included me, Gauhara and Henna Begum.

A certain concubine who'd been inciting Henna to perform her usual mocking skits of the royal household couldn't herself have been older than 16, but was already known for her bold personality. She teased, "We've all heard stories of your tamashas, Henna Begum."

234 ☸ Mistress of the Throne

Henna chuckled. "You'll need a little more opium and another few gulps of wine to get Henna to do a tamasha for you young birds." Usually when Henna spoke in the third person, it meant she'd already had too much opium and wine.

But soon her skit began. She tied a stick around her waist as though it was a dagger and put kajal around her face to mimic a beard. She then sat on the divan, and a eunuch sat next to her as if ready to play a role in the skit.

The eunuch began it: "Oh, Dara Shikoh, what command say you? You have been entrusted to win Kandahar from the Persians."

Henna put her hand to her forehead. "I, Dara Shikoh, command you to find me a sufi who will put a curse on the water the Persians drink the morning of the battle!"

The crowd erupted in laughter, and my heart sank. Dara had left for Lahore immediately after being commanded to do so by Aba. For some reason that continues to baffle me to this day, he opted to take two Sufi mystics to Lahore with him. Apparently during their journey to Lahore they'd prophesied what the fate of their enemy would be.

Egging the skit on, the eunuch intoned: "As I close my eyes, Your Majesty, I can see the King of Persia dead. I'm actually watching the Persians carry their king's coffin to the ground." The laughter increased. "Don't disturb me... I want to see them inter the body completely!"

Apparently Dara believed all this nonsense, even in the absence of any solid evidence: The King of Persia was alive, well and ready for any rematch with the Mughals forces. Though the Sufis had given Dara much in his life, insight into the enemy's weaknesses would not add to these riches.

Then Henna piped in: "Gentlemen, when I close my eyes, I see Mian Mir sitting on the throne of paradise, telling me that I will be in Kandahar only seven days." Soldiers present at this journey had returned from Kandahar and visited their mistresses in the zenana, giving the ladies ample material for mocking.

Henna then placed some of the empty gold vases in her chunni and wrapped it so it looked like a sack of riches. "I am hereby leaving for Kandahar with the riches of the kingdom." Dara left Lahore on 11ᵗʰ February, 1653, the date his astrologers picked as being the most auspicious for the journey. Aba – informed by Dara's runner of this date – sent riches from Delhi to accompany him, including jewels, ammunition, elephants, horses and over one crore rupees in gold for his military treasury. Aba gave Dara 70,000 men for this campaign, 20,000 more than he'd given Aurangzeb. Dara arrived at the outskirts of Kandahar two days later and set up the imperial camp.

Another eunuch playing a part in the skit shouted, "Shall I mount the cavalry across the battlefield?

"No, Jai Singh!" yelled Henna. Among the commanders in Dara's army was the legendary Hindu raja Jai Singh, head of the Rajput state that bore his name, Jaipur. A strong military man with many skills, he soon felt dismayed by the Prince's lack of understanding of military matters. Henna bellowed, "I need neither cannons nor cavalry. Find me an ascetic who'll blow so hard, the Kandahar fort will fall down!"

The women all laughed, and Henna mocked on: "He must spit so hard, the fort walls will crumble under his force." Now the women were falling over one another with amusement. It was well known that day after day, Dara would invite and entertain gurus and ascetics from the region, some self-proclaimed hypnotists, others magicians, each claiming to have powers to win the battle without firing a single shot – in return for enough money.

"Find me the ascetic who with his piss alone will down the Persians!" Henna could hardly contain her own laughter now, as she took a coconut with a hole cut in the middle and held it to her waist, her body turned sideways. "Allow the piss to fall," she cried faux-solemnly, tilting the coconut sideways so its water flowed down like a man's urine.

The night's debauchery ended like a usual zenana party. Aba never visited; I wasn't surprised. I was with Bahadur as the women passed out one by one. "It seems our Dara has become the joke of the kingdom," I said. "Even young concubines are laughing at him. Do you think he actually said such things to Jai Singh and the other commanders?"

Bahadur stopped cleaning my table. "Your Majesty, what was said I don't know, but everyone knows that saints and ascetics flowed all over the camp, each bringing his own disciples, and the Prince was convinced that they possessed supernatural powers and abilities." Bahadur sat sown heavily. "Some were paid 40 rupees and given rations; others were paid in gold, while our army of soldiers watched and waited for Prince Dara to lead them into battle."

I'd heard the stories many times from many people, but had difficulty understanding how Dara could be so myopic in military matters. Days had turned to weeks, and weeks to months, and while the Mughal army played at waiting games for the ascetics to show their miracles, the Persians had begun sending raids in the midst of the night and beheading soldiers in their tents.

I laughed bitterly. "At one point, Jai Singh even warned of mutiny!"

Bahadur nodded. "Yes, I know, Jai Singh and Prince Dara were continuously furious, Jai Singh complaining that the Prince had spent nearly a quarter of the treasury on voodoo, and the military camp had turned into an ascetic's pilgrimage."

Dara ultimately caved in to Jai Singh's demands and stopped the ascetic nonsense. Several more months passed, and at last Dara's army under Jai Singh's command launched an offensive against the Persians in Kandahar that captured smaller surrounding forts around the major fort. On the side of the main fort was a solid granite cliff, over which loomed the citadel that needed to be overtaken.

Jai Singh ordered his men to quarantine the citadel, preventing any goods to flow in or out of the fort, in hopes of starving the enemy.

"Your Majesty, Prince Dara's impatience has been his greatest weakness. He should have listened to Jai Singh when he advised to continue the quarantine." After only a week of the blockade, Dara grew impatient and ordered fire rockets released at the citadel.

I said: "Jai Singh had advised Dara *not* to fire rockets because the fog was too thick, but my ascetic brother was too arrogant."

"Yes, Your Highness. Those whom Allah wishes to destroy he first makes arrogant." The rockets missed their target miserably, only lighting the night sky. The Persians responded with this note to the imperial army.

Our Dearest Young Prince,

Thank you; we've never seen a more brilliant fireworks display!

With Deep Respect,
The Persian Army

This mocking note enraged the usually calm Dara. Wishing to make a direct assault this time, waiting for no cover, Dara demanded his commanders give him ideas about how best to wage such an assault, but none would venture any.

"Do you blame them, Your Majesty?" Bahadur seemed unconventionally open in her criticism of Dara before me. "No commander in the Mughal army had confidence in the Prince. No individual wanted to put his stamp of approval on any of his plans, fearing that a loss would cause the Emperor to lay blame for the failure squarely on their shoulders. The generals were sent by the Kings as chaperones and babysitters rather than subordinates. Any failure of the mission would thus be in their hands; Prince Dara would go unscathed – even by a loss."

The battle dragged on for four hours, and the Mughal army fought with all its might. But lacking a strong commander at the helm, the heterogeneous unit attacked in a disunited way. The Persians, strengthened by their homogenous background and one religion – they were all Muslims – fought as one. The Mughal army retreated in defeat, losing over 1,000 soldiers and another 1,000 wounded.

Dara, wounded along with his men, retreated. To further inflame their passion, the Persians began to play victory music loudly and even had dancing girls come outside in view of the imperial camp. Thus Kandahar was again lost to Mughal India.

Dara had returned earlier this month to Delhi in shame, leading back less than half his army, with the remainder mostly being carried on stretchers or walking with bandages on one or more limbs. Men cried out in great pain as their wounds won the battle over them. Aba heard the sounds of the defeated army from the Rang Mahal and looked out of the window with tears in his eyes. The sight of a suffering Dara was always difficult for Aba to bear. He would banish any failing child – even me perhaps – but couldn't spend a moment without Dara.

I looked out from my apartment that day, too, and saw the army make its way past the Jumna. Much to my dismay, Dara had not succeeded where Aurangzeb failed. Yet, even in loss there was victory, I initially thought. Perhaps after seeing Dara, too, lose this war, Aba would reach out to Aurangzeb and mend fences. He would realise now that this military endeavour was no small task, and that he ought not to blame Aurangzeb for something two other sons, Murad and now Dara, had also failed at. And if the King felt justified in reprimanding Aurangzeb, perhaps he would do the same to Dara, and I'd be able to write Aurangzeb that the King's love was the same for all his children, not partial towards Dara.

We all gathered in the Diwan-i-khas as Dara slowly walked towards the Peacock Throne with his head hanging low.

A voice intoned: "All Hail, Prince Dara Shikoh!"

The Prince walked towards Aba, stood immediately before the throne and performed the necessary salutation. Then he said slowly, "It is with regret, Jahanpanah, that I must report that my army has failed to capture Kandahar from the Persians."

Aba leaned forward sadly, not so much over the loss of Kandahar, but at seeing his son in such a defeated state of mind. He rose from his throne and walked to the Prince, surprising all the nobility in attendance and me as well. Aba then embraced and kissed his son, and said, "You are and always will be the world illuminator, my son! I never cared much for that border town anyway."

Never cared much for that border town? These words kept resonating in my ear, echoing through my head. What had I just seen? Since childhood, I'd witnessed my father's bias towards Dara, but never as profound an instance as this. *He never cared much for that border town?* Why, then, had he banished Aurangzeb to the Deccan and denied him another opportunity to wage battle?

I watched stunned as Dara's frown turned into a jubilant smile and father and son hugged, the crowd hailing Dara's name in the background as if nothing had been lost. What would I write to Aurangzeb? What explanation could I give? Everything he'd said was accurate. Here were father and son rejoicing over a *loss*, while a younger, far less culpable brother lived in virtual exile, governor of a region he didn't even want, like an utter failure?

I won't allow this to go on longer, I thought. *This demands an explanation.* Impulsively I spoke out: "Does Jahanpanah wish all the brothers from the four corners of the empire to return, so the royal family may be reunited after all this time of senseless bloodshed in that arid border town?" I had no idea whether or not this was the right thing to propose, but I wanted to see if my father's anger towards Aurangzeb had perhaps thawed and he might want to see him again.

"No," replied Aba. "They'll remain at their posts. We're fine here" And he kept smiling at his son.

❈ ❈ ❈

My sources were now telling me Aurangzeb was effectively and energetically converting Fatehpur into a major metropolis, making it, in fact, Aurangzeb's 'Taj.' Just as Aba and I had released our emotions building the Taj Mahal and Delhi, it seemed Aurangzeb was releasing his rebuilding Fatehpur, or as he'd renamed it, Aurangabad.

Aurangabad was located northeast of the Portuguese town of Goa. Because it had dry soil and no natural rivers, Aurangzeb created a large water tank four kos in circumference and ran a canal from a nearby village to feed it. Near the tank he built his palace, less impressive than the fort at Delhi, but perfect for the more modest Aurangzeb. He now lived there with his family – and built Raushanara a palace there as well. The Deccan was now looking more like home to him. Far from the Mughal pageantry of Delhi, this city had become elegant yet simple enough to reflect its creator.

24
THE MARATHAS
1st May, 1654

The eunuchs were tittering: "The pearl embroidery will make Prince Sulaiman's eyes glow like a diya on a dark night!" They ran hither and thither, setting one robe after another before me for consideration.

After years of bloodshed, first in Balkh then in Kandahar, the Mughal household was once again abuzz with joy and delight. Dara's oldest son, Sulaiman Shikoh, was to be wed to none other than a Hindu Rajput princess, who was also ironically a niece of Rajah Jai Singh, the ill-fated general Dara had blamed for the loss of Kandahar. Recognising his own myopia in blaming the brave Hindu warrior for the debacle, he'd sought to mend relations by having his son marry the Raja's niece. Yet again, a Hindu bride graced the Mughal household, and Aurangzeb, reeling from the preferential treatment of Dara by their father and also by the mixed marriage between Hindu and Muslim, opted not to attend or send any presents for the affair.

Dara had also made other peaceful gestures to the Rajputs in this time period following the wedding. Soon after his son's wedding, Aba engaged in a border dispute with the Raja of Udaipur. While the mullahs insisted the King attack Udaipur and annex the kingdom, Dara made a surprise visit to the King and mediated with the rajah, ending the conflict with no bloodshed and acceding just a few strips of worthless land to the Mughals.

"The pearls look beautiful, but the King wants emeralds to decorate the turban. Will the pearls match them?"

Bahadur said, "Yes, Your Majesty. Pearls and emeralds were meant to live in harmony, just as man and wife."

The giggling continued as the excitement of the festivities rose. This was the first wedding to take place at our new royal palaces in Delhi. The city was decorated with garlands of jasmine, marigold and paper flags. Royal gardeners had tended the gardens to perfection, trimming the hedges, mowing the lawns and arranging the flower beds.

Women in the zenana competed with one another for resources to beautify themselves; each wore new clothes given to her for this special occasion.

Feeling sensuous from my love of Gabriel, I dared to wear a ghaghara so fine and thin my bosom could be seen through it. For once I didn't care what others might say; I just wore what I felt like wearing. I also wore my mother's pearl necklace she'd received on her wedding day and the matching earrings. For a moment, I felt like I was attending my own wedding.

The festivities were reminiscent of Dara's wedding, which I'd planned myself a generation ago, except that now I felt able to enjoy myself without fear of what others thought. I'd made the ultimate sacrifice for my kingdom, treating the crown as my child, and like other children, it would listen to me and not the other way around. I enjoyed the wine and the opium and allowed the effects to settle into my smile as I greeted visitors.

Aba, Dara and Sulaiman sat across from the Raja Jai Singh as the mullahs read the verse from the Koran. Though she was Hindu, no Hindu ceremony would occur to sanctify the marriage. Rather, the King's religion was to be accepted by all for this occasion. The mullah had both the bride and groom sign the book, and then proclaimed them married.

The remainder of the night, lavish exuberance reverberated through the halls of the zenana. Wines from all over the world were opened and opium was made available for all who desired it. Loud, provocative language and actions were tolerated – and to some extent encouraged – this day, and all who chose to rejoice in any way were given licence to do so.

Later, shortly before day, once the zenana ladies had fallen asleep, I opened my eyes from the make-believe nap I'd been taking. I grabbed a dark towel and folded it in half. It was too thin, so I folded it yet again. Then I placed it around my buttocks and pulled my black pajamas over it to secure it in place. I grabbed then another towel, also dark, folded it only once and placed it around my waist, pulling the front of my pajamas up in order to secure the towel around my stomach.

I turned to my side to see if I looked like a heavy-set, middle aged commoner. Not yet. My breasts were hanging over, not slouching like they would have if I'd truly had a large stomach and a weight problem. I took a piece of dyed silk cloth and cut it in half. I wrapped it tightly around my breasts and then secured it in place with a hair clip. I looked at myself sideways again: flat chest, protruding belly and an overarching behind. This was the look!

I placed a dark black kameez over my torso to cover the artificial curves I'd created. I started chuckling. Most zenana ladies used such techniques to increase their attractiveness, enlarge their breasts and tighten their stomachs. I was doing the reverse.

I then tied my hair up to hide its length, just as I did when I dressed like a boy for Gabe (an odd legacy of my love). Then I wrapped myself in a black robe and slid down the side staircase of the zenana and onto the main street.

Hiding from the few Mughal soldiers combing the streets, I moved from alley to alley, into the outskirts of the town. Soon I was standing at the riverbank.

I disrobed and removed the towels from my stomach and buttocks. (I'd use them later to dry myself.) Then I walked into the river and began to meditate. My legs soon grew numb from the cold, till I could barely feel them. I closed my eyes and concentrated on the one person I knew I was never going to see again, but desperately failed at forgetting: Gabe.

Just as I was told to, I'd brought a memento Gabe had once given me: a pendant with a portrait of the English Queen, Elizabeth I. I held it in my hand and concentrated as hard as I could, as the cold water choked my waist and numbness travelled up my body.

I opened my eyes and looked out onto the river. I saw Gabe's image clearly as if someone had painted his face on the surface of the water. He looked older, as if he'd aged several years since we last saw each other. He was working frantically, as though he had to, but didn't really care to anymore. The signs on the cargo he was unloading read 'Kalikata,' which made sense because he'd told me in his last letter about the villages in that area being reorganised into this town.

I closed my eyes and tried to hear what he was saying but could barely do so. Then I heard: "Don't let any of these break, you wretch!" The voice was classic Gabe. Had he really uttered those words, or was I hallucinating from the cold? I began to wonder.

Another firangi walked next to Gabe, put his hand on Gabe's shoulder and said, "I hear you're leaving a few months from now?"

I was startled. Was Gabe leaving India? If so, I had no doubt in my mind it would be for good. He said, "It's true, friend. I've put my name down to leave for England next season. They need me back."

But why? I myself had told him to leave, and now that he was leaving, I was shocked? I saw his image fade in the river and realised my vision of him was ending. But he wasn't why I'd come to the river this night.

I plucked from my blouse another memento, this one from Aurangzeb – one of the Prophet's hairs he'd given me when I had my accident. I again closed my eyes, focused and opened them a few moments later. In the distance, I now could see Aurangzeb.

He was dividing his land into sections and ordering the jungles cleared, probably hoping to convert the fields into farms for grain, wheat and other valuable crops. He was using the funds he'd been allocated for his governorship, and where he fell short, he was increasing taxes on those in his area. He was trying to convert the Deccan's jungles into granaries!

I now saw him riding on horseback and realised these visions might not be in actual time. He came across a stone structure at a slight elevation a few kos from where he was riding. Aurangzeb motioned to Shahnawaz while looking at the structure. "Is it true that those Hindu temples have idols made of solid gold?"

Shahnawaz Khan seemed not to have recognised the structure was a temple at first; but now that his son-in-law pointed it out to him, it seemed he could see the Hindu architecture in the edifice.

"Yes, Your Highness." Shahnawaz's round, bearded face smiled broadly. "The Hindus spend a lot of gold on the décor of their infidel structures."

Aurangzeb smiled with his mouth still shut. As if he'd just ridden into a gold mine, he looked to his equally intolerant companion to execute his next command: "Well, then I want that temple destroyed and its gold melted to be used for more important purposes, like funding this farming project."

"What about... resistance?"

"Kill anyone who resists, promise clemency for any who converts, and bring all the women of those killed into the harem."

Temples were now to be gutted across the Deccan, I feared. In the bigger picture of what Aurangzeb was doing, temples were the least useful structures, and the Hindus the biggest nuisance. *Interestingly,* I thought, *though he continues to detest Hindus, he doesn't have a problem keeping Hindu women in his harem. It seems he's forcing the wealthy Hindus to relocate to more impoverished sections of the city and give a higher portion of their wealth in taxes. The Deccan slowly begins resembling the horrific empire all of India would be if Aurangzeb was king...*

I suddenly shut my eyes; I couldn't take the horror anymore! I felt helpless to do anything against this brother shunned by my father. I both feared him and feared for him. I slowly walked to

246 ❖ Mistress of the Throne

the edge of the river. I hugged myself against the cold air blowing against my wet body. I wiped myself with a cloth I'd left by the shore and put my black robe back on. I then slipped back into the palace as inconspicuously as I'd slipped out.

✻ ✻ ✻

While gathered in the Diwan-i-khas, we received a letter from Aurangzeb asking Aba for assistance:

> Dearest Aba,
>
> I hope this letter finds you in good health. My warmest regards for you and your oldest grandson, Sulaiman Shikoh, on his marriage to a Rajput princess. I hope she will bear you a great-grandson soon!
> We are struggling here, Aba. This land is full of jungles and pests. To make it habitable I've used all available means, including increasing taxation, but a new enemy, the Marathas, recently attacked us like cowards in the dark and burned our crops to the ground. What's worse, they cremated our fallen soldiers, denying them the proper burial required of every good Muslim to ensure his entry into paradise. I now find myself unable to generate funds to replant the crops and turn the Deccan into an income-producing region of the empire. Not doing so will continue to make this region a drain on the empire.
> Your Majesty, if you wish for me to be honoured with great viceroyalty, then grant me the means to make it so. The few fertile lands in this area are occupied by nobles whose loyalty is important to the court. With the exception of their lands, all here is jungles and pests. I graciously await your response.
>
> Your humble servant,
> Aurangzeb

Sadullah Khan, a natural ally of Aurangzeb and a committed opponent of Dara, immediately exclaimed, "The Marathas must be taught a lesson, Jahanpanah." He had encouraged Aurangzeb many years ago to vie for the governorship of Gujarat, and it was no secret that he'd been dismayed by Aurangzeb's leaving.

"The Marathas have always been in the Deccan, Mirza Khan," shot back Dara.

Sadullah Khan frowned but pursed his lips, not openly challenging Dara in Aba's presence. "They were there even when Aba was living there. Only since Aurangzeb went have they rebelled!"

Sadullah would not be entirely silenced. "Their attack is an attack on Mughal sovereignty, my lord."

"Their attack is against *Aurangzeb!*" yelled Dara, facing Sadullah though Sadullah continued to stand at attention facing Aba, not addressing Dara directly. Dara looked enraged.

I called out, "We must first know *why* the Marathas have attacked. If they have indeed been our allies, what has happened to suddenly upset them?"

Dara pointed at the air with conviction. "I'll tell you why they attacked! Jahanpanah, I would like to present to you Hira Bai." A thin young woman with fair skin and a nose ring walked into the Diwan-i-khas, and Dara continued:

"This woman and her husband, Jaswant Raj, are employed in Aurangabad, she as a female slave to Aurangzeb's harem and Jaswant as a cook. To the world they're his slaves, but they are really my spies."

Quiet chattering began in the court. Aba grinned approvingly, but sat silent.

Dara said, "Through them I've learned what's happened in the Mughal court of the Deccan during the past few months."

The mullahs, Sadullah Khan at their head, stood at attention looking frightened, their heads hung low, anticipating any harmful revelation Dara's spies might bring.

Dara's spies now told the court that Aurangzeb had torn down virtually every Hindu temple in Aurangabad and neighbouring towns, melting any gold looted from them for his treasury. Thousands of Hindu priests had been slaughtered, and many Hindu women forced into the harems of Muslim noblemen, and even, to the shock of many, into Aurangzeb's own harem. Aurangzeb had also levied higher taxes on Hindus of the Deccan and confiscated some of their property illegally.

Hira Bai and Jaswant told us the funds looted were used for Aurangzeb's farming project in the Deccan. According to them, Aurangzeb had embarked on an ambitious project to cultivate the vast jungles of the Deccan into granaries that could be used to produce wealth for the kingdom. Acre upon acre of land was cleared away and given to peasants to farm and cultivate whatever crops were in greatest shortage. Areas once swamplands were now filled with earth to create lush ground for crops, while canals were dug for irrigation to improve harvests.

Hindus as well as Muslims were given the opportunity to cultivate the fields, but the better lands went to the Muslim peasantry. Aurangzeb himself visited the areas and assessed their progress. If a peasant was found to be neglecting his land, he was promptly removed, punished and his lands confiscated and given to a more able individual.

After months of toiling, and with most of the treasury of the Deccan spent on this project, slowly the jungles were clearing away and more fields were taking their place along the countryside. It was autumn now; the crops planted needed to be harvested, sold or traded with neighbouring countries in return for riches.

But Aurangzeb's fortunes took an ill turn on the night of 11th October, 1654, when hundreds of men came out from the woods with machetes, swords and torches and began lighting the hard-won crops on fire.

The Mughal army awoke and mounted a counter-offensive against the rebels, but couldn't see anything in the black smoke that filled the area. But the rebels were unaffected by the dark; the smoke didn't seem to hinder their movements at all, and they soon were killing more soldiers and burning more crops.

After the last of the crops were burned to the ground, the rebels gathered all the Mughal soldiers who'd not yet retreated and piled them into a large heap in the middle of the field. There they cremated the soldiers, denying the Muslims their required religious burials.

Aurangzeb dispatched his army to avenge the dishonour and damage that had been inflicted on him. With his harvest completely obliterated, Aurangzeb now needed more funds to start again. He must have had to swallow much pride to write Aba in the most conciliatory tone he could muster.

The spies fell silent and Aba spoke: "Perhaps we should assign a new governor for the Deccan. Maybe Prince Shuja would do a better job." The nobility gasped in shock! Such open criticism of Aurangzeb by the king himself was uncommon in the Mughal court. While father-son disputes had occurred for generations in the Mughal kingdom, they were always kept in private, leaving bazaar gossip as the only source to learn about who was angry with whom.

Now Sadullah Khan sought to defend his hero from this unprecedented outburst. "Begging forgiveness, Your Majesty, this servant of yours would like the opportunity to speak before you."

Aba nodded, giving the intolerant noble his chance to defend his choice for King of India.

"What has Prince Aurangzeb done that is so outrageous?" said Sadullah. "He's merely acting on your behalf, trying to increase the revenue of your domain. Don't you think this is a wise investment?"

Aba replied: "He was sent to bring wealth, not drain it from other regions. And while trying to create growing fields, he's destroyed temples and churches all along the coastline, killing thousands of innocent priests, worshippers and disciples of other religions. Now, some of them have joined our enemy, the Marathas, making them ever stronger!"

Dara grinned, and Aba added: "They were there when I was in the Deccan as a young officer under my father. But no one feared them then. They were weak! Now, thanks to the many intolerant acts of my worthless son, all my Hindu subjects have begun supporting them, because they too are Hindus. Now they've become a growing threat and menace!"

Aba wrote ferociously back to Aurangzeb:

Dear Aurangzeb,

Your congratulations for the marriage of Sulaiman Shikoh are too late to display any genuine affection. I'm surprised you didn't refer to your new daughter-in-law as an infidel, and merely called her by her title. Yet it seems your hatred for her people has only grown. Are you sure you're happy with this marriage?

As to your request, it is categorically denied. You brought this on yourself. You robbed Hindus, burned temples, and even tore their families apart just to fund your farming project. Allah has decided to punish you for your intolerance, so he has sent the Marathas to burn your fields and slay your men. You're lucky they didn't attack your life.

Furthermore, even though you hadn't heard of the Marathas, I have! They were a small, worthless bunch until you went there; but now because of your poor judgment and intolerance they've grown stronger, convincing Hindus in the Deccan as well as elsewhere that I am not their king and they should find one elsewhere.

Aurangzeb, no doubt you possess the resources, majesty and pomp that might make a future king; but you lack that critical acumen that all just kings must have: the ability to tell right from wrong. You appear to always be good to bad people and bad to good people. Until you learn to do things properly, I certainly will not come to your aid.

Yours,
Aba

I feared the ramifications Aba's letter might cause. With no help from us, would Aurangzeb now attack even more helpless people in his thirst for wealth? Much worse, I wondered what role, if any, my evil sister had been playing in all this.

25

GOLCONDA

11ᵗʰ June, 1656

Sadullah Khan abruptly fled Delhi, and I couldn't help but think he was up to something. I'd hoped for a vision the following nights that would send me to wherever he was going, and caution me about any mischief he might be planning, but to no avail.

I finally opted to once again go to the river, this time with a pearl necklace I'd confiscated from one of Sadullah's concubines as a memento from him. Yet again, I escaped from the rear entrance of the Red Fort in a black robe, hoping to evade recognition by anyone. Yet again I walked into the river, closed my eyes and concentrated on Sadullah Khan's face, his necklace wrapped around the fingers of my right hand.

I then opened my eyes and stared out into the river, the usual fog dissipated in the distance, and the water surface became a large screen.

I saw Sadullah, sitting with another man I assumed was a mullah of noble stature, based on his robes, in a haveli, presumably that of the mullah.

"Doomsday is upon us, Sadullah!" cried the mullah. "All we've ever known is being thrown into the fire by this infidel Dara."

The mullah was a short, old man with a long white beard and no mustache. The beard had been trimmed to perfection, allowing his light-skinned cheeks to be seen. His voice cracked as he spoke: "What is the definition of an infidel, Sadullah? Someone who merely denies Allah? Or is it someone who openly contradicts the teachings of the Koran? Tell me!" Sadullah stared at the mullah. "This I ask because Dara has done both. He even wrote a book, *Mingling of Two Oceans*, where he says Islam and Hinduism are one."

Indeed Dara had written such a book, much to the chagrin of everyone at the court who felt he'd gone too far trying to reconcile the religions. He'd further angered the orthodoxy by then claiming in court that the Hindu texts, the *Upanishads*, were really the *Lost Book of Islam*. Such talk was acceptable in the privacy of the Qadiriya, but public display of such beliefs was very dangerous, and Dara refused to see that.

"And he's always taking the side of Rajputs," added Sadullah. "Even the king takes his side, not realising that Dara's loyalty is not with him, but with the Hindus."

The mullah then leaned closer to Sadullah, as if about to whisper something important. His eyes fanned out over the hall in which he was sitting, presumably to make sure no one else from any other corner of the room could hear him as he spoke to Sadullah. "Sadullah," he said, "I have something to tell you that you must keep a secret." Sadullah nodded, and the mullah said, "The King is demented!"

Sadullah sprang up. To speak ill of the King was treason, punishable by death.

"Don't be alarmed, Sadullah. I'm not the only one who feels this way. There is much you don't know. I tell you the King is demented, my son, and I can prove it!"

"How?"

The mullah paused. Presumably both men were worried someone else might be listening. "Every night a boy visits the Emperor's harem, and it's widely believed that this 'boy' is really a young woman named Chamani Begum."

"Why dressed as a boy?"

"Ah!" shouted the mullah, waving a finger. "Now, 'why' is

the right question, Sadullah. Why would the King need to hide a woman in a boy's clothes? We Mughals have always allowed our Kings to exercise their manhood with anyone they desire – wives, concubines, even first cousins. Why, then, hide a woman?"

"I don't understand."

"He's hiding her in a boy's clothing because she is his *daughter*!"

"Chamani Begum is the Emperor's *daughter*?"

"Yes!"

"I'm confused," said a frustrated Sadullah, his head shaking. "There's Jahanara Begum, Raushanara Begum and Gauhara Begum. I've never heard of *Chamani* Begum."

"What if I told you that Jahanara Begum *was* Chamani Begum!"

"What?"

"Yes, my friend. The King is having an illicit relationship with his own daughter. Why else would he make her the Empress, bypassing all his other wives? Why else are they always together? The King began losing his mind when his wife died, and now his life is nothing more than a hotbed of sin, where incest and orgies occur in the kingdom day and night!"

The words struck me like a knife through the chest, but these rumours now had a life of their own, so what could I do? How many people could I silence? How could I even ask my father to address such a sickening rumour?

"Just imagine, Sadullah. If Dara becomes king, things like this will happen in every street and home in this country! Fathers sleeping with daughters, sisters having affairs with brothers – our daughters will be whores, and our sons will be philanderers. Not one mosque will be left still standing," cried the mullah. Tears began to roll from his eyes. "Idol worshipping temples with their sacred prostitution will take over the land, and the Rajputs will rule while we Muslims are slaughtered and imprisoned!"

"Sir, don't be worried about anything," said Sadullah as he stood up and put his hands on the mullah's drooping shoulders.

"I will go to Aurangabad at once and rally our hero, Prince Aurangzeb, to return to Shahjahanabad and claim his rightful throne!"

Sadullah walked the mullah to the door, closing it as he left. Sadullah mounted his horse and rode towards the Deccan.

I had heard and seen enough. Not realising it, I had started crying and my vision became blurry. I needed to go home and rest.

I thought long and hard that night about how I could secure the support of my other three brothers for Dara's ascension to the throne. I was encouraged by the notion that even if Aba gave up the throne during his reign, no brother would dare attack the capital while he was still alive. Thus, by crowning Dara in advance, he was trying to prevent the usual war of succession. However, what would stop the brothers from attacking Dara once Aba died? Or would any attack be too late? Would Dara already be in such a strong position as emperor that any challenge from a brother would be quelled easily?

I decided to try and convince the other three that Dara was the right choice for the next King of India, and win their hearts and support. This was an ambitious goal for even me, yet if anyone could achieve this, it would be me. Hoping to reach Aurangzeb before Sadullah did, I decided to write to and try to win his support first:

My Dear Brother Aurangzeb,

I know it has been long since I wrote to you last. I know that sending you to the Deccan wasn't right and that in doing so the King acted against your wishes. Yet you have worked tirelessly to turn that cursed land into fertile soil. I also have heard of the horror of the Marathas and the denial of funds from the King. Though you have never asked me, I'm writing to you to offer my help for your efforts. I offer you the use of my allowance and earnings to finance your projects in the Deccan – in other words, to provide everything you need.

In return, I ask, for this time only, for just one thing, brother. I ask that you support our brother, Dara, for the throne of India. I know certain people of high rank are filling your head with crazy thoughts about me and Aba, but let me assure you, they are not true.

These people don't love you; they're just using you to further their own agendas. Do not succumb to their persuasions, brother. They are not your friends.

Please show this world that our family will reject the legacy of bloodshed that's tainted our name for generations. In return for granting me this favour, whatever you wish will be yours.

Your Loving Sister,
Jahanara

Aurangzeb never replied to this letter and might not even have considered the offer I made him. To him, the whole notion of supporting someone else for the throne, especially Dara, was probably unconscionable.

So I still worried for my brothers' lives. Though relatively peaceful, Dara might grow violent in the heat of a brutal war and in the process slay one or more of his brothers. That possibility was very difficult for me to contemplate.

I went to Dara's mansion atop a beautifully decorated palanquin on an elephant. We sat on the steps alongside the Jumna, speaking like friends; but I wasn't here to chatter, but to give him a very stern warning: "If any of my brothers die in wars of succession over the throne of India, I'll poison myself."

Dara suddenly shook his head as if unable to believe his ears. He bent his brows inwards and said, "Who's mentioned anything about killing, sister?"

"I don't care whether it was said," I said, looking towards the river, away from my brother. "You Mughal men have a history of committing treacherous acts against one another whenever it's convenient."

Dara continued to stare at me, and I shifted my gaze directly to him. "You are the crown prince, and will ultimately be king. I need you to promise me," I continued as I walked over to him and folded my hands before him, "that if any of your brothers declare war on you and you are victorious, you will not kill them as punishment."

Dara held my hand in his and stood up, his eyes widening as if with optimism and promise of a better tomorrow. "Jahanara, I promise you that not only will I not slay any of my brothers, I will forgive their offence against me and treat their sons and daughters as my own."

I began to tear with delight, confident in Dara's virtues and honesty. I then asked him for one more favour, a favour I'd dared never to ask my father for fear I'd be viewed unfavourably: "When you're king, Dara, please allow your daughters to marry. Please allow Jani to love a man as you've loved Nadira and Aba loved Ami."

Dara smiled at me, his chiselled, bearded face looking down on me, wrinkles forming on his forehead. "Yes, Jahanara. I've already told this to Aba: Once I am king, every Mughal princess will be allowed marriage, and I will treat not just Jani's marriage as my own, but also the marriages of all of Aurangzeb's daughters. All of Aba's grandchildren will be married the way I was. I promise. This pleases Aba, too."

I began to cry open-heartedly. Had some aunt of mine asked for this when Aba was crown prince, perhaps I this day would have been someone's love, someone's mother and perhaps even someone's grandmother? I wouldn't have had to endure the humiliation of allegations of incest, nor run around in shadowy alleys to meet with Gabriel like a thief. For all the power Nur Jahan held and for all the influence she'd at one point wielded, she'd never thought of the plight of the Mughal daughters as her own, and never once considered that her own grand-nieces were doomed to lives of celibacy because of these ancient traditions. Other princesses wouldn't suffer the way I'd had to. Jani would be someone's love, and through her, I would be victorious.

"Your Highness!" yelled an approaching runner. "Someone is here from Golconda requesting to speak to you. He's badly wounded and being treated by the hakims in the fort. He brings you a message from Golconda."

Golconda, further south from Aurangzeb's Deccan, was home to the world's only known diamond mines. Aba had purchased a large beautiful diamond from Golconda for his Peacock Throne, the Kohinoor. Golconda's capital city, Hyderabad, was famous as a centre for diamond trade for the entire world. In Golconda one could find steel for Damascus blades; swords, daggers, and lances produced here were used throughout the world; and carpets, fish and wheat were produced in large quantities. Maybe the rest of the Deccan was wasteland, but Golconda was fertile, with tobacco and palm trees everywhere.

Golconda was ruled by Sultan Abdullah Qutb Shah, a decent yet aggressive military man. For all the riches of Golconda, he'd resisted the urge to engage the Mughals in battle for several decades. The Mughals, in turn, left Golconda alone, content with their own riches farther north.

I said, "We'll see him in the Diwan-i-khas. Tell the hakims to give him the utmost care, and when he's feeling able, we'll receive him properly there."

What did the presence of this wounded runner truly represent? Sadullah had run to the Deccan to rally Aurangzeb; my letter to Aurangzeb had been rebuffed; and now a representative from a neighbouring kingdom was appearing before us, severely wounded? I prayed to Allah that Aurangzeb had nothing to do with this.

As I sat on my divan later that night, Bahadur prepared my hookah for me. I asked her, "What do you think went on in the Deccan, Bahadur?" The question was rhetorical. My visions had already given me enough information to know Aurangzeb was creating mischief.

"Your Majesty," she replied, "what do *you* think is happening there?" Still readying my hookah, she continued, "Everyone knows how wealthy Golconda is, and with no financial help from the Emperor, I suspect Prince Aurangzeb must've tried to invade it."

"Nonsense!" I sniffed, though I knew what Bahadur was saying was probably true. I just couldn't bear to hear it. "How could he invade our allies and we not even know of it?"

Bahadur looked away. "Your hookah is ready, Your Majesty." She seemed uninterested in talking to me further.

The messenger Khalid Shah appeared the following day in the Diwan-i-khas, badly wounded with bandages on both arms, kneeling on a cane.

Dara said, "This is hardly a way to represent the Sultan, runner."

Khalid's face was severely bruised and swollen face, and the hakims had wrapped his head and jaw in a disfiguring white bandage. It appeared one of his legs and one of his arms were broken as well.

Aba sat on his throne, paying little attention to the court proceedings, leaving Dara to do most of the talking.

"Your Majesty," cried Khalid, "I was sent to bring you greetings from Sultan Qutb Shah, with diamonds from our famous mines and trays of rubies and gems, along with elephants and horses. Our embassy sent 15 people with several dozen concubines and female slaves for your pleasure."

The runner had at last said something of value to my sexually driven father, I thought. Hearing of concubines and female slaves, the aging monarch turned his head towards the runner, his eyebrows raised curiously.

"Our contingent left a few weeks ago from Hyderabad, and we were travelling alongside the jungles in your dominion, en route to this beautiful majestic capital of yours. Khalid paused, unable to bow in honour of our new city. Then he said, "Suddenly we were attacked by a cordon of the Mughal army in the Deccan!"

Dara looked in my direction as if gesturing me to understand that it had to be Aurangzeb who'd ordered this.

"They surrounded us and demanded that we go with them, but we refused. They then tried to chain us and take us with them, but we fought back with our swords and daggers. The army killed our whole embassy, and the concubines all fled towards wherever they thought they could find cover. The riches meant for Your Majesty were confiscated, and I barely escaped. Playing dead, I hid under one of my soldiers and later trekked here on a limping horse that had been badly wounded in the skirmish."

I said, "How do you know the men who attacked you were Mughals and not bandits merely dressed as Mughals?" Dara appeared irritated by my interruption.

The runner said, "Your Majesty, had they been bandits, I'm certain they would have merely looted us. Instead, they tried to kidnap us. They carried the Mughal flag and wore the traditional burgundy tunics."

Dara asked, "What was to have been the purpose of your visit?"

Khalid anwered: "To tell His Majesty that the Sultan of Golconda views you as his brother and wishes you no harm. But war is being thrust upon us by your son, Aurangzeb. He threatens to attack our nation because we've confiscated the cargo of Mir Jumla, a businessman of poor character in our realm."

I'd heard before of Mir Jumla, a Persian businessman who'd made his fortune in Golconda's diamond business. Backed by this fortune, he'd managed to spread his influence over other matters and by now had essentially created a monopoly over civil and military matters, much to the Sultan's chagrin. Qutb Shah viewed him as a growing threat, especially since he'd begun to muster his own private armies within the borders of Golconda. To curtail his power any further, Qutb Shah began imposing fees and levies against his revenue, and he slowly laid restrictions on how many men he could employ in his military service. A distraught Mir Jumla was looking for asylum but afraid to approach the Mughals, fearful that the noble Shah Jahan would rebuff him and the thought of moving to them would further alienate Qutb Shah.

I asked sharply from behind the screen, "But why have you confiscated his cargo?" I wanted to know the real basis for the war, and if Aurangzeb was in the wrong as this runner claimed.

"Your Majesty, Mir Jumla has refused to pay the taxes levied against him. The confiscation was his punishment."

"But we heard," Dara said, "that you seized cargo we had bought from you through Mir Jumla."

Khalid Shah paused for a long moment and the hall fell silent. I was flabbergasted at learning there'd been correspondence between Dara and the Deccan. If Dara was heir to the throne, I still was the queen and bearer of the royal seal.

"Begging Your Majesty's forgiveness, this servant of yours would like to inform you that no sales have occurred between our two kingdoms. Your representative in the Deccan has pried in our private affairs by granting sanctuary to the evil Mir Jumla."

"Runner," growled Aba, "choose your words carefully! You are accusing a royal prince of deceit, a crime punishable by death!"

I found it ironic that though always suspicious of Aurangzeb, Aba now acted as though he felt it a personal affront to allow an outsider to insult a member of the royal family.

"I beg your forgiveness, Your Majesty. But I assure you, no business transaction has occurred."

"You must stay here," said Dara. "You will be our eyes and ears as we continue our investigation of this matter!"

Afterwards Dara, Aba and I continued our discussion in the Macchi Bawan.

"What do you wish to do?" Aba asked Dara.

"We must send a letter to Aurangzeb forbidding him to attack Golconda under any circumstances!" Dara replied, looking towards me. I looked away, embarrassed on Aurangzeb's behalf, but also still somewhat hopeful that this might be a misunderstanding.

I said, "We must also ask him for any proof he may have of transactions."

"So be it!" said Aba.

"That wretch!" yelled Dara. "He should be skinned alive!"

I felt shock at seeing this belligerent side of my once-passive brother.

Dara fumed, "He deliberately disobeyed imperial orders and marched onto Golconda!"

"What orders, Dara?" I spat. "How could I not have been privy to all this?" I felt my influence and authority had slowly slipped from me, just as I'd feared.

Dara said, "I received a letter from Aurangzeb."

"You?"

"Well… it was addressed to Aba, but I read it and replied to it."

Aba looked away, as to dismiss my unmade question. Dara must have realised I'd grown furious.

"The letter said that Mir Jumla wanted to sell cargo to the Mughal Empire, and this is why Qutb Shah seized that cargo."

"So what did you say?"

"I told Aurangzeb to write to the Sultan to release all the cargo in seven days or else military force would be used against him."

"Did you do your own separate investigation into the matter?"

"Investigation?" Dara seemed puzzled. "What do you mean?"

Shaking his head, Aba said, "You authorised military force against a neighbour without verifying the facts?"

"That's not the point, he intentionally misrepresented the facts! What's worse, instead of seven it now appears he gave Qutb Shah only two days to comply!"

"What do you want to do now?" asked Aba.

"I want an embassy to travel to the Deccan, nonstop under the royal seal of the Empress, that attests to the fact that we wish for this military excursion to come to a halt."

Aba, his eyes gleaming greedily, said, "Have Golconda's riches been compromised?"

"If they have," said Dara, "we'll return them and start again. We'll help them repair their empire and repay the families of their fallen from the royal treasury."

Dara looked towards me for support, which I reluctantly gave in the form of a subtle nod. No matter how neutral I tried to be, the lines between right and wrong couldn't be clearer: This war in Golconda was clearly a war of choice, and it must be ended.

While Raushanara, Aurangzeb and Sadullah had formed a team in the south, Dara and I made up a reluctant northern team, and both were vying for the approval of the overly sexualised Aba who, rather than bothering with these matters, would have liked to retire to his harem for enjoyment and pleasure.

26

COMING OF THE STORM

6th September, 1657

I wrote several letters to Aurangzeb trying to explain what had happened and imploring him to confide in me about his true intentions regarding the Golconda debacle. But Aurangzeb seemed to have lost faith in my loyalty and seemed to no longer wish any further communication with me. Banished to the Deccan by Aba, humiliated by Dara and prevented from achieving the prize of Golconda by my royal seal, Aurangzeb also refused to talk with anyone else in my triumvirate.

I was in my apartment still pondering the future of Mughal women during the reign of Dara Shikoh when inauspicious news arrived. "Empress," called out a female servant, "Wazir Khan has sent for you! The Emperor is ill."

I ran from my apartment to the Emperor's chambers.

"Wazir Khan," I said, out of breath, "what's wrong with Aba?"

"I don't know why, Empress, but for some reason, the Emperor hasn't been able to empty his bladder for the last several days."

"What? Is this common for someone at this age?"

"No, Your Majesty, it isn't. But I think some of the aphrodisiacs the Emperor has been taking may be responsible."

While Wazir Khan was respectful enough to refer to the substances as aphrodisiacs, it was widely known that for the last several years, Aba had taken just about every stimulating drug he could find – from Europe, the far east, from Hindus, from hakims – to satisfy his urges. Yes, some mixture of all of these substances, taken simultaneously, had probably caused him to retain urine and made him increasingly sicker.

Now I could see that my father's eyes bore the same look of death I'd seen in Ami's that fateful day in the Deccan. "You must do something!" I shouted. "Call healers from all across the globe if you must, but the King cannot die."

I felt in my core that despite all of Aba's and Dara's assurances, a war would erupt after Aba's death and consume my family. There would be slaughter, tears, and millions of innocent Indians would lose their lives as unwilling participants in the bloodshed. Regardless of who won, India would lose, and the celebrations for the new monarch would occur alongside burials and cremations for the deceased. Though this seemed inevitable, I wasn't ready for it just yet.

The next several days saw Aba's health drastically decline though the royal physicians hovered constantly over him. His legs were now swollen, his mouth so dry he couldn't talk, his stomach swelled to a gross potbelly. To make matters worse, he developed a steep fever. I even thought of writing to Gabriel, but I soon realised such thoughts were futile – he was thousands of kos away, and by the time he received the message and could return to India, months would pass.

I now slept near Aba, thinking how Nur Jahan must have felt when Jahangir was sick. She knew that after Jahangir was dead she'd be banished and exiled, or perhaps worse. Yet my worry was different; I wasn't worried about myself – I never craved riches – I just couldn't shake the feeling that something bad was brewing in the Deccan and would erupt as soon as the King was dead.

I applied moist dressings to Aba's forehead in a frenzy hoping to bring his fever down. I also wondered if perhaps Aba was being misdiagnosed. Rather than suffering side effects of aphrodisiacs, had he caught an illness through one of his female liaisons? With a harem of several hundred concubines and illicit affairs with other women, the King in the past year must have enjoyed several hundred, maybe even 1,000 women from all across India.

I ordered my servants to check all the women who'd come into contact with the Emperor in the last month – no easy task – and report to me anyone who was feeling ill.

Over the next several days, my women fanned out across the harem and examined closely anyone, including nobility, even rumoured to have had recent relations with the King. Women suspected of liaisons were brought in from neighbouring towns and villages in carts, like cattle, and questioned by Bahadur.

All this was done secretly, because news of the King's illness had to be kept private to prevent any uprising. The zenana women were all investigated, of course, and anyone with strange symptoms or some recent illness was examined by the hakims.

On September 12, the servants reported back to me. "We've found none of the women to be unhealthy, Your Majesty. About a dozen have died in the last month, but mostly from accidents; none were sick."

Then, as a matter of last resort, I told Bahadur to find the one other person who might shed light on the cause of the Emperor's illness – Chamani Begum.

"Do you know anything about her, Your Majesty?" she asked. "Where she lives, who she serves?"

"No, I don't."

"Do you even know what she looks like?"

I looked away and said somberly: "She looks like me."

Despite my attempts to keep Aba's illness private, news of it began to permeate the kingdom, and the people wondered even more avidly whether the rumours were true. When the public gathered now at the Jharoka-i-darshan, no King was was present. The rumours were worsening now; some were now openly saying the King was already dead, and that Dara was intentionally hiding this from the public to consolidate his empire.

Dara insisted to me, "Aba must come to the window and prove to the people he's very much alive. They won't believe me or you unless he's with us!"

"What do you want from me?" I responded helplessly. "He can barely openly his eyes. Shall we prop up a living corpse?"

Dara and I now restricted anyone from visiting the Emperor for fear that one or more persons might be spies or hired guns from my other brothers who'd try to take Aba's life to spark a bloody war. But though we intended to protect him, the effect was to feed the conspiracy theories even further, making people believe Dara and I must be plotting something.

On the morning of September 14, Aba was lying in his bed, covered with silk blankets; I was waking from fitful sleep on the Persian carpet nearby; Dara sat a few feet away, still asleep on the gold-studded chair, his turban placed on the table next to him. Suddenly I saw sunlight glare straight from the window onto Aba's face, and it seemed to give him a boost of divine strength, for as the light hit, he opened his eyes and smiled.

"Is anyone here awake?" he asked looking around the room.

"Aba?" I cried. I stood up quickly, grinning and laughing hysterically. "Aba, you're *well*! Allah ho Akbar!" My screams woke up Dara, who looked up still groggy from his uncomfortable sleep on the chair. "Aba, how are you feeling?" I asked.

"Weak."

Dara said, "Well, that's not surprising," and knelt next to the King. "But you'll get better now, I just know it."

Aba seemed very drowsy from the opium the hakims had been giving him. I lamented, "Oh, Aba, you can't know all that's happened in this kingdom of yours during the last several days. Rumours are rampant that you're dead, and that Dara and I have hidden this and are usurping the throne."

Dara whined, "They're saying I care more about the throne than for your health!"

"But I feel fine," Aba sighed.

"Aba," I said, "I know you feel weak, but I think it's vitally important that after eating something you give darshan at the balcony to show that you're alive and well."

Aba seemed perplexed by this request, but we explained to him that only physical proof of his life would quell the rumours and restore stability to the country. Then I advised Aba also to summon all the princes to Delhi and make his wishes for the future of India known to them.

Later that day, though weak, Aba rose to the balcony window and rallied a crowd of several thousand, who may or may not have been relieved to learn that they'd just been spared an unnecessary war for succession. Aba was a popular king, possibly the most popular India had seen in a long time. There could be no substitute for him; each candidate to succeed him was controversial in his own way, and no one before had ever shown the ability to form the broad ruling coalition the current Emperor enjoyed.

As was customary, alms were distributed in the King's name, prisoners were set free and Dara received promotions and rewards for his devotion to Aba. But outside Delhi, the validity of his appearance at the window was questioned, and though all of us children had to know our father was still alive, I knew it would serve some to pretend they didn't know and rally the support of their constituents.

I was lying in my chambers the next day, the sweet scents of flowers and cool water from the Paradise Canal cooling the city's unusually hot September days. I thought to myself how great an idea the canals were, flowing all across the city, every avenue and lane on a boardwalk, and the sweet smell of the river mixing with the north winds, relieving the city's normally dry climate.

An attendant broke into my thoughts: "Bahadur is here to see you, Your Majesty."

When he entered the room, I asked, "Yes, what news do you bring?"

"Your Majesty, I've found Chamani Begum." "Really? Where? Is she still alive?" Bahadur hesitated, as if he knew he had to bring bad news. "Your Majesty, Chamani Begum died a few days ago of swollen legs, a potbelly and a high fever. Her skin turned completely black, and she was cremated at the far side of the town so the fumes from her remains wouldn't blow into the city. It was believed she died of a toxic infection."

I stared confused at the servant. Aba had had those same symptoms, and though he was doing better now, I began to worry he might relapse. After a pause I said, "Who cremated her?"

"One of the untouchables who cleans the gutters. No peasant wanted anything to do with her."

I sighed. This had been the end of Chamani Begum, whom I never knew but whose existence had caused me much unintended grief. A favourite of my father's, this concubine probably could've mustered anything from Aba she chose; yet here she'd died as an orphan, with no relative or friend even to cremate her. Such was the fate of the Mughal concubine, to live and gain praise so long as she had a pleasing physical appearance, but to be discarded afterwards.

"Thank you for your service," I said, handing Bahadur a bag of pearls.

I told Wazir Khan about the results of my investigation and my fears.

"He should go to Agra, Empress," said Wazir Khan. "There he has the Taj Mahal to remind him of his real love. All this debauchery started when he moved away from the Taj. There, he'll turn back to normal, and the change of air will do him good. Besides, now that he's healing, the last thing he needs is for someone to give him more aphrodisiacs or concubines."

Aba's health continued to improve for the next several weeks, and in early November 1657, unsure how long we'd stay there, I had my maids pack all my belongings, and the imperial caravan set out for Agra.

Bahadur said, "Your decision to leave Delhi during the day was quite wise." His words were always wise, so this compliment meant much to me. "With you and the king in Agra with the full might of the kingdom, the people of both cities and the countryside in between will certainly know their king is well!"

I had not thought of that, but clearly this procession would help solidify the impression that Aba was well. I chose to ride on his elephant with him, still afraid for his health, which remained quite fragile.

Leaving Delhi and saying farewell to Chandni Chowk was more difficult than I thought. I felt grieved as if I was leaving Gabriel again. Yet my sorrow was lessened by the thought of seeing the Taj Mahal and paying homage to my mother again.

I could tell by the smell in the air that we'd left Delhi and now were near the Jumna. The riverside had its own unique aroma, and I welcomed the cooler air it brought. I peeked out of the canopy while Aba slept beside me. To my chagrin, I saw the same semi-naked sadhus I'd seen many years ago when I first visited Delhi staring back at me from the shallow edge of the river.

"Farewell, oh maiden!" shouted one of them, grinning stiffly. Others cried, "Farewell, oh ill-fated ones! Farewell, oh ill-fated ones!"

I felt anxious then, as though they knew something of my future I didn't. "Farewell!" they mocked. "You've lost your Delhi." Then others joined in: "Farewell! You've lost your Delhi. Farewell! You've lost your Delhi."

I ducked my head back inside the palanquin, and felt my heart racing. I began to sweat and feel as if someone had grabbed my neck and was slowly strangling me. Eventually our caravan moved past the Jumna riverside, and much to my relief these feelings subsided. The rest of the journey passed uneventfully.

✻ ✻ ✻

I sent Bahadur to Shuja in Bengal to muster Shuja's support and reassure him that Aba was well and in full control of the state. I'd given up reluctantly trying to connect with Aurangzeb, but I tried to reach out to my more timid, less ambitious brothers.

Bahadur met me in Agra to discuss his trip; I greeted him on my balcony overlooking the Taj.

"Your Majesty," he began, "before I could even bring your message to Prince Shuja I was summoned to his audience hall to hear *his* message."

"*His* message?"

Bahadur looked at me soberly. "He's preparing to challenge Dara for the next Mughal emperorship."

This news saddened but didn't surprise me. Bahadur further reported:

"Prince Shuja, seated in his chair in Rajmahal, the capital of Bengal, shouted, 'Abul Fauz Nasiruddin Mohammad Timur III, Alexander II, Shah Shuja Bahadur Ghazi! This will be the name of the next emperor, and so I will be addressed by the people of India!'"

I thought to myself, if ever there was a buffoon who made someone as inept as Murad look like a wise statesman, it was Shuja. Sent to the Bengal as its governor, he'd no talents or accomplishments whatsoever to boast of. Though he was older than Aurangzeb, our father had more respect – though not love – for Aurangzeb than he did for Shuja. Shuja's only distinction throughout his useless life had been that he'd accompanied Ami's remains from the Deccan many years ago. At that time Aurangzeb was too young, and Dara was too beloved to the King to lose sight of the latter for even a short while.

Bahadur went on: "He then ordered the prayers to be read in his new name in the mosques of Bengal, and showed proof of the new coins he'd commissioned. These were to bear his image, side-profiled. He then turned his head to the side, showing off the profile he wished to see on every Mughal coin. His advisors looked at each other in dismay, probably unaware of how to relate further with with their imbecile leader."

"What happened next?" I pressed.

"One of them asked if the Prince shouldn't hold off on the minting until after his coronation at Shahjahanabad, to which the Prince yelled, *Shuja–bad!* That will be the capital's new name."

I thanked Bahadur for his service and asked him to do one more task for me: deliver this message:

Dear Dara,

Our younger brother, Shuja, has defected and is planning to crown himself king. While we both know this isn't possible, his governorship has lent him the blindfold of arrogance and he's even minting new coins in his name. Just as I feared, there will be bloodshed in this generation, too. You must send the army to stop Shuja before he enters the capital and threatens Aba's legitimacy.

Love,
Jahanara

Dara sent his son, Sulaiman Shikoh, with a regimen of 45,000 troops charged to imprison, but not kill, Shuja. Meanwhile, my messenger from Gujarat returned with equally troubling news – of my other brother, Murad.

"'Maruwwajuddin!' That's what Prince Murad's yelling from his fort in Gujarat."

I looked down, ashamed and embarrassed at another brother's defection.

"He calls himself the Titan of Balkh. He says after subduing the Central Asian tribes and almost exceeding our boundaries north, he'll finish the work he started."

Though not so foolish as to mint his own coins, it seemed Murad was also dreaming of ruling the kingdom he wrongfully thought was his for the taking. Like the advisors had in Bengal, hundreds of kos away, the advisors to this incompetent Prince were said to have looked at each other bewildered, unsure of how to bring Murad to reality and remind him that his 10,000-strong cavalry was no match for our army from Shahjahanabad.

Somewhat relieved to know Murad was at least not initiating an immediate march on to the capital, I simply ignored his talk as senseless rambling.

A few days later I received a letter from Dara,

Dear Jahanara,

I'm pleased to inform you that my son has made us proud. Pursuant to my orders, Sulaiman Shikoh's army met Shuja's and he was surprised to see how disorganised the enemy was. Perhaps envisioning an easy victory against a young lad like Sulaiman, Shuja sought to sleep until midday on a divan under a mosquito net, while his leaderless men roasted in the heat on the battlefield.

Finally, on February 14, young Sulaiman's troops descended on Shuja's men from all sides and sent Shuja's chaotic army fleeing in all directions. Sulaiman took the fight right into Shuja's camp and looted his riches, including his illegally minted coins, making off with loot totalling over two lakh rupees.

Shuja was said to have been sleeping when one of his men tripped into him, suddenly awakening him from his sound sleep. The man informed our inept brother that his army was annihilated. In shock, Shuja instructed the soldier to fight to the death – a command the solder then refused to obey!

Shuja then put on a long scarf around his head as if he were a maiden, and mounted on a horse. Unfortunately, thus disguised Shuja managed to escape unscathed. But for now our problem is resolved, and Sulaiman will return home soon.

Love
Dara

I wasn't as pleased as Dara may have hoped. Would Shuja resurface again? And with the two passive, weak brothers acting this way, what must the strong, military genius Aurangzeb be planning? Success or failure, Shuja had succeeded in initiating the first battle in this war, and now others might feel emboldened to do the same. Attacking one's own kin was no longer unthinkable in our own generation.

27
THE STORM
25th April, 1658

Our stay in Agra was cut short by the news from the Deccan that Aurangzeb and Murad had formed an alliance and were marching on Delhi! I tried to quell the approaching storm by reaching out to Aurangzeb, who I was convinced was this rebellion's architect. I wrote him shortly after learning of the alliance between him and Murad:

Dear Aurangzeb,

Aba has recovered from his illness and is now again fully in control of his administration, moving to correct any and all disorders that cropped up during his illness. Your armed advance, brother, is totally unwarranted and paramount to an act of war against your own father. Even if it's directed at Dara, it's still both sinful and unethical, since the eldest son both by Canon Law and common usage stands in the place of the father. If you value your name and reputation and truly seek salvation in this world as well as the next, you must obey Aba and convey any grievances in writing.

Yours,
Jahanara

I received this terse response from him a few days later:

> *My Dear Empress,*
>
> *Aba has lost all true power and control of India. Dara is now ruling the land illegally and plotting to harm his brothers. Anyone who doubts this should just look at how he crushed Shuja in Bengal. He also foiled my attempts at Golconda when victory was at hand and repeatedly poisoned Aba against me. Against such overt hostilities, I have no choice but to take up arms and defend what's rightfully mine.*
>
> *As for Canon Law and common usage, were it so, Aba would never have been king. He wasn't the eldest son of his father, Uncle Khusrau was. Rumour at the time even suggested that Aba murdered Khusrau to remove him and upon seizing the throne slaughtered his brother Shahriar and nephews. To now hide behind tradition and laws is to invite the title of a hypocrite. The best man should rule India, regardless of his order of birth.*
>
> *Yours,*
> *Prince Aurangzeb*

I didn't know who to be more upset with, my father or my brothers. I'd tried repeatedly ever since my father recovered from his illness to convene a summit between all four brothers with Aba as the arbiter, but to no avail. Aba was intent on the notion that merely crowning Dara the heir apparent was all that needed to be done to prevent any revolt.

His reasoning was that no prince would have the audacity to attack the capital while he was still alive, and that by the time of his death, all the military and nobility would be solidly in Dara's camp. I knew his notion was flawed, but I was hesitant to push him on this issue for fear his illness would relapse.

As we rode towards Delhi I began to wonder if I was even justified in blaming my brothers for all of this conflict. After all, what did Shuja do that a generation ago Aba hadn't done? Had he not rebelled against his father? Had his father not rebelled against his own father? Much of a moron as he may have been, Shuja was merely continuing family tradition. Had Aba addressed this bloody tradition earlier and taught his sons to live peacefully, perhaps all this turmoil could have been avoided.

Yet this was indeed Mughal tradition. Unlike other monarchies, there was no clear line of succession, no commonly recognised primogeniture. From our Central Asian ancestry, we Mughals had adopted a turbulent spirit of rebellion and sedition, where anything and everything was considered fair game to gain the throne. '*Throne or coffin*' was the mantra, and all familial relationships were forgotten during wars for the throne.

I felt a clutch in my throat when Aba told me Delhi was in danger of an attack. He wouldn't tell me where his intelligence came from, so I was suspicious of its reliability. Nevertheless, I agreed to leave Agra and march with our caravan to Delhi.

As my body moved from side to side over the rough, still yet-to-be-paved route to Delhi, I noticed Aba snoring loudly under his breath. He was taking copious amounts of opium to relieve the bladder pain that was now normal for him.

From the pocket of his robe I could see the folded letter from Dara dangling. *Should I just read it myself?* I wondered. Though not an offence (I was the queen after all), I held myself to a higher standard than that. Reaching into my father's pocket and reading a private note sent to him was not in my nature.

But could I afford to be kept in the dark? Aba's decision had led us to this point, and should I continue to let him chart the course going forward? As Queen of India, was I to let it crumble and fall into the wrong hands?

Ever since Aba's illness I'd considered trying to sneak out to the river again and revisit my visions. I wasn't sure what I was looking for, because my spies and informants were telling me everything anyway, but I hoped perhaps these visions would give me something new that I could use to save my family. Unfortunately, Aba's health prevented me from leaving his side for even a moment, and thus my desire to visit the river and receive visions went unfulfilled.

I wouldn't pluck the letter from Aba's shirt, I decided. Too much lying, deceiving and snooping had occurred already. I'd gone from being an innocent Begum Sahiba to become the manipulative, self-serving queen I'd always faulted Nur Jahan for being. I remembered asking Nur Jahan once if she'd always been this way and her saying, *You won't understand. This seal, the* muhr uzak, *makes you this way. It makes you constantly suspicious. In this seal lies so much power, to preserve that power you allow yourself to do anything, compromise any principle, violate any tenet...*

Our caravan was nearing Delhi, and I now saw some withering ruins with partial brick walls standing in the distance. Again I felt a shiver overcome me, and I felt like a fish freshly plucked out of water. Would my kingdom end up like those ruins? Would Jani's children end up like the half-naked peasants who were living in mud huts around these ruins?

I had to do something. I couldn't let these foolish young men control India's destiny. I needed to read that letter. Putting aside my reservations, I plucked it from Aba's pocket and began reading:

Dear Aba,

I have just learned from Raushanara that Murad and Aurangzeb are communicating and coordinating with one another to invade Shahjahanabad. What should I do? I've sent all my top generals to Bengal with Sulaiman, and I fear that by the time they return, it'll be too late. Please send me your advice and counsel, as I'm alone in Shahjahanabad with just Raushanara as my ally and saviour.

Yours,
Dara

Raushanara his ally? Why would he trust that witch? *Ever since Aba threw her out of the kingdom, she's been thirsty for revenge. What's*

276 ❧ *Mistress of the Throne*

wrong with Dara? Aba must have kept this note from me because he knows I'd never have allowed him to leave Agra, with the royal treasury unguarded, based on information from Raushanara.

I peeked from my elephant canopy and motioned to the Tatar woman riding on horseback next to our elephant. "Tell the general to return the caravan back to Agra!" I commanded.

As we rode through the jungles between the capital and Agra, I considered what might have happened elsewhere in the empire with my brothers. Was everything that had transpired during the past few months somehow linked? Was Aurangzeb orchestrating everything? He must have done it, and that's why I hadn't heard from him!

I rested my head against the back wall of the canopy and closed my eyes, hoping for a vision of some sort.

I thought of what may have gone through Aurangzeb's mind when news of Aba's health spread like wildfire throughout the kingdom. Maybe he thought Dara, encouraged by me, would usurp the throne. Zealous for power, he was probably flabbergasted and ready to march on to Agra, but how could he? Dara had access to the imperial treasury and a standing army of 120,000 men. Aurangzeb's ill-fated conquest of Golconda had left him with only 40,000 men with virtually no funds.

He knew no neighbours would come to his aid because he'd harassed all of them, the Hindu Marathas by destroying their temples, the Sultan of Golconda by an ill-advised invasion, and neighbouring Bijapur with continued threats of aggression.

So who would help this belligerent brother of mine who was out of money and manpower? Maybe in despair he contacted Shuja and Murad to form an alliance. But why would both of them work for Aurangzeb who was weaker and unpopular, and turn on Dara, who was the clear favourite?

I kept trying to link the pieces together:

Perhaps Aurangzeb promised these two idiot brothers of mine some share of the kingdom – something Aba and Dara would never do. Maybe he thought he could control their armies and whatever funds they had, but in the end wouldn't he turn on them once he won the throne for himself? If so, might Shuja's rebellion have been just a diversion so the army would be in Bengal when Aurangzeb attacked Agra?

Where did Raushanara fit in all this? Could she be part of the plan? Or was she outcast by Aurangzeb and coming to us now because she had nowhere else to go? This last factor perplexed me, and my head was hurting. I didn't want to know more, at least not for now.

My mind began to wander; I couldn't believe this was happening. All the letters and lectures, the talks and meetings, all for nothing! There would be war now, and I knew I couldn't stop it...

My reverie was interrupted by a soldier riding towards the caravan. "Your Majesty, I bring you news from the Deccan," he announced.

"What is it, soldier?"

"Your Majesty, the armies of Aurangzeb and Murad are 50,000 strong. They've defeated our ally, Raja Jaswant Singh, and are marching on to Agra, not Delhi, to steal the treasury!"

"Alas, you were right, Jahanara!" screamed Aba, who'd awakened in time to hear this dire news. So was the original letter sent by Dara warning of an attack on Delhi based on faulty intelligence, or was Raushanara intentionally misleading us? Again, I wondered: Were we purposely made to leave Agra unguarded so Aurangzeb could seize it, or was this a misunderstanding?

Aba said, "Runner, ride to Delhi and convey this information to my son, Dara. Also, tell him to march immediately to Agra. We'll plan our next move from there."

Dara and Raushanara arrived in Agra a few days after we did, much to my dismay, as I was now openly questioning why Dara would trust her during this difficult time. "She should be the last person we talk to regarding strategy!" I yelled to him.

My sister cried, "See, Dara, how she treats me? After all the help I've given you..." She flashed a pitiful, helpless look at him.

I rolled my eyes and pleaded with my father and Dara to not trust her. She was Aurangzeb's ally, I maintained, and not to be trusted in the least.

Dara frowned, "Enough, Jahanara! You talk of family unity, yet this is how you treat our sister? What crime has she committed? She doesn't *have* to be here!"

I tried to make Dara understand that all she was telling him was false information to trap him. But Dara wouldn't budge; he insisted that she'd changed and could now be trusted. I couldn't believe what I was hearing. Why would this person leave her equally scheming brother and help someone like Dara, who all his life had favoured me over her?

"Aba," wept Raushanara, "if you don't believe me, tell me, and I'll drink poison and kill myself."

No doubt this was another ploy of hers. Raushanara'd poison herself because her father didn't trust her? She'd spent her whole life deceiving him and others in our family. But it was working. I could see Aba's heart was thawing.

He turned to me, grabbed my hand and pleaded, "My child, forgive your sister for any offence you think she's committed. She speaks from her heart now, I can feel it." He then grabbed Raushanara's hand with his other, brought our two hands together and said, "We must work together, my children. If we stay together, your brothers will hesitate to walk the path of violence. Forgive and forget what's past, and let's start again. We can do it, my children. Do it for your Aba – do it for Ami."

I was sick to my stomach with all this treachery and gullibility, but what sickened me most was this invocation of Ami. Thank God she didn't live to see this.

✳ ✳ ✳

We were now in the Macchi Bawan, the same site where many years ago I'd helped plan the Taj Mahal. Now I was planning the battle of brother versus brother, my worst nightmare.

Raushanara said, "We have to prevent Aurangzeb from crossing the Chambal River. He has to cross it to march towards Agra!"

I just stood frowning with arms folded, watching my younger sister make detailed suggestions to the King.

"How sure are you he'll cross there?" asked Aba.

"I know it. They've been planning this for months. I overheard the whole thing while I was in Aurangabad."

Dara pointed to the location on a map. "Then this is where we'll plant heavy guns. As they march towards us, we'll sound warning shots, followed by real ones if we have to."

I walked to the drawing of the Chambal river (a tributary of the Jumna located 40 kos south of Agra) and said morosely: "What about *this* area, 30 kos east of where you're planning to place your guns?"

"What about it?" snapped Dara.

"Well, I know from building the Taj that when we wanted to run water for the canals through here, we learned it's incredibly shallow. What if Aurangzeb's army tries to cross here?"

Aba cupped his chin. "Maybe we should plant guns there, too..."

"...That may be overkill," said Raushanara quickly, glancing directly at Dara alone.

"We'll do it, though," nodded Dara, hoping, I figured, to prevent another fight between us sisters.

Now that our plan was in place, the only thing left was to assemble an army of soldiers able to do battle should matters degenerate further and peace overtures be spurned.

Aba responded, given that his own generals were all hundreds of kos away in Bengal, by placing the entire treasury and arsenal of the Mughal Empire at Dara's disposal. More than one lakh of horsemen and 20,000 infantry with 100 pieces of field artillery and 200 European artillerymen were quickly assembled for Dara. Well-armoured elephants and over 500 camels along with subordinates and shopkeepers also were drafted, meant to provide ready resources for the army should it be needed. Never before to my knowledge had a sitting emperor so enthusiastically provided a sitting prince with ammunition and resources for his fight against other princes of the empire.

Dara mounted his war horse amid cheers of 'Allah-ho-Akbar' by Muslims and 'Har Har Mahadev' by Hindus. Aba embraced Dara for an unusually long time, as if Aba knew this might be the last time he saw his son. Dara had given Aba such joy and happiness, that it seemed to have robbed all the love due the other brothers. In that tight embrace lay the seeds of this day – brothers joining hands to fight another brother and their father.

Aurangzeb outnumbered Dara in terms of career soldiers, and those soldiers Dara did have couldn't compare in training and leadership with his enemy brother's. Dara's army was a patchwork of butchers, barbers, blacksmiths, tailors and carpenters, while Aurangzeb's army had 50,000 well-trained soldiers. Dara's forces hadn't endured training in the Deccan's blazing sun, half-submerged in water, crawling on their stomachs for the past 18 months as Aurangzeb's likely had. Dara's minions weren't soldiers, but ordinary citizens.

As Dara was about to ride off, Mullah Shah Badakshi stood in front of him. He said, "Mullah, bless me that I may be victorious today."

Shah Badakshi said, "The people of Hindustan are very malicious, Prince Dara. They deserve a malignant king, not a good-natured man like you."

Dara glowered at Badakshi's words, but then he smiled at his old friend's wishes and rode off with his army to fight.

Shah Badakshi then turned to me. He placed his hand over my head and smiled. I returned his smile. Was he blessing me?

He said, "Your visions will cease from this moment on. At least, nothing they reveal to you will be of any value." He was taking away my visions? How could I help Dara if I couldn't see what the others were doing? Or was it now too late?

He then told me he'd had a premonition the night before that victory was not to be Dara's. Yet he'd been summoned here to say both farewell to Dara and not give him false hope as the other Sufis had done.

The men began chanting "Manzil Mubarak!"

As the army left and the Diwan-i-am emptied, Aba and I watched our Prince's army slowly fade into the darkness and eventually out of sight. I feared I would never see my Prince alive again.

28

MIDNIGHT

22nd May, 1658

I sent Bahadur with Dara's army to report what was happening on the front lines. Apparently, Dara planted his heavy guns across the Chambal river as Raushanara had instructed, ignoring my warning of that shallow stretch of land 30 kos east which was perfect for crossing. He thought guarding that area also might stretch his army too thin, and hoping to repel the rebel forces just long enough for his son and his forces to arrive from Bengal, Dara planted his troops in just the one area.

Meanwhile the rebel army regrouped at the other end of the river. By morning, they were ready to march on to Agra.

Dara was said to have been shocked at hearing the horrific news. He called his entire army to attention and chaotically marched it from the riverside, with the heavy artillery he'd posted on the river front abandoned in the great haste. His artillery now greatly weakened, he rushed his dishevelled army of commoners back to their ill-fated home.

"Where are they now?" I asked Bahadur.

"They're now occupying the great plains of Samugarh. Prince Dara's army has sped past Prince Aurangzeb's army."

I stood pondering what that meant. I was confidant all of Aurangzeb's moves were carefully calculated.

Aurangzeb's army moved gingerly towards the plain, where the decisive battle of Samugarh would be fought. Dara and his men had scouted the battlefield the night before, making sure they understood the terrain. At a distance they could see Aurangzeb's army, readying itself for the following day.

I lay in my apartment in the Agra Fort, able to see the armies in the distance from my elevated residence. I wept alone as if all the life was draining from me. No matter who won, I would lose a brother, maybe two brothers, tomorrow. Nur Jahan's plan had worked: by poisoning Aurangzeb against Aba, she'd gotten her revenge even after her death. Yet in my loss also lay the loss of my mother. There loomed the Taj Mahal, moonlight reflecting off of its white marble walls – illuminating the battlefield where her sons' armies would face each other in battle. *What must her soul be thinking right now?* This battlefield, where the blood of at least one of her sons would be spilled the next day, had once been a hunting ground of Jahangir, my grandfather, for deer, cattle and tigers. Now, his own kin were going to hunt one another.

I knew Aba must be gazing at the same battlefield from his window, praying with every inch of his heart that his peaceful son would develop the courage and military acumen to defeat the military master Aurangzeb. I could imagine him walking over to his chair, opening the Koran, reading verses from it and weeping.

"I'm sorry my love," he would say, looking towards the Taj Mahal. Like me, he too must have felt he'd failed his wife. Perhaps if she'd lived this day would never have come. She could have helped Aurangzeb become a better man. Neither Aba nor I had been able to stem the tide of orthodoxy and intolerance that had seized Aurangzeb's heart after her death.

I didn't know where Raushanara was, but I was sure she'd be smiling at the battlefield; the end was so close. She knew Aurangzeb would win, and then perhaps she'd be empress. After a lifetime spent in the shadows, finally she'd enjoy the limelight.

Yes, all of us Mughals would be looking at the plains from the majestic Red Fort, the glistening Taj Mahal reminding us of our common, deceased relative, while my two brothers look on the moonlit battlefield, perhaps also realising that somehow their mutual mother was watching and would judge them at heaven's gate for their actions.

I awoke early the next day and performed my early morning prayers, facing towards Mecca. The rug under me, I knelt with hands facing up before me, eyes closed.

I'd had Bahadur mount Aba's telescope on the Samman Burj, so I could see the battle between my brothers' armies. I'd studied the stars the night before just as closely. What was our destiny in them to be today?

Soon I saw Aurangzeb's army wave their swords, javelins, daggers and muskets in the air, signalling to Dara's army across the battlefield that an attack might be imminent.

Dara's army arrayed a front row of artillery carriages, behind which he'd set out 20,000 musketeers and 500 camels. Another 28,000 cavalry stood behind them, and in the extreme rear, Dara himself rode atop a massive elephant. His army's right wing offered several thousand men with saffron-painted faces. These were the Hindu Rajputs, I assumed. The left wing contained huge-sized bodies, the Uzbeks, no doubt.

Aurangzeb's army stood in sharp contrast. His soldiers were all career fighters and all Muslims. Each man looked sturdy, wore the same exact uniform and stood in the same posture: back slightly bent forward as if ready to lunge at the enemy. They looked like men thirsty for blood. Aurangzeb was mounted on a grated-metal-armoured elephant; he looked even leaner than when I'd last seen him. Near him Murad, on horseback, also looked confident.

Neither side was attacking yet, each probably hoping to set up a defence. Then Dara's gunners opened fire, barely skimming the front line of Aurangzeb's soldiers. Dara ordered a direct assault, possibly thinking the gunfire had silenced the enemies' own artillery. Both wings of Dara's armies marched in – giving Aurangzeb the opportunity to fire a cannon into the heart of the wings, killing hundreds before they could ever reach the rebel army. Those that did make it – still thousands – now engaged in close combat with the enemy.

Now the Hindu Rajput contingent charged Murad's army. I caught a glimpse of Murad on horseback. He motioned his hand sideways as if ordering his men to 'slice' his enemies. I'd never seen his face spew such hatred.

The Rajput soldiers attacked him, hurling their javelins. Murad fell off his horse and slashed his sword towards the Rajput general, Ram Singh. Ram Singh fell, too, and the two now met hand-to-hand. Murad fell to the ground and the General lunged on top of him, but Murad shielded himself with his own sword. Murad then kicked the General off and mounted the General's empty horse. Ram Singh ran after Murad, but just then one of Aurangzeb's men attacked the general from the rear and fatally wounded him.

Seeing this, the Rajputs ran after Murad and surrounded him. Murad's army tried to fend them off, but the Rajputs formed a giant circle around them and closed in, suffocating his regiment. Murad's regiment seemed less seasoned and well-trained than the rest of Aurangzeb's army. These weren't career warriors, but instead low-class men of unwarlike habits — a bunch of brutes and outlaws who didn't fight as a unit.

As Murad's men ran out of ammunition, the Rajputs went in for the kill, cutting off the heads and arms of as many men as they could. For a moment, it seemed like victory was Dara's, but then the tide of battle began turning, and soon the Rajputs began to fall. One by one, each saffron-coloured face fell, and at last the ground took on a bloody, saffron-mixed colour.

Now red-stained swords and daggers flailed in the wind, and Dara marched forward on his elephant towards Aurangzeb, who was now on horseback. Aurangzeb began to retreat, but why, I wondered? Soon, Dara changed from his elephant to a mobile horse, and chased after Aurangzeb.

"Dara, don't do that, you idiot!" I yelled as if Dara could hear me. I could tell Dara was walking into a trap! A dismounted royal elephant gives an army the false impression that their leader's fallen, and a leaderless army's tantamount to a headless man. Chaos would ensue.

I saw Aurangzeb's men chanting now, probably, "Prince Dara has fallen!" which would further feed the frenzy. Though I couldn't tell what they were saying, the effect was the same: Dara's men looked around to catch a glimpse of their leader, but saw his empty, decorated elephant, further disillusioning them.

The rebel soldiers pushed back against the imperial army now, and the butchers, bakers and carpenters now ran for their lives, assuming no doubt that if they stayed and fought, the rebel Prince who'd now be King would execute them all. Thus, all Dara's men either died or fled, leaving him alone with a small cordon of bodyguards in the middle of the battlefield. Fearing for his own life, he ran towards the countryside. In the shade of a neem tree he took off his helmet, so depressed and exhausted, he just sat on the ground, unwilling to move at the sounds of enemy kettledrums now approaching his way...

I watched this entire battle from the fort, as if it were an elephant fight in the royal arena. Seeing my worst fears come true, I paced back and forth, not sure what to do next. I ran to my father, who I knew must be equally distressed at seeing his favourite son defeated on the battlefield. I found Aba was lying in bed, staring silently at the ceiling, tears and fear in his eyes.

"Aba!" I screamed. "How can you lie in bed at a time like this? Say something, Aba! What is Dara to do now? Say something!"

But Aba just lay there, unwilling and unable to offer any advice. From that moment on, he must have known his reign was over. No matter what he did in the coming days to stop Aurangzeb's advancement, he would eventually be captured by this son, removed as emperor and probably executed – if he were lucky.

Dara got up and rode on to Delhi, bypassing Agra with the hopes, I'm told, of meeting Nadira and their children there, continuing his flight and perhaps regrouping, though he was now fully cognizant of the fact that Agra would fall and he could do nothing more about it. Meanwhile, Aurangzeb approached the gates of Agra, but refused to enter. As Aba had a generation ago, Aurangzeb merely waited outside for the astrologers to offer him an auspicious date to enter. But he sent his army and commanders inside to loot Agra, take control of the treasury and offices and ask us for a formal surrender.

Alamgir would be his new name now that he would soon be the next Mughal King of India. At last the years of his despair had ended. No longer would he have to receive imperial permission before making decisions; he could attack and destroy as he pleased. And at last he could spread Islam as he saw fit.

Like any army since the beginning of time given such latitude, Aurangzeb's men wreaked havoc all over Agra. Men and women ran through the streets, young women were kidnapped, men were slaughtered and goods were stolen as his army unleashed its wrath on Agra for supporting Dara. These families had sent their men to fight against Aurangzeb's army, and time for retribution had arrived, so the army exacted revenge on the helpless public who'd unwillingly taken indirect part in this family feud.

"Aba, you must get up; Aurangzeb's men are marching towards the fort!"

Aba just lay there, murmuring to himself, "All is lost, all is gone!"

I shook my father repeatedly, begging him to snap out of his despair and take charge like the brave soldier he'd once been and could be again, but to no avail. Aba was thoroughly broken, knowing his Dara would now soon be dead, and that the kingdom he'd built would fall into the hands of the one son he'd always tried to keep it from. His parents had given him a safe and secure India, but he would be the Mughal to turn it over to a monster. He had nothing to say, no defence to give, no solution to offer.

I finally gave up pleading with my father and ran to the Diwan-i-khas. I had the guards seal the gates of the fort and plant armed guards along the periphery. If Aurangzeb was going to take the fort, it wouldn't be without a fight. But then another idea came to me...

That night I wore my black robe disguise one last time, not to visit the river that had given me my visions for the past few years, but instead to visit the man who now controlled most of our lives, Aurangzeb.

I was told he was sleeping alone in his imperial tent. His wife, Dilras, had died a few months before, earning from him only a few moments of silence, but certainly no tears. His children were still in Aurangabad with his other wives, while he, as always, was alone. He preferred his own company – non-judgmental (of himself, anyway), loyal and dependable.

I rode with Bahadur at my side, helping guide me to Aurangzeb's tent. There I dismounted and entered the tent while Bahadur stood guard outside.

I touched his shoulder, waking him from his deep sleep. Aurangzeb started, sat up and lunged towards me with his dagger.

"It's I, Jahanara!" I said quickly. Aurangzeb moved back and laid down his dagger. "I was forced to dress this way to evade recognition, brother. How are you?"

Aurangzeb looked at the ground. Having won the greatest prize by committing one of the greatest sins – fighting an older brother – and now waiting to commit more, what might his state of mind be, I wondered. "I know, Aurangzeb, that no one in Hindustan is happy tonight, not even the victors."

Aurangzeb listened glumly, his discombobulated hair and messy night clothes adding to his demeanour.

I said, "Hindustan lost many of its sons today, and before the war is over, so many people will have died that the wood for cremation and land for cemeteries will all be used up. Aba has lost control of himself; he's devastated by the fear that further bloodshed awaits us. And no one who can stop all this but you, my brother."

Aurangzeb then softly said, "There is nothing I can do."

"I don't ask that you compromise in any way, Aurangzeb. You've rightfully won the throne of India as the brave soldier you are. But I suggest to you an offer: that you divide the kingdom into four parts: Dara for Punjab, Murad for Gujarat, Shuja for Bengal, your oldest son for Deccan, and you take the rest, with full title to the throne!"

"I refuse to give that infidel an inch!"

I'd fully expected Aurangzeb would scoff at the idea of giving Dara anything. "But even if you won't give Dara Punjab, will you allow him to at least live there in peace, as your subject?"

Myriad emotions crossed Aurangzeb's face; then at last he said, "I'll think it over."

I just stared at my brother for a few minutes. In utter silence, neither of us spoke a word. I then rose to leave, but said quietly as I turned away: "I'll open the doors to the fort tomorrow, Aurangzeb."

Aurangzeb suddenly gazed at me in amazement. He couldn't have expected me to give up the fort so easily. At last he gave me the respect he hadn't yet at this meeting: He looked me straight in the eye.

I said, "Please visit Aba just once. He needs to know you mean him no harm. I'm not opening the fort for an enemy, Aurangzeb, but for my brother, who's come home." I wished him a comfortable sleep, hoping he would allow his heart a measure of calm.

Aurangzeb stared at me dumbfounded; I walked out of the tent in my disguise and rode back to the fort. His heart, I was hoping, would soften. In childhood, before me he'd always melted like ice on a hot day.

The next morning all Agra braced itself for the arrival of Alamgir, as he would now be known. Soldiers lined the path from the rebel camp to the fort's main entrance. Slowly, led by his heavily decorated elephant, Alamgir's procession moved towards the fort. Aba and I looked through the Samman Burj at the procession, cautiously optimistic that the new king would grant a humble pardon to the former one and begin his reign with mercy and compassion.

I ordered the gates opened so that as Alamgir rode in he'd see an open door, symbolising my love for him. Emotionally, I knew closed doors were what my fateful brother was used to, but this time I opened the doors for him personally even if the sitting emperor couldn't. I was now in full control, having sidelined Aba for his own good.

"All Hail! Emperor Alamgir" shouted his men repeatedly as he rode through.

Aurangzeb smiled and nodded to his men, who for the past several years had probably endured every hardship and test he could put them through, all for this moment.

Alamgir dismounted from his elephant after entering the Red Fort and walking with a small contingent of armed soldiers to the Diwan-i-khas, where Aba sat on the Peacock Throne with me and Raushanara at his side. I wouldn't be hidden behind a marble screen today; too much was riding on the events that would occur in this hall for me not to be seated in the open, and I didn't feel I could trust my disillusioned father to keep the situation from degenerating.

"Greetings, Aba!" called out Aurangzeb triumphantly, without asking his blessing as he had in the past.

"Greetings, my son!" Aba rose like an old stallion staggering to his feet. "I'm so pleased to see you. You have made me proud!"

"Really? Prouder than you are of Dara?"

Aba had no reply to his son's cruel jibe.

Aurangzeb's gaze swept the hall dramatically. "And where *is* Dara, anyway? He ran from the battlefield like a mouse!"

I couldn't help but worry; these weren't the words of a forgiving brother.

"Whatever is his fate will happen," sighed Aba.

"Men are masters of their own fates, O King," smirked Aurangzeb. "And only the foolish blame their weaknesses on nature. I'm here to tell you that I, Alamgir, will control my fate. I won't let circumstances control *me*."

Aba said weakly, "However you wish to proceed, the choice is yours."

"Yes it is, isn't it?" beamed Aurangzeb. "Guards, please escort my father to prison."

Without hesitation I shouted, "*No!* What is this, Aurangzeb?"

"What is it, you ask?" he shot back in disgust. "This is I, preventing my own downfall by a manipulative father! Look at this letter he tried to sneak to that infidel Dara!"

He waved a note in the air and then threw it at my feet.

Dear Dara,

Stay in Shahjahanabad. There's no lack of money or troops. I'll see to matters here.

Aba

I said, "He couldn't have written this, he was barely lucid until this morning!"

"You lie! You all lie!!" cried Aurangzeb.

"Yes, brother," Raushanara now sneered, "they're liars, all right! I saw with my own eyes these two devising plans to imprison you after they've won your favour!"

I looked at my sister in disgust; of course Raushanara had been manipulating events all along, most importantly Aurangzeb to not reconcile with us so she could take my place as empress. But what could I do? I knew Aurangzeb – now Alamgir – would never believe me over her. His mind was too corrupted already by power and revenge, and nothing I said or did would reverse his decisions now.

He ordered, "Guards, please also escort the Empress to the prison with my Aba!"

I was hurt but not surprised. I'd go with the guards and my father to my new home.

"I'll take *that*!" rasped Raushanara, snatching the muhr uzak from my hand. Then she ran to the new emperor, and the two laughed together.

"It worked!" crowed Aurangzeb. "You misguided Dara to the Chambal river, to falsely locate our crossing, and it was all worth it! "You'll make a terrific empress," he added, looking at me as the guards led Aba and me away.

"And you a wise emperor, my brother," Raushanara glowed. "You, a wise emperor!"

29

PARADISE LOST

29th September, 1658

O ur time in prison passed slowly; another year, and now we were a year closer to death.

Aba didn't enjoy the fast, simple death his brothers had enjoyed when he executed them. Indeed, his death wouldn't be as tranquil as any Mughal emperor's before him (or even after him, perhaps).

Aurangzeb had us under house arrest in the Samman Burj, the once imperial apartment that was home to Aba's nemesis, Nur Jahan, as well as his beloved wife. Our once boundless empire had now shrunk to a few yards.

Though not meant to torment his aging father, Aurangzeb's decision to imprison him in the Samman Burj resulted in giving the deposed King a clear view of the Taj Mahal, which now he could see but not touch, a brutal reminder of what once was, but never would be, again. From here Aba mourned his wife even while admiring his own architecture. Aba's architectural pursuits had reshaped India, giving it monuments I was sure would long outlast our times. Yet for all the glamour and glory he'd brought on the empire, he couldn't prevent the tide of dissent and calamity that had brewed in his own household.

Shortly after being crowned 'Al-Sultan al-Azam wal Khaqan al-Mukarram Abul Muzaffar Muhi ud-din Muhammad Aurangzeb Bahadur Alamgir I,' Aurangzeb freed me and offered me a place in the fort – not as empress, of course – to live out my remaining days. I instead chose to stay with my father, knowing his final days would be his worst and that I couldn't enjoy luxury while knowing he was living in a decrepit state. I would remain with him in the Samman Burj, looking at the Taj Mahal with the same haunting admiration as my father, asking both guidance and forgiveness of my mother for not being able to fend off the bloodshed she'd predicted a generation ago would consume our family.

Many years passed after the battle at Samugarh, and I spent them blaming myself for everything that had happened. Perhaps I could have done more to convince Aurangzeb I was *his* ally, and stopped Raushanara from further manipulating him. Even my affair with Gabriel had given Raushanara ammunition, allowing her to spread vicious rumours of incest about me, further pushing Aurangzeb and the orthodoxy away from me and weakening my position as empress.

During this imprisonment, Aurangzeb's attitude towards me seemed strange. We didn't talk; no written or verbal communication occurred. However, through guards appointed to Aba in the Samman Burj by the new Emperor, I lobbied for more amenities for Aba. I could never ask Aurangzeb directly, I'd simply ask the guards, knowing they ultimately would ask the Emperor himself.

"This place is too big for two people," I once told a guard. "Either move us to a small cell or allow the former Emperor to have his entire harem join him here."

Within a week, all his harem ladies, wives and concubines, were gracing the formerly majestic apartment with their presence. Another time, I asked for special dishes for the former Emperor, and a private cook; these requests, too, were rapidly agreed to. Though I was no longer empress, Aurangzeb still treated me like one in some ways.

Aba wasn't allowed to write letters to anyone but Aurangzeb, and those letters wavered from cheap flattery to threats of outright revolt against his own son. Aurangzeb would respond in kind now that Aba had no control over him and no longer required the respect of silence and submission he'd given Aba previously all his life.

Mullah Shah Badakshi paid us a visit over a year after our imprisonment, reluctantly allowed to do so because of his 'mullah' status and his political connections with the orthodoxy – a group that now enjoyed unprecedented power.

I told him kindly, "You took great pains to come here, mullah."

He replied, "The pains I may have suffered are nothing compared to the pains you, the Emperor, and the rest of India are suffering every day, Your Majesty."

"I am no longer royalty, sir, so you need not address me as Majesty."

Mullah Shah quickly responded: "To me you will always be royalty, Your Highness. The current Emperor and Empress cannot even wash the floors you walk on!"

The chief eunuch appointed to guard Aba, Itibar Khan, glanced over at the mullah, indicating by his disapproving facial expression caution against any language against the Emperor. But Mullah Shah, caring nothing about his own well-being, added, "I am here to partake in the mourning for Dara Shikoh's death."

Dara Shikoh was killed shortly after Aurangzeb had become King of India. While on the run, Dara's wife Nadira died, and a depressed Dara simply stopped running. Encouraged by his men to keep evading Aurangzeb's troops, he reluctantly continued his march, only to be betrayed by his own men and eventually captured.

I looked down sorrowfully as the mullah spoke, unwilling to think of what Dara must have endured at the hands of his vengeful brother. Dara's head was presented to Aba and me at our dinner table by Aurangzeb's instructions; he'd committed this heinous act at the behest of Raushanara.

Mullah Badakshi told me Dara's final moments were also his finest. After his capture, the Prince was paraded down Chandni Chowk on a weak, miserable old elephant covered in filth. Robbed of any jewellery or riches, he simply wore a coarse-textured garment and a turban wrapped in a Kashmiri shawl.

The intent was to humiliate the Prince and show the triumph of the Emperor; but in every quarter of the city where he was paraded, the people wept as if their own king had been killed. The crowds that gathered in his honour were immense, and people cried out his name, tears flowing down their faces. Not only Hindus, the land's Muslims also wept, as if the glory days of Islam in India were now over.

Finally Dara dismounted the filthy elephant and was brought before the Red Fort in chains. Just then, a crazy fakir who was known for standing in that particular spot began taunting the Prince: "Oh, Prince Dara, as a master you always gave me donations. But today you have nothing to give me, do you?"

But then the crowd turned quiet, and Dara looked directly with his bloodshot eyes at the fakir. All those present watched, as he lifted his hand to his shoulder, pulled off his dingy shawl and threw it to the fakir.

The fakir fell to the ground and begged Dara's forgiveness. Then the Prince was taken immediately to a secured location, where he was subsequently executed.

We continued to stare at the ground, unable find words. At last Badakshi looked towards Aba, who sat in the corner staring at the Taj Mahal. He said, "How is the King, Your Majesty?"

I turned my head towards Aba and smiled, "He's fine, given the circumstances. He likes to stare at my mother's tomb. It reminds him of her, and of the love they shared."

"Love has no place in India anymore, Your Highness."

"It still does, I'm sure, just not in the open as before," I said. "Aba became immune to news of death after Dara's. When they told him how Aurangzeb killed Murad, Aba didn't react."

"There's still hope, Your Majesty; Shuja still evades capture."

"Shuja won't last long, Mullah. We'll hear of his death, too, one day soon."

We spent these years waiting – to live, to die, for a liberation that seemed would never come. We never spoke of the future because it was unclear if we even had one. I grew in spirit, too, during this time, realising that self-guilt and shame were consuming me and stopping me from doing what I'd always sworn to do – take care of my family. Though I'd aged well my whole life, for the next seven-and-a-half years my age would catch up with me. Wrinkles began to form, my face began to sink in, and my hair started to turn white.

I'd learned that Dara's orphaned daughter, Jani, was being mistreated in the Red Fort at Delhi. Frequently taunted by Raushanara and not allowed proper schooling, her life was slowly turning into a waste as she was becoming the primordial example of what inevitably becomes the life of a Salatin. I implored my father to write to Aurangzeb and request that she be sent to the Samman Burj in Agra, to spend her days with her grandfather in imprisonment, where at least she'd be safe.

I don't think Aurangzeb harboured any ill will against Jani or any of Dara's other children, but he gave full freedom to Raushanara to torture them, a role she relished greatly. When the new King received the request for Jani's extradition to Agra, he promptly fulfilled it and allowed her to join us in captivity.

With Jani now living with me, I found a new purpose in life. I began raising her as my own daughter, tutoring her and teaching her Persian, Arabic and even a little English. I taught her about the Koran, architecture, music and arts – an education even Aurangzeb's children were being denied because of strict orthodox rules banning poetry and music in the court. I never understood how men who claimed to love God could have such a rigid, narrow vision of him.

Aba saw reflections of Ami in Jani's smile, once we finally got her to laugh after several years of verbal and emotional abuse by Raushanara. This was my new family – Aba, Jani and me – living together like a seemingly normal family, but haunted by the harsh truth that our loved ones had been slain by our own relative, Aurangzeb.

I now found myself abandoned on this rudderless raft slowly drifting into oblivion. All the good we'd done, the change we sought to bring, was being slowly reversed by my ruthless brother. The love we shared among ourselves was all the magic we could experience. Enfolded in our self-contained universe, we took our only solace in being invisible to this new world Aurangzeb was creating.

On 7th January, 1666, Aba again turned very weak and ill. Again his legs began to swell, and he developed a high fever. He kept growing weaker, and I knew now that nothing I could do would save him. Still, Jani and I hovered over him around the clock, applying cool bandages to his forehead to lower the temperature, making khichdi to help him regain his strength, but to no avail. Hakims and European physicians came, but nothing seemed to work.

Almost two weeks later, Aba lay on the balcony off the Samman Burj with his head on my lap, staring straight at the Taj Mahal; close by Jani held her grandfather's hand. As the sun set for the night, the white Taj Mahal seemed to radiate a golden hue, and Aba began telling me of the age-old saying Akbar left about his famed city of Fatehpur Sikri: "The world is a bridge; walk over it, but do not make the mistake of building on it." Aba was about to cross the bridge, and yet what he'd built would live on for centuries after him, reminding the world of what he'd felt for his wife and what love meant to him.

He recited words from the Koran, gave thanks for a thousand gifts, but also asked forgiveness for a thousand sins he may have committed in his life. Only now, as he lay dying, did the screams of Shahriar and his nephew ring in his ears.

"I'm sorry, Aba," he cried violently as I tried to console him. "I'm sorry I killed your sons and grandsons! I'm sorry! This is all my fault! Allah, please have mercy on my children. Please don't punish them for my sins!"

It was, of course, Aba who despite his many good attributes, had begun the sinful tradition of massacring one's own family in quest of the throne. He'd even rebelled against his own father. Was Aurangzeb his punishment for these sins, or was further punishment waiting for him in the next world?

He saw ghosts of a leprosy-inflicted Shahriar standing on the balcony staring at him. Frightened, Aba moved his head away, this time claiming to see his young nephew Dawar Baksh, who was just a boy when Aba ordered his execution.

"Jahanara, my child, help me, I see ghosts!" he cried as the life drained from him. "How could I have been so cruel as to kill a man already sick from leprosy? How could I have killed a child... my own nephew... just for the throne? Jahanara... give me a path to salvation, my child! Please, show me a path!"

He sobbed in panic, truly believing the ghosts of the dead had arrived to haunt him and demand answers for sins he'd committed.

I remained calm, cradling his head in my lap. I then whispered something in Aba's ear, so softly no one else present, not even Jani, heard what I said. I then wrote something on a sheet of paper and had Aba put his imprint on it. I tucked it in my blouse and held my father's head on my lap, and we watched the sunset together. Now Aba was at peace.

Aba stared smiling at the Taj Mahal. I was keenly aware that he'd not see the next sunrise, and quite frankly, I hoped he'd die at that time and suffer no more. I knew it tortured Aba to see how death always evaded him, instead visiting his loved ones: Dara, Nadira Ami and – for a brief moment – me. No longer able to watch death from a distance, it seemed he decided to pull death into his own embrace finally, to escape his own misery.

He slowly spoke, still staring at the inviting golden Taj Mahal: "You know something, my child? Everything I did since your mother died, I did because of her. I built in hopes of celebrating my love for her through architecture, but it was never enough. From sarcophagus, to buildings, to entire cities, every time I was finished, I felt alone again. I even bedded many women hoping that perhaps one of them, just one, would be able to make me feel the way your mother had, but it never happened."

Jani and I just listened, giving our dying loved one the opportunity to say his last words in peace: "True love really does come only once. You can't reproduce it. It can't be bargained for or compromised. Once you find it, nothing else will suffice. Anything else you see or try will fall short of expectations."

I thought of Gabriel. Had I moved with him when he wanted, I'd be in the arms of my true love today. I might even be someone's mother or grandmother, but alas, I'm living here in penury. The previous year I'd received word that Gabriel died in England in the Black Plague in London. While everyone else fled London, he stayed to help the people and died in the process. Having no more tears to shed, I now merely remembered and mourned his passing in my own, private way.

Aba was breathing hard through his mouth now, panting as if desperately trying to hold onto life. But true to his intuition, Aba breathed his last that night, a smile frozen on his face, his eyes still open. He was 75.

It was difficult to imagine that this was the face Nur Jahan and my mother had fought over. These lips had once commanded armies, ruled a nation and directed masons from around the world to build the most glorious monument India had ever seen. Behind the wrinkles of his skin had once been the young boy who yearned physically and emotionally for a 16-year-old daughter of a noble, and upon winning her, spent the next 14 years worshipping their love.

When he built the Diwan-i-khas in Shahjahanabad, he had engraved all over its ceiling, 'If there is Paradise on Earth, it is this; it is this; it is this.' Yet here he was, having died a slow miserable death, having been made to watch every branch of his family tree slowly fall to the ground as his intolerant son, a known enemy of art, music and architecture, undid everything Aba had worked for. The days awaiting India would be tumultuous, and his citizenry would pay a heavy price for their new King's bigotry. Aba's paradise would be lost in the whirlwind of intolerance and fanaticism that took hold during his son's reign.

30

FATE OF THE INNOCENTS

23rd January, 1666

News of Aba's death was sent to Aurangzeb immediately, and much to the surprise of everyone at his court, he quickly dispatched his son, Muazzam, to Agra to prepare the funeral, and he himself changed into white robes of mourning. This meant the court would mourn the former Emperor's death.

Though I wanted a full state funeral for my father, the guards present would not allow this. Instead, a small funeral party escorted Aba's body to the grave. Thirty-five years after the death of my mother, I would yet again be the only child to escort my parent's remains to its burial site, a status that brought both honour and anguish to me.

At noon the following day, the sandalwood box bearing Aba's remains was removed – head first – from the majestic Red Fort he'd remodelled a generation ago and taken to the Taj Mahal, with me, Muazzam, and Jani as the only relatives attending. It was Aba's wish to be buried next to his wife so he might lie in eternity with her; this request Aurangzeb approved; he even agreed to fully finance a beautifully decorated marble sarcophagus for the deceased Emperor.

Aurangzeb visited the Taj two weeks later and offered his respects to both our parents, now permanently interred in the same mausoleum. Dressed more like a fakir than a king, he chose to walk on foot over to the Red Fort to visit me, his sister he hadn't seen or spoken to for many years.

I hoped that as he walked he'd see the devastation in the eyes of the public. All India wept for the deceased King, a monarch who had brought India to its Golden Age, despite his personal faults. Now apprehensive about their future in a land ruled by mullahs, Hindus especially wept for their Muslim King, realising life would now only be harder for them and their children. I hoped Aurangzeb would be taken aback by this reaction, and also sad to know how much everyone had loved the man he'd grown to hate.

He slowly walked into the fort, and rather than sit atop a throne in the Diwan–i–khas, he walked straight to the Samman Burj, where I sat composed and silent on a golden divan, waiting to speak to my only surviving brother at his request.

"Greetings, *Emperor* Alamgir," I said in a mildly mocking tone.

Aurangzeb looked like he had no idea what to say to me. In childhood he'd been putty in my fingers. Now he couldn't look me straight in the eye since this was the first time he'd seen me after having killed all three of his brothers and numerous nephews, including Dara's oldest son, Sulaiman.

"How have you been, Jahanara?" he said slowly, staring straight at the ground, his spine bent forwards.

"It's been difficult," I replied, "but Jani and I have managed. I wanted to distribute a thousand gold coins to the poor in honour of Aba, but your eunuch Itibar Khan took it from me and said I can't do that until you say so."

"Of course it'll be done, sister!" he said suddenly, adding: "And I will add another 12,000 rupees of my own. And you'll be happy to know that I gave Muazzam the specific orders to inter Aba's body right next to Ami's."

I probably confused him by my evident lack of appreciation for his gesture, but I knew Aba would never have placed his own grave in that particular location. In the entire Taj Mahal, the location of Aba's grave is now the only asymmetrical part. How little Aurangzeb knew of architecture or the arts in general! But perhaps the sloppy location of my father's grave was his most appropriate contribution to the majestic monument.

"I also had a beautiful monument built in Aurangabad in Dilras' memory, sister," said Aurangzeb.

"I know," I replied. "It's called Bibi ka Makbara, right?"

"Yes! You must visit it."

I had no intention of ever seeing it, having heard from one of the concubines who did visit it how poorly it was designed. Like the Taj, it too was made of pure marble, with four towers and a central dome. But it looked like a comedian's distortion of the Taj; the proportions were all wrong; the width of the towers was too wide for the top dome; the top of the central dome, too large for the base. Like Aurangzeb's love for Dilras, it was clumsy and disproportionate. Whereas my father designed every brick of his monument with love and attention, Aurangzeb designed in haste, only so he could upstage Aba. Aba's Taj was a product of love; Aurangzeb's Makabara a product of envy and vanity. The two monuments reflected their creators' feelings towards their wives and reaffirmed to me how every architectural glory of my father's – and mine – was a product of genuine love for another human being.

Aurangzeb and I stared past each other for a few more minutes, neither knowing what needed to be said or how to move past the bloodshed that had divided us.

"I hope Ami takes better care of Aba than I did!" Aurangzeb blurted out, and he broke down and began to weep. He fell to my feet and to my amazement buried his weeping head in my lap, just as he had many years ago when Dara attacked him, and I took a blow to protect his little body from harm.

I stared straight ahead, not looking down at my weeping brother, but unable to keep myself from crying. My lips quivered and tears rolled down my cheeks.

Aurangzeb had never wept easily. Quite likely this was the first time he'd wept since receiving those ten lashes for poisoning Manu many years ago. It was as if with Aba's death his last hope also died, that one day somehow Aba might grow to love him.

"I killed my own Aba!" cried Aurangzeb as his tears wet my pajamas. "*I* did it. Allah will never forgive me. Ami will never forgive me!"

Instinctively I moved my left hand from my side and placed it on Aurangzeb's head, as a blessing and comfort to him in place of our parents'. Aurangzeb slowly gained control over his tears, but he remained at my feet, saying he felt more comfort there than he had anywhere for many years.

At last I whispered, "Get up, brother. Before he died, Aba gave me something for you."

I reached into my blouse and pulled out the folded piece of paper, the letter 'from Aba,' written by me when Aba asked me to find him a way to salvation. I wrote it, but he'd put his imprint on it, and it had brought him peace:

My Dear Son Aurangzeb,

You and I are both sons of Allah, and he has chosen a path for both me and you, so who are we to judge each other? When I was young I committed a sin: I rebelled against my father and killed my brothers. Perhaps that's why Allah took your Ami away from me and kept me alive for so long – so one day I might know how horrible it is for a son to rebel against his father or a child to kill another child.

 I don't resent or fault you for anything, my child. You only did what I taught you, and for that I apologise to you. I will pay for my sins perhaps more when I die, but I don't wish for you to think I die wishing you ill. I forgive you for any and all offences you have committed against me. I ask that Allah open his doors of paradise to you, and that you may be a better father to your children than I was to you.

Love,
Your Aba

Aurangzeb looked up at me, red-eyed. "Aba is forgiving me?"

"Yes, brother. It's over. Our long nightmare is over. It's time to begin again. Ami and Aba are both praying for you."

Aurangzeb wept deeply, as if letting go of a lifetime of sadness and depression with his tears. Ashamed, embarrassed, humbled, he would never know how to repay Aba for 'his' words, nor know that the words were really mine, and it was I who'd realised that the salvation of both my brother and father must rest in a reconciliation, albeit posthumous. The nightmare had to end; for the future of India depended on it, and I'd known I was the only one left who could do it.

Aurangzeb finally wiped away his tears, got off his knees and sat in a chair, holding both my hands in his. He said: "I want all my brothers' children to live with me as my children, sister. I want Jani to marry my son Mohammad Azam, and you to preside over the wedding. Will you give her hand in marriage to my son?"

This gesture surprised me, but I said, "I will, but only if you'll allow all of your daughters to marry freely. I ask that you end this tradition that denies marriage to Mughal daughters."

"Consider it done!" he said. "In fact, since Jani is marrying my son, I think Dara's younger son Siphr would be a good match for my daughter Zubdat-un -nissa."

And not only the two he mentioned, but also before long, five of Aurangzeb's ten children would marry children of my deceased brothers.

"I have one more request, Jahanara," he continued after a short pause. "I ask that you come home with me now, to Shahjahanabad, and reassume your role as Empress of India."

This request truly amazed me. I said, "What about Raushanara?"

Aurengzeb had learned earlier that year about Raushanara's orgies, and even learned she'd concocted a secret plot to overthrow him in favor of his nine-year-old son. Realizing she was no true ally of his, but just using him, he banished her from his palace (though she would remain in the capital for a few more years).

He said, "She could have never been the empress this country needs. Now come, sister, let's go. Let's take care of our parents' kingdom together."

I was still unsure that joining Aurangzeb was the right course of action. Something in me resisted the urge to accept the offer, even though it would take me back to the majestic Chandni Chowk, a monument to my love for my Gabriel. But I decided I would accede to his request – on one condition: "I'll always be allowed to criticise and question you, regardless of what the issue may be."

"Of course, sister!" he retorted.

"And you will never harm any member of our family again, least of all the children of the deceased brothers."

"Of course! I swear on the Koran I will not!"

I knew the next reign would be very difficult for India's non-Muslims, and that I was the only person who could possibly protect them. I knew my brother still had a selfish and narrow spirit, who in seeking his own salvation might remain oblivious to the concerns of the outside world. Scrupulously following the letter of the Koran, he would strictly enforce his narrow interpretation – even on non-Muslims – and regard any deviations as direct threats to his own soul's salvation in the afterlife. In a nation of many creeds and interests, such a man would be a nightmare if left unchecked.

I would go with Aurangzeb and fulfill my commitment to Nur Jahan: to always see a reflection of my father in the emperor and help him rule India. I would protect India from all threats, just as I had many years ago in Hugli.

Aurangzeb, for his part, would avoid harming any more relatives, a promise he kept for the rest of his life.

That night we both sat in the same palanquin atop a decorated elephant, each staring out onto the landscape as the beast slowly rode out of Agra. We didn't look at each other, just stared at the great monument glowing in the moonlight – the Taj.

I was leaving my Ami and Aba for the first time ever. I'd never deserted my Aba before, pursuant to my vow to my mother, but now that he was with her, I was free to go. There were newer battles to be fought, hearts to be healed and causes to be furthered. I couldn't rest now.

As we rode into the night the Taj faded but never completely disappeared, as if even from the grave my more tolerant parents were making their eternal presence known through the glow radiating from the monument. Aurangzeb had won the kingdom, but lost himself doing it. This much even he must have known as he rode away. Tears flowed down his face as he looked at the monument that now housed the parents he'd never see again.

Each shedding tears, but having no more words to express our feelings, we made our way to the capital, to put together the family now so dispersed. I would do the healing, if Aurangzeb would merely not get in the way.

AFTERWORD

Mistress of the Throne is a work of fiction, but it's rooted in actual history. Jahanara Begum was seventeen when her mother died and though there were numerous other wives whom Shah Jahan could have installed as the empress after Mumtaz Mahal's death, he opted instead to elevate his daughter to such a prominent position. European travellers to Mughal India at the time write about Jahanara – her feud with Raushanara, her burning accident, and her role in trying to prevent bloodshed for the throne.

A picture emerged from all of these accounts of a very mature, level-headed individual who reluctantly accepted the role of empress and used it to benefit her family and her kingdom. As her family feud began to deepen, I was astonished to learn that Aurangzeb and Dara both revered Jahanara, even more than their own father, with whom Aurangzeb had a feud till his dying day.

The more I researched her, the more I began to realise that Jahanara was one of the greatest unsung heroines of Mughal India. Her contributions were greater than perhaps even her mother; she helped bring Shah Jahan out of his melancholy and helped supervise the building of the Taj as well as the city of Delhi, which today is the capital of India. Thus, she possessed her mother's timely beauty and calm demeanour while also possessing her father's sense of architecture.

Rumours of her incest with the king troubled me. However, as I delved deeper into the origins of such rumours what I found was that these were chronicled mainly by European travellers during

Aurangzeb's reign and it remains suspect that perhaps the intention of such rumours was more to malign the deposed Shah Jahan than record actual events. Still, I found myself torn as to how to reconcile this disturbing rumour about a woman who seemed remarkable in every other way. I thus created a case of mistaken identity and used that as a way to describe this claim.

When one thinks of Mughal women, the names of Nur Jahan and Mumtaz Mahal are catapulted to the top. However, the character of Jahanara also deserves a prominent place alongside these two women.

Had Jahanara been born a man, she undoubtedly would have been the king after Shah Jahan. She possessed the intellect to rule and enjoyed the popularity to maintain a coalition. The weakening of the Mughal Empire and subsequent rise of the East India Company which led to almost two centuries of colonial hegemony would possibly have been avoided. Hence, it was Mughal India's insistence on treating men with a more prominent place than qualified women that added to the eventual collapse of the kingdom.

The agonies of losing a parent at an early age, becoming a surrogate to younger siblings, and of never being able to marry are very human emotions. Thus, beyond the majestic pageantry of the Mughal times, Jahanara emerges as a very ordinary figure living under extraordinary circumstances.

It is a common fact that as per Emperor Akbar's decree, no Mughal princess was allowed to marry. I thought hard about the torment this must have caused a young adolescent princess whose own parents shared a romance that was legendary even in its own time. When I learned that Aurangzeb had asked Jahanara to return to Delhi after Shah Jahan's death and from that moment onward, princesses were being allowed to marry, I immediately wondered if Jahanara may have had a role in this policy reversal. Why would Aurangzeb, on his own, reverse the policy? What difference would it make to him? But to Jahanara, it would mean that she succeeded in preventing other princesses from living a celibate life. This made more sense to me and I tried to capture this in my final pages of *Mistress of the Throne*.

Finally, I was moved to learn of how it was Jahanara that convinced Shah Jahan to write a letter granting Aurangzeb an apology. Even a non-vengeful individual would have scoffed at the thought of forgiving her captor and the murderer of her family. Yet, in offering Aurangzeb forgiveness, Jahanara once again tried to heal her family and the nation at large. This, I felt, was her greatest contribution to the Mughal era.

Whatever one may deduce from her life as depicted in this novel or in works of history, one fact is indisputable: she was more than just a queen. The majestic Chandni Chowk which today is the main avenue of commerce for Delhi, was designed by her; the Red Fort from where the annual Indian Independence day celebrations are launched, was her design; and Mughal princesses before her were not allowed to marry, but after her did and became mothers of prominent future kings. She never could marry, so she married the throne, devoting her whole life to preserving it. Nonetheless, somewhere along the path of history, her name was lost. Alas, we celebrate her life in this book and bestow on her the appropriate title, *Mistress of the Throne*.

A CONVERSATION WITH
RUCHIR GUPTA

1. What made you write this book?

I was inspired to write this book when I began reading other works of historical fiction on the Mughals. I find this time period in Indian history very fascinating. This was one of India's first pluralistic societies and the culture and opulence of the court was the thing of legends. The time period I write about was not explored much in contemporary literature. Though we knew the story of the Taj Mahal, the effect of Mumtaz Mahal's untimely death on her children was never truly explored, and I felt that it would be interesting to explore how her children, Jahanara in particular, regained their footing and shaped India.

2. What part of *Mistress of the Throne* is fact and what part is fiction?

Mostly all of what you read is fact. There are some areas where I intentionally changed the facts to allow for better flow of the story and add more thrill to the characters. Specifically, Nur Jahan was not imprisoned in Agra, but instead several hundred miles away in Lahore. Thus, her involvement with shaping Aurangzeb is suspect, though it is difficult to assume that Aurangzeb's imprisonment by her at a young age did not have some deleterious effect on his personality that ultimately shaped his character. The character of Gita is purely fictional and created to provide a background for Dara's initial hatred for Aurangzeb. It also serves to anchor Dara's love for Hinduism on an intimate level. Manu was indeed a Hindu wife of Shah Jahan, but the poisoning incident as well as her interaction with other characters was purely fictional and again, meant to showcase the passions of Dara and Aurangzeb. All of the other major characters are rooted in actual history. The interactions I created were done in such a way that the characters *could* have interacted that way, but there is no proof to argue one way or the other.

3. How did you go about researching about the main protagonist, Jahanara?

There isn't much written about Jahanara. I relied heavily on books from European travellers to India during that time. It is through them that we learn about the rumours of incest between her and the king, the burning incident, and the arrival of Gabriel Boughton to help her recover. It is also true that she was the closest child to the king and ultimately the Empress of India. Her conflict with Raushanara and Aurangzeb is also mentioned in both Mughal chronicles as well as European ones. Actual letters between Aurangzeb and his father were used and translated to serve as a basis for the letters contained in the book. Though not all letters are verbatim translations, I tried to preserve the tone and message of each letter in this book. For descriptive scenes showing the opulence, I used Mughal paintings and well as chronicles to describe the scene.

4. You show Jahanara having mystical powers that allow her to see what is happening in other places. Why did you do that?

I originally had written the book in the third person perspective, but my editor felt that writing from a first person perspective would allow the reader to connect more deeply with Jahanara. Thus, I was in a quandary as to how best to show what is happening outside of Jahanara's immediate vicinity. We know from history that Jahanara and Dara were both members of a movement known as the Qadiriya order and members of this movement claimed to have special telepathic powers. Thus, I gave Jahanara special powers that allowed her to see what was happening in other parts of the kingdom. Again, there is nothing in the recorded history to suggest she did *not* have such powers. I simply exercised poetic licence to give her these powers to allow for a better read.

5. **Tell us about your writing process for a book such as this.**

For any historical fiction book, I think research is key. My project begins with an initial interest in a character and then I do extensive research on that character, making an outline of the major events in that person's life and the people he/she interacted with. If, after making this outline, I find that the person is indeed very fascinating and not enough has been written about them, I start writing the book. For each event in the outline, I write a chapter and this gives me my 'skeleton' for the book. I then link the skeleton with fictional material that allows me to make the events flow. For example, in this book there was a clear sense of intolerance and rage in Aurangzeb from a young age. There is also a documented history of him being imprisoned. Thus, I fictionalised his years of captivity as being abusive and leading to him becoming a pious, intolerant, vengeful adult.

Other titles by Srishti

- 34 Bubblegums and Candies
- A Dilli-Mumbai Love Story
- A Feeling Beyond Words
- A half baked love story
- A Life that you knew..
- A Little Bit of Love...
- A Little Love Incident
- A Roller Coaster Ride!
- A thing beyond forever
- A Walk Down the Lane...
- An Unequal Harmony
- And then it rained....
- Anyone Else but you
- As Long as I Love you...
- Because you Loved me..
- Beep you! you BeepHole
- Boundless Saga of Love
- By the River Pampa I...
- Can't Cook a Love Story
- Corporate Atyaachaar
- Dancing with Maharaja
- Everything you Desire
- Forever in these pages
- From Cubicles 2 Cabins
- Heartbreaks & Dreams!
- I am Broke....! Love me
- I am Still Committed..
- I Know What Women Want
- I will Love Once Again!
- If God went to B-School
- If I Pretend I am Sorry!
- In Course of True Love
- It Happened that Night
- It Should Be u!! My Love
- It wasn't Love at First
- It's all About Love...
- Jab se you have loved me
- Journey of two Hearts
- Just Like in the Movies
- Life is What you Make it
- Love Happens Like that
- Love Power Politics!!
- Love, Life & A Beer Can!
- Love, Life and Dream on
- My Beloved's MBA Plans
- My Love Never Faked...
- Never Say Good Bye
- Nobody Dies a Virgin
- Nothing for you my Dear
- Nothing Lasts Forever
- Of Tattoos and Taboos!
- Ohh! Gods are Online
- Oops! 'I' fell in Love!
- Ouch! that 'Hearts'..
- Reality Bytes 'Bites'
- She is Single I'm Taken
- Something in your Eyes
- Spicy Bites of Biryani
- Sumthing of a Mocktale
- That Kiss in the Rain..
- The Dev-D Syndrome...
- The Equation of my Love

- The Funda of Mix-ology
- The Guardians of Karma
- The Homing Pigeons
- The Idiot-Dudes.....
- The India I Dream of
- The Journey to Nowhere
- The Legends of Amrapali
- The Off-Site Tamasha
- The Other way Round
- The Paperback Badshah
- The Quest for Nothing!
- The Secrets of the Dark
- The Storm in My Mind
- The Thing Between U & Me
- Those Small Lil Things
- Three Times Loser....
- What... if not I.I.T.?
- When Life Tricked me..
- When Strangers Meet
- When You Became My Life
- Where the Rainbows End

Non-Fiction
- Bluejay Teach Yourself Hindi
- Mastering English from Day One
- What They Don't Teach at School
- Why You Can't Lose Weight
- Do This Get rich
- Manage Your Manager